TWO DOWN . . .

Smailes knew something was wrong as soon as he strode up the path and saw the front door standing ajar. He rapped on it forcefully and called out, hesitating only a second before pushing the door open with a foot and feeling it swing open freely. He stepped quickly into the dim hallway and caught his breath, fighting an instinct to vomit.

At the bottom of the stairs the body of Howard's mother lay facedown in a dark lake of blood, a huge exit wound in the middle of her back. Her flowered housecoat was bunched obscenely around her thighs; the force of the bullet in her chest must have literally lifted her off her feet and spun her backward.

Smailes stood transfixed for a moment in horror, then leapt over the body and bounded up the stairs two at a time, yelling Howard's name as he did so. . . .

THE LAST DEFECTOR

Tony Cape

BANTAM BOOKS

NEW YORK · TORONTO · LONDON · SYDNEY · AUCKLAND

THE LAST DEFECTOR

A Bantam Falcon Book / published in association with Doubleday

PRINTING HISTORY

Doubleday edition published July 1991
Bantam edition / June 1992

FALCON *and the portrayal of a boxed "f" are trademarks of Bantam*
Books, *a division of Bantam Doubleday Dell Publishing Group, Inc.*

ISBN 0-553-29755-4

Published simultaneously in the United States and Canada

Bantam Books are published by Bantam Books, a division of Bantam
Doubleday Dell Publishing Group, Inc. Its trademark, consisting of
the words "Bantam Books" and the portrayal of a rooster, is
Registered in U.S. Patent and Trademark Office and in other
countries. Marca Registrada. Bantam Books, 666 Fifth Avenue, New
York, New York 10103.

PRINTED IN THE UNITED STATES OF AMERICA

RAD   0 9 8 7 6 5 4 3 2 1

for Mary

THE
LAST
DEFECTOR

Darnell Roberts leaned across the bench seat and paid off the car service driver with a five, leaving him a good tip. The radio continued to churn out samba music, so he slid out of the door without speaking and stepped into the sudden cold of night. He oriented himself to the dark columns of buildings, picked out his sister's block and swaggered toward it. Windshield shards crunched under his feet as he crossed the parking lot.

Roberts wore the standard equipment of inner-city black youth—white hightops with sport laces tucked, not tied, stovepipe black jeans, sweat top with the hood up, ski hat, parka. He had a hundred and seventy dollars and half a gram of powder cocaine in his pocket, an evening's pay. He hesitated as he saw the glow of cigarette tips in a Monte Carlo parked next to the walkway. It could be competition, even the law. He kept walking, not looking around.

In the dim light of the lobby he saw the scrawled note that the second elevator was out of service and swore under his breath. One working elevator for ten floors, and it was broken half the time. He headed for the stairwell. At least it was only three flights.

He was pleased to have a real job again, feeling useful, getting paid. He had taken the dumb rent-a-cop thing to please his sister, the parole board. He couldn't take the yessah-nosah bullshit, the joke pay, and was glad the weird spics and their bribe at the diplomat building had gotten his ass fired. As it turned out, the five bills he had palmed were enough to give him a cushion until he hustled the job with Gomez's captain. Another month of that kind of crap and he would have been back on rock, he knew it. Now he just pushed it for Gomez, but felt good enough not to touch it himself. Crack—you were king of the universe for ten minutes, then your whole world shriveled right down to how you were going to score again. Powder was an easier high, more controllable, and it was part of his pay.

Roberts mounted the steps slowly, ignoring the stale smells of urine and marijuana. Stairwells of buildings like these were a major hangout—you could come across almost anything—but it was late, almost three, and no one was around. He entered his sister's landing, fishing for a key in his pants. Just another week or two with all her damn kids, then he'd get his own place.

He saw the butt of an aluminum suitcase holding open the door to the garbage room, but paid it no attention. He reached his key to the lock as the pneumatic shriek of a silenced revolver burst the air. The bullet entered beneath his armpit, blowing out through his heart and chest, killing him instantly. Footsteps paused briefly over the body, then hurried away to the stairs, then were gone.

Derek Smailes got out of his chair and went into the bathroom to check the condition of the ice in the plastic bucket. He was hungry but had been too nervous to eat earlier, and now it was too late. He returned to the lamp table and checked the equipment in the drawer for the tenth time, sitting down to mutter a fragment of nursery rhyme, listening to the sound quality, then rewinding the sliver of tape and closing the drawer. Still he couldn't stay seated.

He rose and peered out of the heavy curtains into the

airshaft that the concierge who had shown him the room had called an "atrium." He turned and looked around. It was one of the Plaza's smaller and cheaper rooms, but there was plenty of antique furniture and a crystal chandelier, and enough rococo plasterwork to satisfy a dowager. He walked back into the bathroom, relieved himself, then fixed himself an extremely weak Scotch. He caught his reflection in the mirror, blinked twice, then shook his head in disbelief. Here was Derek Smailes, former provincial cop turned junior security man at the British Mission, waiting in one of the world's most exclusive hotels to hold a clandestine meeting with a Soviet diplomat that might alter the course of East-West relations. He found himself unable to suppress a blurt of laughter, but then just as quickly caught himself, his senses straining. Then he heard it again, a weak but distinct rapping sound.

Smailes crossed to the door in six long paces. He wiped his palm on his suit pants before turning the handle, opening the door as the stocky, agitated Russian pushed past him into the room.

2 _____

"Czecho job," said Howard, unable to suppress a smirk of triumph. "Or East German. Could be your East German."

Howard held up the circuit board between a thumb and forefinger and tapped it lightly with the tip of a long, slim screwdriver, like a conductor admonishing his orchestra. Then he tossed it down carelessly on the cluttered surface of the workbench.

"Course, means it's old. Pretty crude all round, really," he said, attempting to sound uninterested.

Derek Smailes watched his colleague closely as he leaned with his elbows on the edge of Howard's bench, his face cupped in his hands. He sensed the glee with which Howard was consolidating his discovery, and the schoolyard bravado with which he tried to discount it. Smailes looked across at Howard's assistant, Kevin Butterworth, who was standing at Howard's elbow. They both looked away as they tried not to smile.

Howard Grundy was a short, bulbous man in his late forties with a big head, paunch and buttocks. He was balding and his thick-lensed glasses hid baggy, protruding eyes. Howard always wore blue work clothes and his belt was cinched so tightly that a girdle of fat was extruded from each side of it. From the belt hung various accoutrements of his trade—walkie-talkie, beeper and technician's toolkit. He still wore heavy policeman's shoes and socks, after almost ten years as a civilian.

Smailes stood up and passed a hand over his mouth. It smelled of baked dirt from his crawl along the heating duct. "How can you be sure, Howard?" he asked.

"Know the cookbook," replied Howard casually. "The Minsk wireless school from the early seventies, where Ivan used to train the East-bloc charlies." Howard picked up the circuit board again and trained a gooseneck lamp on it. "Look here," he said, using the screwdriver as a pointer.

"Look at the design—sort of obvious but weird. You've got your diodes top left and capacitors and crap below and these antique inductors down there, all hand-soldered—it's a standard Minsk menu. I've seen a couple before—I dug one out of the East Berlin consulate five years ago and another was sent to me last year which the local boys yanked out of the ambassador's house in Prague. That's why I'm saying Czecho or East German—assembled when they were still Ivan's bad boys, of course."

Here Howard gave a broad wink. Clearly, he was one of those intelligence types who believed the rapid unraveling of the Cold War had been an intermission, rather than a final act.

"How does the rest of it work, Howard?" asked Butterworth, genuinely interested.

Kevin Butterworth was a big man like Smailes, an MI5 trainee who was completing his U.S. tour by accompanying Grundy on his annual security sweep around British installations in America. In his middle twenties, Butterworth had worked in Smailes' department at the New York Mission for the past five months, and the two had gotten along famously. Kevin Butterworth was a Londoner with a milk-white complexion and vivid red hair, and, although he was a fast-track graduate trainee, he'd been a modest and deferential assistant, treating Smailes as a mentor. In Smailes' view, he'd shown the makings of a first-rate intelligence officer, combining an agile mind with a canny sense of office politics. He was, in fact, in every area the opposite of Graham Booth, the dashing and bumptious young Welshman who had recently replaced him.

With great relish Grundy explained the technology they'd found—how the voice-activated mike relayed its data to the storage and compression unit in the microchip. Transmission through the large encryption unit—definitely of Soviet make, he pointed out—was activated by a polling signal from outside the building, probably from a passing car, perhaps once a day. The size of the batteries in the power pack meant the thing could probably last a year or two without being serviced. And given the burst technology used, it was almost impossible to turn up in a standard sweep, he added proudly, brandishing his trophy again.

"But how well does it work, eh? That's another question," he said to himself, almost as an afterthought. He set the circuit board down, carefully this time, removed his glasses and wiped his nose and eyes with a wide handkerchief. Then he pressed the glasses back on the bridge of his nose and looked from Butterworth to Smailes quizzically, a half smile on his face.

Derek Smailes had known Howard Grundy for more than fifteen years, from the time when Smailes had been a raw CID recruit and Grundy an instructor at the detectives' academy in Hendon, North London. The paths of the former policemen had diverged, then crossed again years later at an MI5 listening post in Hertfordshire, then again in New York, by which time Smailes had become a security officer with the British Mission and Grundy a senior technician with the joint operations unit. Now the two officers and their young assistant were standing in the basement of the British safe house in Mount Vernon, a working-class suburb just north of New York City. The basement served as Grundy's warehouse, barracks and workshop during his stay.

Howard Grundy, technically still on permanent assignment to the Sandridge listening post, actually spent a large portion of his time touring the world, conducting security sweeps at British installations far and wide. Grundy had been recruited much earlier than Smailes, and was already a somewhat legendary figure in the service. A bachelor, Howard lived with his widowed mother outside St. Albans, and electronics was his only passion. He was widely considered one of the best in the business, on either side of the Atlantic.

Smailes straightened up and looked around Howard's crowded workshop. Behind him ranks of steel shelving held bins of components and the occasional amputated contraption trailing intestinal wires and tubing. Dusty fluorescent tubes hummed overhead, which Howard augmented with adjustable task lights along the Formica workbench that ran the length of one wall. At the far end of the workshop a steel door led to the storage room where Howard kept his most valuable equipment— his spectrum analyzers and other scanning equipment, night vision pieces and interception gear. At the other end was a wash basin and simple camp bed where Howard claimed he occasionally slept if he was working late. From the razor and toothbrush next to the mirror, Smailes knew that Howard only kept his clothes in the third floor suite and regularly chose the security of his electronic dungeon over any other bedroom in the house. Kevin Butterworth was no doubt installed in one of the guest rooms on the second floor.

Butterworth caught Smailes' roving eye and smiled broadly. The truth was, all three Britons were feeling immensely relieved and Kevin seemed eager to give Howard further opportunity to expatiate.

"What's this gadget then, Howard?" Kevin asked, pointing to a device standing on a tripod on an overhead shelf that looked like a pistol mounted with a telescopic lens. It looked new and expensive and Smailes wondered momentarily why it wasn't stowed in the lockup with the rest of Grundy's prize gear. Smailes groaned inwardly at the question. He had had enough electronics for one day; it was almost six and he was getting hungry.

Before he could answer, the walkie-talkie at Howard's belt let out a squawk, and Grundy pawed for it, pushing the volume wheel as he did so.

"QST, QST. Read you, Harvey. Go ahead," he said.

Through a burst of static Smailes and Butterworth heard a heavy New York accent announce he was on the Throg's Neck, ETA twenty minutes. Howard held the radio to his mouth and gave a ten-four for the Peking Kitchen, six-thirty. Butterworth cast his eyes to the ceiling and Smailes looked at Grundy in wonder.

"My pal Harvey from Queens," Howard explained sheepishly. "We're friends from the ham circuit. Works for a phone company and gets me all this gear when I'm in town," he said, indicating the paraphernalia on his belt. "We're eating Chinese. Hey, Kevin, Derek, you want to join us?"

Butterworth laughed politely and said he'd fix something upstairs. Smailes thanked him also, but said he had plans.

"What did you ask, Kev?" Grundy continued. "Oh, that thing, yeah. Latest in laser mikes," he said, reaching up to caress a black telescopic leg. "Loaner from a friend with the Cousins. A beauty, isn't she? I'm going to take her apart later tonight—got to give her back before we go to California. Of course, it'll be five years before Curzon Street will spring for one, wait and see. I was just saying . . ."

"Look, Howard, I've got to get going," said Smailes. "Can you write your report by Monday? I'll go in to Ralph first thing. And you and Kevin had better stick around a day or two. There may be some debriefing, you know . . ."

"No problem," said Howard, beaming. "We're in no big hurry, are we, Kev?"

"Absolutely not," said Butterworth, folding his arms across his broad chest and giving Grundy an indulgent smile.

*   *   *

The truth was they had almost not found the bloody listening device at all. Howard had arrived at the beginning of the previous week to arrange the annual sweep, which Grundy, Smailes and Butterworth had conducted over the course of three evenings throughout the multiple floors of the British government offices. It was a painstaking process, since the British diplomatic facility in New York, located on First Avenue just north of the United Nations, was one of the most elaborate anywhere, comprising four separate government departments. The UN Mission, which occupied the eleventh floor, operated as a foreign embassy and also housed the MI5 station and the secure communications area known as "the fort." The tenth floor was exclusively the United Kingdom Consulate, largely a visa and passport factory. The ninth housed the British Government trade offices, together with the staff of the JAO, the joint administrative office that oversaw the other three departments. It also contained the Secret Intelligence Service's New York field station, which operated under the cover of the Devon and Cornwall Development Office. As usual, the routine sweep had turned up nothing.

At the end of the week, Howard and Kevin had traveled up to Boston on schedule, after which they were due to visit San Francisco, then Butterworth would return to London before the Christmas break. Grundy would then travel on to Fort Meade in Maryland for his annual visit to NSA, the largest electronic intelligence-gathering facility on the planet, and as such, Howard's earthly paradise. Grundy had confided to Smailes that if he visited NSA during the annual holiday lull, it was easier for his counterparts to show him around. Smailes did not doubt the NSA visit was Grundy's secret incentive for his annual U.S. trip.

Logically, Smailes had thought it was the last he would see of Howard Grundy for another year. Then the following Monday he had been reviewing the weekend sign-in sheets supplied by the lobby guard when a discrepancy struck him. Telephone company repairmen had been signed in on Saturday morning to visit the Portuguese Mission on the twelfth floor, but the guard had scribbled the floor number as eleven. The eleventh floor's sole occupant was the United Kingdom Mission to the United Nations, where Smailes now sat in his office. It was an odd mistake, and on closer examination, Smailes did not recognize the handwriting as that of Oral Yates, the regular Saturday guard. Further inquiries with the Portuguese counselor revealed that no repair work had been ordered or performed, by which time Smailes began to grow alarmed. He put in a call to Mort Janowitz, head of the building management company, but he was away from his office, so he went to his file cabinet to retrieve Yates' phone number from his personnel file.

Smailes spread the file in front of him, checked the number and punched in the digits, smiling as he did so. When Smailes had first arrived in the U.S. three years earlier, it had taken some time for him to grow used to the bizarre profusion of names, so different from the Anglo-Saxon uniformity he was used to. Two early favorites belonged to a U.S. diplomat at the UN named Crouch Schticking, and to an FBI agent he had met who was called Roman Violin. They were both supplanted, however, the first time he had cause to refer to the personnel file of Mr. Oral Love Yates.

Oral Yates was a diminutive, sixty-year-old black man of massive personal dignity and granitelike integrity who was deacon of a Pentecostal church somewhere in Brooklyn. Smailes could only assume his middle name had been bestowed by unsuspecting, God-fearing parents in token of their faith, which the adult Yates had chosen not to drop for similar reasons. Yates had been a civilian employee with the Police Department before retiring on a city pension to head up the building security force. Although he was employed by the management company, he worked closely with the building's senior tenant, and with Derek Smailes in particular. The two men had always gotten along particularly well, Smailes felt.

Yates' reassuring baritone answered the phone, but

his news was unsettling. Yates had indeed been absent on Saturday to attend the wedding of a relative, and his regular replacement had been unable to double up. Accordingly, Yates had arranged for a stand-in from their usual security firm. A memo should have been sent, he added. Had Smailes not seen it? Was there a problem? Quickly, Smailes told him of the discrepancy in the sign-in sheets, his suspicion that security might have been breached. Smailes heard a quick intake of breath. Yates promised to look into the matter and get back to him immediately. He did so within half an hour, and his report only confirmed Smailes' fears.

The weekend replacement turned out to be one Darnell Roberts, whom Yates' police contacts revealed to be a convicted felon who had been released from Rikers Island only seven weeks previously. Yates expressed his mortification over the incident and said he had reached Mort Janowitz, who wanted Smailes to call him immediately. Was there anything else he could do? Smailes had enormous respect for Oral Yates and could hear the pain in his voice. He asked him to report to him personally before his shift began the following day. He called Janowitz and spoke with him briefly, then walked across the corridor to the office of Ralph Van Deusen, his boss, who had sufficient status to have both a private office and a nameplate on his door. He knocked and went in. Van Deusen raised his pinched features from a sheaf of documents as he entered.

"Ralph, you see a memo from Janowitz that Mr. Yates was going to be replaced by a temporary guard Saturday?" he asked unceremoniously.

Ralph Van Deusen put down his papers with a gesture of forbearance and glared at his intruder. He was truly one of the more odious people Smailes had ever worked for, and Smailes sometimes suspected he had only won the coveted New York posting so early in his career because more experienced officers knew better than to serve with him. Van Deusen was a Rhodesian in his early sixties, a senior C Branch bureaucrat who had bailed out of his homeland during the civil war of the seventies and resumed British citizenship. He had parlayed his experience with the Rhodesian security service into a job with MI5, and had at first served with the prestigious K Branch, the counterintelligence service. Something had gone wrong shortly thereafter, however, since he had been reassigned to C Branch, or Locks and Safes, as it was known internally, and had shortly afterward undergone a messy divorce. He had recently begun a second four-year tour as head of Five's New York station, and Smailes had been crushed when he had not been reassigned the previous year. London had probably decided to keep him out of the way until his retirement.

Van Deusen had an unnaturally pink complexion that shone in artificial light, and fine gray hair that he kept clipped to military length. His nose and chin curled toward each other, and his eyes were narrow and suspicious. He had two peculiarities that were particularly objectionable to Smailes. Over the protests of his coworkers, Van Deusen smoked a dozen or so Churchillian cigars a day, and his office was always filled with their poisonous smell. The other was the vicious racial prejudice for which his countrymen were justly infamous. One of the reasons Smailes dealt almost exclusively with Yates or his assistants was because Ralph found it impossible to speak to them with civility. He was physically unable to pronounce the word "Zimbabwe," by which name Rhodesia was now universally known, as if in its alien consonants he heard the thunder of tribal feet across his ancestral land. It took Smailes most of his reserves to remain deferential toward him.

Van Deusen looked at him defensively. "Yes, I'm sure I did. I initialed it for Madge to copy and circulate to you, probably Thursday. You didn't see it?" He leaned forward to press the button on his handset to summon Madge from her adjoining office. "Is anything wrong?"

Before Smailes could answer, Madge Ryan entered the room, her eyes averted, and Van Deusen asked her brusquely about the Janowitz memo in his out-tray at the end of the previous week. Madge was Van Deusen's downtrodden secretary, a spinster in her late thirties who had worked for C Branch her whole career and had accompanied Ralph from London. She could be alternately officious and self-pitying, although Smailes had noticed she seemed more jaunty of late.

Madge disclaimed all knowledge of the document, and Ralph rummaged in that morning's accumulated papers in his out-tray without success, then began to lift papers and files from his in-tray below. Reddening slightly, he pulled out a memo halfway down. Smailes could see a note clipped to it.

"How the hell did that happen?" said Van Deusen, almost to himself.

"I don't know, Ralph," said Madge, reddening also. "But I'm not supposed to look through your in-tray. You've told me so yourself," she added defiantly.

"Ralph, I think we've got to get Howard back here," said Smailes quietly. "Madge, will you excuse us?"

That afternoon Smailes circulated a memo to the senior officials of all four departments that indicated a break-in might have occurred on the eleventh floor and that no office or telephone should be regarded as secure until a second security sweep could be completed. Minutes later, he took a flustered call from Quentin Smith, the SIS station chief on the ninth floor. The hostility between MI5 and SIS flourished at all levels of their interaction, and Smith's tone indicated that he held Smailes personally accountable for the suspected breach.

"Look here, old man, the fort's okay, isn't it?" he asked. All the members of the diplomatic corps relied on the eleventh-floor cipher rooms for their communications with London.

"Quentin, you'd have to be Houdini to get in there, you know that," said Smailes. "But until we can give the all-clear, I think you should be prudent."

Smith swore softly under his breath and hung up. Unless of course there's been collusion, Smailes said to himself, thinking the unthinkable.

Smailes pushed his chair away from the desk and put his feet up on Graham Booth's chair. Booth, Kevin Butterworth's replacement, was the new graduate trainee who now shared the office with Smailes and was the fourth C Branch member in the New York station. He was out riding shotgun with the diplomatic bag to Kennedy and wouldn't be in until the following morning. Smailes looked over at his Manhattan street map on the wall and stretched. Actually, he doubted collusion. It certainly wasn't necessary to pull off a break-in, which he had already begun to figure out in his mind.

It had to involve the weak link of the deadbolt code, Smailes was convinced. Although he had lobbied vociferously for its removal, a digital pad in the lobby controlled the main deadbolt lock into the eleventh floor office suite, in addition to the receptionist's buzzer. Smailes had argued that the six-digit code could be easily stolen by a sharp-eyed delivery person, but the diplomatic ranks who were issued the code had successfully overruled his protests. Perhaps, Smailes thought, he might finally prevail.

Yates' absence and his replacement by a stand-in had obviously leaked. The timing of their original sweep was probably also known. The mislaying of the Janowitz memo had prevented Smailes from warning Saturday's duty officer that Yates would not be patrolling the lobby. The phony workmen had somehow convinced the Saturday guard they were legitimate, and had gotten him to unlock the eleventh floor instead of the twelfth—his own stupidity had made him unaware of the discrepancy on the sign-in sheet. On Saturday morning the duty officer, who was always a senior "comm," as the British called their cipher clerks, was doubtless back in the fort. Intruders possessing the deadbolt code could be into the mission in seconds. Surveillance cameras covered the major thoroughfares and most sensitive offices on all three floors, but the monitors in the operations room were not ganged to recording tape—it had been deemed an unnecessary expense. If intruders had indeed penetrated the eleventh floor, there was no videotaped record of them doing so. If none of the duty staff had emerged from the fort during this interval, the intruders could have bugged half a dozen offices in the thirty-five minutes that the sign-in sheet indicated they had been in the building. He doubted the break-in team had journeyed to the ninth or tenth floors, although it could, of course, not be ruled out. But it certainly looked as if he, Howard and Kevin would have to repeat the whole bloody sweep again.

Further details were supplied by Oral Yates the following day when he presented himself dolefully at Smailes' office. Yates and Janowitz had traveled personally to the security company's offices in Valhalla, New York, to debrief the owner, who had pulled Darnell Roberts in for questioning the previous evening and summarily fired him. Yates wore an impeccable blue uniform similar to that of the UN security force, a stiff white collar and a black tie. His hair was receding and his temples were flecked with gray. He prepared for his account by shifting uncomfortably in his seat and adjusting his black-framed librarian's glasses on his nose.

"It's a broken play, Mr. Smailes," said Yates eventually, aware that Smailes' baseball knowledge relieved him of the need for further elaboration. "Can't fault Valhalla Security at all, except maybe putting in such a new man." He shook his head gravely.

In Yates' account, Darnell Roberts' criminal record had escaped security review on a technicality, a parole board waiver in his file. After initially stonewalling, Roberts had confessed Saturday morning's events after being threatened with the law. He admitted he had at first challenged the two workmen because their papers indicated they were to be admitted to the Portuguese Mission on the eleventh floor whereas his floor plan told him it was on the twelfth. The leader of the two then said they knew where they were going, handed him a clipboard and told him to check the second page. Underneath the work order Roberts found five hundred-dollar bills held by the clip. The temptation for a minimum-wage jockey like Roberts had been too great and he had unlocked the eleventh floor on his elevator console without further protest. Roberts had had little more to add except that the thirty-five minutes for which the workmen were signed in was accurate, and that he had only unlocked the single floor. He said the men were both middle-aged Hispanics, and that the older of the two, the leader, was seemingly missing some finger joints on his right hand. The owner had fired Roberts and wanted to know whether Janowitz or his clients wanted to press charges.

Smailes had been playing with the cap of a ballpoint pen during this account and slowly raised his eyes.

"What do you think, Mr. Yates?" he asked.

"No point," he replied. "Court system in this city has collapsed. Roberts could bargain any charge down to nothing and walk. Tell Valhalla Security to notify his parole officer. It's the best we can do."

Smailes exhaled slowly, knowing Yates was right.

"You think they got in, Mr. Smailes?" Yates asked.

Smailes nodded slowly.

"Anything stolen?"

"No, but I doubt that was the purpose. No sign of any office door being forced, but that doesn't tell me anything either."

"You didn't tell your duty man to keep his eyes open?"

Smailes tossed the pen cap down on his blotter and smiled weakly. "We lost your memo, Mr. Yates. I knew nothing about it."

Yates blew out his cheeks and shook his head slowly.

"A broken double play," said Yates, extending his metaphor.

Smailes picked up Grundy and Butterworth from the Boston shuttle on Friday, and Grundy was predictably buoyant at the prospect of finally tracking down a real bug in the New York facility. During the drive from La Guardia to Mount Vernon he was silent and attentive as Smailes rehearsed for him the circumstances of the break-in. Then he made Smailes backtrack over the major points. Half an hour? One floor? No alarms tripped? The fort occupied the whole time? He thought for a moment, then pronounced the new sweep a piece of cake. They would start after lunch and be finished by dinner, he claimed.

"We'll do your phones, your perimeter offices, deputy ambassador, chancery, first secretaries on down," he pronounced. Then he paused and asked self-importantly, "You know why they did it, of course? The timing, like?"

"Not really," Smailes admitted. He looked up into the rearview mirror and saw Butterworth listening intently, his eyes round with attention.

"Geneva," said Howard casually, looking down at the Bronx rooftops from the elevated expressway.

"What do you mean, Howard?" asked Kevin from the back seat.

"Foreign secretary's there right now. You wait, after his visit, they'll announce consultations in Washington, and you know he'll come through New York. The steam's starting to build out there, all right."

Smailes knew what he meant. Meeting under UN auspices, NATO and what was left of the Warsaw Pact— that is, the U.S. and the Soviet Union—had begun to make unexpected headway at the European Stability Talks in Geneva. It now seemed possible that the process of conventional force reductions begun in Paris three years earlier might now be extended to accomplish the virtual demilitarization of the European mainland, including the withdrawal of all but token U.S. and Soviet ground troops. The United Kingdom, as the primary European ally of the U.S., was intensely involved in the negotiations. Both sides were desperate to know the true state of thinking of their adversaries—and of their allies, Smailes realized as an afterthought. Since the talks were UN-sponsored, Britain's UN ambassador, Sir Michael Horsforth, was doubtless in the highest foreign policy loop. Grundy might well be right about the timing and motive. He caught Butterworth's eye in the rearview again and gave him a grudging shrug of acknowledgment.

*   *   *

The following day Howard began by having Butterworth monitor all the major phone lines out to the junction box in the stairwell, thereby eliminating the most obvious way to bug a building. Howard and Smailes began a methodical testing of individual phone sets. After half an hour Butterworth joined them back in the operations room behind the receptionist's station and announced that all the lines checked out, and Howard made a theatrical gesture. Then he picked up his spectrum analyzer in its foam-lined aluminum case.

"Time to modulate, boys," he said jauntily.

They began with the deputy ambassador's suite, Grundy planting his equipment on a desk in each room and scanning slowly through the entire radio spectrum, his eyes fixed on the circular screen and its jumping gauge that indicated frequency. Occasionally at the sign of a peak he grew excited and would yell "Modulate!" and Smailes and Butterworth would take turns reciting jingles and rhymes, but always there was a simple explanation—a powerful radio station, a television channel, a police dispatcher. After two hours they had swept all but the least sensitive offices, and Howard had grown discouraged.

"We've got to do the ambassador's office, then the fort," he said. "Only places we haven't tried."

Smailes reminded him that the alarm controlling the door to Sir Michael's suite had not been tripped or tampered with, but Grundy insisted.

"You checked the door locks for break-ins, Derek?" asked Butterworth carefully, avoiding affront to Smailes' professional vanity.

"Course I checked the bloody locks," said Smailes, exasperated. "But look, be my guest, check 'em again," said Smailes, and Butterworth disappeared into the corridor.

"Come on, it's got to be somewhere," said Grundy. "Them blokes didn't come to read the meter."

Smailes went to the operations room to punch in the code that disarmed the door to the ambassador's suite, then joined Grundy in the corridor. They walked slowly back together and Smailes used his pass key to let them into the conference room that formed Sir Michael's outer office. As Howard unpacked his gear and plugged it into the wall, Butterworth joined them again, shaking his head. This time, within seconds Howard's screen was jumping like a seismograph.

"Jesus, Derek, modulate!" said Howard.

Smailes complied and Howard snapped on his headphones, listening intently. His face broke into a wide grin and he hit a switch on top of the equipment.

"And everywhere that Mary went, the lamb was sure to go," said the speakers on the machine, in time with Smailes' lips.

"Gotcha," said Howard, reaching for the wand that would pinpoint the bug. Within minutes they had them both, two simple harmonica bugs about the size of large coins, concealed beneath the carpet at either end of the room. Howard tossed them in his hand like winnings. "Knew they had to be here," he said smugly.

Butterworth had a troubled look on his face, and Smailes knew why. "Howard, it means they got the alarm," said Smailes.

"Not necessarily," said Howard, pointing at the fiberglass tiles of the drop ceiling. "Let's look outside."

In the corridor opposite Sir Michael's secretary's office was a storage closet. Smailes unlocked it and flipped on the light. There were fresh smudges high on the wall near an air intake grille, above two cases of paper towels.

"They got in through the plenum," said Howard, "along the heating duct, picked out a tile and dropped down into the conference room."

Kevin Butterworth was bending down to examine the lock in the door handle. "Jesus, Derek, look at this," he said, pointing out tiny striations where someone had gone at the lock with a pick. Smailes had checked all the office doors, but not the storage rooms. He swore under his breath, furious that he had missed such simple evidence.

"Missed it completely," said Smailes. "Goddammit."

"I missed it too," said Butterworth, commiserating.

"You're supposed to miss it," said Smailes angrily. "You're a goddamn trainee."

"Don't be so tough on yourself, Derek," said Howard diplomatically. "We got 'em. No harm done."

Moments later, the two former policemen and their young assistant were standing in front of the bank of monitors in the operations room, Smailes still smarting at his oversight. Grundy was examining the two tiny bugs under a desk light, pointing out their design to Butterworth, but his expression had clouded.

"Amateur rubbish," he said, frowning. "Look, Kevin. Look at these batteries—don't have a couple of weeks of life. I dunno. See, Derek," he said, wheeling around. "I dunno if we got everything here."

"What the hell is it, Howard?" asked Smailes, irritated.

"This stuff's got no power and no range, but these boys were pros. Don't fit, Derek. I think these could be decoys. I think we've got to keep looking."

"I think he could be right, Derek," said Butterworth, very carefully.

Smailes swore again and indicated the video screens with a sweep of his arm. "If we'd just had these things hooked up to a recorder, like any bloody village bank, we could have watched the whole show, couldn't we?" he said defensively. "See, that conference room has a camera." He pointed at a screen in the top row.

"I know, I know," said Grundy, conciliating. He turned and looked up at the screen for a moment, cocked his head, took off his glasses and pressed his eyeballs. Then he looked again, more intently.

"Jesus, Derek. Look at that picture quality! It's twice as good as any of the others."

Smailes looked again. Grundy was right. Of the dozen monitors, the picture of the ambassador's conference room was easily the sharpest. Howard and Kevin were already hurrying out of the door.

They found it straightaway. Howard pointed out the tiny wires leading from the camera case mounted above

Sir Michael's inner door, coiling around the steel bracket and disappearing into the drop ceiling. They dragged a desk and a chair over to it and Kevin held the chair steady as Howard clambered up. Then he slowly unscrewed the side of the camera unit and whistled. He was beside himself with delight.

"Clever. Oh, very clever! Here, grab this stuff as I hand it down," he ordered.

When the equipment was spread out on the desk, Howard explained what the burglars had accomplished.

"See, they took out the old videcon camera and hooked up this job, a CCD piece," he said, holding up a small black video camera the size of a cigarette packet. "That's why the picture was so much clearer. So you've got a big cavity left, enough for all this." Howard pointed to a bulky power pack, a circuit board that held the storage and transmission components, and the large encryption device. "Let's find the mikes, Derek. I've unhooked the leads. Then we can go home."

"Howard, why didn't your scanner find it?" asked Butterworth.

"Because it uses your compression-burst technology, see, so it only gives out RF once a day, when it's transmitting. That's why they stuck in the decoys, so we'd go away when we found them, thinking that was it. These fellas were top drawer."

Smailes was a big man but he was less rotund than either Grundy or Butterworth, so he volunteered for the crawl along the heating duct from the intake grille in the closet. It was filthy and precarious work, but he quickly found where the ducting had been cut away for access into the plenum, and where the mike leads had been fed over the composition tiles. Butterworth jiggled them for him from below, and Smailes slowly pulled in both mikes from their positions in the drop ceiling, one above the conference table, and the other from above Sir Michael's desk.

Howard's excitement was infectious and Smailes now felt less angry with himself as he stood in the operations room, brushing the dirt from his hands and clothes. Kevin Butterworth had initiated that most British of celebrations; he was making tea.

"Bloody good show, Derek," said Howard. "You look like you need a cuppa."

"You bet, Howard," he replied, finally allowing himself a grin.

3

Derek Smailes emerged from Grand Central into a torrent of shoppers and traffic. A small battalion of people stood in the shallows, beckoning for cabs. He had chosen not to go home and change, and had plenty of time, so he decided to walk. The New York winter had not yet turned raw.

He strode confidently up Fifth Avenue, pleased with himself and his prospects for the evening. He was due at the apartment of his girlfriend, Clea Lynch, for dinner at seven-thirty. Clea had no doubt contrived another unlikely gathering from her large acquaintance, and despite his protests, Smailes loved her cooking. Their relationship was approaching its first anniversary, and since the nights they spent together were still irregular, he knew that tonight they would make love. He quickened his pace.

He strode past the floodlit, Teutonic heights of Rockefeller Center, the skaters in the plaza below the massive baubled tree, and headed for the giant snowflake suspended over the intersection at Fifty-seventh. The stores were still open and the sidewalks were mobbed, so he had to jog and weave along. It was his favorite time of year, and New York was at its best—the air was bracing, the mood was festive, and everywhere the thrill of spending was in the air. You could almost forget that in New

York City there were a million people on welfare, and five dope murders a day, if it was quiet.

Clea's apartment was on Madison in the Seventies above a florist's shop, and was one of the more desirable units in the British inventory, comprising as it did a two-bedroom, two-floor flat that the Americans called a "duplex." Clea had used her influence as second secretary admin with the joint administrative office to secure it, although she had to share it with a mousy simultaneous translator at the UN named Felicity Rowe. Smailes shuddered to think what it would rent for on the open market —probably double the thousand dollars a month that Clea and Felicity paid for it.

Clea buzzed him up and greeted him effusively at the door, holding floured hands away from him as she leaned forward to kiss his cheek.

"Darling, you're early. How nice," she said, standing aside so he could enter. Smailes stepped into the living room and saw the table was already set. Various bowls and plates of food stood on the counter of the galley kitchen.

"Can I do anything, Clea?" he asked, taking off his raincoat. He had never been able to reciprocate Clea's "darling." It just didn't come naturally to his lips, and in extremis he would grab for more tepid substitutes such as "honey" or "sweetie." Clea, for her part, never used any other term, and in fact used it indiscriminately with anyone from her considerable acquaintance whom she knew or liked moderately well. It was part of the theatrical quality of her personality, which Smailes secretly loved.

Smailes hung up his coat and looked at Clea in admiration. Slightly taller than average height, Clea Lynch was a broad-hipped, small-breasted woman with a white, almost translucent complexion. She had high cheekbones, green eyes and full lips, and the kind of beauty that could support a simple pageboy haircut. Her hair was dark brown, fine, and perfectly straight. She was twenty-nine, and by any standard, a beautiful woman in the prime of her life.

Clea had resumed her work in the kitchen, negotiat-

ing the preparations with her elbows held away from her
and her hands hovering like white birds. She was wearing
an elegant gray gabardine jumpsuit, obviously brand new,
beneath a bright yellow apron. She had a vaguely per-
plexed expression on her face.

Smailes steered his way past one of Clea's enormous
house plants and walked toward her, watching her with
amusement.

"You look nice," he said.

"Oh, I've had this for ages," she lied, glancing down.

"What's this?" he asked mischievously, peering into
a bowl.

"It's marinated tofu, darling. We're having Japanese
bean curd and tempura." Smailes commented that it
looked like a lump of drywall compound, sitting in a pool
of motor oil. Clea looked at him archly, refusing to be
drawn.

"It's very nutritious and very low-calorie, for your
information, Meatball," she said. Clea was a committed
vegetarian and pretended not to understand Smailes'
flesh-eating propensities.

"How about something high-calorie?" asked Smailes,
moving past her toward the refrigerator. "You got any
cheese in here? I'm half starved."

Another of Clea's peculiarities was her colorful political views. Stuck on the freezer door was a large magnet
that read "Sandino Lives!"

Clea had rinsed the tempura batter from her hands
and came toward him to greet him properly. "Oh, you're
such a brute, Sergeant Smailes," she said. "Open the
wine, will you, darling, and pour one for me?" She
reached up to kiss him, but pulled back in alarm.

"Good grief, Derek, you're filthy! Where have you
been all afternoon, down a coal mine?"

Smailes suddenly realized that his face was probably
still a mess from his crawl along the heating duct. "Re-
arranging the basement out in Mount Vernon," he said
casually. "Did I get dirty?"

"You certainly did. And your hair, too. Go and take a

shower. They'll all be here soon, and you'll just be in my way here."

"Who's coming?" asked Smailes. He retrieved a bottle of white wine from the refrigerator, opened it, and reached down two glasses from the cabinet.

"Some of your favorites," said Clea. "Felicity and that new boyfriend I told you about, the one who works at Hambros. Tyler and Dennis. And Lyle, of course. Lyle Pitkethly left a message that he's definitely coming."

Smailes grimaced. He liked Tyler and Dennis, but Lyle left him distinctly cold, and he was unsure about Felicity's new beau. He headed toward the stairs with his glass.

He stood in Clea's bedroom, peeling off his clothes. He could see the tiny plastic spindles scattered about where she had clipped the price tags from that afternoon's purchases, probably less than an hour earlier. He shook his head and smiled, wondering how he had ever ended up with a woman so far removed from his own background. At the same time he knew that their disparity in upbringing was a major source of their attraction. Clea was an Oxford graduate who had attended a public school that included lesser royalty on its rolls, but she had a defiant, unconventional nature that Smailes found thrilling. How else could she be attracted to him, an ungainly ex-policeman with two A-levels? And while she demonstrated many of the assumptions that went with her station in life, there was not a trace of snobbery about her. On the rare occasions they had discussed the prospects for their relationship, Smailes had expressed skepticism that it might survive the more class-polluted atmosphere of Britain, but such talk made Clea angry, and was contrary to her natural optimism. In consequence they avoided the topic—after all, Smailes had another year to serve in New York, and Clea almost three.

Smailes himself had another motive for not broaching the subject, even with himself. The truth was, despite himself, he was in love with her, and the realization exasperated him. He had expected his infatuation to diminish

ine, but in fact, as they approached their anniversary, it remained as strong as ever. He could not determine whether this passion was dependent on its very
illicitness—he was after all a peasant, shagging the
squire's daughter—but he certainly manifested a dangerous array of symptoms. Suspecting Clea was ultimately
unattainable, Smailes just hoped he was keeping them
successfully hidden from her.

He scooped the plastic tags off the carpet and
dropped them into the wastebasket, wondering about her
foray of that afternoon. Shopping was Clea's avocation,
which she was able to indulge seemingly at will thanks to
a supplement to her salary provided by her father, a
wealthy former Tory MP turned financier. It was a
weekly, almost daily ritual that Smailes had witnessed on
a number of occasions, an exercise in focused discrimina-
tion so intent that it made the act of purchasing almost an
anticlimax, except that it allowed the whole process to
begin over again.

Unable to contain his curiosity, Smailes crossed to
the dresser and opened Clea's lingerie drawer, checking
for new acquisitions. He saw nothing he recognized, but
became aware of a constriction in his throat as he brushed
her collection of cotton, silk and lace with the back of his
hand. Feeling guilty, he closed the drawer and sat on the
bed to remove his cowboy boots, socks and pants. Naked,
he reached into the huge closet to hunt for Clea's kimono-
style bathrobe. As he cast through her clothes, a trace of
her cologne greeted him, arousing him further. He found
the robe and covered himself, noticing as he did so a large
carrier bag thrust into the far corner on top of the chaos of
shoes. He squatted and examined the legend; it was from
the Lone Star Emporium, and his heart leapt in excitement. Clea knew of his love of country music and western
clothing, and this was probably his Christmas present,
something absurdly expensive from a fancy Greenwich
Village boutique. He resisted the temptation to look inside.

In the living room Clea's dinner guests had arrived.

Clea was still standing in the galley kitchen, sipping and talking conspiratorially with Dennis Dicenzo. Felicity was sitting crumpled on the couch next to a barrel-chested fellow in a blue blazer who was stabbing a broccoli branch into a bowl of dip. Tyler Dawes was seated opposite on a chair, talking quietly with Lyle Pitkethly, who was waggling one long leg across another, and playing with the tassel of a loafer. Everyone seemed to be drinking wine except Tyler, who was drinking Scotch. Smailes headed toward the kitchen to replenish his glass. He wanted to throw his arms around Clea and greet her properly, but knew he had missed his chance.

"That's better," she said, looking at him critically.

"Hello, Derek," said Dennis, offering a rather weak handshake. He was a tall blond man, handsome in a boyish way, wearing an elegant black cashmere sweater.

"Dennis," said Smailes, smiling, then tilting his head and opening his mouth to the light as a joke. Dicenzo, who was a dentist, laughed politely.

Smailes poured more wine and Clea tugged him out into the living room in front of the coffee table.

"Derek Smailes, this is Barry Boyd," she said with an elaborate gesture. "Barry works on Wall Street for a British bank. You know, Barry, Derek went to Cambridge, too," she said impishly.

Felicity's muscular companion rose and offered Smailes a beefy hand. "Really? Which college? I'm Tit Hall, land economy, eight years back. Rowing blue, Pitt Club, Union Society and all that . . ."

Despite himself, Smailes had reddened, but he didn't allow Clea the triumph of an angry look. Sensing his discomfort, Clea squeezed his hand to indicate that Barry, not Derek, was her intended target.

"I did a year at the Tech," he said flatly, "back in the nineteenth century. Police football league, Baron of Beef, Mill Road laundrette," said Smailes, and they all laughed. He returned her squeeze, rather too tightly. "I'll get another chair," he said.

"Not necessary, darling," said Clea, and made a

proprietorial gesture. "Everyone sit down. Dinner's ready."

Clea made a valiant attempt to orchestrate conversation during dinner, but the bizarre medley of personalities she had concocted was a strain on even her formidable talents. Barry in particular kept making braying, inept remarks that displayed an impressive range of Neanderthal views, causing Tyler to chew ever more slowly and look across at Clea from beneath his brows. Thankfully Barry seemed to be in the throes of an early bestial passion, since he enticed Felicity into a leering "early night" and they disappeared together up the stairs. Dennis and Clea worked on clearing the table and resumed their private conversation in the kitchen, leaving Smailes to talk with Tyler and Pitkethly. Smailes glanced over at Clea and Dennis, feeling intrigued, although not threatened. The reason was that Dennis and Tyler were lovers, so he felt no rivalry from either of them.

He began to pay attention to the conversation next to him, aware that he could not quite say the same about Lyle. Pitkethly was an affable, courteous man and Smailes knew his only excuse for animus toward him was that he had been an early flame of Clea's when she first came to New York. He was a tall, craggy East Coast Brahmin, a former State Department type who now worked in the UN Secretariat. He was in his late thirties and wore the standard off-duty garb of the U.S. diplomatic corps—striped oxford shirt, chinos and loafers. He was a staunch Republican and was complaining to Tyler Dawes about the pace of the Geneva arms control talks, which he claimed had been misnamed European Stability Talks, since their effect would be destabilizing. Dawes was disagreeing with him with a patronizing wave of his hand.

"Lyle, when was the last time a Soviet broke into your car and stole your cassette deck?" he asked sardonically.

Tyler Dawes was an intellectual jazz pianist with a mind like a flashbulb and a forbidding, lethal wit. He was

also black. Smailes had been dismayed to disco~~ver~~
Dennis and Tyler's relationship, not only homosexual but
interracial, pushed the envelope of his liberalism. In
Cambridge he had always been viewed as a dangerous
radical, but this, after all, was New York. Tyler made him
feel off balance, and he was aware that he tried slightly
too hard around him, currying favor with him in an uncharacteristic, almost fawning way, as if to erase his
prejudice by overcompensation. In return, it seemed to
Smailes that Tyler barely tolerated him, although he affected a superior manner with almost everyone, including
Clea. He was an attractive man in early middle age, with
light, coffee-colored skin, Caucasian features and short,
Afro-style hair that was beginning to turn gray. He wore
conservative clothes with incongruous touches—tonight
he was wearing a gold medallion over a brown turtleneck
and sport coat. Smailes had noticed that when he had
been drinking, like tonight, his educated voice began to
assume the accusatory cadence of street talk.

. "Admit it, Lyle, the Soviets just ain't the primary
threat to this society. Drugs and poverty are. Lemme ask
you something," he said, reaching again for his tumbler of
Scotch, not waiting for Pitkethly to reply. "What's the size
of the U.S. defense budget?"

"In round numbers? About three hundred billion,"
replied Pitkethly.

"An' what's the size of the federal deficit?"

"About a hundred and fifty billion, I think," said
Lyle, allowing himself to be drawn.

"An' what percent of the defense budget goes to Europe, even with all the troops we got left in the Persian
Gulf? Around half, right?"

"That's right."

"So we finally pull out of Europe, we wipe out the
deficit like that, right?" he asked, snapping his fingers.
"We'd have some money to put toward the real problems
we got."

Pitkethly was obviously goaded by this logic and explained patiently that the cost of defending Europe was

the same principle as buying an insurance policy for your house. It was expensive, but it protected the most valuable thing you had, and like it or not, U.S. postwar policy had brought the Western world its longest period of peace and prosperity in modern history.

"So you saying we shouldn't do business with the Soviets at all?" asked Dawes.

"No, I'm just saying it's all moving far too fast," said Pitkethly. "And I don't like the negotiating positions the U.S. has been taking."

"Such as, Lyle?" asked Smailes, finally joining in. There was a pause while Clea and Dennis, having finished up in the kitchen, brought their coffee over and joined them. At this juncture Pitkethly squandered whatever debating points he had accrued by indulging the classic American weakness for polysyllabic jargon.

"For a start it's excessively scenario-dependent," he said angrily, "and it's ignoring the crucial question of penetrativity."

"What the hell are you talking about, Lyle?" asked Tyler, but Pitkethly ignored him, growing more animated.

"Terrain enhancement, for instance, could easily buy two weeks after mobilization and ought to be leveraged, but Wilkes has dealt it over unilaterally as part of this absurd security zone idea."

"What's terrain enhancement, Lyle?" asked Clea politely.

"Oh, just some defensive systems we have in what used to be West Germany," said Pitkethly awkwardly.

"Like what?" asked Tyler, amused.

"The specifics aren't important."

"Well, *I'd* like to know," insisted Tyler, wide-eyed.

Pitkethly gave in. "Well, there are some antitank measures like plastic pipe beneath the fields that you can pump explosive slurry into, booby traps in the autobahn sidings and overhead gantries, things like that," he said dismissively.

Tyler Dawes waved an exultant hand in the air. "Only someone from the U.S. Department of State could describe pumping explosive under farmland as an *enhancement*," he said, and everyone laughed, including, eventually, Pitkethly. He turned to Smailes.

"Derek, what do you think? I don't think Tyler's being entirely serious." Smailes thought for a moment and returned to Pitkethly's analogy of the insurance policy.

"Seems to me the premiums should go down in times of less risk, Lyle. Look at the problems the Soviets have got. They've got ethnic wars throughout the South, individual republics queuing up to secede, and the economy's still a shambles. Seems there's still much more weaponry in Europe than is needed, on both sides, despite the cuts we've had," he said.

"Look, I'm not opposed to some more limited build-down," said Pitkethly, trying to sound reasonable, "but the Soviets are always going to be our adversary, let's not pretend about that. Oh sure, they cooperated over the Gulf, but that's only because they're desperate for our credits and technology, and it suited their agenda. And with the Germans reunified, I just don't think fifty thousand American ground troops are enough counterweight. I think it's entirely misleading to call that a 'precautionary level.' It's too small to be a precaution against anything."

Smailes tried to respond but Tyler issued a loud hoot at the term "build-down" and it seemed the discussion would get no further. Dennis interceded by telling Tyler it was time to leave, and Dawes did not protest, draining his glass and standing unsteadily. Pitkethly rose also and went to hunt for his jacket. Within minutes Smailes and Clea were alone.

"Sometimes I think you disagree with Lyle just on principle," she said, turning out the lights.

"Sometimes I do," said Smailes, smiling.

He undressed and sat up in bed, pretending to look at a magazine, waiting for Clea to emerge from the bathroom. He thought of Dennis and Tyler, how he wished he could be more relaxed around them, because he genuinely liked them both. Clea came back into the room wearing an alluring, high-collared nightgown that was ob-

viously nev~~~~~~~~~ with tipping~~~~~~ somehow missed in his hasty
search earlier. Jne sat down on the bed next to him.

"So what were you *really* doing this afternoon, Mr.
Smailes?" she asked innocently, running her hand into his
hair. Smailes frowned because he was going to have to lie
to her. Clea, of course, knew Smailes' affiliation, but his
training had been too strict and his sense of professionalism too keen for him to be able to divulge any details of
his work to her. He repeated his story about clearing out
the basement of the Mount Vernon house.

"On a Saturday? Of course, darling," she countered,
although not harshly. Smailes had explained his reticence
to her in the past by citing the disparity in their security
clearances. As an MI5 officer, Smailes had the highest,
Top Secret clearance, whereas Clea, a junior administrator, had clearance only at the first, Classified level. She
had accepted this justification with a certain theatrical
resignation and did not usually challenge him further. She
changed the subject by congratulating him in a lowered
voice on the restraint he had shown with Barry, Felicity's
new boyfriend. Smailes laughed, and although he did not
feel much like conversation, said casually, "Tyler was certainly putting it away tonight. And he was giving poor
Lyle a hard time." Then, with more urgency, "Come on,
sweetheart, get into bed."

Clea moved around to her side of the bed and
climbed in beside him. "That's because he was celebrat-
ing. He just found out today he's sero-negative."

"What?"

"He tested negative for AIDS. He and Dennis are so
relieved they're almost delirious."

"Ah, *that's* what you and Dennis were talking about
in the kitchen," he said. "Has he had the test too?"

"Doesn't need it. Tyler is the promiscuous one, or
was. Tyler took the test without telling him. Dennis feels
like they've been reprieved." She reached up to switch
out the light above the bed. "Anyway, since when have
you been so concerned about 'poor Lyle'?" she asked.

Smailes caught her wrist as she settled beside him

and kissed its flesh softly. When they had not made love for some time, Smailes had to literally force himself to go slowly. Clea brought his face up to hers and kissed him lovingly, running her hand down his flank to his hip.

"Actually, there's something I always wanted to ask you about Lyle," he whispered into her hair.

"What's that, darling?"

"How was his penetrativity?" He gasped slightly as her knuckle dug into his ribs.

The chairman of the Socialist Party of the Soviet Union strode noisily onto the landing of his hunting dacha, stamping the mud from his boots. He cradled a shotgun broken in the safety position and two borzoi hunting dogs yelped excitedly at his ankles. Standing aside, he fumbled with a game pouch at his belt as two much taller men entered behind him. In the icy draft from the open door the breath of the three men became a white fog. Eventually he freed the bag and handed it with his shotgun to the more bedraggled of his two companions. The man, obviously a bodyguard, was dressed in a civilian suit and was covered in mud. He closed the door and retreated miserably toward the kitchen, followed by the dogs.

Nikolai Sergeyevich Rostov, the president of the Soviet Union, grasped the elbow of his friend and military intelligence chief, Grigori Chumak, to steady himself as he removed his leather hunting boots. Rostov was a short, compact man in his midfifties with a flat Slavic face and steel gray hair cropped close to his skull. He wore an expensive leather hunting jacket and knee breeches. Chumak, by contrast, was a massive, corpulent figure, with thick black hair brushed back in waves from a high forehead. He had a large nose and red complexion, and wore a heavy military sweater and parka, and enormous rubber waders. Chumak in turn struggled out of his boots by grabbing the banister for support, as Rostov stood looking down at the people in the sunken living room below. Eventually both men padded to the wooden stairs in their socks and descended.

Nikolai Rostov's dacha at Zavidovo was a modest affair, a relic from his earliest days on the Central Committee, which was now used only as a hunting lodge. Its unfinished pine walls and scalloped banister rails contributed to an Alpine look. An open fire of birch logs burned low in the grate before a hooked oval rug. His wife, Sonia, sat reading in a warm-up suit on the simple sofa, her legs tucked beneath her. Two military men stood to attention as Rostov crossed toward her. She did not look up.

The Soviet president gave an impression of constrained energy, crouching slightly and walking with his weight forward on the balls of his feet, like a wrestler. Without looking at the two soldiers he waved an arm as he sat down and said, "As you were," and the two men relaxed slightly. Chumak took up a position at the bottom of the stairs, his face flushed from his exertion and the sudden heat of the dacha. He clasped his hands behind his back and rocked slightly on his heels, looking at the two uniformed men in amusement.

Lieutenant General Alexei Dolghorukov, the senior of the two soldiers, cleared his throat and spoke. He wore the heavy, double-breasted uniform of a Soviet general, the gold wheat-sheaf insignia on the collar and the two gold stars on the epaulets indicating his rank. Like Rostov he was a stocky, block-jawed man, with a pink complexion and thick gray hair parted neatly on the left. His Russian was formal and correct, spoken in a clipped Moscow accent.

"My office managed to reach me, Nikolai Sergeyevich. You wish to review next week's position papers? Naturally, the chief of staff will first—"

"You have the data I requested?" Rostov interrupted. The president was from the Transcaucasus region and spoke Russian with a thick Krasnodar accent.

"Yes, yes, certainly," replied Dolghorukov, slightly flustered, reaching behind him to where his aide held open a leather briefcase. "Only in the normal course—"

"Let me see," said Rostov impatiently, taking from him a manila folder. He glanced at the papers quickly and then raised his eyes to Chumak, who walked across to the sofa and took the file from him.

Chumak examined the documents laboriously, blowing out his cheeks and pawing through the papers noisily. Sonia Rostov did not move during this exercise, sitting motionless beside her husband, her eyes averted in a magazine. She did not turn the pages. Eventually Chumak looked up at Rostov and shook his head lugubriously.

"Now what about the correct data, comrade general?" asked Rostov angrily.

Dolghorukov flushed scarlet and said that in terms of the Geneva negotiations, these were the correct data. Glancing quickly at Chumak, Rostov snapped his fingers as if inviting a prepared speech. In a reedy voice surprising for such a big man, Chumak rehearsed the weapons categories agreed on in Geneva, and the classification protocols. In which case, Dolghorukov's data were deliberately misleading, he said. Did Dolghorukov not agree? Like Rostov, Chumak spoke with a southern twang in his voice.

The general did not speak but reached behind him to his aide, who produced a second file. Dolghorukov handed it directly to Chumak, who reviewed it slowly, a smile broadening on his face. Eventually he nodded and handed it to Rostov. Rostov stood and fished in the pocket of his breeches for a pen. He scrawled something across the first page in the file, then handed the packet back to Dolghorukov.

"You see, comrade, there is nothing to be feared from the truth. Present only these files to the chief of staff. You may leave."

At this point Rostov turned his back on the two soldiers and walked over to the fire. With a grunt he stooped and stirred the embers with an iron poker, then reached for more logs from the basket to his right. The two military men mounted the steps awkwardly, and retrieved their peaked caps from the bodyguard, who had reappeared on the small landing, the worst of the mud brushed from his suit. Only when the door closed did

Rostov stand and look at Chumak. Chumak's expression was the first to break, and soon both men were roaring with laughter.

Sonia Rostov finally looked up. "I don't understand you, Nikolenka," she said anxiously. "Summoning him on a Saturday, receiving him here of all places, you and Grigori going hunting like that at the last minute. Then leaving me here with them for hours. What am I supposed to do, go and sit in the kitchen? If you distrust him so, why do you provoke him?"

Rostov's laughter subsided and his expression stiffened. As if on cue, Chumak stopped laughing also.

"I'll provoke who I damn well please," said Rostov, his voice hardening.

Howard Grundy struggled out of the yellow utility van and hitched up his pants, feeling the radio flap against his hip. Then he kicked the door shut and slid open the side gate, retracting a tool belt, equipment case and folded tripod. He clipped on the belt and reached in for a "Maspeth Telecom" hard hat, which he planted awkwardly on his head. It was too small for him and almost fell off as he turned to look up at the partially completed apartment tower in front of him.

Grundy proceeded up the cement stairwell without incident, pausing at the fourth-floor landing to gather his breath. Then he ventured onto the concrete expanse of the unfinished floor, now bristling with thickets of aluminum studs strung with wiring. It was late afternoon and he had evidently arrived during a construction lull, since the site was deserted apart from a couple of heavily clad workmen crouched above the incandescent ball of a welding torch over in the far corner.

He scouted the south wall, peering through the empty window wells at the twenty-three-story white building five hundred yards away. He eventually chose a window partially obstructed by a compressor rig that offered the most promising line of sight, and carefully unpacked the laser mike and coupled it to its tripod. He had just adjusted height and trained the gun against the distant building to catch the pinprick reflection on his chest when a voice behind him called, "Hey you!"

Grundy's blood froze. He turned to confront a beefy-looking foreman in a hard hat and lumber shirt, the buttons of which didn't close over his paunch, revealing a soiled patch of stubbly undershirt.

"You Maspeth Telecom, surveying them access lines?"

"Right," said Grundy.

"Shoulda checked in," said the foreman. "Lemme get this outa your way."

The foreman reached for the handrails of the compressor and wheeled it into the center of the floor. "Call down to the third if you need me. Name's Bob," he said over his shoulder, heading away toward the welders.

"Sure," said Grundy, trying to sound as American as he was able. He waited until his heartbeat slowed to a manageable thump and resumed his calibration of the mike. He trained the gun at a fourth-floor window of the big building opposite, eventually finding the reflected beam again on his shoulder and adjusting the angle delicately until the pinprick was caught in the tiny parabolic dish. Then he coupled the leads to his captured recording gear and touched the volume wheel. His heart leapt as the bar meter jumped into life. Sound! He damn well knew it! The Soviets couldn't build a vacuum seal if their lives depended on it!

_4_

Derek Smailes had not been disappointed by New York. For years the United States had been for him the focus of unspecified yearnings, and it was the offer of a New York posting that had swayed his initial decision to enlist, despite the ambivalent circumstances of his recruitment. New York, the crucible of America's vast energies, would provide him with a distilled experience of the country, he believed, and he had leapt at the opportunity. Yet when he finally arrived, after a tiresome year of induction and orientation in Britain, the reality was far more challenging than anything he had anticipated.

For his first few weeks in New York, Smailes was literally reeling from culture shock, emerging from the collegial redoubt of the British Mission into a city whose pace and menace were far beyond anything in his experience. He commuted daily by train from Mount Vernon, where he had been installed in the safe house pending permanent arrangements, and spent a good deal of time in retreat, trying to understand his new culture through the medium of television.

Smailes had undergone a standard induction in London, despite having been personally recruited by the head of K Branch. After an endless series of interviews and panels, his training consisted largely of five months of lectures at the Berkeley Street training center in Mayfair, the topics focusing heavily on Five's history and its shibboleths—the British Communist Party, the Comintern, British fascism. However, one series of presentations had particularly enthralled him—the history of Britain's special relationship with the United States.

The U.S. lectures were delivered by a dubious-looking academic from Keele named Smethwick, whose long hair and beard seemed particularly provocative in the context of MI5's vacuum-sealed lecture room. Smethwick, however, was a virtuoso in U.S. history, and delivered two-hour lectures without notes that Smailes found completely engrossing. The key to understanding the contradictory phenomenon of U.S. cultural hegemony, claimed Smethwick, lay during its revolutionary period, when the U.S. colonies threw off the tyranny of British rule and established the first constitutional democracy in history. At one end of the country, he explained, there was an extraordinary group of high-minded patriots who provided intellectual leadership for the rebellion, then crafted a blueprint for the democratic exercise of power unsurpassed in human history. At the other end were back-country farmers selling provisions to the highest bidder, invading British or American. Such a marriage of idealism and venality was the unique American character, best personified by Thomas Jefferson, visionary author of the Declaration of Independence, who nevertheless defended his ownership of slaves on economic grounds. Smethwick claimed that the consummate modern expression of this dichotomy was the career of Richard Nixon— no other culture in the world could have both created Nixon and impeached him. The overarching impact of these conflicting American values had made the U.S. at once both vilified and revered throughout the world.

Smailes would remember Smethwick's words as he tried to decipher the messages on American television. The game shows and power dramas were already familiar to him, but the variety programs were entirely new, if only because the principals would often announce com-

mercial breaks, then appear in the commercials themselves, which Smailes found totally confusing. These
commercials were in themselves a revelation, since the
restraint and implied taste shown by network programs in
areas like language and nudity were completely abandoned in corporate America's advertisements. Cheerful
housewives menstruated gaily into sailor pants, followed
by poker-faced front men proclaiming a particular un-
guent able to reduce their hemorrhoids from the size of
an oceangoing barracuda to that of a small dinner trout,
with accompanying fisherman's gestures. Most striking of
all was the contrast in news presentation, where the traditional British sobriety was replaced by wisecracking
troupes of anchor people and weathermen. In his first few
weeks it was the weatherman, above all others, who reduced Smailes to gaping wonder. In Britain, television
weathermen practiced their calling with funereal reserve,
as if the British climate were a collective tragedy that
could only be borne through a delicate screen of euphe-
misms. In New York the weathermen bawled and
shrieked their wares with a thigh-slapping enthusiasm, as
if the weather was just another commodity to be pitched.
The whole spectacle struck Smailes as demeaning and
undignified, until he grew used to it.

Slowly, Smailes began to appreciate the liberating
properties of U.S. society and its mercantile ethic. The
contrast between the class-defined environment of the
mission and the greater world of New York City grew
increasingly more acute, and Smailes found himself
choosing friends and companions from outside the expatriate world, where nuances of accent and class had no
significance. He made friends in the FBI field office and
in the constellation of intelligence and security people at
the UN, and part of his early attraction to Clea was that
she, too, avoided the "expats," as the British called them.
And whereas at first he felt intimidated by the city's de-
generacy, by its very implausibility, he soon began to relish its commodious diversity. This last was its most
treasured property, since Derek Smailes—the copper's

kid, the literate cop, the Americophile—had been out of step his whole life, and in New York City, it was simply impossible to be weird.

Smailes was sitting in the cabaret bar of a dingy hotel slightly too far uptown on Lexington, watching Rudy Kabalan negotiate his way back to their booth. Kabalan passed in front of a small stage where a trio was setting up its instruments, unsteadily balancing two drinks and a large plate of hors d'oeuvres. He eventually set everything down and maneuvered onto the bench, pushing a plate piled high with chicken wings and shrimp into the center of the table.

"Help yourself," he said. "I'm definitely going to call this dinner."

"What do you mean, Rudy?"

"I joined OA," explained Kabalan. "Overeaters Anonymous. Realized I gotta do something about this," he said, grabbing his enormous girth. "We're talking two ninety. I do this contract with myself, see, where I designate three meals a day in advance. This is gonna be my dinner."

"I see," said Smailes noncommittally. He had put on some weight himself since coming to New York, and was now almost two hundred. He sipped his beer and glanced at the stage, where the trio had swung into the theme from *Ghostbusters*. "You're late," he said casually.

Smailes looked over at his companion and waited for him to finish a chicken wing. Rudy Kabalan was a huge, physically unattractive man who had cultivated Smailes since his earliest days in New York. He was a former CIA operative who now styled himself a "freelance information dealer," who made it his business to know as many intelligence and security types as he could. Kabalan had appalling taste in clothes and was wearing a tight-fitting brown leisure suit that was too small in the shoulders and neck and made him look bullheaded. He was in his late forties, had thinning, wiry hair and a dark complexion, and could have been Arabic, Latin, or even black. In fact, he was part Venezuelan and part Lebanese, and the Company still used him a lot for contract work, he claimed, because of his languages. Smailes doubted it was the only reason. In his phone call to Smailes earlier that Monday, he had explained he had just got back into town after a month in Tegucigalpa, straightening out some logistics. Kabalan had called the Honduran capital "Tea-goose."

"Yeah, sorry about that," he replied presently. "Some PR flipped a U-Haul on the Drive and nothing was moving south of Ninety-sixth Street. I got a scanner so I took a detour down through East Harlem. And you know what I see? I'm stopped at a light around a Hundred Thirtieth and see this buck climbing out of a red Beemer, vanity tags, spoilers and all that shit, with a pistol and ammo belt wrapped around him. Broad daylight! It's friggin' Dodge City up there. Vanity tag says the guy's street name is Shortstop. You believe that?"

Smailes knew that Kabalan had not summoned him to his Manhattan haunt to complain about the behavior of local drug dealers. "What's up, Rudy?" he asked.

Kabalan wiped his fingers on a paper napkin and ran a tongue along his front teeth. "You see the piece in the *Times* Sunday, the thing about the McLean Cartel?"

"Sure," said Smailes. The article had been the lead story in the magazine, profiling the activities of the antiarms control group that had begun making loud noises in Washington. The lobby had been formed in late summer by some defense industry and right-wing Congressional types to oppose signing any new accord with the Soviets. It had an official, tongue-twisting name, but the press had quickly dubbed it the McLean Cartel after the hotel in suburban Washington where the founders had gathered to announce its formation. The concept avowedly had been to create a "recession cartel" along the Japanese model, to spread the effects of the prospective downturn in their industry. It was also clear that aggressive lobbying was part of its agenda.

"They begun hassling the Brits yet, then?" asked Kabalan.

Smailes smiled and shook his head. "There's no need, Rudy. The British government is going to get plenty of heat domestically if the PM goes along with this latest U.S. proposal. You think it's going to fly?"

"The security zone idea? Sure. Very clever pitch."

"What do you mean?"

"I think the basic concept was Rostov's. He threw Wilkes a hanging curve and Wilkes took it out of the park, claims it's his own idea. See, it's been one of the more far-out items on the American agenda for years. Imagine, a five-hundred-kilometer demilitarized zone through the middle of Europe! It's a concept the Americans can get hold of. And it takes care of a lot of problems with one shot. It solves the issue of what to do about former East German turf when the Soviets finally yank their troops out. Sure, Germany stays in NATO, but Rostov can save face by telling his public, and his military, that they didn't sacrifice twenty-odd million lives in the war for nothing, that now they've got this buffer zone all around their western border, guaranteed by treaty. Czechoslovakia and the Balkan states will love it, since it guarantees the removal of Russian troops from their soil. The Poles will probably accept some Soviet forces on their territory as insurance against Russian isolationism. And it allows the Western nations some solid pretext for drawing down their defense budgets, which they all wanna do. Believe me, it's gonna fly."

A primary activity of Kabalan's that summer had been to nurture Smailes' burgeoning interest in baseball, and from the lessons Kabalan had given him in New York's ballparks Smailes needed no further elaboration of the hanging curve analogy. He knew the curveball down and in was almost impossible to hit, but any hitter worth his salt would not miss the curve that a pitcher hung up by his belt.

"Let's face it," Kabalan continued, "with the egg-heads talking another world recession and the dollar on the skids, arms control is the only game in town. The Middle East's cooling off and the Geneva talks are beginning to move, so Congress is not about to start banging the pork barrel or get in the way. 'Peace dividend' is the new Beltway buzzword, believe me."

Smailes took a shrimp from the plate between them and looked away at the three-piece band, who were just winding up a number. He remarked with some surprise that the lead singer, who played an electric keyboard, had only one arm. The drummer, an old lizard of a guy who must have been almost seventy, wore an improbable dark brown toupee. He looked like a twenty-eight-year-old who'd led an extremely difficult life. The drummer put down his sticks and reached for brushes.

"So seriously, they're not hassling you? Nothing weird going on?" said Kabalan.

"Who wants to know, Rudy?"

"A client," he replied offhandedly.

Smailes reflected that Rudy's timing was peculiar, given that he had only turned in Grundy's report on the discovery of the bug to Van Deusen that morning. He was aware he had to be on his guard around Kabalan, whose precise allegiances were impossible to call, although he could be a mine of information and was the kind of maverick to whom he was drawn. Smailes repeated that he knew nothing, but would let him know if he heard anything unusual. He finished his glass and rose to leave as the one-armed vocalist began crooning something about doing it his way.

Ralph Van Deusen sucked his cigar until the tip glowed red, removed it carefully with long, almost feminine fingers, then exhaled a jet of smoke. He looked down again at Grundy's report, then across at Smailes. From the pained expression on his face, he was obviously about to do something contrary to his nature, and was taking time with preparations.

"Congratulations," he said eventually. "The ambassador's impressed. It seems they might very well have got away with the whole thing. You agree with his speculation about its origin?"

The vestiges of Ralph's Rhodesian accent were still distinct, and he pronounced the word "embessedor."

"I don't doubt Howard knows what he's talking about, the design and everything, and the Soviets or their former surrogates are the most logical culprits. But it could be either side, when you think about it, if their wireless design is so easy to identify and copy. Either way the connection has got to be the latest stuff happening in Geneva. The Soviets desperately need intelligence, but the Americans must be dying to know if we'll go along with them. Looks like the installation crew was Cuban, and Lord knows, both sides have plenty of those boys on board."

Van Deusen made a scoffing gesture with the hand that held his cigar. "You think the Americans might have planted this? That's ridiculous, Derek. If the CIA wanted to bug this place they could strong-arm any junior diplomat to plant something during office hours. They're in and out of here all the time."

"You have a point, I suppose," said Smailes.

"How they got in is more the question. Where's the leak, Derek?"

"There doesn't have to be one, Ralph. I've said all along that deadbolt code could be stolen by someone watching its use. It's only six digits. No keys were used, looks like, since the lock to the closet door was forced." He handed Ralph a copy of his memo authorizing another change in the code, and a separate memo asking Ralph to back him up with a further appeal to JAO to scrap the deadbolt keypad altogether.

Van Deusen glanced at them, then growled, "They knew the layout well enough. How d'you explain that?"

"Pretty standard in a building like this," Smailes countered. "As far as I know, the perimeter offices have the same layout on all the floors. We only customized the fort. I was more concerned initially about the timing, with Mr. Yates out like that, but that could have leaked in a number of places, or even have been a coincidence." He paused. "Of course, I could get out the VSA and start to question people one by one."

Van Deusen looked up sharply and Smailes knew he would have to chew on this one. Smailes' use of the Voice Stress Analyzer had been highly controversial when he first arrived in New York. He had seen it demonstrated during his training in Berkeley Street and had agreed it was vastly superior to the polygraph, which most of the British service still favored. Unlike "fluttering," the VSA required no wires or special training. It simply measured microstresses in the voice which were present when someone lied, and could be used without the subject's even being aware of it. After a series of thefts soon after he arrived, Smailes had procured one and used it to identify a locally employed woman in the visa section who had begun stealing increasing amounts of cash. It had been a quick and relatively painless investigation, but many career people had been indignant at Smailes' tactics and had complained bitterly about the totalitarian methods of the security service. The VSA had remained locked in his safe ever since.

"No, I don't think that will be necessary, Derek," said Van Deusen quickly. "I agree there's no obvious reason to suspect a leak."

"I'm going to follow up with the security guard," said Smailes. "Mr. Yates is getting me his address. Maybe we can get a better description of the two Latins, more of a sense of affiliation. Lustig at the FBI might be able to help out, get them short-listed."

At this juncture Van Deusen's secretary, Madge, came into the room and stood timidly in the doorway, holding a document. Van Deusen ignored her.

"Seems like a waste of time, Derek," said Van Deusen forcefully. "And I'm damn sure we don't want to go blabbing to the FBI."

Smailes was still angry that the break-in team had almost succeeded, and couldn't understand Ralph's opposition.

"Look, Ralph, it's the only lead we got, and I don't see how—"

"Okay, okay," interrupted Van Deusen irritably, looking up at Madge. "What is it?"

She stepped forward quickly and dropped the document on his desk. "You left this in the copy machine, Ralph," she said, turning on her heel. It was the original of Grundy's report. Van Deusen glared at the door as she closed it, then went in his desk drawer for a file and made a production of writing a note in it.

"I deliberately check her every so often," he said, in a typical attempt at self-justification. It was classic Van Deusen, turning an elementary personal error into an imputation of disloyalty against his staff. Van Deusen stuck the huge cigar back in his mouth like a giant pacifier. Smailes kept his expression impassive.

"Will you sign off on the JAO memo, Ralph?" he asked.

"Absolutely," he said, without removing the cigar, so his mouth flapped around it. "No one can object to scrapping the stupid system now, even if the horse has bolted."

Back in his office, Smailes found Graham Booth scanning their copy of the Grundy report, and had to endure his bantering accusations. Booth wanted to know why he hadn't been included in the team for the second sweep, since it had been certain to turn something up.

"Because you would have bleated like a goat if I'd violated your precious weekend, Graham," Smailes retorted angrily. Booth had barely been on the job three weeks, but already felt emboldened to challenge Smailes directly. He was a self-opinionated Welshman with dark curly hair, chiseled features, the build of an Olympic diver, and boots that were entirely too big for him. If Kevin Butterworth represented one dimension of Five's graduate entrance program, Booth represented its opposite—a clever, immature kid in his first suit, who thought he was God's gift to the intelligence community. Smailes was going to have to endure his company for six months and regarded it as a personal mission to bring him down a peg or two.

"Not if I'd known we were going to find something," said Booth, as if that made a difference. "You've got a phone message," he said, indicating a pink slip on Smailes' desk.

Smailes picked up the slip and groaned. Howard had phoned in asking him to call his beeper number. Why couldn't Howard agree to have a phone installed in the Mount Vernon basement? Smailes knew it was where he would be. Howard probably wanted an update on his report, to know whether he would be required in person or whether he and Butterworth could make tracks back to Boston. They probably could, thought Smailes, punching in Howard's number, waiting for the screeching tone, then punching in his own. He hung up and almost immediately Howard called back.

"You in your workshop, Howard?"

"Naturally," said Howard, and Smailes rolled his eyes.

"Well, it doesn't look like Ralph wants the story in person, Howard, if you're wondering—"

"No, no, that's not what I'm calling about, Derek. I want you out here right away, see what I've got." Howard was talking rapidly in an unnatural, high-pitched voice. "I think we can put one back on Ivan," he said excitedly.

Caleb Wilkes, the president of the United States, stretched his feet out on the coffee table and flicked the report with the end of a pencil. Seated around him were his five most senior aides, their dark suits contrasting sharply with the expensive white upholstery of the Oval Office. Wilkes, a rugged, telegenic man in his early sixties, was the only one in shirtsleeves, and the only one with his feet on the table.

Each man was holding a copy of the council of deputies report on the activities of the McLean Cartel. Wilkes' inner council increasingly used this informal grouping of its deputies to define the polarity of opinion within the

Administration and generate policy options. "So what do you think, John?" said Wilkes presently, looking across at his director of central intelligence.

"Option B is your safest course, Caleb," said the DCI, folding one blue pinstriped leg over the other. "I think the analysis is fair-minded, but overstated. This outfit is basically the predictable collection of ex-spooks, defense industry hucksters and the lunatic Right. They've got no one within three tiers of policy at Defense or State, and no credibility on the Hill. Oh sure, they've got a couple of think-tank types on the board, but everyone knows it's basically a bunch of arms makers trying to stop us sinking their gravy boat. I just can't justify a destabilization exercise. Option B, ignore them, that's the most sensible course."

Several heads began to nod, but Wilkes' chief of staff, a redheaded Texan, spoke up. There was a mournful pessimism in his voice.

"Do you think that's wise, John? These are extremely delicate times. We gotta carry not only international public opinion, but Congress, the entire policy-making establishment and the American people too. God knows, if they step up the doomsday stuff, start guerrilla tactics, create a lot of anxiety . . ."

"It won't matter," said Wilkes, holding up his hand. "John is right." He looked away at a portrait of John Kennedy on the wall, as if summoning inspiration. "The safest bet is to keep an eye on them, and ignore them."

"And why won't it matter?" asked the chief of staff, persisting.

Wilkes put his report down on the coffee table and waved at the DCI, without looking up. "Tell him, John," he said casually.

"Because anyone who matters at State, at Defense, or on the Hill has been indoctrinated on the Lvov protocols, and knows that all this stuff about abandoning deterrence is alarmist crap," said the CIA director forcefully.

The three other dark-suited men in the room, who included the secretary of defense, nodded in agreement.

No elaboration was needed. It had been a highly irregular and daring move when the defense secretary had met the previous month with Soviet chief of staff Sergei Kapalkin, the head Soviet arms control negotiator. The cover had been a routine inspection by American officials of a missile battery in Lvov, Ukraine, but the real agenda had been a recognition by both sides of the need to break the deadlock in Geneva. General Kapalkin had traveled to Lvov in total secrecy, and the result of the meeting had been a historic agreement by each side never to trust one another. In concrete terms, the Lvov protocols had committed both sides never to negotiate further reductions in their bedrock deterrent force, their second-strike capability, their massive mobile ICBM systems, which each side now had mounted both in silos and on high-speed military trains. It was an acknowledgment that the threat of mutually assured destruction was the ultimate guarantor of peace in the world, that a MAD world was a safe world, and that the promise of nuclear obliteration should be enshrined forever as sacred East-West doctrine. In view of this secret accord, the great reformers Wilkes and Rostov had agreed to proceed with further reductions in conventional forces in Europe, and sudden breakthroughs had followed.

Wilkes looked again at John Kennedy's charismatic smile. He was a good bit older than Kennedy when in office, he knew, but almost as good-looking. He turned to face his skeptical disciple, and his face hardened.

"This bastard Rostov is no goddamn social democrat, I know that. You think I'd do a deal with a Communist asshole like him, without something like the Lvov agreement in the bank?"

The expletives compressed the air in the room like gunshots, and the men seated around him flinched. No one, however, rose to the rhetorical question.

"Neither do the American people," he said forcefully, signaling that discussion was over.

"What about the allies? When are they gonna learn about the Lvov deal?" asked the chief of staff recklessly.

Wilkes looked up sharply. "In due course," he said. "In due course."

The junction of Broad and Wall in New York's financial district was completely deserted. A freezing rain fell in clouds as a lone pedestrian made his way toward a parked car, leaning against the downpour behind his umbrella. He opened the passenger door then reached up for the catch, collapsing the umbrella and ducking into the car in one motion.

"Jesus Christ," said Lyle Pitkethly. "I'm drenched."

Oscar Tufano did not look at him, but reached a cigarette up to his mouth.

"Do you have to?" asked Pitkethly.

"You said we got a change to the plan?" asked Tufano in a heavy accent, turning toward him. He was a dark-complected Latin of average height, balding, with a flattened lump for a nose.

"We've got to get close to the guard."

"This not part of my job description."

"I said it might be."

"I donno."

"You want me to go elsewhere? I could easily go elsewhere."

"You got the address?"

"Yes."

Tufano changed the subject. "I done the bomb. Half a kilo Semtex, simple. I hit the safe like you say, dead easy."

"Well?"

"Market is thirty thousand," said Tufano, looking out at the rain.

"I know," said Pitkethly, reaching into his raincoat for a fat envelope and placing it on the dash. "The address is inside."

Tufano turned to look at him, raising the cigarette again to his lips. It burned close to the back of his hand since his index and ring fingers were missing their top two joints.

"How soon?" asked Tufano.

"Soon."

"This is the last?" he asked.

"I'll let you know," said Pitkethly, opening the door and thrusting his umbrella out into the rain.

5

Lieutenant General Alexei Dolghorukov leaned forward to throw the security switch beneath his desk and call the meeting of Krasnaya Zvezdochka to order. There were a dozen or so senior military men in the office, which he had managed to keep despite losing his general staff position in Rostov's latest "reorganization." Since his political supporters had won his appointment to the restored rank of chief of Soviet forces in the European theater, last held by Ogarkov, the spacious third-floor office on Frunze Quay in Moscow had remained his. It was an honor to which he hoped he was equal.

Dolghorukov watched in silence as his guests, none of whom was below the rank of lieutenant colonel, rose slowly to their feet. Then he opened the meeting with a curious ceremony. The fluted teak panel behind him held an enormous map of the Moscow military district. He stooped and released a catch at its base, then pushed the panel up into the ceiling like the lid of a giant rolltop desk. He reached inside and pulled the cord of a small fluorescent tube, then crossed to a safe beneath the large window, extracted a porcelain figurine and placed it on a plinth inside the lit recess. Then he stepped aside so the officers could view the scene. The room had come quietly to attention.

What Dolghorukov revealed was a shrine to the glory and continuity of the Russian army. The central figure was a reproduction of Count Aleksandr Suvorov, Catherine the Great's greatest general and Czarist Russia's most celebrated soldier. Below were two smaller representations of Kutuzov and Zhukov, vanquishers of Napoleon and Hitler respectively. Beneath them was the statuette depicting Minin and Pozharsky, heroes of the seventeenth-century defense of Moscow against the Poles, astride their rearing mounts. The original stood outside St. Basil's Cathedral in Red Square. Only Zhukov was a postrevolutionary figure.

Dolghorukov looked up and cleared his throat, then snapped his fingers in annoyance at the official portraits of Rostov and Lenin on the teak panel opposite. A major general broke ranks and reached up to the Rostov portrait, turning it to face the wall. When he was back in position, Dolghorukov ordered a presentation of arms and the military men saluted the shrine in unison. On the command "Order arms!" the salutes snapped back down. On command again the soldiers relaxed, taking seats and reaching for cigarettes. Dolghorukov pushed aside one of his four telephones, sat on the corner of his desk and faced them.

Krasnaya Zvezdochka, or Red Insignia, was the official historical society of the Soviet officer corps, of which Alexei Dolghorukov had become a guiding light. He began by welcoming a guest to the meeting of the Moscow chapter, Major General Anton Palov from Lvov in the Ukraine. General Palov, he explained, was deputy commander of the Carpathian military district and was on a short visit to Moscow. At his introduction, Palov, a dark-skinned, slightly built officer with wiry hair, inclined his head slightly. Dolghorukov then reviewed their agenda—a slide presentation of the battle of Kursk, the pivotal Soviet victory in the Great Patriotic War, and a discussion of Premier Rostov's latest arms control proposals in Geneva. The reaction in the room was instantaneous.

"I propose we reverse the order, comrade general,"

said a plump infantry colonel heatedly. "Who can concentrate on the glories of our past when our future is being bargained away? Do you have further developments to report?" There was immediate assent in the room. Dolghorukov held up his hand.

"Comrades, I understand your concern, believe me. Yes, I was present at a meeting where the latest position papers were approved. There will be announcement no doubt tomorrow, or early next week . . ."

"And . . . ?" said the colonel, to a background of agitated murmurs.

Dolghorukov paused for effect, looking away out of the window at the building opposite. When he turned again to the meeting there was pain and anger in his voice.

"Rostov proposes to accept the American offer of a security zone in central Europe. In return, the Soviet armed forces will be reduced by a further five hundred thousand men within two years. Seventy-five percent from the European theater, ten percent overall from officer ranks—"

"You mean in addition to last year's cuts?" asked the colonel. "That's impossible. It would mean an overall reduction in troop strength of more than forty percent . . ."

Dolghorukov continued. "Troop ceilings on foreign European territory to be reduced to precautionary levels of fifty thousand men, each side. Tank strength to seven thousand. The Bundeswehr will be limited to two hundred fifty thousand men on former Federal Republic territory. And we will entrust the defense of our western border against imperialism to twelve divisions."

Pandemonium broke out, with half a dozen officers trying to speak at once. Eventually Dolghorukov managed to restore order, and acknowledged Palov, who got to his feet to speak, his voice shaking with emotion.

"Comrade general, though my initial response is disbelief, I have to assume that what you say is true. And frankly, I feel it is time for us to do something. The Russian army will not have witnessed such derisory troop numbers since the defeat of Napoleon! Twelve divisions for the defense of our own western districts? We hold double that number in the former East German territory alone! Return another fifty thousand officers to civilian life? How? Where? There is no housing, there is no parallel employment! What is this man thinking?"

Several other hands were raised and Dolghorukov acknowledged a major general from the rocket forces, a gray-haired old bureaucrat with thick black eyebrows bordering an enormous brow.

"I agree with our comrade from Carpathia. The officers in this room alone command tens of thousands of men. This has gone far enough. We must organize resistance, protest through our representatives at the highest level . . ."

"Like who?" asked the plump colonel woefully. "Kapalkin has been co-opted as chief negotiator, and Ermakov is a tame bear." The hawk-browed major general turned angrily to Dolghorukov.

"Alexei, what do Anatoli Petrovich and Georgi Vladimirovich say?" he asked, referring to Dolghorukov's invisible protectors, the presidential council conservatives Anatoli Grishkin and Georgi Tumanov.

"What can they do?" said Dolghorukov with an anguished shrug. "They are in the lesser faction." He used the term of historical doom, the *mensheviki*, the minority.

Derek Smailes could not believe his ears. He was leaning over a small cassette recorder on Howard's bench, listening to conversations in Russian. Howard stood aside, beaming.

"See, I knew their vacuum technology was lousy," Howard said gleefully. Smailes looked around at him sharply, then frowned.

"Did you know anything about this, Kevin?" asked Smailes sharply. Butterworth was leaning with his rump against Howard's workbench, his arms folded. He gave a baffled shrug at Smailes' question and shook his head.

Howard had been almost wild with excitement when Smailes arrived at the Mount Vernon basement, and it took considerable coaxing for Smailes to get his story straight, since it emerged with all kinds of time lurches. Sometime over the weekend, it transpired, Howard had decided to field-test the bugging equipment they had found in the mission to determine whether it was any good. He claimed he had noticed the Soviets were replacing windows on their diplomatic apartment building, the twenty-three-story white monstrosity in Riverdale, northwest of the city—he had seen the work proceeding while driving by to a friend's on the Upper West Side, and it had intrigued him. It stood to reason the Soviets were using their own materials and labor for such a sensitive job, and Grundy could tell they were installing vacuum-sealed security glass. It was a perfect opportunity to field-test the equipment and try out his borrowed laser mike at the same time, since it could intercept through leaky glass up to half a mile away. Some elementary reconnaissance turned up an apartment tower under construction six blocks away, and after his pal Harvey came through with a van, hard hat and equipment belt, Howard decided to try and score one for his own team.

According to Howard, the previous evening he had showed up with his laser mike rigged to the captured recording gear, and waltzed up through the partially finished tower block, shooting across at the Soviet building from the empty window wells. And sure enough, throughout the seven floors the Soviets had completed, there were all kinds of leaks. At that time in early evening many of the flats were unoccupied, but he had gotten good resolution from one apartment on the fourth floor, and two more on the seventh. Since he had looked like a telephone company employee, none of the other workers at the site had paid him much attention. Howard was triumphant—the recording gear they had captured was revealed as top quality, certainly a lot better than the Soviet window seals. And who knew, maybe he had gotten hold of something important.

Smailes had asked whether Kevin Butterworth was in the house, then summoned him down to the basement to hear a condensed version of Grundy's stunt. In his opinion, it offered Kevin an important example of the kind of freelance operation to avoid. Smailes frowned again as he hit the Rewind button on the tiny machine. In his opinion, the whole stunt was ludicrous, and could easily have backfired if Grundy had been apprehended by either the Soviet or American authorities. He winced at the thought of the FBI response if the British had been caught in such an idiotic prank on its turf, or the outraged protests the Russians would have handed up at the UN.

"Howard, don't you think you could have run this by me first?" he asked testily.

"Didn't know it would come to anything, did I?" said Grundy defensively. He clearly felt he had not exceeded his authority.

Smailes hit the Play button and the three Britons listened to the intercepted conversations again. The first was hardly a conversation—rather, a series of muffled shouts and grunts to the accompaniment of one of Tchaikovsky's more boisterous overtures. Smailes spoke no Russian but did not need the female participant's "Da! Da! Da!" translated, since it was clear she would reach her climax at about the same time as the music. The second intercept was more prosaic; an earnest Russian voice explaining something while an early *Dallas* episode ran in the background. A radio also seemed to be playing somewhere. Smailes heard the names "J.R." and "Ray Krebs" pronounced in a thick Russian accent. The third conversation was the longest and clearest, without background interference. A man and a woman were holding an animated discussion about unknown matters. Smailes caught the names "Tatanya" and "Irina," and occasional English words like "New York Hospital" and "baseball." All in all, it seemed meager fruit, hardly worth jeopardizing the special relationship for. Howard, however, was pleased as Punch. Smailes looked across at Butterworth, then back to his colleague Grundy and sighed. He did not have the heart to admonish him further.

"Yeah, well, I suppose the first thing is to get it translated, see what it's worth," said Smailes. "At least we know we could get more if it was warranted." He wasn't sure he sounded convincing.

"So does Van Deusen want any more explanation about how we found this stuff?" asked Butterworth, indicating the dissected remains of the bugging gear. "Only, we've still got a whole floor to do in Boston before the California leg, and I've just found out I'm supposed to check in at Curzon Street by the twenty-third," said Butterworth. "Looks like I'm going to spend the next six months there."

Smailes smiled to himself. He had recently filed a glowing evaluation on Butterworth, which had probably been instrumental in the decision to transfer him to headquarters so quickly.

"That's terrific news, Kevin," said Smailes. "I'll have to give you my survival tips."

"I'd appreciate that," said Butterworth.

"No, it doesn't look like Ralph's interested. Let's give it another twenty-four hours, then make your plans," he said, punching the Eject button and stuffing the tape into its slim plastic case. "Howard, I'll let you know what this turns up," he said, with as much enthusiasm as he could muster.

The taxi lurched onto Park and headed south, bouncing over craters for half a block until the driver slammed on his brakes with such force that Smailes had to grab for the back of his seat for support. He looked over at Clea and they both laughed. At this time of night it was probably quicker to take the subway, but they both avoided it at all costs.

"So where are you taking me tonight, if I may ask, Mr. Smailes?" she asked mockingly, fixing her green eyes on him from beneath the perfect brows. Smailes felt a surge of desire for her, but looked away casually. The most erogenous part of Clea's anatomy for Derek Smailes was her larynx. She had a resonant contralto voice and perfect diction, and spoke English with a kind of sensual precision he found irresistible.

"The Shalimar," he said. "I hear it's terrific. Great vegetarian menu."

"It's not on East Tenth is it?" she asked, knowing from his look that she was right. "Honestly, Derek, you're hopeless. All those restaurants have the same kitchen, you know—they're knocked together in the back."

Smailes had realized soon after he arrived in New York that the city was the eating man's destination resort —the range and quality of restaurants was simply superb. He had recently hit a trove of Bangladeshi emporia in the East Village that were outstanding—excellent cuisine, mountainous portions, and very cheap. He considered making a comment about The Shalimar's sexy waiters, but thought better of it.

The occasion was Derek and Clea's first anniversary, which they had acknowledged in an offhand manner that afternoon on the telephone, and then had agreed to go to dinner. Smailes settled back in the stalled taxi and thought again of how they had met, the unlikely course of their romance.

It had been the annual staff party at the consul general's townhouse, which Smailes had attended without any particular expectation. He had been single for almost six months since he had stopped seeing Special Agent Sheila Delaney, and was aware he was feeling restless. However, he had an informal personal rule about co-workers, most of whom were married anyway. He had naturally noticed Clea Lynch soon after her arrival that summer, since she was not the kind of woman you could overlook. The Five station and JAO overlapped in a number of areas, and Clea had always been friendly and polite when he had cause to speak with her on the phone. But they had had almost no personal contact, and Smailes automatically assumed she was unavailable.

During the party he stayed fairly close to the people

he knew best, generally the support staff rather than the diplomats, and was thinking of calling it an early night when he noticed Clea Lynch over by the cocktail table, cornered by Ralph Van Deusen. Smailes joined them and introduced himself, at which Clea gave him a dazzling smile that made his heart quicken. Ralph was going on and on about some university prank involving himself and Clea's father, and Smailes was suddenly aware that the two of them knew each other. Ralph had plainly had too much to drink, and since his bellicosity swelled in direct proportion to his alcohol intake, he was by this stage actually bellowing at Clea, and roaring with laughter at his incomprehensible story. Clea shot Smailes a despairing look, and he manfully interrupted with questions about her work. Clea engaged him gratefully, and Ralph suddenly realized that the conversation had veered away from him, that he had begun talking to himself. He muttered an embarrassed remark about good old days and then retreated, looking for other victims.

As soon as he was out of earshot, Clea said, "What a prick!," which endeared her to Smailes hugely. She explained that Ralph had known her since her schooldays, he had been at Oxford with Daddy, as she put it, but that he made her flesh creep. She looked at him squarely and asked, "You work with him, don't you?," which let Smailes know she must have made some note of his existence. He explained his role in the security office vaguely, and the two of them talked animatedly for the next hour, pausing only at intervals for more drinks. Clea was wearing an exquisite floral dress, blue pumps and a delicate cologne. He found her extremely easy to talk with, intelligent, provocative and funny, and was soon aware of a growing attraction to her. Then, as the evening wound down and he wondered how to advance this encounter to a next stage, she said to him artlessly, "Let's go home together." Smailes felt a lurch in his stomach and a flush of color to his face, and remembered saying hoarsely, "Okay," or something like that. Their relationship had never looked back.

Later, when they had begun to exchange intimacies, Clea confessed that she had had to break off with her latest lover, Raul, to continue her relationship with Smailes. He was an Argentine waiter at a Ninth Avenue steakhouse, and their relationship was suffering "communication problems," she conceded. However, she had liked him much better than her first boyfriend in New York, the U.S. diplomat Lyle Pitkethly, she explained. She had never had much to say to Lyle and could no longer take him seriously once she discovered that his idea of relaxation was to wear his loafers without socks on weekends. Smailes told her of his affair with Sheila, whom he had met through their mutual friend at the FBI, Bob Lustig, how he felt there was finally too much a cultural barrier between them, despite his prejudice in favor of Americans. Smailes told her he sympathized with the inevitable communication difficulties of a committed vegetarian and a steakhouse waiter. What did she eat when she went over there? he wanted to know. Clea responded archly that the restaurant had a salad bar, and called him Meatball, a nickname which unfortunately stuck. Smailes secretly loved it when she insulted him.

The cab freed itself from its traffic swamp somewhere below the Pan Am building and hit an unexpected sequence of green lights. Smailes felt for Grundy's tape cassette in his raincoat pocket, but before he could speak Clea began a long lament about her day. She was particularly indignant about the CG's recent behavior—he was being such a baby about this limousine business, she said. Smailes commiserated. In his opinion it had been an entirely pointless exercise when the deputy ambassador and the CG had been notified they were to lose their chauffeur-driven Jaguars for budgetary reasons. Sir Michael got to keep his Rolls after all—it was deemed a representational vehicle—and the CG and the deputy had been incensed at the slight. The savings from the switch to domestic vehicles were probably insignificant, and Smailes had been told the whole point was simply for the new gang in Whitehall to throw its weight around a little, to show the mandarins at the FO who was in charge. Clea, as JAO second-in-command, had taken the brunt of the CG's bile. She told Smailes that the dealership had finally called to say the new Lincolns were ready to be picked up, and she had circulated the news to the CG, the deputy ambassador and Ralph. Smailes had in fact already seen the memo and was planning to pick up the cars the following morning.

He also knew that a major element of Clea's complaint was her overall weariness with the nature of her work. In the normal course of events, Clea, an Oxford graduate, would have been an A-stream entrant into the civil service, and by now would have been anticipating promotion to first secretary somewhere on a political desk. But because of her unconventional background, Clea had been admitted to the less prestigious executive or E stream, and had had to prove herself in a string of administrative positions, with the promise that at some unspecified date she could retake the full entrance exam and be upgraded. Clea never expressed overt regrets that she had chosen to take almost three years off after university to travel Europe, then work for a drug rehab program in South London, but Smailes wondered what she really felt. It was clear that the tedium and indignity of being a glorified clerk was beginning to irk her.

The cab had pulled up outside The Shalimar by the time Clea had finished her account of the day's events, and Smailes went into his pocket and held up Howard's cassette. He had given the question of translation some thought, and had concluded that Clea's flatmate, Felicity, was his safest bet. As far as he was aware, almost no one at the British Mission spoke Russian, except perhaps the first secretary on the East Europe desk, and he wanted to avoid any fallout from that direction. Felicity, after all, worked for the UN, not the British, and was likely to remain discreet about the task.

"Can you ask Felicity to translate this for me, sweetheart?" he asked casually, holding the cassette out to her.

"Of course," she replied. "What is it?"

"I'm not sure, to tell you the truth. Something Howard Grundy wants me to get translated."

Clea took the cassette and put it in her bag. "It's an eyes-only Top Secret," he said awkwardly.

Clea looked across at him sharply. "All right, I understand," she said quickly, turning to open the taxi door. "Are the waiters good-looking in here?" she asked over her shoulder.

Karl Busch was standing in the middle of the showroom, waving a fan of papers at a "joe," a rookie salesman who was trying to leave by a side door without being seen. "Hey, Micky," he yelled, and the young man approached sullenly. "Get me the keys on these two, will you?" he said, tearing off sheets from the triplicate forms. The salesman, who looked all of nineteen, slunk off toward the offices in back. "Okay, Mr. Smalls," said Busch. "Gonna be all set here in just a minute."

"Smailes," said Smailes, tapping his foot against a metal desk in irritation. He had handed over the teller's check a good forty minutes ago. It seemed paperwork, no matter whose, always took forever. He looked down the length of the dealership, at the row of identical desks with their phones and computer terminals, bisected by the sleek Lincoln Continental that stood alone in the middle of the showroom. At its far end was the general manager's glass-walled office. Smailes could see him looking out on his domain, smoking and talking on the telephone. Busch, the leasing manager, came over to where Smailes was seated and smiled uneasily. "Sorry, Mr. Smailes. I dunno where all the joes got to today. Must be on strike," he said.

Smailes turned and looked at the plaques on the wall. It appeared the latest sales award had been shared by Frank "The King" Carbone and Dan "The Silk" Sullivan. "That's all right, Mr. Busch," said Smailes. "What was the delivery hold-up, anyway?"

"Custom phone jobs always take time, Mr. Smailes. You go to your stretch limo, your phones are standard, factory equipped. In the town cars we got to have 'em installed. You understand."

Smailes nodded. There were only a handful of Manhattan dealerships that had UN security clearance, and Smailes had worked with the UN general services division to line up Eastside Lincoln in the Seventies off Third Avenue. The two disgruntled British diplomats had expressed no interest in actually choosing their new models —that had been left to himself and Van Deusen. Derek Smailes, once the paperwork was finally complete, was planning to drive each in turn down to the British garage at Forty-ninth Street. It looked like the exercise was going to take the whole morning.

Busch was too agitated to sit down. He was a short man with a helmet of frizzy hair and an expensive blue suit who wore a gold identity bracelet that drooped onto the back of his hand. Smailes speculated about the size of his commission on such an order—at least a month's diplomatic salary, he reckoned.

Busch's joe finally returned with four sets of keys, and it was only then that Smailes thought to ask the obvious. "Where do you keep these machines until people pick them up?" he queried.

"Out there," said Busch, pointing across the street to a row of shiny cars that were parked diagonally across the opposite sidewalk, like horses tethered to a rail. "We bring 'em out of the shop every morning. One of the hazards of doing business in Manhattan," he explained.

"Let's go and look, then," said Smailes, taking the keys and signing one last form that Busch produced.

Smailes had picked out the model on the dealership floor, and had ordered two identical town cars in dark blue. They stood side by side, gleaming in the pale winter sun. Smailes wrapped his raincoat around him and peered in the driver's window of the first. He thought the fuss would die down once the diplomats saw them—they were handsome cars, even roomier than the Jags.

He left Busch standing on the sidewalk and climbed in the driver's seat, whose brown leather was still covered in plastic. He turned the ignition key to contact, punched the radio and heater buttons, cranked the gearshift back and forth. He picked up the handset of the cellular phone, hit the Talk button and listened for a dial tone. Then he looked at the instrument panel, fiddling with the stalks on the steering column as he did so. He hit the window button on the armrest and leaned out to Busch as it glided down.

"You'd better explain all this to me," he said.

"Certainly," said Busch, maneuvering around to the passenger door. Smailes hit the electronic lock release and Busch clambered in beside him.

"All right," said Busch. "You got lights and indicators here . . ."

"Wait a minute," said Smailes, spotting an anomaly. "The mileage reads eighty-two," he said. "The machine I picked out in the showroom said three or four. Why the big difference?"

Busch looked uncomfortable and feigned surprise, craning across to look at the odometer. "Oh, must be some delivery mileage. Maybe we got these from a dealer upstate, or something." He sounded unconvincing.

"No way, Mr. Busch," said Smailes. "Factory-direct —that's what the UN agreement says. Are you telling me you got these cars from somewhere else?"

"I really don't understand, Mr. Smailes," he blustered, but Smailes was already climbing out of the first car to inspect the second. Its odometer read seventy-eight miles. Busch had arrived beside him.

"Okay, Mr. Busch. What's the story?"

Back in the showroom, Busch made a production of inspecting his sheaf of paperwork. Finally he found a document that jogged his memory.

"Oh, that's right. We got overloaded with a rush installation job for the Secretariat, and we had to sub out the phones to a shop on Long Island. They're very reliable. We use them all the time . . ."

"You did what?" said Smailes, horrified. "You drove these cars out to a subcontractor on Long Island, and you weren't going to tell me? This was not part of our agreement, Mr. Busch. I think you'd better let me get that check back."

Busch had begun to panic. "No, no, it was my mistake—an oversight. Everything's okay, believe me. Look, you can bring them both back into the shop and inspect them yourself, if you like. Happens all the time. This is a very reliable supplier we use. The UN people know about them."

"Save it, Mr. Busch," said Smailes, angry at the attempted deception.

They hoisted the first car on the hydraulic lift and Smailes walked beneath it, holding a caged light bulb on the end of an extension cord. A couple of mechanics in stained blue overalls regarded him curiously at first, then returned to work. Smailes looked around the underside of the chassis carefully, but saw nothing unusual. When the car was lowered he repeated the exercise under the hood. He understood little about the profusion of equipment he saw, but nothing looked obviously out of place. Busch stood tensely at his shoulder.

Then they switched cars. Busch stood at the controls of the hydraulic lift and as the second car rose in front of him, Smailes hoisted his light bulb and walked beneath it, looking like the Statue of Liberty in a raincoat. At first he thought he was seeing things, but then he stepped closer and saw a sight that made his blood freeze in terror. Clamped to the right rear suspension unit, directly below where a passenger would sit, was a small cake of pink plastic, attached with bright red wires to a tiny digital receiver. Even with his limited experience, he knew immediately it was a bomb. With his heart in his throat he staggered out from beneath the suspended car, grabbed Busch by the sleeve of his expensive suit, and propelled him toward the swinging door into the showroom. Busch tried to protest and resisted as Smailes pushed him through the doors into the fluorescent cavern.

"There's a fucking bomb on that car!" he yelled in a

strangled whisper, not releasing Busch's arm. "There's a fucking bomb, I tell you!"

The color drained from Busch's face and he reached for the phone on the nearest desk. "Oh my God," he said, not looking at Smailes.

Smailes snatched the receiver and slammed it down. "We'll do this my way, mister," he said, his thoughts racing. "No police. Who the hell knew you'd subbed out this job anyway?"

Several heads farther down the showroom had turned at the commotion, and Smailes could see the manager emerge from his glass lair at the far end of the room. His heart was pounding and he was fighting to order his thoughts. The bomb had a digital receiver, not a clock, which meant it was radio-controlled. It would probably not be detonated until the culprits were sure it was occupied. They were all right. There was probably plenty of time.

"What's the problem, Karl?" asked a suspicious voice. Smailes looked up to see a chubby, red-cheeked man in a gray suit looking at them down a cigarette. He wore his black hair carefully parted with Brylcreem. Car salesmen had to be the last breed still using it.

Busch kept his voice to a suppressed bleat. "This customer says there's a bomb on the Continental he's picking up, Mr. Weingrad. He's with the British government. I didn't see, but I suppose . . ."

Weingrad's jaw dropped and his eyes hardened. "Call the cops, Karl. Right now."

Smailes put his hand forcefully over the handset again. "No way," he said, "unless you want to see your UN account go down the toilet."

"Call the police," Weingrad repeated.

"Look, you people are responsible," Smailes said angrily. "You subbed out the phone job to Long Island, in direct violation of our agreement. Play it my way or I'll see you never lease another car at the UN, period."

The manager's eyes narrowed and he hesitated. "That bomb is radio-controlled, not time-controlled,"

Smailes continued. "There's time. I'm not sure, but I think I can get a British expert over here right away. Ten to one this is the Irish. We can dismantle it quietly, no publicity, no propaganda for the IRA. Let me make a call, try and get him here."

Weingrad had evidently made a rapid evaluation of his UN account, since he pushed the phone over to Smailes. "Okay," he said. "Make your calls. Only if it don't work, we call the cops, understood?"

"Understood," said Smailes, desperately fishing in his wallet for the number of Howard's beeper. The truth was, Howard and Kevin might have already left, and his whole plan was futile.

He found the pink slip with the beeper number, punched in the string of digits, and hung up. There followed a yawning silence as Weingrad stoked up another Merit Ultra Light and scowled at Smailes. He no longer looked so red-cheeked. The handset rang and Smailes grabbed it, identifying himself immediately. It was Howard, sounding affable.

"Kev and I just on our way to La Guardia, the beeper goes off. I say, 'Fancy that.' I tell the taxi driver pull over. What's up, Derek?" he asked.

"Howard, can you do a bomb?" he asked quickly.

Howard remained courtly. "I dunno, I've had some instruction, but no, I've never built one myself. What do you have in mind?"

"No, I mean, can you defuse a bomb?"

The buoyancy drained from Grundy's voice. "What do you mean, Derek? What's going on?"

Smailes quickly explained the circumstances, his wish to avoid publicity. The car was on a hydraulic lift, he explained, and the bomb at eye level.

Howard was obviously scared. "I dunno, Derek, I've got no tools on me. I've never done one in the field . . ."

"Please, Howard," Smailes pleaded. "The IRA get headlines on this one round the world, it's as bad as if the bomb went off. I could put together a package of tools. Will you give it a try?"

Grundy was the kind of man whose loyalty made him incapable of resisting such a direct appeal, and Smailes knew it. Reluctantly, Howard asked for directions and said they'd be there as soon as possible.

Smailes hung up and turned to the showroom manager. "Let's evacuate this place," he said.

The two salesmen, Smailes and Butterworth stood next to the parked limousine on the sidewalk opposite, watching the entrance next to the overhead doors by which Howard Grundy had entered twenty minutes earlier. Grundy had said little to Smailes when they arrived, dropping his suitcase at the curb, taking the packet of tools from Busch, and giving Smailes a forlorn smile. Then he hitched his pants and headed across the street, looking like the loneliest man in the world. At that point, Butterworth leaned over to Smailes and said quietly, "He's dead scared, Derek. Listen, when this is over, we've got to talk."

Smailes looked at him quizzically and said, "Sure," but Butterworth had turned away to resume his vigil.

As the minutes ticked away, Smailes began to feel increasingly uneasy. The way he had pitched his appeal to Howard, he had effectively left him no option. That the bomb might go off and kill him was not possible. It was simply unthinkable. Howard, after all, was the best.

Two dozen or so employees stood around up the street, chatting and smoking, glad of the break from their routine, as if bomb scares were a daily occurrence. The manager had only announced "suspicion of a bomb" over the public address, which obviously no one had taken seriously. Busch had stationed a couple of salesmen at each end of the block to discourage pedestrians from entering. Traffic still sailed by, oblivious.

Eventually, the door opened and Howard emerged, his bald head lowered. His hands were empty and he walked unsteadily toward the four men. Smailes could see dark patches inside his coat where sweat had soaked his shirt. He raised his face to Smailes painfully.

"Can't do it, Derek," he said in an anguished voice. "Hands are shakin' too much. One of the leads looks loose, but I dunno, it could be a trick. Every time I go after that detonator, I don't know I'm goin' to trip it. You'd better get the pros."

Beads of sweat glistened on his forehead, and he removed his glasses while fishing miserably for his handkerchief in the blue work pants. His eyeballs stood out like the testicles on a Doberman.

Smailes turned to Busch. "Call the police, Mr. Busch," he said flatly.

Smailes walked slowly up the block to Third Avenue with Howard, supporting him with an arm around his shoulders. Butterworth followed a pace behind, carrying both suitcases. Smailes would not listen to Howard's self-recrimination. He told him it was not his fault, that he, Smailes, should not have coerced him, that he'd tried his best. They still had a chance to contain the publicity. The important thing was they'd found it, no one had gotten killed. They had foiled the first IRA bomb attack on the U.S. mainland, after all. There was nothing to feel guilty about.

Kevin Butterworth drew level with them. "He's right, Howard," he said. "You did your best."

Howard stood at the corner of Third trying to gather himself as the uptown traffic poured past. Smailes knew that whatever they said was useless, that Howard was not about to forgive himself for failing to come through in the clutch. Howard looked at his watch and said something about another plane in an hour. Smailes told him to go and drink some tea before taking another cab.

"Ask for two teabags, Howard," he told him, as Grundy picked up his suitcase and began to wander off down the block.

Butterworth tarried. "Look, I can't talk now," Smailes told him. "I've got to get on to Ralph. Can you call me from Boston, or California?"

Butterworth hesitated, glancing down the block to

where Howard was disappearing into a coffee shop. "Okay, I suppose so," said Kevin.

Smailes grabbed him by the arm. "Make sure his nerves are okay before you get on another plane," he said.

"Right," said Butterworth, heading off after Grundy.

Smailes made calls from the booth on the corner as the sirens grew closer. He spoke first with Van Deusen at the mission, then with Lustig at the FBI, then with Van Deusen again. By the time he hung up, the New York City bomb squad had arrived, and Smailes decided to stand back and watch the show.

The bomb team had not had a live device to tackle in some time, and went about their task with gusto. They parked their huge yellow command vehicle up the street from the dealership, and quickly set up barricades. A uniformed officer with a walkie-talkie held a hurried conference with Weingrad and Busch, then started directing droves of other officers who had arrived in squad cars from all directions. They apparently decided not to block off Third and Second Avenues, but quickly secured the street and evacuated the bystanders to the blue barricades at each end. Then they went about clearing out all the office buildings in the line of sight. Some of the office workers emerged looking frightened, but most seemed to take their reprieve in a festive spirit and headed off toward shops, bars and subways. A few chose to swell the small crowd that had gathered where Smailes stood at the Third Avenue end of the street.

Smailes quickly intercepted Busch and the foul-tempered Weingrad, both of whom had made the mistake of leaving overcoats in the dealership and were beginning to skip and dance with the cold. He explained forcefully the deal the British were proposing—the car would be described to the press as an unassigned vehicle for the UN pool, and the British would not lodge a formal protest about security violations. Smailes would be left out of it— they would claim Busch had found the device during a routine inspection. The FBI had already been told the real circumstances and would square it with the police, he explained. They would arrange for the UN to go along. Weingrad looked poisonously at Busch, whom he was obviously holding directly responsible, but nodded angrily. Smailes asked a few more questions, and then withdrew as he saw a lieutenant in plainclothes climb out of an emergency services squad car, speak with a uniformed officer, then approach the two men. Outside the command vehicle the bomb team was apparently ready to make its first reconnaissance of the facility itself.

Smailes stood back behind the crowd of onlookers and watched as a figure dressed like an astronaut in an asbestos suit waddled down the street from the command post near Third. He entered the small door next to the folding gates with difficulty. A moment later a faint motor was heard, and one of the gates was slowly retracted onto its overhead tracks. The spaceman then reappeared and walked unsteadily back up the street.

Craning his neck, Smailes could then see the tiny robot vehicle mounted with a video camera as it made its way down the street. Instacam vans from the local TV stations had arrived, and news producers yelled angrily at bystanders to stand aside so their cameramen could get a clear shot. The toy car disappeared into the garage for several minutes, and the crowd gave up an incongruous cheer when it reemerged. After another interval, the spaceman made a second trip down the street, carrying a small toolcase. This was the tricky part, Smailes was aware, and he moved away around the corner. A short way down the block, two reporters stood before cameras in pools of intense light, filing preliminary reports for the early news shows. They looked like an arcane priesthood, making offerings before bizarre, one-eyed deities. Next to the first of them, Weingrad stood to one side, stamping out a Merit Ultra Light in preparation for his anointment. Smailes hoped he was not about to fluff his lines. He turned again and looked up the street. The spaceman had staggered out onto the street. He removed the fish bowl on his head, tucked it under his arm, and gave a thumbs-up sign. The crowd let out another cheer. Smailes moved away down the block, counting the cash in his wallet. He would make one more call to Van Deusen, then he had an expensive cab ride in front of him. Executive Mobile Telephone, Busch had said, Islip, Long Island.

6

The taxi burst out of the Midtown Tunnel at about sixty and swung across toward the ramp for the Long Island Expressway. It had needed three attempts before Smailes found a cab that would take him, and then it was only because he had persuaded the driver, who spoke almost no English, that Islip was "just past Queens" and that he would also provide the fare back to the city. The driver's mugshot on the glovebox identified him as Yussuf Khalil, and made him look like a serial murderer. As Smailes climbed in he noticed a tiny portrait dangling from the driver's rearview mirror. He craned forward to see the shaggy smile of Yasir Arafat.

Van Deusen had supplied one last piece of information when Smailes called through with news of the all-clear. It appeared Executive Mobile Telephone was owned by Raymond Cooney, whose brother Michael was a prominent Noraid fundraiser and had been a St. Patrick's Day grand marshal the previous year. In theory, MI5 had no jurisdiction in North America. In practice, the security service maintained extensive files on Irish republican sympathizers, particularly in the New York and Boston areas, which they used to pressurize domestic law enforcement agencies. The intelligence seemed to confirm the obvious—that somehow an IRA cell had learned of the presence of the two British vehicles at the Cooney shop, and had taken the opportunity to plant a bomb on one. If the analysis was correct, it would mark the first time the IRA had attacked British personnel outside Europe, and could signal a frightening escalation of their campaign. Smailes had had little time to discuss ramifications with Van Deusen, but he could tell from the intensity in Ralph's voice that the news of the discovery had sent shock waves throughout the British colony. Smailes reflected that his cultivation of agents at the FBI station was finally paying off—he could never have leaned on the dealership people to suppress the British involvement without an FBI guarantee to back him up.

The Palestinian cab driver leaned over his shoulder a couple of times to ask, "How far this place?" and each time Smailes reassured him it was just a few more miles. Lunchtime was one of the few periods in the day when traffic on the expressway actually moved, and they made good progress. Presently Smailes saw the exit for Central Islip and told the driver to turn off. They had to stop a couple of times for directions, but eventually found Executive Mobile Telephone on a corner lot in a small industrial park. Smailes told the driver to wait and leave his meter running.

The cellular phone company occupied a prefabricated cement building adjacent to a woodworking shop. There was a parched square of grass in front of a glass door and office window, next to a steel garage door. Smailes approached the office door, noticing that the bottom half was in fact a plywood panel held in with screws and duct tape. He pushed and went in. Behind a glass-topped counter sat a large elderly woman with a pink complexion and a halo of blue curls, reading a magazine. A cigarette was parked in an ashtray made from a large brass cog in front of her. She looked up pleasantly.

"Can I be helping you, sir?" she asked in a broad Irish accent.

"Ray Cooney in?" asked Smailes mildly.

"You interested in a car phone, sir?" she asked.

"No, it's a personal call."

"You're not a salesman?" she asked, growing suspicious of Smailes' accent.

"No, I'm with the British government," said Smailes, noticing her expression change. "I'd just like a word if I might."

The elderly lady kept her eyes on Smailes as she lifted the handset in front of her and punched the intercom button. "Raymond, step in and see a visitor please," she said, and Smailes heard her amplified voice echo in the workshop beyond. He looked around the cramped office, at the banks of filing cabinets with their display stands of various cellular phone models. The connecting door opened abruptly and a muscular-looking man with wiry red hair and a red mustache entered. He wore a plaid work shirt and blue jeans.

"Yes?" he said to Smailes carefully, shooting a quick glance across at the woman. Smailes realized she was probably his mother.

"Mr. Cooney?" asked Smailes, going into his wallet for his Home Office ID. "I'm Derek Smailes with the security department of the United Kingdom Mission. I wonder if I could ask you some questions?"

"About what?" asked Cooney, staying on his side of the counter.

"About the two Lincolns for the British government that you did the phone installation work on recently."

"First I know about it," said Cooney. There was an Irish lilt to his accent, though it was less broad than his mother's.

Smailes continued. "Yes, well, there was an explosive device found on one of the vehicles this morning. I wondered if you knew anything about that."

Cooney's eyes hardened. "Step back into the shop, will you, Ma?" he said, not taking his eyes off Smailes. "I'd better talk with this gentleman alone."

The old woman gave a frightened glance over her shoulder as she retreated with her magazine through the connecting door. When it closed Cooney said angrily, "Now what the **hell are** you talking about?"

"The two town cars from Eastside Lincoln that you just did the installation job on, you're trying to tell me you didn't know they were for the British government?"

"Damn right I am," said Cooney, going to a filing cabinet behind him. "Those two Lincolns, you're saying? That went out Monday?"

"That's right."

Cooney had produced his invoice. He flicked to a sheet stapled beneath and placed the paperwork on the counter. "See, two JVC units, the work order says. No mention of who the customer is, see?" he said, spinning the form around so Smailes could inspect it.

Smailes glanced down. There it was, plain as day, Lincoln Continental Town Cars, UKMISS. "You're saying you don't know that UKMISS means the United Kingdom Mission, Mr. Cooney?" asked Smailes sarcastically.

Cooney grabbed the paperwork, stared at it, then looked up again at Smailes. "That's exactly what I'm saying, mister. Exactly what are you trying to suggest?"

"That when you realized you had two cars in here destined for the British government, you let it drop to your brother, or maybe one of his pals, and then you looked the other way when they did some modifications. That's what I'm suggesting."

Cooney lost his temper, and held a finger up in Smailes' face. "Look here, Mr. Smiles, whatever your goddamn Brit name is, I'm tellin' you I knew nothing where these cars were going. There was no tampering with these vehicles under my roof." Cooney paused briefly, then said with less certainty, "Or if there was, it was without my knowledge. I suppose it could've been last Thursday night, when they did the safe."

"What?"

"We were broken into last Thursday. They took the payroll. You didn't see the goddamn door? Look." Cooney pointed and Smailes turned around to look again at the hastily patched panel in the glass door. As he turned back

Cooney was searching through a different drawer of his filing cabinet and eventually produced a copy of an incident report where the break-in had been reported to the local police. Smailes' expression did not change.

"Look, if you're not convinced, I'll show you." Cooney led Smailes through the workshop door. Five or six men sat around on drums and boxes, eating sandwiches and smoking. A silver BMW and a green Mercedes stood in the middle of the floor. Cooney's mother was seated on the only chair and looked up anxiously from her magazine as the two men entered.

Cooney led Smailes over to a large Dumpster on wheels, and pulled back the cover. "See," he said, and Smailes peered inside at the mangled remains of a small safe. Its door lolled open like a bruised tongue.

"Okay?" hissed Cooney, leading Smailes back into the fluorescent glare of the front office. By the time they resumed their positions, Cooney had regained himself a little.

"Listen, mister, you better get your facts straight before you go throwing accusations around. I knew nothing where these cars were going after Eastside Lincoln. My brother neither. And for that matter, my brother's activities in this country are perfectly legal, which is more than I can say for what your government's doing in Northern Ireland."

"Any of your workmen see those work orders, Mr. Cooney?" he asked.

"Maybe," said Cooney cautiously.

"You got any republican sympathizers on the payroll, Mr. Cooney?"

"Get lost, mister. Get off this property."

"They all got green cards, Mr. Cooney?" he asked, baiting him. Cooney snapped, and came around the counter at him.

"Get your fucking British arse off my property, mister. Get the fuck out."

Smailes held up his hand, retreating. "Save the insults, Mr. Cooney. Save them for the FBI and the INS.

They'll be around shortly, I can promise you," he said, closing the door behind him. Cooney stood at his door glaring at him, and Smailes retreated down the cement walkway to where the cab was waiting.

Yussuf wound down the window. "Back Manhattan?" he asked.

"Back Manhattan," Smailes confirmed, grimacing as he saw the numbers on the meter.

Derek Smailes pulled off the New York State Thruway and steered the Ford station wagon with its diplomatic plates down Route 17K toward Newburgh. Oral Yates had found him the lobby guard's address right away, but Smailes had had to get in line until a British vehicle became available. Like most diplomatic personnel, Smailes owned his own car since the government picked up garage fees, the biggest expense of keeping a car in New York. The use of private cars had been an important revenue source in his CID days, but for reasons that were unclear to him, it was impermissible to use personal vehicles on government business. That meant you waited for a mission car or you took taxis, and it was Thursday afternoon before the travel section of JAO phoned through and told him a vehicle was ready.

The truth was Smailes had almost forgotten his request by the time the call came through from the dispatcher. The previous twenty-four hours had been consumed by the suppressed pandemonium that the discovery of the limousine bomb had caused. On his return from Islip, Smailes was summoned to a hastily convened meeting of the security committee, an ad hoc group that comprised Van Deusen, Smith from the SIS station, Bates, the head of chancery at the mission, and the deputy CG from the consulate, a Victorian relic named Asquith. It was an informal grouping that hardly ever met, and had certainly never had to handle anything as outrageous as a potential terrorist attack. Ralph chaired the meeting and did a fairly good job of placating the terrified diplomats. Smailes reported his findings from the Islip trip, including his opinion that the Cooney brothers were responsible, and had staged the break-in the previous week as cover. Smith had appointed himself communications officer and waved a sheaf of decrypted cables from London. Special Branch wanted more precise information. The Yard was considering sending out a unit from its antiterrorist squad. K Branch was clamoring for a full report. Van Deusen looked irked that Smith had invaded his turf, but obviously had his own hands full. He explained that he had notified heads of security at all other UK missions in the U.S. to perform a full security review in case the New York incident was part of an offensive. All four men then turned to Smailes and asked him to give a blow-by-blow account of the incident again.

Afterward, Smailes had to confess he hadn't minded his turn in the limelight. His tour in New York had become so routine it made his Cambridge police days seem like the Wild West. He rehearsed the morning's events patiently, giving his interpretation where he thought appropriate. No one contradicted him. He gave his opinion that if he had not noticed the discrepancy in the odometer readings, the likelihood was both limos would now be sitting in the British garage, awaiting their inauguration. Smith chimed in that the British ought to rescind their agreement with the Lincoln dealership and lease replacement cars elsewhere, but Smailes explained the deal he and Ralph had struck with Eastside's management in exchange for their co-operation with the press. There was no question of complicity in that corner, he maintained. Everyone agreed that the denial of a propaganda coup to the IRA was the most satisfying outcome of the day, and they agreed to order two more town cars from Weingrad's outfit. Smailes agreed to attend in person while phones were installed. On the British front, they agreed to brief the senior mission diplomats on the day's events, and draw the line there. The fewer people that knew, the less chance of leaks. Everyone agreed. Smailes promised to generate a full report by the end of the day.

In fact, Smailes did not complete his report until the

following morning. He and Ralph had spent the better part of the afternoon in phone conference with other British missions, with the FBI, and in particular with the UN, where Smailes had the task of hosing down a furious Egyptian diplomat in the general services division who was fielding press calls about the bomb incident. Eventually Smailes raised his voice and said he thought the Egyptian would understand the terrorist mentality, that publicity was what they craved, and the diplomat fell silent. Smailes pleaded with him unctuously, and the aggrieved bureaucrat finally acquiesced to the sanitized version. Smailes hung up and turned to the stack of phone messages to which Madge kept adding on his desk.

Ralph spent a good part of the afternoon on the fort's secure line to London, checking in with Smailes at intervals. If he was pleased with his deputy's work that day, he did not find time to say so. In the frenzied activity, Smailes hardly noticed.

Derek Smailes took a deep breath and let it out slowly as he eased the government station wagon down the broad avenue toward the low gray hills on the far bank of the invisible Hudson. When Smailes had quizzed Yates about Roberts' address, Yates had shaken his head and described Newburgh as "South Bronx-on-the-Hudson," where Roberts lived with a married sister, which had been a condition of his parole. He said it was a shantytown where poverty and drugs were as bad as anywhere in the city, a sinkhole where the state dumped migrant farm workers from upstate after they hit the welfare rolls.

Smailes could appreciate the description, despite the beauty of the physical setting, for as the wide street descended toward the river, the neighborhood grew steadily worse. Car dealerships and furniture warehouses gave way to boarded-up supermarkets and clothing stores. It was a dark December afternoon, and only the liquor stores and the check-cashing joints seemed still in business, their lights shining weakly through closed concertina gates. Huddles of men in parkas and woolen hats stood around, and the occasional battered sedan reared and bucked over the roadway. Smailes noticed that the police drove huge four-wheel-drive vehicles, like armored cars.

Yates had told him to drive straight through the town until the road gave out, turn left, and you couldn't miss it. Smailes swung the wheel left as the main street hit the river road next to an incongruous new office building. It looked completely empty. He looked up the river to where the Newburgh-Beacon Bridge strode across the huge span of gray water. A tiny freight train on the far bank wound beneath it, heading for the city. It would have been an idyllic sight, were it not for the abandoned, boarded-up gas station below him, and the grim apartment towers two hundred yards away.

Smailes pulled sharply away from the river, up a steep cobbled street and into the parking lot of the first building. A youth in a ski hat and a parka sat on the expired shell of a Buick, watching Smailes as he climbed out of his Ford.

"You know an Earlene Roberts lives here?" he shouted, giving the name of the sister.

The youth appeared not to have heard him, so Smailes yelled again, "You know Earlene Roberts?"

The youth slid off the hood of the dead car and sauntered toward him. "Fi' dollars watch you car," he said. Smailes was about to answer sarcastically, until he noticed how few of the cars in the lot were actually in running order. He went in his wallet carefully and took out a five.

"Apartment 4-C," said the youth, taking the bill. "Elevator's broke." He turned away to resume his lookout post and Smailes headed across the expanse of decayed tarmac toward the building entrance, feeling uneasy.

He held his breath up the three double flights and was relieved when he stepped out onto the fourth-floor landing. He found apartment 4-C and leaned on the bell. An urchin, no older than six or seven, opened the door on the safety chain. She wore a stained red T-shirt and underpants. Her hair was braided in tight cornrows.

"Is Darnell Roberts home?" Smailes asked.

"He dead," said the girl.

Smailes was momentarily lost for words. "Is his mother home?" he found himself saying.

"She dead."

At this an older child, twelve or thirteen, pushed the young girl out of the way and looked out at Smailes angrily.

"Go 'way, mister," she said. "My mom say don't open the door to no one." She began closing the door. Smailes stuck his foot next to the jamb.

"What happened to Darnell Roberts?"

The older child grew frightened. "You get lost or I call the cops, mister. You get lost or I start screamin'."

She took a lungful of air and Smailes withdrew his foot. The door slammed sharply, and Smailes could hear bolts being thrown. He retreated back down the stairs warily.

Outside in the lot, the ski bum regarded him indifferently as he walked over to his perch.

"What happened to Darnell Roberts?" he asked.

"Got no idea," said the youth. Despite the different culture, the scene was immediately familiar to Smailes, the ex-cop. He went in his wallet and held up a twenty. "Now you remember?" he asked.

"You the cops?" asked the youth.

"Insurance company," said Smailes.

The youth reached for the bill and stuck it in his jeans pocket.

"Got taken out, night before last. Dude was waitin' for him in the garbage room when he come home round three. Least that's the way I heard it."

"They catch the guy?" Smailes asked.

"No way. Coupla guys was sittin' out here in a car, got a look at him. Say he was a beaner, forty or fifty, medium heavy, carrying an aluminum suitcase. They din' see no car."

"So who was he? What's a beaner, anyway?"

"You know, PR. From the island. Cops are sayin' it's a dope hit. They say Darnell started runnin' poison for

Gomez, started slidin' on the payments, Gomez paid him off. I don't see it that way myself."

"Why not?" Smailes was suddenly aware how cold it was. A wind was picking up off the metallic surface of the river. He folded his raincoat more tightly around him.

The ski bum looked at Smailes with a mixture of suspicion and contempt. He was clearly skeptical of Smailes' description of himself as an insurance investigator.

"I din' know Darnell that good. He only moved in with his sister 'round Thanksgiving. Sure, maybe he was running dope for Gomez—he's got the main action over on Liberty Street. But I know Darnell weren't stupid. You slide on payments to Gomez, you dead. Beside, Gomez don't have no middle-aged guys on his payroll. His guys don't carry guns in no suitcase. They carry 'em like this," he said, sticking a hand down the front of his pants. "Way I see it, it was a nark hit."

"You mean drugs?"

"Naw, nark, snitch. You know, informant. See, Darnell got out of Rikers last month. His sister tell me he done seven months for stickin' up a gas station off the thruway. You tellin' me he got out after seven months for armed robbery? He gotta suck somebody for that. Maybe he narked on someone inside to get out early, and they called the hit on him. That's the way I see it."

"When does the sister get home?"

"Round five. She works the cafeteria over at West Point."

Smailes thought for several moments. "Where's the police station?"

"You turn at the new buildin' into Broadway. It's on your left. Can't miss it."

"What's that building for?" asked Smailes pointlessly.

"Don't start me lyin'," said the youth, turning away.

Viktor Vasilyevich Kott sat in his office on the ninth floor of the Aquarium, looking down at the south runway of the

Khodinka military airfield below. A giant six-engine Mriya gathered speed and lumbered into the sky, in seeming defiance of all natural law. To his left, the chimney of the crematorium gave out a gasp of gray smoke flecked with ash.

The Aquarium was the Moscow headquarters of the Glavnoye Razvedyvatelnoye Upravleniye, or the GRU, the chief intelligence directorate of the Soviet general staff. Major General Viktor Kott was its first deputy chief, making him the second-highest-ranking military intelligence officer in the land. Viktor Kott glanced up at the plane rising slowly into the leaden sky and reflected upon a career that had enjoyed a similar, unlikely ascent.

Like his more celebrated forebear Feliks Dzerzhinsky, Lenin's secret police chief, Viktor Kott was of Polish origin. He had risen through the commissioned ranks of the Special Forces, the Spetsnaz, before transfer to the operational arm of the GRU's Fifth Directorate, then eventual promotion to the Aquarium itself. But he was a Pole, and he knew that this last move, together with subsequent elevations in rank, would never have come about without his combined determination and the invisible patronage that sustained him. Thus his chances for top office, always slim, had been destroyed when Dolghorukov, his protector, had been cashiered by Rostov earlier that year. It was one thing he had to concede about Rostov—he had uncanny political instincts. And he would certainly need them if he were to prevail where the earlier band of so-called reformers had so miserably failed.

Kott looked around the spartan surroundings of his office and reached into his desk drawer for a cigarette. Unlike other senior GRU officers, Kott kept his office deliberately spare and free from trophies. The only exceptions were a blurred, framed photograph near the door and a glass display case on the bookshelf behind him. The glass box contained three spent casings from the rifle bullets that had really killed President Kennedy, and was a gift from the Cuban intelligence chief, Raul Castro, in gratitude for services Kott had rendered over the years.

The framed photograph was a poorly exposed shot of a corpse strapped to a stretcher, which was about to be pushed by a man in overalls into the blinding mouth of a huge oven. Except on closer inspection, the corpse appeared to be alive, and was straining its neck muscles as it yelled in wordless agony. Insiders knew this to be a photograph of the last moments of Colonel Oleg Penkovsky, the British agent and the GRU's most notorious traitor, who had been burned alive in the very crematorium outside Kott's window. For visitors to Kott's office it stood as silent reminder of the fate that awaited all those who betrayed the service, should they be caught.

Kott lit his cigarette and inhaled. In his station he could, of course, choose an American or British brand, but smoked instead Hercegovina Flor, the acrid cigarettes Stalin used to crumble up as pipe tobacco. Russian cigarettes, he knew, made him less obtrusive, which was the principle that governed all his behavior. Viktor Kott was a small, wiry man of fifty-seven, with lank gray hair worn longer than was customary with military men. This, too, was part of a chosen style, as were the limp synthetic clothes and cheap plastic shoes he favored. Since his early GRU service had been under cover in European capitals —a trade representative in London, a Tass correspondent in Bonn—he could no longer take the chance of ever wearing uniform, lest a former Western acquaintance bump into him in Moscow and retroactively blow his cover. Consequently, many Aquarium staff knew neither his rank nor his position. His favorite cover presently, whether in Moscow or traveling to visit his illegals, was as a chauffeur. Many was the time some deputy resident or self-described Viking had beaten his chest in the back seat of a Zil, not knowing his driver outranked every GRU officer in the world, bar one. It was a preferred way of gathering information.

Kott drew on his cigarette and reflected further on the meteoric rise of the man who now led the three hundred million people of the Soviet Union. Certainly, Nikolai Rostov had surprised almost everyone when he vaulted from obscurity into the vacated presidency after the sudden death of the discredited high priest of *perestroika*. More obvious successors had been unable to build enough coalition to muster a majority in the Supreme Soviet, but Rostov, a political chameleon from Krasnodar, had adopted the mantle of an intrepid reformer while seducing the old guard with the offer of several seats on his presidential council. Even with the formal dissolution of the Communist Party, Rostov's socialists had managed to outflank both the democratic alliance and the New Leninists by seizing control of the neo-Party rump in the Congress of Deputies and the vast patronage machine which was its historical prerogative. But Rostov had only two years before he would have to face a real election, and by Kott's reckoning, even less time to improve the lot of Soviet consumers. Otherwise he would be swept away by the same tide of fury that had finally destroyed the health of his predecessor.

Personally, Kott did not count Rostov out. He seemed to have daringly shortened the leash on the military leadership, demoting the defense ministry to candidate status on his council and appointing a neophyte chief of staff. As for the KGB, for all Kott could tell, it was still trying to restyle itself as a giant welfare agency. And the appointment of Grigori Chumak as GRU Navigator, its overall boss, was another inspired move, in Kott's view. Wherever he could, Rostov had installed members of his own Krasnodar mafia in positions of power, landsmen who owed their position uniquely to him. Chumak, though he looked more like a Georgian gangster than an intelligence chief, had been Rostov's Navigator in the Transcaucasus. He had apparently protected Rostov when a nasty procurement scandal had burst in their district, and Rostov had in turn favored him over the customary KGB *apparatchik* as Navigator for the entire system. It signaled to all that Rostov would take intelligence and advice only from those whom he trusted utterly. And if the boldness of his foreign policy was sincere, Kott reflected, he was going to need all the trusted advice he could get.

Viktor Kott's ruminations were interrupted by an almost inaudible rap on his door, and he looked up cautiously.

"Come in," he said quietly.

It was Borya, his cipher clerk, being melodramatic. Borya, like all GRU cipher clerks, was the personal slave of his commanding officer, and led a life as cosseted as any harem eunuch's. Since the unprecedented defection of Igor Gouzenko from the Ottawa *rezidentura* in 1945, GRU cipher men, who knew their masters' secrets more intimately than they did themselves, never left a military installation unescorted. Kott had personally picked Borya from the Vatutinki cipher center when he was nineteen, and the pair had been inseparable ever since. Like Kott himself, Borya would end his days here at the Aquarium, firstly in the pensioner's apartment building, and finally, inevitably, as another belch of gray smoke from the stack of the crematorium. After a lifetime in the GRU, there was no other way.

"Yes, Borya," said Kott.

"A numerical message for you, comrade general," said Borya, signifying his displeasure by his unusual formality.

Kott's expression did not change, but he registered an internal flicker of alarm. His personal numerical code, incomprehensible even to Borya, was only ever used by one person. It meant he would have to descend personally to the Aquarium basement to retrieve the message. Borya had been quite correct to deliver the news in person.

"All right, Borya," he said indulgently. "I'll be right down."

The door closed and Kott reflected wryly on Borya's loyalty, his sense of injury at receiving a message so secret he was not allowed to decipher it. He was also a brilliant technician, Kott knew, and herein lay a crucial mistake of Chumak's. Owing either to the speed of his appointment or for other reasons, General Grigori Chumak had not brought a personal cipher clerk with him from the Trans-caucasus, but had picked a man from the Aquarium staff. Which meant he used a house code for personal transmissions, which Borya the Tireless, his Borya, claimed to be on the point of breaking.

7

Clea Lynch strode out from her apartment in her characteristically determined fashion and began waving purposefully at the uptown traffic for a cab. She was in a buoyant mood for a number of reasons, in sufficient spirits to countenance the dreaded trek out to Brooklyn. It was so typical of Derek Smailes, man of the people, to take a stupid apartment in an outer borough when there were plenty of quite acceptable units available in town. Still, it was a move he had made long before her arrival, and she knew he preferred to live out there, in his own perverse way.

The transcript she carried in her handbag had made no sense to her, but even if it had she would have had no opportunity to discuss it with him, which irked her. In fact, the enforced silence about the exact nature of Derek's work was the single most irritating aspect of their relationship for her, an issue she was unsure how to resolve. Whatever she decided to do about it, she knew any frontal assault was doomed. On that score, men were all the same: never dare impeach their precious "professionalism," their puny core of self-worth.

All in all, Derek Smailes was the most challenging project she had ever set herself. The truculent outsider within the Establishment, he was still terrified to put a foot wrong, and obviously scared to death at the prospect of ever mustering another commitment to a woman, presumedly because of that failed marriage back when he was barely out of his teens. She was aware she intimidated him, but hoped she had begun to convey that she found him totally acceptable as he was—brave, principled, intelligent man that he was. But for all his steadfastness, Derek was curiously insecure, always deprecating his looks, his abilities, his prospects. Clea had realized quite recently that this was his only major flaw, and knew then with her head what her heart had told her all along —that she did genuinely love him, that he was the man she wanted. Her problem was how to let Derek Smailes arrive at the same conclusion.

Her eventual success, she knew, would depend largely on developing patience, and on not losing heart over temporary obstacles. Her secret conviction was that she had already won him, that he loved her as deeply as she loved him, and the awareness thrilled her. Which was another reason why, as the yellow cab pulled over and she bounced onto the seat, she felt particularly pleased with herself.

Smailes got caught in traffic on his return from Newburgh, and it was well after office hours when he checked the car back in and returned home. He had hardly taken off his coat when the phone rang and it was Clea, asking whether she could come over. Since Smailes' Brooklyn Heights apartment was a rare venue for them, he had wondered what her real motivation was for the trip from Manhattan. Actually, his apartment wasn't really in the Heights, but on Adams Street across the tracks of Cadman Plaza on the approach road to the Brooklyn Bridge. His skepticism evaporated, however, as soon as Clea arrived, still wearing her formal office clothes. He secretly loved it when she visited him in his lair.

"So where were you all afternoon?" she asked finally, seated on his sofa and sipping a glass of wine. Smailes pulled a face as he set his glass of beer down on its coaster. Try as he might, he simply couldn't get used to the stuff.

"Had to take a trip up to Newburgh. Security check on a building employee," he said casually.

"Where's that?"

"About fifty miles north, up the Hudson. Must've been a nice place, once."

"It wasn't anything to do with that bomb you found yesterday, was it?" asked Clea, looking at him carefully over the rim of her wineglass.

"How the hell did you find out about that?" he asked sharply, sitting up.

"Stuart Bates told me this afternoon, when I asked if he knew why the cars hadn't been delivered yet," Clea announced triumphantly. "Since I couldn't get hold of you to ask." Then her tone softened. "God, Derek, weren't you scared stiff? You could've been killed."

The news that the head of chancery had blabbed to his girlfriend the story of his big success both exasperated and pleased him. On the one hand, it confirmed how far some diplomats could be trusted with restricted information. On the other, it relieved him of the burden of further dissemblance, and allowed him finally to share something of import with the single person who meant most to him. He checked carefully what Bates had revealed, then replayed the entire incident for Clea, omitting only some of the technicalities of the security committee's decisions. Clea listened with rapt attention.

"So what do you think? Who was it meant for?" she asked eventually.

"Either one of them, my guess," said Smailes. "The button man would have waited outside the garage until he saw the booby-trapped car take off with a diplomat in the back. He'd give it a few blocks, then detonate it by remote. God knows how many people might have been killed in addition to the people in the car. Although the police confirmed something Howard suspected—that one of the wires had been shaken loose in transit, so it probably wouldn't have gone off. But that doesn't change the murderous intent."

"Honestly, those people are such pigs," said Clea forcefully. For all her left-leaning views, Clea drew the line at terrorist attacks on civilians. This was a relief to Smailes, since he knew they could have little future together if they disagreed on such fundamentals.

"Keep it to yourself, okay, honey?" Smailes cautioned. "Bates was out of line telling you anything, you know."

"I know. I can keep a secret," she said primly, finishing her wine. "On which subject, I've got something for you."

Clea opened the elegant leather handbag resting against the arm of the sofa, and removed a small manila envelope. She fished inside and handed Smailes Howard's tape cassette and a folded transcript. Smailes had forgotten all about them.

Clea got up, picked up their empty glasses and headed toward the kitchen.

"Have you got anything edible in the refrigerator, Meatball?" she asked. "I'll make us something."

"I dunno, hunt around," said Smailes, opening the folded papers.

Clea stuck her head back into the living room. "Can I stay the night?" she asked.

"Yes, absolutely," said Smailes, looking up with a broad smile. Clea hesitated and Smailes was aware of a sudden, electric charge in the room, and he felt a tremendous urge to jump up and put his arms around her and tell her how much he loved her. But the moment passed, Clea went back into the kitchen, and Smailes settled back into the sofa and unfolded Felicity's transcript. He remained fairly convinced that Clea would find such an avowal embarrassing. Listening to her noises from the kitchen, he found himself wondering what it would be like to be married again, but angrily dismissed the thought. He was quite sure that whatever Clea Lynch's short-term plans were, marriage was not among them, and certainly not to a plebeian like him.

The transcript only confirmed his suspicions that Howard's intercept had been a worthless, harebrained prank. Felicity had commented demurely on the first "conversation," that it was "indecipherable," but seemed to represent "sounds of passion." He thought of the hapless young woman in the paws of the evil banker Barry, and shuddered.

The second conversation was largely a monologue by a "middle-aged male," who was lecturing his partner on the political significance of the early *Dallas* episode they were watching. According to this Soviet expert, there were many clandestine Marxists still active in Hollywood, of whom the *Dallas* scriptwriter was apparently a representative. He explained that the luckless Ray Krebs personified the heroic struggle of the proletariat against his brothers Bobby and J.R., who in turn symbolized the worst predations of capitalism. Felicity had not offered an opinion about whether the man was being serious or not.

The last conversation was the longest and most involved. A Soviet diplomat called Mikhail, or sometimes Misha for short, was discussing with a woman called Tatanya, presumably his wife, some hospital tests their daughter Irina had completed earlier that week. Felicity commented that she could infer from the conversation that the girl was in her early teens. The transcript of the conversation unfolded page after page, and reading it was a somewhat harrowing experience. It transpired that after suffering repeated attacks of dizziness and nausea, Irina had been diagnosed as suffering from the early stages of amyotrophic lateral sclerosis, an incurable, degenerative illness also known commonly in the U.S. as Lou Gehrig's disease, after the famous Yankee baseball star who died from it. The wife seemed almost incapable of believing the news, and kept insisting on further tests. Her husband Mikhail said it was unnecessary, the report from the specialist at New York Hospital was conclusive. The couple then held a painful discussion of Irina's life expectancy, and her prospects for treatment on their return to Moscow. It appeared their tour of service in New York was about to expire. Smailes reread the entire transcript, then set the document down thoughtfully as Clea reappeared, carrying two plates of what appeared to be a pasta and vegetable dish.

"What's this, then?" he asked, eyeing his plate suspiciously.

"You'll like it, darling," she countered. "You want another beer?"

Clea was retreating to the kitchen. "No, wine," he called after her. "I'll never get used to this alcoholic ginger ale they sell here."

Clea paused by the door. "You can buy British beer in the shops, you know, darling," she said with a hint of mockery.

"I know, I know," he replied irritably. "But the prices they charge, what with the exchange rate, it's nearly two quid a bottle."

Clea looked at him condescendingly and said, "You're not so badly paid, Derek Smailes. You could afford decent beer once in a while."

He felt awkward—money was always a difficult subject between them. For Smailes, the value of money was directly related to the discomfort and inconvenience of having to earn it; for Clea, he was painfully aware, it bore no such obvious relation. He looked at her uncomfortably.

"Sweetheart, it's not that I can't *afford* beer at two pounds a bottle," he said. "I just can't *enjoy* it at that price." Clea rolled her eyes and disappeared into the kitchen; his explanation was obviously incomprehensible to her.

She returned with two glasses of wine and for a while they ate in silence. Clea really was an excellent cook—he had no idea carrots and onions and cabbage could taste so good. At one point she gestured at Felicity's transcript with a fork.

"Anything interesting?" she asked.

"Naw," said Smailes. "Waste of time really," and they fell silent again.

He had cleared away the food and returned with coffee before he noticed anything unusual in her manner. He put down his cup and was about to say something when he saw she was grinning to herself, as if at some secret they had not yet shared.

"What are you smiling at, Clea? You look like the cat that just ate the canary."

"You didn't ask me why I was seeing Stuart Bates today yet," she replied coyly.

"I thought you said, about the cars."

"No, no, that was incidental. He asked to see me."

"Whatever for?" asked Smailes, a little alarmed. The head of chancery of the UN Mission had no obvious business with Clea's department.

"They want me to take the competition. In March," she said, setting down her cup triumphantly.

"What?"

"The competition. The full entrance procedure. If I pass, I'll be upgraded to A stream. Bates says there's an opportunity on the Western European desk here at the mission . . ."

Smailes maneuvered quickly across to her side of the couch and took her hand. "Oh Clea, that's fantastic news! In March? And they'll let you come back to New York and join the diplomatic staff?"

"That's what he said. Darling, I can't tell you how thrilled I am! I go back in the middle of March for two months training in Whitehall. Then back here, if everything goes well. I think they offered me that because, well, they know about us." Here she lowered her eyes, then looked up again suddenly.

"Only, Derek, what happens if I don't pass?"

"Sweetheart, don't be ridiculous. Of course you'll pass. You would have passed years ago, when you first entered. Well, congratulations, you clever girl," he said, holding her by the shoulders. "It's long overdue. Only, why didn't you tell me when you first got here?"

"I tried to call you all afternoon. Then I thought it only fair to get your news first. You're the big hero, after all." Clea put her cup down and dabbed her mouth with the napkin she was holding. "This isn't the kind of congratulations I want. Come here and give me a kiss."

He felt intensely proud of her, but experienced a sudden surge of insecurity. What if, in her new diplomatic station, she now found him beneath her? The anxiety distracted him slightly as he felt the soft pressure of her lips on his and her hand run up the inside of his thigh.

Graham Booth was the last person Smailes wanted to meet first thing the next morning, before tea and the overnight news summaries. Booth was one of those unwelcome, early-morning effervescent types, and Smailes groaned inwardly when Booth stepped into the empty elevator car with them. He insisted on a formal and profuse introduction to Clea, even though the two of them had spoken on the telephone several times. Then, as the two men entered their office, Smailes saw that the overnight cable traffic had subsided to normal levels, and he had no immediate respite from his partner's wisecracks about bags under the eyes and "active diplomacy." Smailes was appalled by Booth's presumption, and reflected he would be relieved when the clever little bugger's tour was up and he finally had his office to himself again.

He drank his tea and walked across the corridor to Madge's office to inquire about Ralph's schedule. He had Howard's transcript in his portfolio and was resolved to dispose of the matter as quickly as possible. He also had to update Ralph on the news about Roberts, the stand-in security guard.

Madge's face was set as she sat hunched over the morning mail. Her expression did not change as she looked up, although Smailes noticed she was wearing a little discreet makeup, and her graying hair had recently been cut in a slightly less severe style.

"He's been in since seven-thirty, Derek. Asked to see you as soon as you came in," she said, without inquiring his business. Smailes had noticed that Madge always referred to Ralph as "him." He could not imagine what her life was like—living alone in a foreign city, working for a man she despised.

Smailes returned briefly to his desk for his portfolio, then crossed to Ralph's door and knocked. He heard the grunted acknowledgment and entered. Ralph was seated behind his desk in a cloud of cigar smoke. He looked up briefly, then down again at the papers on his desk.

"Sit down. Sit down, Derek," he said, waving a hand in the air.

Presently he looked up, pointing his cigar at Smailes like an ugly bazooka. He sucked it and the tip glowed red.

"Didn't get a chance to speak with you Wednesday, and yesterday afternoon I couldn't find you," he said, making it sound like an accusation.

"Drove up to Newburgh, Ralph, to check on the security guard. Some interesting news there, too . . ."

Ralph proceeded as if he hadn't heard him. "So I wanted to be sure to see you first thing. That was an incredible piece of work, discovering the bomb like that, and having the presence of mind to contain the publicity. I think we averted a big disaster there." Smailes shrugged in a gesture of false modesty.

"No, no, you should take the credit. The deputy ambassador and the CG wanted to be sure I thanked you personally. You obviously saved one of their lives." Smailes said nothing, knowing that Ralph must have also seen the report that indicated the bomb was defective.

"They even wanted me to phone London to find out whether there was some special bonus or award you could be given. That's what I've been doing this morning. Unfortunately, it's outside civil service regulations." Ralph imparted this last information as if it caused him genuine regret, although Smailes could tell that this entire exercise was sticking in his craw.

"Anyway, they insist on writing a personal commendation for your file, which I'm going to send through this afternoon. I wanted you to see it before I send it down for signature."

Van Deusen turned the paper on his desk so Smailes could review it. Despite himself, Smailes blushed at the fulsomeness of the tribute. It almost read as if he had given his life in battle.

"Thanks, Ralph. It's really not necessary," he managed to say.

"Right, well, that's done," Van Deusen said to himself. "Your friend Lustig called from the FBI yesterday afternoon. Three of the men on that chap Cooney's payroll were undocumented aliens. They're being deported back to Ireland and Cooney will face some kind of fine. But it's all they can pin on him, they think."

"Clever," said Smailes.

"Yes, I agree," said Van Deusen, "although I think I convinced him that the Cooneys were obviously responsible, and they're considering a tap on Michael Cooney's phone, perhaps even surveillance. Maybe they'll turn up something that will stick."

"Not if the Cooneys are as good as I think they are," said Smailes. "But I suppose it's the best we can hope for." He always felt awkward discussing operations with Ralph, since only the thinnest of veneers disguised their mutual distrust. As far as Smailes was concerned, Van Deusen was the archetypal deskman, with only the vaguest notion of how an investigation proceeded in the field.

"What did you say about Newburgh?" Ralph asked.

"I drove up there yesterday afternoon, when I could get hold of a car. Seems this replacement guard, Roberts, was murdered three nights ago outside his apartment. No suspects."

Van Deusen removed the cigar from his mouth slowly and sat back in his swivel chair. "Really? Did you speak to the police? Is there a motive?"

"Sure. The local police say he was working for one of the neighborhood drug heavies, and got killed for shortchanging him. They have a description of the killer, a middle-aged Hispanic, medium build. Interesting, don't you think?"

"No, why?"

"The leader of the team that broke in here was a middle-aged Hispanic, wasn't he?"

"Could be coincidence," said Van Deusen suspiciously. "Did you speak with anyone else?"

"Yes. I spoke with a . . ." Smailes fished for the right term. ". . . a neighbor. He said he thought Roberts might have been an informant when he was in prison, and someone bought a contract on him."

Van Deusen screwed up his face in distaste. "Jesus, Derek, I think we ought to tell Mort Janowitz we never want to use this security firm again, don't you? You just can't trust anyone." Clearly Ralph had heard all he wanted to hear about Darnell Roberts.

"Write an update for your report and let me see it before you file it," he said. "And once again, congratulations—"

"Ralph, there's something else I've got to show you," said Smailes, opening his portfolio. "Take a look at this." He handed the transcript across the desk and Ralph stuck the cigar stub back in his face so he could take it with both hands. He began flicking through it irritably.

At that moment, Madge Ryan stuck her head through the connecting door and said, "Derek, Kevin Butterworth's on the line for you. You want to take it in your office?"

"No, no, I'll take it in here, if it's okay with Ralph."

Van Deusen signified his assent without looking up from Smailes' document and presently the handset rang. Smailes picked up the receiver.

"Kevin! Where are you?"

"San Francisco," said Butterworth's distant voice.

"Blimey, you're up early. What's new?"

"I've changed my reservations back to London and have a twelve-hour layover in New York on Tuesday. Can I come spend the night on your settee?"

Smailes smiled. "Hey, your travel allowance should stretch to a hotel room, you know, Kevin," he said.

"I know. I need to talk to you. Remember?"

"Oh, right," said Smailes, recalling Butterworth's comments outside the Lincoln dealership. "My Curzon Street survival guide, right?"

"Right," said Butterworth hesitantly.

"What time shall I expect you?"

"Plane lands about seven-thirty. About nine?"

"Fine," said Smailes. "See you then. How was Boston?"

"Routine."

"Okay, next week, then."

"Next week," said Butterworth, hanging up.

Ralph Van Deusen eventually looked up from the transcript with a pained expression. "What the hell is this?" he asked.

Slowly, and with some discomfort, Smailes recounted the story of Grundy's use of the captured bugging gear to gather the intercept at the Soviet building in Riverdale. He was aware of how improbable the whole thing sounded.

Van Deusen was mortified. "Good God, man! Did anyone see him?"

"Apparently not. I just thought, maybe we should run it by Alan Sparks. Perhaps he could identify the players . . ."

At Sparks' name, Van Deusen sat upright. Alan Sparks was the SIS deskman in charge of babysitting the Soviet colony in New York, which was one of the largest and most intelligence-oriented of any in the world.

"Absolutely not," he shot out. "This is all gobbledygook, as far as I can tell. And someone could get into very hot water over it," he said, meaning that he could. "Is this the only copy?"

"Yes," said Smailes.

Van Deusen gripped the transcript tightly so the pages buckled, and gave one of his rare, brown-toothed grins.

"Don't worry about it further, Derek," he said. "It might get mislaid in the burn box, you never know."

Viktor Kott swam slowly back to the shallow end of the huge outdoor pool in Gorky Park, keeping only his nostrils above the surface for warmth. Hardier souls lumbered along the marble surround, barely visible through the rising vapor. Viktor Kott, however, had none of the traditional Russian padding against the cold. He had, in fact, not gained a pound since winning his divisional featherweight boxing title at the age of eighteen. He touched the rail and stood briefly. One more lap, he told himself, then the fallback.

The coded message he had retrieved from the basement cipher room had said simply "87," one of the personal meeting codes. He had almost expected this first venue to be a blind, so the good general could check on his timely compliance. Kott did not doubt that one of the oblivious bathers around him had monitored his attendance, which would be reported in due time. The fallback, after all, was twenty-four hours away.

As soon as Kott heard that his numerical code had been used, he knew the situation was extremely grave. And he had already begun to pull together the outline of a plan he had nurtured for just this contingency.

Throughout the weekend, Smailes could not shrug off his feeling of irritation that Ralph might be about to deep-six the information that Howard had taken such risks for. It was not that he believed the intercept had any great value, he just believed that its existence, if only its confirmation that the Soviets made lousy security glass, ought to be reported through proper channels. He also knew quite well that Ralph's motivation was only partially fear of embarrassment. Van Deusen had been a Five bureaucrat for too long not to register instinctive resentment as soon as Smailes invoked the potential interest of their senior colleagues from the Secret Intelligence Service. The truth was that MI5 people loathed the snobs in Six, as SIS was also called, and regarded them as spoiled inhabitants of a protracted adolescence. In their turn, the espionage gurus of SIS looked on their MI5 colleagues as uncultured flatfeet in shiny suits. The image suited Smailes just fine, since that was approximately how he saw himself, but desk jockeys like Van Deusen had spent their whole careers smoldering at the patronage.

Smailes showed up at the British offices Monday morning to find the whole place had more or less suspended work in anticipation of the Christmas holidays, which began in three days' time. Ralph himself, he remembered, was taking two weeks off in the Caribbean, where he went at intervals to play golf and hunt divorcées. His absence seemed to have rendered Madge practically festive, since she wandered across to Smailes' office to chat with him lightheartedly about his plans for the holidays. The roguish Mr. Booth was nowhere to be seen.

Alone again, Smailes rapped his knuckles on his desk, then made one of those impulsive decisions which had occurred too frequently in his career to be deemed uncharacteristic. He picked up his phone and called Alan Sparks, who invited him down to the SIS station cordially and without hesitation.

Within the civilized redoubt of the British Mission, the Devon and Cornwall Development Office on the ninth floor was a yet more serene island of privilege and gentility. Expensive tastes, upper-class accents and calm prevailed, or so it had seemed to Smailes on his rare visits. On this occasion, he noticed that Sparks' perimeter office was considerably more spacious than his own, and had a fine view across the East River to the low Queens skyline opposite. Sparks was a man with a certain sense of humor, who kept a large formal portrait of the Queen on his wall, flanked by unflattering file shots of the KGB and GRU New York *rezidenti*. Beyond this adornment, his office, furnished in modern style in chromium and vinyl, was bare. He proffered a warm greeting and offered Smailes a chair and tea, which were accepted gladly.

Smailes did not doubt that Sparks was one of those diplomatic Britons who insisted on importing his tea directly from London.

Smailes looked across at his colleague's battered face and smiled. He reckoned Sparks was perhaps ten years older than himself, although he looked older. His forehead and eyes were deeply lined, and the thick sandy hair, kept unfashionably short at the back and sides, stood up like a prow from his skull. Sparks dressed with careless eccentricity, and was wearing an expensive gray suit with an old striped tie that was too short. He was a tall man of medium build, with a spherical paunch that rested like a bowling ball in his lap.

Smailes liked Alan Sparks, and although he had only met him on a handful of occasions, he felt as if he knew him fairly well. The fact was, Sparks' colorful history was something of a legend in British intelligence circles, and inevitably affected people's dealings with him. Smailes wondered whether he himself would not appear considerably more ravaged, had their positions been reversed.

Alan Sparks had apparently distinguished himself early in his career on the German desk at London Central, then later with the Berlin field office. Back when the temperature of the Cold War had still been set at deep freeze, he had been sent over the Wall on some tricky cover operation involving a small network in the defense ministry. Something had gone wrong and Sparks had been picked up by agents of the Stasi, the dreaded security police, and held in East Berlin for questioning. Like the professional he was, Sparks had held out, asserting his diplomatic immunity. Until, that is, the Stasi drafted a particularly brutal interlocutor, who spoke German with a thick Russian accent. The Russian agent had weakened Sparks by all manner of deprivation techniques, then broken him with a particularly sadistic ploy. It seemed that Sparks had been returned to his interrogation room bound and gagged, and then was tied to his chair. The Russian, a small, wiry man with pitiless eyes, had then removed his service revolver and taped the barrel into

Sparks'- mouth. At each refusal to his barked questions, the Russian would pull the trigger of the gun. Sparks broke after the third empty chamber, and then spilled his entire operational knowledge, as most men would have done immediately. He was dumped back at Checkpoint Charlie in a dreadful state, and when he was returned to London he suffered some awful breakdown from which it took him almost a year to recover. He was finally rehabilitated away from the front line in New York and given the largely passive task of watching the Soviet diplomatic colony come and go, which had won him the rather unkind nickname of Alan Spooks. He was a divorced bachelor, and it was well known that his nerves were still bad and he drank too much, but it appeared London felt he was owed something in view of his ordeal. To Smailes, it seemed Sparks' experiences had rendered him considerably less conceited than the rest of the people he knew in Six, and he felt relaxed with him. He was fairly confident he could squeeze the information he wanted out of him, without tripping any alarms.

After Celia, Sparks' elderly assistant, had set down a fine china tea service on his desk and poured tea for both men, Sparks looked across at Smailes mildly and offered him a compliment.

"That was a terrific piece of investigation, Derek," he said, "turning up the listening equipment like that."

Smailes took a long sip of his tea and set his cup down carefully. "Thanks," he said. No mention of the limousine bomb. It seemed Quentin Smith might have done a better job of containing that information than Stuart Bates in chancery had done.

"What's your guess?" Sparks continued. "The Sovs trying to get an inside track on the Geneva positions?"

"That's as good an explanation as any I can think of," said Smailes. "Although I can think of better offices to bug than Sir Michael's."

"No doubt they can too. They've probably got a crew on it."

"Actually, that's why I wanted to see you, Alan," he said.

Sparks swiveled around to gaze across the river, then back to face Smailes. "Oh yes?" he asked politely.

"I've got a friend in the FBI here. We have a few beers every so often. He tells me a KGB wireless expert came through last month, and is staying in Riverdale. Maybe there's a link."

Sparks sat upright. "A KGB piano man? Staying at the White House? Not that I know of."

"My friend said his operational name is Solovyov. Staying on the seventh floor."

Smailes had no need to press his friend further. He had risen from his chair and walked across to the wall that held the Queen's portrait. "Excuse me, ma'am," said Sparks, apparently seriously. He flipped a catch and turned the portrait aside on its hinges, revealing a small wall safe. With his back obscuring Smailes' view, he turned the tumbler, opened the door and retracted a fairly fat manila file. Then he closed the safe and sat down again. "Now what floor did your friend say?" he asked.

"Seventh, he was fairly sure."

Sparks spread the file in front of him. As Smailes had hoped, the occupancy of Soviet residential and diplomatic facilities was routine intelligence for Sparks' office. Sparks leafed through several pages of floor plans, then scanned one particular document carefully. Eventually he passed it across to Smailes and shook his head.

"Nope, not that I know of," he said. "I can't be a hundred percent, of course, but my information is that no one has moved onto the seventh floor in more than six months."

Smailes glanced across the plan, registering the names of individuals and couples penciled in the boxes for each apartment. Some were underlined in pink or yellow. Then he saw what he wanted. In the southeast corner apartment were penciled the names of Mikhail Siskin, UN diplomat, Department of Disarmament Affairs, and his wife Tatanya, translator, Soviet Mission. Neither name was underlined.

"Well, it could be my guy was misinformed. It's not his primary field. What does the underlining mean?"

"Pink is KGB, yellow is GRU," Sparks explained. Smailes glanced at the floor plan again as he handed it back. "Jesus, there's as many underlined as not. Is that accurate?"

"A rough estimate is that fifty percent of the Soviet colony are active agents. Not to mention the expectation that every member of the colony will cooperate if requested. Yes, they're a busy bunch, all right."

"How do you update all this information, Alan?" he asked. It was the kind of question he would not even float with a different member of the SIS station, but he knew Sparks would not take offense.

"Well, unofficially, between you and me, old man, it's low-level agents in place that spoon up this stuff. You know, caretakers, cooks, people like that. The Sovs pay their people dirt, you see, and they're all desperate for some hard currency so they can stock up on consumer goods before they go back. It's never been too difficult."

"And the intelligence affiliations?"

"We make it a point to assume that every Soviet is an active agent until we can corroborate from several sources that he's not. Safest way," he said. "What was the name of your wireless chap again?"

Smailes fished desperately in his mind. He'd made the name up on the spur of the moment.

"Er, Solovyov, I think . . ." he said.

"First name and patronymic?"

"Sorry."

Sparks scrawled something on his desk pad. "I'll crunch it through Data Center, see if we can come up with anything."

He reached for the elegant, willow-pattern teapot. "After the holidays," he added with a smile. "More tea?"

8

It was impossible to mistake the massive triumphal arch at the entrance to Kutuzovsky Prospekt as anything but a monument to victory. More impressive than its counterpart, the Parisian Arc de Triomphe, the arch held the chariot of winged "Glory," pulled by six magnificent bronze horses. Erected by the czars to commemorate their defeat of Napoleon, the statue had been partially destroyed by Stalin and hidden away in the grounds of a Moscow monastery. It had been lovingly restored by Brezhnev, however, in gratitude for the army-backed coup that had installed him, following Khrushchev's hamfisted attempts at reform. It now stood as eloquent tribute to the enduring, untarnished institution of the Russian Army, which had guaranteed every Soviet leader's position since the foundation of the state.

A black official Volga, itself a commonplace sight, approached the arch through light traffic from the government dachas in the northwest suburbs. In the rear of the car sat General Alexei Dolghorukov, former deputy chief of staff, and his protégé, Major General Viktor Kott of the GRU. Dolghorukov's bodyguard and aide was driving, his face as expressionless as stone. As the car moved slowly around the traffic circle, the older general could be seen gesticulating wildly at the statue, then turning to harangue his younger colleague. Kott appeared to pay no attention, staring straight ahead, then turning to gaze impassively out of the window. As the car pulled up at the traffic light at the entrance of Kutuzovsky Prospekt, neither man appeared to notice a battered-looking delivery van that pulled up briefly beside them. Neither did they notice that the van's twisted radio antenna, actually a mangled wire coathanger, was held in place by a brand-new mounting, which swiveled slightly to adjust its angle as the two vehicles stood briefly side by side.

The plunge room of the Sandunov *banya* was filled with mountains of privileged white male flesh and the aromatic fragrance of birch. From time to time a bather would stagger naked from the steamroom and dive into the cold green water, disturbing the murmured conversations around him. Then he, too, would retrieve a togalike toweling robe and join the recumbent figures around the walls, savoring the sensation of a million pores slammed shut.

Behind a fluted Ionic column that was beginning to mold from its base, two short figures were stretched on marble benches, talking quietly. They were General Alexei Dolghorukov and Anatoli Petrovich Grishkin, New Leninist party boss in Leningrad and minister of military-industrial production, one of the most powerful conservatives in the Soviet Union. Grishkin, who had helped secure Dolghorukov's continued voice in policy following the recent "reorganization," was about the same age and build as his rival, Rostov, but with longer, silvery hair. Eventually he raised himself on an elbow and said forcefully, "All right. All right. But I don't know if Tumanov will buy it."

Dolghorukov said nothing, but struggled to raise himself into a sitting position. He planted his bare feet on the marble tile, then leaned forward until his face was close to Grishkin's.

"Either Tumanov buys it, or we move without you," he said in an angry whisper. Then he got to his feet, found his balance, and walked slowly toward the changing rooms.

Anatoli Grishkin remained motionless for a long time, resting his head on folded arms. Then he, too, got slowly to his feet, standing unsteadily. As he did so, the white toga slid to the floor, revealing a heavyset white body with thick black hair on the chest, limbs and pubis. He stood for another long moment, lost in thought, then stooped to retrieve the robe, wrapped it around him and headed for the exit.

As he moved away, the prostrate form of a bather on the opposite side of the bath raised his head slightly and cocked open an eye to watch him.

The deafening roar of three hundred tank exhausts split the air, the diesel smoke black with oil as the drivers gunned their engines. A dirty wash of light had begun to streak the eastern Ukrainian skyline as dark figures scurried through the compound, buttoning tunics as they ran, looking for their platoons. In keeping with motorized infantry rules, no one would inform the company commanders until the first tanks rolled whether this was a maneuver, or finally, war. The adjudicator from Moscow kept out of sight behind a high brick wall as he strode with the deputy district commander toward the huge steel mesh gates at the compound entrance.

Alexei Dolghorukov almost had to trot to keep pace with the lithe form of General Anton Palov beside him. The two men were dressed in army greatcoats and were deep in conversation, which did not end even as the adjudicator's armored personnel vehicle, flying its white flag, drew up beside them, signaling that the maneuver was ready to begin. Eventually, Dolghorukov clapped the smaller man on the shoulder, and the two figures shook hands briskly. Then the general climbed into the umpire's vehicle, which sped away. Palov gestured to the two soldiers standing at the compound entrance, who threw open the gates. The tank engines roared even louder and the war game commenced.

*   *   *

Kevin Butterworth paid off the outrageous fare and clambered out of the taxi to help the driver lift his luggage from the trunk. He was even beginning to dress like Derek Smailes, he told himself with a smile, wrapping the trenchcoat he'd bought in San Francisco around himself before hitching his garment bag onto his shoulder. Then he picked up the heavy cases and walked unsteadily down the sidewalk toward the entrance of Smailes' building.

He saw the squat figure standing in the shadows as he approached the patch of light outside the doorway, but ignored it until the man suddenly stepped forward.

"Hey, mister, you gotta time?" asked the man.

Butterworth registered alarm, knowing better than to put down his case to check his watch. He lifted his arm with its heavy case, rotating his wrist with difficulty. Then the man lurched forward and made a grab for it.

"Hey, what the hell . . ." said Butterworth, resisting.

He caught a glint of gunmetal, but far too late to save himself, and looked up helplessly as the gun roared and the bullet struck him in the chest. The second bullet caught him as he fell, and then the killer was running toward a car double-parked outside the entrance, which a moment later was gone.

Adams Street had to be the noisiest bloody thoroughfare in all of Brooklyn, Smailes told himself in annoyance, tapping the volume pad on his remote to hear the news announcer better. The traffic swarming up to the bridge made an insistent roar, not to mention the almost continuous sirens and the occasional backfiring of the wrecks that people still drove in the outer boroughs. Smailes muted his set as the commercials came on, then as he restored the volume he heard a couple of particularly vicious backfires from the street below and swore to himself. When the sirens grew so insistent he could hardly hear a thing, he snapped the set off in irritation. He stretched out his legs and looked up at the ceiling, then the blood in his veins turned to ice. Blue and red lights played alternately on the surface above him, and he dashed for his door.

Three police cars and two ambulances were pulled up at reckless angles outside the building. A group of tenants huddled in the lobby, and a small crowd of bystanders had gathered next to the first ambulance. On the sidewalk, Smailes saw a burst case, a discarded garment bag. Then he saw the medical technician about to close the rear doors of his ambulance.

"Hey, just a minute!" he yelled, running forward. The ambulanceman hesitated, and Smailes saw the inert form on the stretcher inside, a red lake in the front of the raincoat, an oxygen mask over the face.

"Kevin!" he yelled, but a muscular arm pulled him away, and the ambulanceman slammed the door.

Smailes turned to confront a New York City cop as the ambulance lurched away, its dreadful siren whooping into life. "Stand aside, sir," said the cop. "Give the guy a chance."

"I know him," said Smailes pathetically. "He's my friend."

"You knew the guy?" asked the cop. "Here, speak with the lieutenant."

The cop led Smailes back to the sidewalk where a plainclothes officer was listening to a uniformed patrolman as he pawed through the contents of a wallet.

"Lieutenant, this here's a friend of the victim," he said.

The lieutenant, a sharp-faced Italian with a broken nose, looked up. "You knew this guy? Butterworth?"

"He was coming to stay with me," said Smailes helplessly.

"From where?"

"California. He was on his way back to London."

"He was English?"

"Yes."

The lieutenant waved the wallet in exasperation. "Jesus, people gotta learn. The guy wants your case, you let him take your case. That way nobody don't get shot. This is the third drive-by this month."

"Drive-by? What happened?"

"That old guy saw it," said the lieutenant, indicating a shaken-looking elderly man in a blue overcoat who was standing against the side of the building, talking with another policeman. "Party gets out of a cab carrying three cases, mugger steps out of the doorway here, tries to snatch a case, party resists, takes two shots in the chest. Mugger runs to car right over there, partner drives him away."

"Did he give a description?"

"Nothing worth nothing. Average build, dark jacket, bald. Who knows?"

Smailes turned around in desperation. The second ambulance was beginning to pull away.

"Which hospital are they taking him to?" asked Smailes.

"Long Island College. But hold on, sir, there ain't no hurry. Your friend's a DOA, no question. I'm sorry. Look, let me get your name and maybe you could answer some questions . . ."

Christmas began very inauspiciously for Derek and Clea. The shocking murder of Kevin Butterworth plunged Smailes into despair, since he could not help but hold himself partially responsible. Butterworth had been coming to visit him, after all, and it was Derek Smailes who had ignored conventional wisdom and had chosen to live in a marginal Brooklyn neighborhood. The days before Christmas itself were taken up with the awful duties of notifying Ralph in Jamaica and then his bosses in London, arranging for the repatriation of Kevin's remains, then holding several long and painful conversations with Butterworth's family in Finchley. There was so little to say that offered any comfort. To maintain that Kevin had had a brilliant future before him, that his death was a tragic waste, sounded the most vapid of clichés, though both were true.

In addition, there was an aspect of the murder that made Smailes deeply apprehensive, although he had not mentioned his doubts to either Ralph or Curzon Street. Kevin, after all, had made a particular point of trying to meet with him in private, claiming there was a matter he needed to discuss with him. What was the prospective topic—how to survive the bruising politics of headquarters? Hardly sufficient motive to alter his travel plans from the West Coast, Smailes thought. And if he counted Roberts, the security guard, Kevin Butterworth was the second person murdered recently before Smailes had had the chance to speak with him. That seemed one too many murders to be coincidental.

Then, at the last minute, Smailes and Clea had to cede Clea's apartment, their preferred venue for the holiday, to Felicity and Barry, since Barry had decided at the last moment not to return to England, and Felicity implored Clea to be allowed her turn alone in the apartment. It was not a major inconvenience, but it put Clea in a bad mood since she disliked having her plans disrupted and claimed to be frightened of traveling to Derek's apartment alone since Kevin's murder. Then Smailes, predictably, left his Christmas shopping far too late, and almost got dragged into an incident on the tube that could have landed him in court as a witness. It only renewed his determination to stay away from the subterranean nightmare of the subway system at all costs.

On Christmas Eve Smailes procrastinated most of the day before taking a taxi into Manhattan. In truth, gift-shopping for Clea intimidated him even when he was in decent spirits, and he spent a fruitless two hours in the Fifth Avenue department stores, braving the hordes to cast indecisively through racks of blouses and sweaters. Eventually, he conceded defeat and ended up in Tiffany's, where he spent far more than he had intended on a set of pearl earrings. By the time he emerged it was late, so he stopped off at an expensive deli for a meal, by which time it was almost eight and there was not a taxi for hire within five miles of midtown. Smailes cursed to himself and headed for the subway at Fifty-ninth and Fifth, where he joined the desultory throng waiting for the downtown train.

It was a long wait. Most shoppers and workers had gone home, and the platform filled up slowly with the usual New York collection of misfits and ordinary folk trying not to appear anxious. Next to Smailes a drunken office worker slouched against a pillar half asleep, his suit crumpled and collar open, exposing a gold chain which drooped down his chest. Nearby a long-haired Hispanic in a studded headband and leather jacket toed the warning strip, muttering and swaying in time to a muted ghetto blaster balanced on his shoulder. Other passengers stood around restlessly, avoiding eye contact. Suddenly, everyone's attention was caught by a commotion at the far end of the platform, and Smailes turned to see three black youths heading toward him. They were shouting raucously and pushing people out of their way. They stopped at one point to hassle a thin youth in a red down vest who was pretending to read a magazine. Then just as suddenly they dropped him and headed on in search of further quarry.

Smailes stiffened as the three youths approached him and thrust the jewelry box containing Clea's earrings farther down into his raincoat pocket. He was feeling understandably jumpy about street crime, and try as he might, he had not found a way to live in New York and avoid racial tension and resentment. Aggressive black teenagers represented the single most menacing aspect of life in the city, and like everyone else he knew, Smailes was on guard whenever he found himself around them. Derek Smailes was a big man and doubted he was a potential target, and he figured the mean-looking Latino with the boom box was probably also safe, but the drunken clerk looked like a sitting duck. The three young blacks screeched something at Smailes as they passed and one even faked a punch, but suddenly a train came crashing into the station and people crowded forward in relief. Smailes saw one of the youths point to the drunk, who staggered forward as the train halted and entered the same car as Smailes and the Latino.

At first, Smailes thought they were in the clear, since the black youths had boarded an adjacent car and did not immediately appear. The Latino remained oblivious, muttering into his radio as the office worker fell asleep in the seat next to him, lolling forward precariously as the train careened along. Then all of a sudden the din of the train swelled as the car's connecting door was thrown open, and the three youths appeared, jeering over their shoulders. Smailes stiffened again as they turned into the car and watched their leader carefully, trying to gauge whether he could successfully kick him in the groin from a sitting position, if it was necessary. Two of the three young men jostled past, however, and took up positions by the double sliding doors. The third hung from a strap between Smailes and the drunk and closed his eyes. The train began to slow for a station.

What happened next took place in a blur. As the train stopped, the youth standing next to Smailes wheeled and lunged at the drunk, wrenched the gold chain from his neck and tossed it to his two partners by the doors. The Latino leapt from his seat and felled the youth with a vicious punch, then knelt on his neck and proceeded to slap handcuffs on him, screaming all the while. A workman in a stained jacket and lumberjack cap, whom Smailes had not noticed before, had picked up the boom box and was yelling their position into it. Over by the door, another plainclothesman dressed like a derelict had floored another of the youths. The third had gotten away. The Latino was clearly the team leader, since he was screaming down the car, "Mirandize that fucker!" He then took pains to read his own victim his rights, snarling the words at the prostrate figure as he continued kneeling on his ear. He identified himself as Lieutenant Something of the Transit Police.

Smailes sat back in awe as the drunk straightened up and gave him a broad wink. The lieutenant looked over at Smailes and asked whether he had witnessed the incident. If so, it was his duty as a New Yorker to step forward and testify against the muggers, he claimed. Smailes shrugged and said he had been too scared, he had looked away. The lieutenant narrowed his eyes at him and was about to respond when a young woman down the car piped up and offered herself as a witness. At the next station the whole troupe got out, including the "victim," now surprisingly steady on his feet. Then the train moved on again and passengers went back to their books and magazines, as if the whole event was run of the mill. Smailes' heart was still racing, and he marveled at the blatancy of the sting he'd witnessed. The word "entrapment" actually entered his mind briefly, but left again just as quickly. In this city, after all, law enforcement needed all the help it could get.

It was after nine on Christmas Eve when Smailes finally got back to the flat, and Clea was extremely agitated, saying she had been worried about him and that he ought to have called if he was going to be so late. Smailes apologized and recounted his story, then excused himself to hide her present. In his bedroom, he could see a large, decorated box poking out of his closet, and smiled. Despite his somber mood, he had not lost his childlike excitement about Christmas.

The next morning Derek and Clea sat up in bed, drinking coffee and opening their gifts. Clea professed joy and admiration for his taste in jewelry, and left the room briefly to try on the earrings in front of the bathroom mirror. Smailes had opened a scarf from his mother and was manipulating a small padded envelope that he knew from its handwriting came from Tracy, his teenage daughter. He fished out a card and a small, gaily wrapped package. He tore off the paper and found a tape cassette of the Oak Ridge Boys, one of his favorite country groups. He remembered Tracy's scorn when they had discussed music the last time he had seen her, and waved the cassette in the air.

"Now that's devotion," he said ruefully.

Clea wasn't listening. She was opening an envelope

from her father and extracted a small card. As she did so, a check fell out and tumbled onto the bedspread between them. Smailes retrieved it and handed it over to her, turning it the right way up as he did so and noticing its small parade of zeroes. Clea feigned surprise.

"Oh, it's a check," she said, apparently crestfallen. "I wish he wouldn't."

Clea's hypocrisy about her family's money, and particularly the regular gifts from her father, irritated Smailes. "Well, you don't have to keep it, you know, honey," he said, a little harshly.

"Oh no, Daddy would know if I didn't cash it," she protested.

"Well, you could run it through your bank account and donate it to the Coalition for the Homeless, or something," he said, not letting her off the hook.

"Oh no, that would upset him even more," she said, with complete disregard for logic.

"Clea, just admit you expected the gift. In fact, you've come to depend on them."

"Derek, that's not fair," she said, a little tearfully, knowing it was completely fair. She crumpled up the card and the check and stuffed them back into the envelope, then swung her feet out of the bed.

"I'm going to get more coffee," she said, turning away from him. She did not get up, however, and when her shoulders began to rock quietly he knew that she was crying. He immediately regretted his harshness. Who was he to ruin their Christmas?

"What is it, sweetheart? I didn't mean to hurt your feelings." He reached over and rested his hand on her back. She turned and looked at him miserably.

"Honestly, Derek, I don't know why you bother with me. I must be everything you despise."

"What on earth do you mean?"

"I'm a rich, shallow, spoiled bitch. I know that's what you think."

"Like hell that's what I think. I know what I think, thank you very much."

"Well, what do you think?"

He was momentarily lost for words. "Well, I think you're a wonderful, warm, compassionate woman who is a little ashamed of the fact she has rich parents and a privileged upbringing. It's not your fault, you know, and it's not a crime to admit you appreciate their generosity. No one I know thinks you're shallow or spoiled, except maybe yourself. Look, I'm sorry I spoke unkindly. It's just, Kevin getting killed like that, it fills me with a kind of impotent rage. I shouldn't take it out on you."

"You really cared about him, didn't you?" Clea asked.

"He was a great guy. And there's something I never told you. He had arranged to come and stay with me because he wanted to see me privately. I never found out why. And between you and me, I'm not convinced his murder was a botched mugging."

"Whyever not?" said Clea, sitting up sharply. "Honestly, Derek, that's so creepy."

"Kevin Butterworth was a bigger man than me, wasn't he? Must have been all of sixteen stone. Not your obvious mugging target, was he?"

"But didn't that witness see the man try to grab his suitcase?"

"I suppose so," said Smailes doubtfully, wanting to change the subject. "Listen, have you forgiven me?"

Clea sat up, brushed away some remaining tears, and put her arms around him. She felt chagrined because it wasn't her strategy to wring testimonials out of him, but felt heartened by his words. "Of course I have. Listen, Derek Smailes, you're so good for me, I don't deserve you."

Smailes held her at arm's length and looked in her eyes. "Yes, well, the feeling's mutual," he said, with all the sincerity he could muster. He knew he wasn't very good at intimacy, but was gratified by the opportunity to tell her something of his real feelings, and that she had forgiven him. And in truth, her occasional outbursts of self-loathing only increased his respect for her. He felt a surge of tenderness and tried to draw her into an embrace. Clea, however, pulled away.

"You haven't opened my present yet, Meatball," she said, her old mischief restored. "It's in the closet."

"I know," he said. "I saw it last night. I already know what it is."

"Liar," she said, as Smailes struggled with the enormous package. Eventually he removed the wrapping paper and eagerly tore the string off the Lone Star Emporium box. He couldn't believe his eyes. It was a full-length, brown and tan buckskin jacket with a four-inch fringe along the arms and yoke. It must have cost a fortune. He immediately threw off his pajama top to try it on, holding his arms away from him to inspect the fringe. He loved it.

"Clea, you're crazy. You're wonderful. This is fantastic."

He looked up to see a curious, alluring look on her face. She was slowly unbuttoning the front of her high-necked nightgown.

"Yes, but it looks awfully silly with those pajama bottoms. Why don't you take them off and get back into bed, cowboy?" she said.

Smailes almost suffered a nasty injury as he fell over in his haste to comply.

Viktor Vasilyevich Kott stopped his battered Lada at the traffic light outside the illuminated nine-story Tass building on Herzen Street, glancing once in the rearview. As the light changed, he accelerated quickly through the gears past the darkened gray basilica of the Church of the Great Ascension on his left. Then he suddenly slowed and swung the wheel left, then right again, the tires squealing as he jogged around the back street to Koltso Boulevard. As anticipated, he just made the light before it changed and swung left again onto the tree-lined, circular avenue, then began driving more calmly. Glancing again in the rearview, he saw no pursuit car caught at the light, and smiled. He had not been followed.

Ever since his enlistment by Dolghorukov, he had insisted that further operational contact be left to him. There was simply no way the ruling cabal of Krasnaya Zvezdochka could not by now be under surveillance by the Chekists, and, in Kott's opinion, these plump generals were too arrogant and slow-witted to know how to spot a tail, let alone evade one. Kott, however, knew Moscow as well as any man alive, and his fieldcraft was unrivaled. He knew he was not being followed.

In truth, he had almost expected the overture and would not have resisted, even if he had been able. Dolghorukov controlled him as surely as he himself controlled Borya, or any of his agents. He actually sympathized; in his view, the country had not been properly led since Stalin.

Dolghorukov, predictably, had complained about "complexity," but also knew he had to concede operational details to Kott. The plan had cohered in its final details only a short time earlier. Although an ideological, the worst kind of agent, he knew the recruitment he had made on his last trip to New York would prove invaluable eventually. The unexpected bonus was that the approach to the McLean Cartel fanatics had borne such unexpected fruit, giving him the kind of operational reach that would have been unthinkable in other circumstances. He had every confidence in his senior agent, his Viking, an outsider like himself who shared his instinctive resentment toward the machinery of power. And as for London's New York field office, he did not count it any threat. He knew that as surely as if he had made the worthy Mr. Sparks suck a bullet from his revolver all those years ago, instead of scorched metal and air.

Lyle Pitkethly's apartment looked like it had been designed by a top-end motel consultant. British hunting scenes hung on the walls above an expensive imitation leather couch and some furniture that might have been antique, but wasn't. A folder rested on the glass coffee table like a room-service menu, its corners aligned perfectly with the table beneath. Pitkethly was seated on the couch in his shirtsleeves and with his tie loosened, talking into the phone with some animation. He finally unfolded his long limbs and stood up.

"Yes, well, there's been some unprofessionalism on your end too, if you ask me," he said angrily, picking up the telephone and pacing about with it.

"Absolutely not," he said presently. "It's taken care of."

Pitkethly paused. "I said it's taken care of," he repeated quietly. "No, I leave tomorrow," he said.

Pitkethly sat down again with the phone on his knee, listening intently to some litany from his respondent. Then he permitted himself the vestige of a smile.

"Don't worry about her," he said. "She's cooperating fully." Then he hung up and placed the telephone down carefully on the folder, nudging it with a knuckle until it, too, was perfectly aligned with the rectangular surface beneath.

9

Derek Smailes was sitting in his office at the end of his first week back at work after the long Christmas break, discussing his update for the Roberts file with Graham Booth. The paperwork had come back via Madge earlier that day, and Smailes was trying to instruct Booth on how to fill out the transmission sheet for the comms. Smailes had largely recovered from the shock of Butterworth's murder, but was aware of a sense of agitation, and not only because a smooth-cheeked trainee like Booth was presuming to give him advice. His social obligations that evening included his first meeting with Peter Lynch, Clea's father, who was passing through New York on his way to a meeting in Washington. Clea and Derek were scheduled for dinner at seven-thirty; it was a prospect that Smailes did not relish.

"So perhaps we should have questioned more people in the block of flats," Booth was saying. "You know, there could be different versions out there."

Smailes kept his reply scrupulously polite. "These people are not the most talkative bunch, Graham. I think we got all the info there we're going to get. And Mr. Yates . . ."

"Oh yes, what did he say?" asked Booth, interrupting.

"Well, he did some checking through his own contacts in the police department, and it's confirmed that Roberts had started working for the local drug boss."

"Well, if that's what Yates says . . ." said Booth magnanimously, and then the phone on Smailes' desk rang once, signifying an internal call.

Smailes picked up the receiver. "Smailes," he said.

"Derek," said Ralph's voice. "Step in, will you? You have a visitor."

Smailes checked his watch. It was after four-thirty on Friday, an odd time for a meeting. He wondered momentarily whether word of his unofficial contact with Sparks had gotten back to Van Deusen, but dismissed the notion quickly. So far, he had not acted on his identification of the anonymous target of Howard's intercept, beyond some preliminary research. Mikhail Siskin had not been listed in the UN directory of permanent missions, but he had found him on the UN's own staff roster. Siskin, it seemed, was a relatively big cheese; his entry had described him as assistant undersecretary in the Department of Disarmament Affairs.

Smailes stepped across to Van Deusen's office, opened the door without knocking, and recognized the guest instantly, although his back was turned.

"Hello, Roger," he said, closing the door quietly. Roger Standiforth, head of MI5's K Branch, looked over his left shoulder and gave his thin-lipped smile.

"Hello, Derek. How are you? Do take a seat." He gestured carelessly to the vacant chair at the other end of Van Deusen's desk. Ralph was watching Smailes closely, a tight, smug expression on his face. Standiforth paused to light a cigarette, then smiled unconvincingly again. "You're looking well," he said. "It's been a few years, hasn't it?"

Smailes sat down, his mind racing. Standiforth was an individual who provoked violent and conflicting emotions within him. Patron and nemesis both, Roger Standiforth was responsible for recruiting Smailes into the security service, and almost getting him killed at the same time. Then he had relegated him to the backwater of C Branch, after enticing him with the promise of life at the sharp end. What on earth was he doing in New York? Standiforth was in charge of domestic counterintelligence, and had no direct authority over C Branch or its overseas outposts. And if the rumors Smailes had heard were correct, he was no friend of Van Deusen either, having climbed up through the K Branch hierarchy after Ralph's own demise.

But his presence in Ralph's office was clearly significant, and Smailes involuntarily straightened his tie and smoothed his hair as he sat down. Were retirements, or even promotions, in the offing? Smailes stared across at Standiforth with a look of studied indifference.

Roger Standiforth was aging well. The pale blue eyes were a little more deeply set beneath the patrician brow, and the creases cut more emphatically alongside the raptor's nose. The sleek fair hair, however, was thick, and only lightly streaked with gray, and he still comported himself like one accustomed to issuing orders. He narrowed his eyes imperceptibly at Smailes and raised his cigarette to his mouth without looking at it. He drew on it carefully, then exhaled through his nose. For his part, Smailes examined the gallery of photographs on the wall behind Roger's head; Ralph with Sir Michael, Ralph with the foreign secretary, Ralph partially obscured by the modest bouffant of a former prime minister.

"So how is New York? To your liking?" asked Roger, glancing down to pick a fleck of ash from a charcoal trouser leg. "I must say it seems you've been doing terrifically well."

"Sure. It's a great place. How's London?" Smailes retorted, a little too quickly. As usual, he found Roger's tone patronizing.

"Oh, business as usual, I'm afraid," said Standiforth wearily. "No one has told the espionage commissars the Cold War is over, I'm afraid. Which is why I'm here in New York, you won't be surprised to learn."

"Really?" said Smailes, attempting to sound interested.

At this juncture, Roger reached forward and lifted the cover of a manila folder which rested on Ralph's desk. The file was edged in blue, signifying a HUMINT, or human intelligence source. He extracted a document and held it up so Smailes could view it. It was a copy of Howard Grundy's Riverdale intercept.

"This made extremely interesting reading. Ralph sent it through by bag just before Christmas. In fact, it's had the old souls in Curzon Street in a bit of a flap."

Smailes stiffened. Ralph had gone behind his back to send the intercept through to London, and he suddenly felt exposed on several fronts.

"Yes, well, it seemed a bit of a stupid stunt at the time, to tell you the truth," said Smailes, prevaricating.

"Not at all, not at all. Nothing ventured, you know. We had a little chat with your pal Grundy when he came home, and we gave him a pat on the head, actually. Ralph tells me it was translated by a British employee at the UN. Is that correct?"

"Yes," said Smailes, gripping the arms of his chair, disoriented. He wasn't sure he liked the description of Howard Grundy as his "pal." He had no idea where this discussion was leading.

"In fact, we've decided to recruit the chap," said Standiforth mildly, as if he were issuing a dinner invitation.

Smailes was stunned. Recruit who? Howard? No, Siskin? How? A joint effort through the SIS station? What the hell was Curzon Street thinking? The recruitment of foreign nationals as intelligence assets had nothing to do with MI5, whose purview was exclusively domestic security. Was Roger playing an elaborate joke? He looked across at his pointed, impassive features, then around at Van Deusen, whose fixed, self-satisfied expression had not changed since Smailes entered the room. He noticed for the first time that Ralph still wore quite a tan from his Caribbean vacation.

Roger retrieved further papers from the blue-rimmed file and waved them confidently in the air. "Yes, the party's name is Mikhail Siskin, you'll be interested to know. Mikhail Karlovich Siskin. Clean diplomat. Brilliant, meteoric career. Used to sit as Soviet rep on First Committee and the Disarmament Commission. Served three years then joined the bureaucracy as number-two man in the Department of Disarmament Affairs. In fact, Data Center has come up with quite a case history on Comrade Siskin, and it turns out he's someone the new chaps in Whitehall would be most interested in hearing from. Disarmament expert, you see, and what with all this palaver at Geneva . . . In fact, there's a couple of things in particular they'd like to ask him."

Smailes could not contain himself. "Roger, why are you telling me all this?"

Standiforth looked genuinely surprised. "Oh, I thought you realized. We want you to recruit the fellow. We want you to enroll Mikhail Siskin as an agent in place, then have him come across . . ."

Smailes thought he was hallucinating. Standiforth's voice receded into the distance as the blood rushed into his ears and his heart rose up in his chest. He slumped back and stared from Standiforth to Van Deusen and back again, his head nodding like a toy dog mounted in the back of a car. Roger's mouth flapped away wordlessly. Slowly, he regained himself.

". . . so all in all, it seemed like a good fit," Standiforth was saying.

"You want me to enroll the guy?" Smailes interjected. "You want *me* to recruit this . . . whoever he is . . . Siskin?"

"We thought you could give it a stab," Standiforth said reasonably. Objections crowded into Smailes' mind so fast he had to struggle to enumerate them.

"Look, Roger, I'm sorry, but what if Siskin is an intelligence agent? I mean, what if this whole thing is a provocation? What if he's really clean, but protests to his ambassador and provokes an incident? Then what? And anyway, I'm C Branch, remember? I'm a lock-and-safe man. You know, copy machines, automobiles, that sort of thing. I've already been passed over for counterintelligence, remember?" he added pointedly.

Standiforth held up a hand indulgently. "One thing at a time, Derek. Obviously, the first thing we suspected was that Siskin was a dangle. As I said, we debriefed Howard Grundy very carefully and are satisfied that his intercept was completely random—there's simply no way this information could have been planted. Siskin is clean all right, and in normal circumstances, there's no reason to suspect he would cooperate. And after all, with our new spirit of international trust and openness, defections are really a relic of the past, aren't they? There just aren't the same incentives anymore." Here Roger paused to append a quick, sharklike grin. "But in Comrade Siskin's case, we're holding a couple of trump cards. Namely, the illness of his daughter, and the fact that his second tour expires in July."

Standiforth thrust his fists away suddenly to adjust his French cuffs, then looked down at the papers in his lap.

"It is a little-known fact that a team of British neurosurgeons in East Grinstead has recently made a dramatic breakthrough against sclerotic illnesses, particularly in younger patients. As I said, Comrade Siskin's tour expires in July, and unfortunately for him, enlightenment has not yet fully dawned in the recesses of the Foreign Ministry, and particularly not in its Foreign Cadres Department, which still vets all diplomats at the conclusion of two consecutive foreign tours. Since it appears Comrade Siskin has been a somewhat unpredictable spokesman for the Soviet agenda during his term in the Secretariat, it is unlikely he will win another overseas posting for another five to ten years. In Moscow, Irina may not live that long. Now, why wouldn't someone in Siskin's position in the *nomenklatura* simply apply for treatment in Britain? Because we have already taken pains to ensure that the work of the East Grinstead team receives no further publicity. And after he learns of it from you, you will make it clear that any independent overtures of his will be rebuffed. No, the only hope for Irina Siskin will be for her father to cooperate with us. What we would prefer is that he remain in place until July, then come across as his tour expires. The whole family, of course. New identity if he wishes, ministry pension, naturally. We expect him to be the last defector of this particular type . . ."

"Ralph, why me?" asked Smailes weakly.

Standiforth turned to Van Deusen and indicated that he wanted the file on his desk. Then he thought twice and said, "Ralph, why don't you explain?"

It was at this point that Smailes realized that Ralph's smug expression was actually a mask he was maintaining through a supreme effort of will. As he spoke, the gall he really felt became obvious.

"Well, London's been very impressed with you lately, Derek," he began unctuously. "Finding the bugging equipment, then the limousine bomb. Normally, in an unusual operation like this, the head of station would take charge, and in fact, I am to be in overall command of the operation." Here he paused to look over at Standiforth, who nodded slightly in confirmation. "But the operational contact is to be left up to you. It was felt there were, well, similarities. You're about the same age, you have daughters the same age, he may feel easier with you because of that."

Standiforth gestured that he wanted the file on Ralph's blotter after all. Smailes shifted position to squint at it. He realized it was his personal file from the central registry in London.

"As Ralph says, he will be in overall control, and all details must be worked out between the two of you. But the task may need considerable improvisation, and we have a lot of confidence in you, Derek. Your training evaluations were uniformly sound, with particularly high marks in the psychologicals. The file does say something about 'difficulty with authority,' but Ralph assures me there have never been any problems on that score." He gave a quick, gleeful smile at the two men, then looked down again, disqualifying any dissent. The expression on his face made him look like a self-satisfied greyhound.

"Now clearly, at another time, we'd send over the enrollment committee to handle the whole thing. They're the boys based in Bovingdon who debrief all our East-bloc chaps, you know. But in the current climate, they'd never get out of London without ringing alarm bells. Lord knows, the KGB have more watchers on the ground than we do. So, if we wanted to proceed, if we wanted to prevent this little nugget simply washing away downstream, it had to be someone in place, and everything pointed to you, Derek. You see, no one will suspect you. You're not even an intelligence officer, after all, technically speaking."

Up to this point, Smailes had been basking in the unaccustomed flattery and was jolted by the put-down. Van Deusen, conversely, brightened at this last remark and nodded vigorously a couple of times in agreement.

"And if Siskin squawks?" Smailes asked.

"There would be an apology, you'd be brought back to London. Nothing serious," said Standiforth.

"I'll need backup. Are we going to use Smith or Sparks on this?" he inquired.

"No," said Standiforth sharply. "We're going to leave SIS out of this completely, both here and in London. Sparks might have been an asset once, but not now. And Smith isn't rated very highly either, between you and me. Percy has spoken with the DG and the cabinet secretary, and they both agree. Percy and I will run the operation from London, Ralph from this end. The fewer indoctrinated the better, you see."

This last remark suddenly clarified the entire scenario for Smailes. If Roger and Percy Price-Jones, the deputy DG, had strongarmed both the DG and the cabinet secretary into approving the scheme, it meant MI5 had won benediction at the highest level to poach on its rival's most hallowed preserve. Price-Jones was the second most powerful man in Five, and the cabinet secretary, who chaired the Joint Intelligence Committee, was the prime minister's permanent liaison to the intelligence community. Smailes had heard that the new PM had knives out for the mandarins at the FO, and here was concrete proof. It was also an open secret that the Gaffer, as the DG was affectionately known, was planning a summer retirement to his Derbyshire estate, and this was probably Price-Jones' opening salvo in the succession struggle. It was similarly well known that Price-Jones had Standiforth in his hip pocket, having put him up for his first "gong," an OBE in last year's birthday honors list. Motives suddenly became clear—a chance for Roger and Percy to mount an interagency coup, to fly their flag over the enemy fort, and to advance their careers as a consequence. Smailes never ceased to marvel at what a British civil servant would do for a title.

"So have a look, Derek, will you?" said Standiforth, handing over the blue file. "We have no doubt you're up to it, but let us know if you disagree. Look, think about it overnight if you like. I suggest we convene again around ten, tomorrow. On a Saturday, we'll have the place to ourselves, I don't doubt?"

Standiforth raised his eyes at Van Deusen, who nodded brusquely. Smailes flipped open the folder and looked at an eight-by-ten glossy of Mikhail Siskin. He looked as if he were in his early forties—great bald dome of a head, black walrus mustache, small, sad Slavic eyes. He felt momentarily offended by the "same age" remark. Exactly how old did Roger think he was?

"Okay. I would need a lot of briefing. I'd need to know exactly what we want from the guy, exactly what deal we're offering."

"Absolutely," said Roger. "I'm planning on staying here for a week, or as long as is necessary."

"I'll think it over," said Smailes, rising to leave.

"One more thing, Derek," said Standiforth. Smailes turned and looked at him quizzically.

"Yes."

"I believe you're having dinner with Peter Lynch tonight."

Smailes was nonplussed. "Yes," he managed to say, evenly.

"Which implies you have more than a professional relationship with his daughter, I presume," he said archly.

Smailes felt like telling him to mind his own business, but thought better of it. "That's right," he said, waiting for Standiforth to explain himself.

"We were on the same flight yesterday, that's all. We belong to the same club, you see. Known him for years. Never misses an opportunity to pump me for gossip, you know. Ralph, I think it's time to update Derek's personal file, don't you?" he said, brandishing the manila file and turning to Van Deusen knowingly.

Ralph ignored him. "Peter Lynch is in town? No one told me anything. Where is he staying? I must give him a ring. We go back years."

"Oh, the Waldorf, I think he said. Some place way outside the range of the British Treasury, that's for sure," Standiforth said with a wave of his hand. "You should see the place they've booked me into. Way up north on Lexington Avenue."

"Yes, well, life can be rough, Roger," said Smailes, turning to leave.

Smailes returned to his office and sat down in a daze. His sense of unreality was so strong that for a moment he did not recognize anything in the room. Then his vision began to focus. On his telephone receiver was a taped note from Booth: "Filed the Roberts update. Clea called. Said going home to change, give a call. See you Monday. Graham."

Smailes walked to the safe that was set into his wall cupboards and locked away the Siskin file. Then he returned to his desk, gathered himself, and dialed Clea's apartment. There was no reply, and her answering machine was turned off. He swore softly and dialed his own number, listened to his recording, then punched in the code to access his messages. There were none. He called

Clea's number again and Felicity picked it up on the second ring.

"Was that you earlier, Derek? I'm sorry, I was in the loo. Clea asked me to give you a message. By the way, was that thing I translated for you all right?"

"Yes, fine. Thanks a lot, Felicity," he said casually, not wanting to pursue the subject further. "What did Clea say?"

Smailes listened with mounting irritation as Felicity recounted how Clea had come home in a whirlwind and had begun making anguished protests about having nothing to wear, when the phone rang and it was Lyle Pitkethly. Lyle had just returned from UN business in Africa and Europe, and Clea had told him her news, including her prospective promotion, and Lyle had invited her for a celebration drink. Clea had dressed hurriedly and gone off to meet Lyle at the Glades. Felicity did not know the place, but had been told that Derek did, and was asked to tell him to meet them there. Then they could go on to their dinner date from there, Clea had said. Smailes cursed to himself, but managed to thank Felicity courteously and hang up.

He felt annoyed and confused. Obviously, he could tell Clea nothing of what had transpired that afternoon, but he wanted to see her and did not like the idea of sharing her on that particular evening, and especially not with Lyle Pitkethly. He thought momentarily of staying at the office to study the Siskin file, then calling the Glades later on for their dinner plans, but realized he was being childish. He locked up, checked in his keys and took a taxi fifteen blocks across town.

The Park Glades was a fern bar near Columbus Circle that had become a regular haunt of Clea's since Tyler Dawes had begun playing there in late summer. Like most New Yorkers, Tyler lived in a tiny apartment where there was no room for a piano. In return for unlimited rehearsal time, therefore, Tyler had elected to lower his dignity and play light jazz there three evenings a week. It was a favorite venue for Clea and her entourage, and in normal circumstances, Smailes would have welcomed the opportunity to relax there with her for an hour before an event like meeting her father. In his current state of mind, however, he wanted to get the evening's events over with as quickly as possible.

As soon as he entered the bar, Smailes was struck by how at ease the ruling classes were with each other, despite disparities in culture. Clea and Lyle were seated in a booth at the far end of the lounge, playing with the swizzle sticks in their cocktails and laughing at some shared joke, oblivious of their surroundings. Smailes maneuvered past a copse of ficus trees at the end of the bar and headed toward the boatsized piano that stood next to a tiny patch of dance floor. Tyler was seated at the keyboard, eyes half closed, playing a liquid Cole Porter tune. He was wearing a white shirt and tie, beneath a colorful Zulu caftan and pillbox hat. Without altering his expression or looking down at the keys, he nodded slightly at Smailes as he passed, and Smailes responded with a brief smile. Clea had looked up from her drink and was beaming at him.

"Derek, darling, you got the message. Lyle simply insisted. Come and sit down," she said, sliding along the bench seat to admit him. She looked, predictably, marvelous, and he felt momentarily ashamed of his earlier pique. Somewhat to his surprise, Clea had chosen a rather daring maroon dress that was a bit more décolleté than was her custom. She wore an elegant silk scarf at her neck, but it only seemed to draw more attention to her modest cleavage. Pitkethly, by contrast, looked stiff and awkward, and shook hands formally, as if they were about to open a business meeting. Lyle was wearing his blue blazer, but had made the concession of loosening his yellow polkadot tie. Smailes did the same, as Michael, one of the regular waiters, came over wearing a bright, professional smile.

"Beer, please, Michael," he said. "Something British," he added, with a quick smile at Clea. "So what have you been up to, Lyle?" he asked.

Any lingering ill will he felt toward Clea left him as

she found his hand under the table and squeezed it. He looked at her and felt a sudden rush of pride that this beautiful, animated woman was his companion. Then he turned his attention back to Pitkethly, who was explaining that he had just got back from Secretariat business at UN outposts in Luanda, Nairobi and Geneva. Smailes saw an opportunity.

"So what's the inside word on the Geneva talks, eh, Lyle? Did you get to talk with any of the players?" he asked casually.

The question appeared to exasperate Pitkethly. "If you ask me, it's developed into a game of gin rummy. Whatever you can lay on the table, we'll match it and raise three of a kind. God knows, they're talking about an April summit between Wilkes and Rostov in Oslo, if they can resolve the remaining issues."

"You don't seem too pleased, Lyle," Smailes commented.

"Absolutely not," said Pitkethly quickly. "What's the big hurry here? These are extremely complicated issues, and if you ask me, Wilkes and Rostov are railroading the whole process for the sake of their domestic agendas."

"They're not doing the actual negotiating, are they, Lyle?" he asked.

"They're providing the impetus," said Pitkethly moodily, and fell silent.

Smailes turned again to Clea and saw an impish look on her face. "Did you hear about Derek's heroism in saving the British ambassador's life, Lyle?" she asked.

"What are you talking about?"

"That UN vehicle that had the bomb defused right before Christmas? Did you hear about that?"

"Yes. I saw the headlines while I was away. An unassigned pool vehicle was all the story said. No details. I was going to check into it when I get back into the office next week. What are you saying, Clea?"

Clea was ignoring the pinching that Smailes was giving her beneath the table. But he wasn't pinching hard, and Clea obviously knew Lyle would learn the whole story as soon as he reported back to the UN. In fact, Smailes was quite proud of the whole incident, and Clea knew it.

"Well, it wasn't. It was one of two cars for the British Mission, and Derek found it. They're going to put him in for the George Medal."

Here Smailes snorted with laughter, and Clea joined in. Pitkethly, however, was horrified.

"You're not serious? How the hell did it happen? God, Derek, where did you find it? In your garage?"

"No, at Eastside Lincoln."

"Eastside Lincoln? My God, we're going to have to take a look at pulling their clearance. What actually happened?"

Smailes embarked on a modified version of the events at the Lincoln dealership, and had almost finished when he felt the pressure of Clea's foot on his beneath the table. He looked up to see Dennis Dicenzo, Tyler's boy-friend, smiling down at them. Dennis was wearing an ex-pensive-looking leather jacket and elegant tailored pants, but his face had a haggard look.

"Fancy meeting you all here," he said. "Tyler didn't say he was expecting you. Mind if I join you?"

"No, please," said Lyle, sliding in to the wall to make room.

It was obvious Smailes was going to have no time alone with Clea that evening, and his attention began to wander back to the Siskin file lying in his safe, when Tyler decided to take a break and came over to join them. He pulled up a chair and hugged Dennis. The pillbox hat was cocked at a raffish angle on his head and he seemed in a lighthearted mood, and when Dennis asked him whether he had practiced much that afternoon, Tyler looked sheep-ish and said he had stayed home to watch the football on television. When Dennis protested that Tyler didn't like football, Tyler laughed and said he enjoyed watching the players in their tight pants, and everyone laughed with him. Then Tyler commented that Dennis looked gaunt.

Dennis Dicenzo took a long sip of his wine and began a tale of his own.

It transpired that Dennis, out of concern for those less fortunate than his regular clientele, worked a day a week in a free dental clinic at a hospital somewhere in deepest Brooklyn. The clinic treated a lot of patients from Little Odessa, the Russian émigré enclave at Brighton Beach, and that afternoon's shift had been his most harrowing to date. It seemed an elderly Jewish woman had attended, complaining of severe pain in her mouth. On examining her, it became clear to Dennis that the old lady, who had arrived only the previous month from Smolensk, had never visited a dentist in her life and was in urgent need of full-mouth extractions. Although she spoke no English, the old lady seemed to understand and readily agreed to have her few remaining teeth pulled. Other questions about experience with medications seemed to defeat her, however.

Undaunted, Dennis and his assistant had given the woman two large injections of lidocaine and were waiting for the anesthesia to take hold, when the woman's head began to swell and turn beet red. Within fifteen minutes, her head had assumed the size and hue of a basketball, and Dennis and his assistant were in a blind panic. Dennis summoned the senior orthodontist, who summoned the hospital anesthesiologist, who summoned the hospital administrator, and soon the tiny room was crammed with anxious medical men, none of whom knew what to do. The old Russian lady remained unperturbed throughout her ordeal, however, resting calmly in the dentist's chair with her huge, alien head, her hands folded across her chest, seemingly prepared for any eventuality. Finally, after almost an hour, the swelling began to subside, and the danger receded. The medical people departed, badly shaken up, but as they left and the lidocaine began to wear off, the old lady grabbed Dennis by the arm and pointed at her mouth, indicating that she expected him to proceed. With some difficulty, he had done so, and had learned something about the fortitude of the Russian soul in the process.

Everyone seemed to appreciate Dennis's story, and so Smailes thought he would try a turn. He recounted a slightly embellished version of the events of Christmas Eve, the improbable undercover squad and its arrest of the young black hoodlums. His story also seemed to go over well, except with Tyler, who seemed uninterested throughout the account and looked away at its conclusion, a sour look on his face. Smailes realized with some dismay that the tale might seem racially motivated to Tyler, and felt guilty. Try as he might, he couldn't quite seem to get it right with the man.

Clea, however, was having a wonderful time, and had apparently come to a decision.

"Listen, everyone. My father's in town for the evening. Derek and I are having dinner with him and are going over to meet him at the Waldorf. But why don't I invite him here for a cocktail? I'd love him to meet everybody." Clea indicated with a sweep of her arm her sense of proprietorship over the scintillating company. No one raised an objection and she retreated busily toward the public phones near the washrooms at the rear of the lounge. Smailes was trying to think of something to repair whatever injury he had caused Tyler, but was interrupted by Pitkethly, looking down at his watch.

"God, is that the time?" he asked. "I have a dinner date myself tonight," he said, adding an uncharacteristic, wolfish grin. "Tell Clea I'm sorry, okay? I'll be in touch." Dennis stood aside to let Lyle slide out from his bench, and as Lyle lifted down his coat from its hook he said to Smailes, "Let's talk next week about that business with the car, okay, Derek?" Smailes nodded, and Pitkethly left.

Clea, Derek and Peter Lynch were embarking on their main course at a basement-level bistro just off the glass canyon of Sixth Avenue. Peter Lynch had insisted on the venue, lavishly praising both its chef and "Provençale" menu. Smailes squinted down at his plate and balked. The food was so artfully arranged it seemed an act of vandalism to disturb it. It also seemed that in restaurant French, "Provençale" had the secondary meaning of "small." Lynch attacked his lamb cutlets with gusto, however, so Smailes hesitantly followed suit.

Smailes had been surprised by Clea's father. Peter Lynch was one of those boyish Englishmen whose features did not particularly age with time, but only grew coarser. Although in his early sixties, Lynch's curly, medium brown hair was still full, his complexion ruddy and his nose and ears slightly too big, like a clown's. He was tall and rangy, a completely different physical type from Clea, and wore expensive, untidy clothes. His hand-tailored Italian suit was rumpled from travel, and although his red silk tie was cinched tightly, the collar curled and stuck out, as if he had lost the stays. He clearly doted on Clea, whose manner with her father seemed to fluctuate between entreaty and rebuke. But it had not been a difficult evening so far, and Lynch's taste in food and wine was clearly superb. Clea had not begun her own meal yet and was berating her father about the "dreadful vultures" with whom he did business in New York.

"Nonsense," said Lynch airily, waving his fork. "Acquisition is the major instrument of business reform these days, my girl."

"Asset-stripping is a better word for what your people do, Daddy," said Clea, although not harshly. Lynch paused to sip more wine. They were well into their second bottle. Lynch had insisted on buying champagne at the Glades, in celebration of Clea's prospective promotion.

"So how do you like your work in New York, Derek?" Lynch asked. Smailes stiffened, not knowing how much Clea had told him.

"Not something I talk about much, Mr. Lynch," said Smailes politely, but with a note of warning.

"Must be a sod to work for. Ralph Van Deusen, I mean," said Lynch, through a mouthful of food. "Has he gotten any better?"

Smailes shot a quick, evil glance at Clea, then remembered that Van Deusen and Lynch were old acquaintances. "I really wouldn't know, Mr. Lynch," said Smailes, more firmly. As a former member of Parliament, Lynch had to know that any discussion of Smailes' work was off limits. Lynch continued in the same tone, seemingly oblivious.

"Call me Peter, for goodness' sake. Only he called me a couple of hours ago at the hotel. Must've heard I was in town. Asked me to go for a drink. I could've invited him this evening, but well, I felt it wasn't fair to you two." Smailes winced at the thought. "So anyway, I said I'd have lunch with him tomorrow. I'm not expected down there until six or something."

Clea had picked up on Smailes' unease and said quietly, "Derek's not allowed to talk to you about his work, Daddy. You should know that."

"Of course, of course. Didn't mean to put you on the spot, old man. Only commiserating, you know. He's such a damned cold fish."

"So where are you off to anyway, Daddy? You wouldn't tell me on the phone," asked Clea, changing the subject.

"A conference," said Lynch. "Sponsored by some outfit calling itself Friends of the Western Alliance. Arms control, I think."

"I didn't know you were interested in arms control, Daddy," said Clea pointedly.

"I'm not, particularly," conceded Lynch. "But it's an all-expenses-paid thing, and they wouldn't leave me alone, so I finally agreed. Something about forming a network of European business people."

The name rang a bell for Smailes, who had been searching his mind. "Isn't that one of those right-wing Washington groups opposed to any further treaties with the Soviets?" Smailes asked.

"Bloody well hope so," said Lynch. "Wouldn't go if it wasn't. This ruddy chap Wilkes is going to scrap the Western deterrent for the sake of his budget deficit, if we don't watch out. Clea, did I tell you that you're looking terrific this evening? Derek must be good for you. You want more wine?" he asked, reaching for the bottle.

Clea's cheeks and bosom reddened slightly as she put her hand over her glass modestly. Smailes realized that the compliment from her father was what she had been waiting for all evening.

"Are you still active in the Conservative Party, sir?" asked Smailes, his formality continuing despite himself. "Clea told me you used to have a seat."

"Well, certainly, I always go to conference and we're a major contributor, that is, my firm is, but I haven't been active on a constituency level in some years, no."

"Any plans for a comeback?"

Lynch was amused by the compliment, and put down his cutlery to respond. "Well, I had a marginal back in the early seventies, you see, which I lost thanks to Heath and his three-day week. Then I fell out with the local committee, and by the time the party was properly led again, I'd gotten rather too immersed in the City, I'm afraid, to consider asking the central office for another stab. Sometimes I think about it, though," he conceded.

"You were a supporter of Mrs. Thatcher, I gather," Smailes persisted.

Lynch seemed genuinely shocked by the remark. "My God, man," he said, "she was sent by heaven to save us!"

Clea found his face and rolled her eyes at the ceiling. They were huge with amusement.

Later, in the taxi, she grabbed his arm and hugged him, and Smailes was aware he'd passed an important test. "You were wonderful tonight, darling. He's not the easiest man to get along with," she said.

"It's great to be alone with you, finally," Smailes said, returning her embrace and slipping his hand inside her coat. "You looked awfully fetching tonight."

Clea pouted a little. "Well, if you had a sister like mine, you'd understand if I'm a bit competitive," was all she'd say, shifting slightly at the movements of his hand.

She checked to see that the cab driver was watching the street, then drew him close and they kissed. Derek squeezed her gently and her breath grew more shallow.

They had both had plenty to drink, and Clea rubbed his neck amorously. "I'll make your favorite breakfast tomorrow as a reward. I'll even cook bacon," she said dreamily.

Smailes straightened, removing his hand. "Look, I'm sorry, but I can't stay tonight, honey. I should have said. I've got to go back to the office and look at some paperwork. It'll take me hours. There's a special meeting tomorrow I just can't get out of."

Predictably, Clea's feelings were hurt. She sat up in the swaying cab. "That's a drag, Derek. Couldn't you have said something earlier?"

"There was hardly an opportunity."

"Honestly," she said angrily. "If you weren't planning to spend the night, you could at least keep your hands off me."

"Sorry."

After a pause, she added accusingly, "I bet it's to do with Roger Standiforth, isn't it?"

Smailes was shocked. He had no idea Clea even knew of his existence. Before he could respond, she said, "I know he's here. I made his travel arrangements, didn't I, and the chargeback was to a Home Office code, which means he's MI5, isn't he?" Smailes hated it when she grew knowing and vindictive.

"I don't know who you mean," he said stiffly. "It's just a special departmental . . ."

"Honestly, Derek Smailes, you don't fool me a bit," she said angrily, as the taxi slowed in front of the flower shop. She accepted his kiss grudgingly, but as she stepped onto the sidewalk she wheeled around with more to say. "Listen, when I become a proper diplomat, my security clearance will be upgraded and you won't have any excuse to tell me lies anymore, will you? Then what will you do?"

Smailes was lost for a reply.

10

"And a budget of five thousand dollars a month," said Smailes, "all voucher restrictions waived."

Ralph's jaw fell open. "My God, man, you've got to be joking. How on earth do you expect . . ."

Roger raised a pacifying hand. "Wait. Just wait a minute, Ralph. I think Percy has some discretionary funds that might stretch to this, and I can see Derek's point about paperwork."

"Right," said Smailes. "What do you expect me to do every time an expenditure comes up, call a meeting of the budget committee and go racing around after signatures? Let's set up an imprest fund with an independent cashier if you like, but civil service regs have got to go out the window on this one."

"Well, I suppose Madge could . . ." Van Deusen responded reluctantly. Van Deusen's hesitation was entirely predictable to Smailes, a preview of what he could expect throughout the whole operation. He tried to meet Standiforth's eyes, but Roger looked away deliberately.

It had been after eleven the previous evening when the taxi dropped Smailes on First Avenue's deserted mission row. A doleful Oral Yates had admitted him to the lobby and unlocked the elevator for him, and he had eventually roused Hugo Brook, one of the senior cipher clerks, to let him into the mission. Hugo was watching a videotape of a football match in the operations room, and Smailes exchanged a few words with him while he made a pot of coffee. Then he asked him to keep the volume down and went through to his office next door. He carefully extracted the material from his safe, took a long swallow of coffee, and began reading.

His eventual decision was never really in doubt. Sometime during the meal with Clea and her father he had looked across at her and realized that if the relationship was to have a future, his career was somehow going to have to keep pace with hers. On the one hand, Roger's offer had a suspiciously familiar ring to it: Smailes was being dispatched as point man on a precarious mission whose outcome was moot. If Smailes succeeded, Roger would get much of the credit, whereas any failure could be blamed on the inexperience of the operative the British had been obliged to use. There was a part of Smailes that relished the prospect of the consternation that his refusal would provoke, and he pretended to toy with the idea. On the other hand, he knew that Roger's offer was in effect a dream come true. It had long been his ambition to work in K Branch, which operated where the real friction between competing powers took place, and if the Siskin mission succeeded, Smailes would be ideally positioned for transfer and promotion. He really didn't need the rationale of Clea's own elevation in rank as a pretext, and secretly knew it.

He also had a less formulated, more personal reason for wanting to assume the mission. He somehow knew in his bones that the murder of Kevin Butterworth was not a random street crime, that it was somehow linked to information that Butterworth had intended to share with him, and that if Smailes was ever to get to the bottom of it, he needed to continue to burnish his star at Curzon Street. It had even crossed his mind that Butterworth might have had something to express about Howard's modus operandi that would have thrown additional light on the intercept he had gathered. And at the risk of looking foolish,

Smailes had determined to broach the issue with Standiforth himself.

The file on Siskin was reasonably complete. Born in Karaganda in the remote Kazakhstan republic soon after the end of the war, he had become a party member in his teens and had shown outstanding academic promise both at the local high school and technical institute. Then came transfer to the capital and the Moscow University Law School, a singular move for a provincial student, the file noted. After becoming a specialist in international law, Siskin had enrolled in the elite Moscow State Institute of International Relations, known commonly by its Russian acronym, MGIMO. While the anonymous author of the Siskin file noted that many MGIMO graduates went on to careers in the KGB, particularly the First Chief Directorate, its overseas department, Siskin had developed genuine expertise in disarmament issues and after a stint in the foreign ministry in Moscow had been transferred to New York as first secretary and permanent representative to the UN Disarmament Commission, an adjunct of the security committee. The file noted he was regarded as a relatively open-minded diplomat who did not slavishly toe the Kremlin line, which was one reason he was subsequently recruited into the Secretariat's Department of Disarmament Affairs. Siskin, it appeared, was one of four assistant undersecretaries and was in charge of the studies division, and all indications were that he took his responsibilities as an international civil servant seriously. There was no reason to presume any collaboration with Soviet intelligence agencies, and no known peculiarities of background or behavior. The file noted the existence of a wife and daughter, although there were no photographs of either.

Smailes read through all the material twice, then studied the inscrutable face in the file shot once more. Comrade Siskin certainly looked a lot more challenging than deadbolt codes and limousine leases. A disembodied image of the huge bald prow with its heavy brows and piercing eyes stayed with him through his midnight taxi ride back to Brooklyn, and hovered in the dark before him as he waited fitfully for sleep.

Roger had gone Celtic the following day, in honor of a civil service Saturday. He wore a knobby Aran sweater beneath something expensive from the Outer Hebrides, with leather on its elbows and cuffs. Ralph, it seemed, was sartorially trapped somewhere in the middle sixties and wore a ribbed sweater in baby blue over a lemon golf shirt and burgundy slacks. The outfit might have blended well on the links at Montego Bay, or wherever he'd been, but looked odd in a British government office. Smailes had elected casual wear also, and was sporting a commando sweater, blue jeans, and his old lizardskin cowboy boots. He had actually taken his new buckskin jacket down from its hanger in the closet, but had had second thoughts at the last minute.

Roger's first suggestion was that they repair to one of the interview rooms in the fort, for security reasons. Smailes readily agreed, but smiled inwardly to himself. Security had apparently not been a major concern during Roger's initial presentation in Ralph's office, and Smailes did not doubt that the existence of built-in recording facilities in the interview rooms was a consideration. Roger had doubtless already begun the reflexive procedure of covering his own behind.

Smailes' first request as the three men took their seats in the tiny, windowless room was that the other two refrain from smoking, except on breaks. For a reformed smoker like Smailes, the idea of being trapped in that airless box with a couple of addicts like Ralph and Roger was obnoxious. Roger readily agreed, so Ralph had no choice but to grunt his compliance. He cleared his throat a couple of times in annoyance, producing a noise that sounded more like a child's injured bleat than an adult cough.

"Well?" asked Roger amiably, after the three men had spread papers in front of them.

"I'll do it," said Smailes, "on the following conditions." He then enumerated his terms—the deputing of

Graham Booth to the operation for its duration, unrestricted and exclusive use of a diplomatic vehicle, and his budget requirement. Roger listened impassively and Ralph did not balk until money came up. Smailes had to use further arguments before a decision was reached.

"Look," he said forcefully, "however the first contact is made, we'll need somewhere secure and relatively close by for further meetings, won't we? I can hardly ask him to come here, or out to Mount Vernon, can I? That means either a hotel room, or an office. Preferably the latter. And that means money, regular money, doesn't it?"

Ralph saw the reasoning. "You can stretch to that, Roger?" he asked doubtfully. Standiforth gave preliminary consent and they agreed on the establishment of an imprest fund through Ralph's office, with Smailes providing monthly accounting statements.

"And remember, Derek, you don't have to spend it all," Standiforth warned. "Now, a few conditions of my own."

Roger went on to stipulate that communication between New York and London was to be by bag only. It might be inconvenient and slow, but it was the only assuredly secure method. Any increase in cable or telephone traffic, even if their encryption systems held, could be noticed by the Soviets and might arouse suspicion. London had reliable word that KGB stations around the world were on heightened alert because of the delicate state of international relations, and nothing must happen in New York that might attract attention.

"On which subject," Roger continued, "there is to be an extremely tight bigot list on this operation. I concede you need operational support, Derek, and I took the precaution of clearing Booth in advance, before I left. In London, only myself, Percy and the DG will be indoctrinated at Curzon Street. In addition, only the cabinet secretary and, of course, the prime minister. Whomever he chooses to tell is up to him. But I will lean on the cabinet secretary to keep operational details secret even from the

JIC. Percy has begun deputing for the DG there, and I think we can prevail."

This last information was news to Smailes. If Percy Price-Jones had begun sitting in for the Gaffer on the Joint Intelligence Committee, then the DG must be closer to retirement than he had suspected, and Price-Jones within striking range of his job and the knighthood that went with it.

"So operational rules will prevail from now on. Siskin's code name is Colin. Derek, you are George. Ralph, Bruce. I suppose we need to pick names for Madge and young Mr. Booth. Any suggestions?"

Smailes had to concede later he felt a frisson of excitement at this point, as they bandied code names about like characters in a bad movie. Roger seemed to perceive the mood of levity, however, and added gravely, "One final thing, before we begin on the background to this whole decision. The Cousins must know nothing of it. I cannot stress how important this is. I have explained that if the overture to Siskin backfires, there will be an official apology and you, Derek, will be recalled, in seeming disgrace. However, if the Americans were to learn that the highest levels of the British government had approved such an action in advance, there would simply be hell to pay, with God knows what consequences. Understood?"

"Absolutely," said Ralph.

"No problem," said Smailes meekly. He had no intention of divulging to Standiforth, or to anyone else for that matter, the call he had made before their meeting had begun, or why.

The meeting lasted most of the afternoon, with a long break for lunch that Smailes ordered in from a delicatessen. The session went well, and Smailes was enthralled by the story of international distrust and deception that had fueled the British decision. When he stopped to think about it, he grew nervous about the delicacy of the mission he was about to undertake, and felt out of his depth. But then he would think back to the recording to which he had listened the previous night, the final thing he had done before locking up and taking his taxi home. The original taped intercept was still in his safe, in fact, and although Smailes understood no Russian, he had listened intently to the conversation between Siskin and his wife, and the anguish and despair in their voices, unimpeded by any background noise, were crystal clear. Given his feelings for his daughter, Smailes knew Comrade Siskin would listen very carefully to whatever the British proposed. Smailes had handed the tape over to Standiforth in his office at the conclusion of the day's briefing, and he had thanked him almost absently, saying he would send it through to London to double-check the translation.

It was at that point Smailes pushed his door closed and took the opportunity to confide some of his doubts about the Butterworth murder. Standiforth conceded the whole thing was a "dreadful business," and listened attentively as Smailes outlined the circumstances of Butterworth's change in travel plan, and his thwarted attempt to meet with Smailes in private.

"What are you saying, Derek? That Kevin Butterworth was killed to prevent his speaking with you? That seems a little farfetched, doesn't it?"

"I don't know, Roger. Does it?"

"About what? Any idea?"

"No. Except that he'd been touring on Howard's sweep for the previous month or so. Maybe something concerning that."

Standiforth thought for a long moment, seated with a long leg across Smailes' desk, drawing deeply on a cigarette. "Listen," he said eventually. "Howard Grundy is probably the most talented, most trusted technician we've got. I can't tell you how trusted. We spoke with him at great length, and we're sure this intercept is completely genuine. But for all our sakes, we'll take particular care with checking Comrade Siskin's bona fides, all right? Be as thorough and as painstaking as you wish. Have you told Ralph of your concerns?"

"No," said Smailes.

"All right," said Standiforth, not elaborating further, but cupping his hand under his cigarette to catch its ash.

"I say, do you have an ashtray anywhere?" he asked.

Smailes walked slowly up the slight incline toward the Second Avenue garage where he had left his car, lost in thought. Satisfied that Ralph and Roger had departed to their various abodes, he stopped at a phone kiosk, checked his date book and rang a number. There was no reply, so he called home and accessed his messages. He got Rudy Kabalan's voice, and smiled at the brusque New York accent. "Derek. Rudy Kabalan returning your call, Saturday morning 'bout eleven. Sure I can see you, whenever. I gotta be at the Two Flags diner in White Plains around six, and I'll go there a bit early to catch a bite, so you could meet me there. Otherwise, I got my kids tomorrow, so call me and we'll fix something for next week." Smailes checked his watch and saw that it was a little after four. He quickly made up his mind, then went for his car.

The Two Flags diner was a classic variant of a vanishing breed, and looked like a railroad car with turrets set back from a highway connector just outside the Westchester community of White Plains. An American and an Italian flag fluttered from twin flagpoles above the main door. Smailes pulled his nondescript Plymouth into the parking lot, climbed the steps to the entrance and ordered coffee and a bran muffin. He took a seat by the window so he could scan the view, but didn't have long to wait. Rudy Kabalan showed up about five minutes later, wearing a sky blue warm-up suit with a New York Giants logo under a darker blue parka. He looked like he'd lost some weight. He swung into the booth across from Smailes, took off his coat and ordered a diet soda, saying nothing until it had been placed in front of him. As the waitress receded down the aisle, he asked, "What's up? Baseball season don't start for another coupla months."

Smailes was trying to free his back teeth from some bran muffin and took a moment before replying. He took a swallow of coffee and said eventually, "Where do I find Vasily Malinovsky?"

Kabalan's eyebrows arched and he actually stiffened a little. Taking his time, he asked casually, "Vasily Malcontent. Whaddya want with him?"

"A little advice," said Smailes. "Can't go through Langley on this one."

Derek Smailes had in fact made his first unilateral decision as point man in the Siskin operation. No matter what kind of briefing Roger could supply, and no matter how carefully they reviewed confidence-building measures, Smailes knew nothing could compare with what he could get from the horse's mouth. Vasily Malinovsky was, in fact, the most celebrated Soviet defector of recent times. A former KGB station chief in Helsinki, he had come across to the British with his whole family some ten years earlier, and had initially provided a priceless stream of intelligence that allowed the British to plug some damaging leaks in both the Admiralty and the lower levels of SIS. Eventually, the Cousins had gotten their turn, but Malinovsky had fared less well with the barons at Langley. Whether out of bureaucratic inertia or because Malinovsky could not support his allegations with concrete facts (he had always been with the European section of the First Directorate), the CIA chiefs largely ignored Malinovsky's claims of wholesale Soviet penetration of U.S. intelligence agencies. Probably for financial reasons, Malinovsky elected to settle in the U.S., but over time his complaints against U.S. complacency in the face of the Soviet threat grew more and more hysterical. Détente, the Sino-Soviet split, unilateral reductions in arms—all were ploys, in Malinovsky's analysis, designed to erode Western preparedness for the final, cataclysmic Soviet thrust. He began to publish articles in military journals, and was even the co-author of a book trumpeting the same doomsday scenario. Eventually, Malinovsky inherited the fate of many prominent dissidents and defectors living in the West—that of an embittered and ignored Cassandra, violently disillusioned by his adopted society.

In Malinovsky's case, there had been some tragic post-scripts—a teenage daughter dead from a heroin overdose, a wife an invalid and alcoholic, a son a juvenile delinquent. The British had had no dealings with him in years, but it was known he lived somewhere in the eastern United States. It was generally agreed in British intelligence circles that his life would not have come apart so disastrously if he had chosen to stay in Britain.

Kabalan was biding his time responding, a devious look on his face. He sucked some Coke through a straw, then said, "Remember what we spoke of last time, that McLean Cartel thing? You got any news on that front?"

Clearly, Rudy was trying to barter. Smailes decided to stick his neck out a little farther.

"You tell me who wants to know, and maybe I've got something."

"A client."

"Which client?"

Kabalan hesitated. "Wilfred Thayer," he said eventually.

Derek Smailes was no expert in high finance, but needed no further description of Thayer, the patriarch of the most prominent banking family in New York after the Rockefellers and the Morgans. His bank, Manhattan Liberty, was one of the largest and most profitable in the country, he knew for certain. Smailes could only speculate why someone like Wilfred Thayer would hire a character like Rudy Kabalan.

"I met a British businessman recently," said Smailes. "He said he was on his way to a meeting in Washington sponsored by Friends of the Western Alliance. Said he'd come under some high-pressure lobbying. Something about a network of European business people."

Kabalan looked disappointed. "Sure, it's a PR front, a cartel spin-off, trying to stir up trouble in the allied capitals. They've got some direct defense industry loot and technical backup from freelancers at Langley and Fort Meade. A lot of noise and air," he said dismissively. Then, uncannily, he added, "What else?"

It was Smailes' turn to hesitate. Then he took a breath and told Kabalan of the mission break-in and their discovery of the sophisticated bugging gear. Looked like Soviet handiwork, but it could also be a third party dressing it up that way, he said, to deflect suspicion if it were found.

Kabalan brightened at this information, and sat back with his arms folded across his massive chest, a self-satisfied expression on his face. An elderly waitress shuffled by and Kabalan flagged her down. He ordered a diet platter and asked Smailes whether he'd like to join him. Smailes demurred. Then Rudy pointed to the crumbs on Smailes' plate and told him he ought to be careful, eating such junk.

"Rudy," Smailes protested, "bran muffins aren't junk. Even I know that."

"Bran muffins, angel food, Twinkies, it's all the same," said Kabalan, knowingly. "Addictive. I think you're in denial, Derek."

Smailes was about to shoot back a reply when he noticed the mischief in Rudy's eyes, and realized he was being teased. Rudy changed the subject.

"I'll work on it, Vasily Malcontent's address. I'll get in touch. And you get a discounted price. Five bills."

Smailes balked. "I thought we just traded information, Rudy," he said irritably.

"Yeah, and for that, you get a fifty percent discount. This is my business, remember? Don't try and tell me this is coming out of your own pocket."

Kabalan had him on that count. He reached down his coat, a heavy blue windbreaker which in England would once have been known as a reefer jacket, but which Clea had made him buy from a mail-order catalog and was called a "weekender."

Smailes stood aside as the waitress slid two scoops of tuna and cottage cheese on a limp bed of lettuce under Kabalan's nose. "See you around," he said.

"Sure," said Rudy. "And Derek. Congratulations on the limo bomb."

Smailes wheeled around but Kabalan had already begun poking at his dinner with a fork. He was momentarily alarmed, but not particularly surprised that Rudy's contacts in the FBI had told him the true story of the Eastside Lincoln incident. It was one thing you had to concede about Kabalan—his sources were impeccable.

Out in the parking lot, Smailes felt disoriented. It was after five-thirty and he knew Clea would be expecting him, but he did not particularly feel like turning up at her apartment empty-handed, given the note on which they had parted the previous evening. Flowers were the obvious thing, but if he drove back to the city now, the florist beneath Clea's apartment would be closed by the time he got there. He squinted down the road to an intersection two hundred yards away where there seemed to be a row of shops. He decided to reconnoiter.

He was fortunate to find a Korean grocery, the type with a giant yuppie salad bar and coolers for everything from gourmet beer to roses. He actually considered a dozen long stems, until he saw the price, and finally stumped for a big bunch of yellow, Oriental-style chrysanthemums. He paid for them and wandered back up the long highway ramp toward the diner, now illuminated like some exotic sailing vessel in the night.

He had parked close to the steps leading up to the entrance, and looked up as he fumbled with his keys to open the car. Rudy was still seated in the window booth, across from a muscular-looking black man with a Zapata mustache and a gold chain the gauge of a tow rope around his neck. Rudy's formidable companion, who was also wearing an incongruous clear plastic shower cap, was apparently annoyed about something since he was making vehement gestures and appeared to be shouting something Smailes could not hear. Smailes turned away, and as he did so he noticed that the car parked next to his was an impressive-looking red BMW with smoked windows, multiple antennas, and all manner of custom accessories. He glanced down and saw a vanity license plate that read SHORTSTP.

*   *   *

Ivan Ivanovich Prokhanov stumbled along in his boss's wake, trying to pick islands of firmness in the marshy terrain. Rostov paid no attention to the difficulty of the ground, ploughing ahead with his shoulders hunched forward in his characteristic, bullish way. The dogs foraged ahead excitedly, repeatedly doubling back to leap and yelp at the skirts of their master's leather hunting coat. Rostov ignored them also.

In contrast to their last hunting trip, on which Prokhanov had ruined his best suit, today, he was more appropriately dressed in his Ninth Directorate field uniform, since he had at least been given a little warning of the excursion. Truthfully, he hated this Zavidovo detail— they were miles from the official dacha at Barvikha with its proper security and communications equipment. On such hunting trips he had only a two-way radio for contact with the outside world. Rostov absolutely refused patrols by helicopter or armored vehicle.

And today's trip seemed particularly bizarre. Rostov cradled his shotgun in the safety position, but when they had startled a bevy of quail just two hundred meters back, he had barely glanced at them as they burst into the air. The dogs had clamored and barked, but Rostov had turned back to whatever invisible trail they were following. Now he suddenly turned west toward Copper Lake, a region in which he had never hunted before, to his bodyguard's knowledge.

To say that Ivan Prokhanov did not trust his boss was an understatement. Rostov's reputation, both at home and abroad, had grown into that of a quick-witted and confident politician, a worthy successor to Gorbachev, nimbly negotiating the twin minefields of domestic reform and international détente. Prokhanov saw another side of him —vain, despotic and unpredictable, grimly determined to hold on to power at any cost. In fact, in the humble opinion of Colonel Ivan Prokhanov, KGB, Nikolai Rostov was no different from any other Soviet leader you care to mention.

After another kilometer the terrain began to ease and Rostov quickened pace and was beginning to extend the distance between them. Prokhanov jogged a few steps to gain ground as his boss disappeared over the crest of a small rise. Catching up, Prokhanov found Rostov was following a narrow trail which angled down toward the birch-lined banks of a small lake. The scene was completely deserted.

As he entered the trees, Rostov halted. He turned to wait and Prokhanov spoke for the first time. "Hold this and wait here," he said, handing over his shotgun. Prokhanov hesitated. The first rule of guarding any member of the leadership was never to allow the principal out of your sight, even if ordered. He moved a little to the right and caught sight of gray water between the silver tree trunks, and of Rostov's back as he approached the bank of the lake. Then he saw another sight that made him freeze in terror—the motionless figure of a fisherman holding a rod and line, who turned his head as Rostov approached, as if expecting him.

Prokhanov remained as close as he dared and still be out of earshot, and then experienced another shock. The fisherman was none other than Grigori Chumak, Rostov's military intelligence chief. Prokhanov could just hear his thin laugh as Rostov drew alongside, adjusted his dress, then began to urinate in the lake. Clearly, on this particular day, Chumak's fishing was about as serious as Rostov's hunting. The two men moved closer together and began to converse. Prokhanov could not hear their voices.

The implications began to dawn on him. A clandestine meeting between Rostov and the GRU boss? So carefully arranged? For what purpose? The KGB and the GRU were the deadliest of rivals. What would his masters at the Lubianka pay to know what was being discussed? Or even for the knowledge that such an encounter had taken place? Prokhanov swallowed slowly and flushed a little at such illicit thoughts. The reward would be more than his entire annual salary, he was sure.

Suddenly, his reverie was interrupted by the sound

of crashing footfalls. Grigori Chumak and Nikolai Rostov were picking their way through the trees toward him. He stepped back to the small trail as Chumak, wearing a green camouflage jacket, approached him. Prokhanov felt his face still flushed.

Uncannily, Chumak seemed to read his thoughts. He clamped a massive hand on his shoulder and ordered in his reedy voice, "Name and rank."

"Prokhanov, Ivan Ivanovich, Colonel," he said, suddenly fearing for his life. He could see Rostov a little farther down the trail, standing with his hands clasped behind him, his back to them.

"What is penalty for breach of confidence in the Ninth Directorate, Colonel Prokhanov?" Chumak asked.

Prokhanov gulped. "Execution by firing squad, comrade general," he said.

"And with whom did Nikolai Sergeyevich meet on his hunting trip today?"

Prokhanov needed no prompting. "No one, comrade general," he replied quickly.

"And with whom did you speak, colonel?"

"No one, comrade general."

"Excellent, Ivan Ivanovich," said Chumak, with a sudden, predatory smile. "Excellent." Then he clapped him on the shoulder again and squeezed hard.

"You see, I have a plan that could make you a hero of the Soviet Union," he said. Then he laughed again, a curious piping laugh for such a big man.

11

Smailes glanced up briefly at the towering marble slab of the UN Secretariat, then entered the General Assembly building by its delegates' entrance at Forty-fifth Street. He passed through the massive chandeliered lobby with its Diego Rivera mural and rode up the escalator to the elevator banks on the second floor. Disembarking at the fourth, he headed for the West Terrace of the delegates' lounge, then stopped to turn into the men's room. An African diplomat in an ankle-length batik robe and a shark's tooth necklace emerged at that moment, pausing to hold the door open for Smailes as he entered.

Derek Smailes enjoyed his rare excursions to the UN. Not only was he always affected by its aura of flat-earth idealism, but he enjoyed the reminder it provided him of the statistical insignificance of the Caucasian tribe to which he belonged. He felt he became invisible there, and could observe without being observed, or at least of being judged of any consequence. Tonight, however, he was nervous. He was wearing his most conservative dark suit, and paused in front of the washroom mirror to adjust his tie and check his breast pocket for the invitation that the UKMISS press officer had obtained for him. Then he cleared his throat and sauntered into the hallway toward the junior Maltese diplomat at the lounge entrance. He showed his pass and wandered in.

The West Terrace was a high-ceilinged reception area with a wall of windows that gave an impressive view across a concrete pergola surrounded by Henry Moore sculptures to the midtown skyline. Smailes stopped by a column of yellow velour curtains to look out at the illuminated art deco spire of the Chrysler building. Then he turned and walked up to the bar station, and ordered white wine. The lounge was beginning to fill up.

The occasion was one of the first diplomatic receptions of the New Year, a pro forma bash hosted by the Malta Mission to salute international advances in arms control. Protocol required that the UN disarmament reps from the various powers attend, and the British team had high hopes for an initial contact. After a little argument, it had been agreed Smailes should go in alone, without Van Deusen or Booth. Realizing his mouth was dry, Smailes swallowed a little of his Chardonnay.

Servers of diverse nationalities circulated, hoisting platters of hors d'oeuvre: tiny, triangular wedges of Norwegian salmon, marinated chicken, new potatoes with sour cream and caviar. Smailes took a small plate and helped himself, edging carefully toward the back of the room as delegates continued to arrive. There were stocky East-bloc types with belligerent-looking wives, smoking strong tobacco; Latin American and European diplomats in expensive suits, and Caribbean and African representatives in both traditional and Western dress. And then he saw him. Instantly recognizable from his file photo, Mikhail Karlovich Siskin stood just inside the entrance, accompanied by a dumpy-looking woman in a dark gray suit, speaking quietly with some sumptuously dressed Africans. Smailes maneuvered to get a better view, but at that moment the diminutive Maltese ambassador stepped forward to speak at the podium, and the delegates crowded forward to listen.

The Maltese ambassador looked a little like Al Pacino, if Al Pacino were built like a jockey. He wore a tuxedo, and had to crane a little to speak into the podium mike, delivering the predictable homily to his government and its sponsorship of global initiatives like the international law of the sea and the pan-European conference on aging. International disarmament was apparently another major concern for the enlightened leadership of Malta, and the ambassador invited all those present to join him in a warm expression of appreciation for the advances already sustained in Geneva. A polite ripple of applause followed. Then the ambassador asked the chairman of the UN Disarmament Commission, a Hungarian diplomat with a face like a bloodhound, to make further remarks, before the gathering could return to the serious business of the evening. Smailes' attention wandered as the Hungarian, in halting English, gave a crude synopsis of the progress at Geneva, and reiterated the hope for a multi-power summit meeting in Norway before the summer.

As the speeches ended, the room thinned out as the delegates coagulated into clusters for drinking and gossip. Smailes tried not to appear conspicuously solo, and latched on to a group of Europeans and Arabs who were discussing something incomprehensible in French. Smailes stroked his chin and nodded sagely from time to time, signifying assent. Eventually, as more people drifted away for dinner in the adjacent restaurant, the crowd grew more sparse and Smailes saw his opportunity. Siskin detached himself from his own group, and wandered over to the now deserted bar station to replenish his glass. Smailes waited until Siskin had made his order, then he hastily scribbled something on his cocktail napkin, set down his own glass, and sauntered up behind him.

"Mikhail Siskin?" he said quietly.

"Yes?" said Siskin, wheeling around. He was wearing an inexpensive blue suit, a nylon shirt with a curling collar, and a blue silk tie fastened in a fat Windsor. There was both suspicion and hostility in his voice.

"I was sorry to hear about Irina. I think I can help."

The dark eyes met his searchingly, and Smailes could see both pain and fear in them. Always say "I," Roger had said, never "we." It was more personal, more reassuring.

"What do you mean? Who are you?" Siskin protested

quietly in good, accented English. His eyes darted right and left in panic.

Smailes said nothing, but dropped his napkin onto the bar table between them. "Call me. Ask for George," said Smailes, turning to leave.

"How dare you! I will protest this . . . this outrage to my ambassador," Siskin said in a forced whisper, but Smailes had already left.

At the entrance, Smailes turned to look back briefly. He could no longer see the napkin resting on the bar, but he could see the back of Mikhail Siskin, who had returned to his group. He was gulping a swallow from his cocktail, and talking anxiously with his dumpy female companion, who Smailes did not doubt was Tatanya. As he headed toward the elevators, Smailes gave a little skip of excitement. The contact had gone perfectly, like a dream. Now all they could do was wait.

Smailes had briefed Graham Booth carefully and at great length the morning after Roger Standiforth had returned to London. He took him into the secure room in the fort, sat him down and spelled out the whole mission, or, at least, as much of it as Booth needed to know from his end. Predictably, Booth was ecstatic at being brought in on such a high-stakes operation, and thanked Smailes profusely for his inclusion. Smailes told him to save it, and, lying, said it wasn't his idea. Booth was entirely too jumpy and excited for Smailes' liking, and he took great pains to explain as patiently as he was able how sensitive the mission was, and how crucial was the need for discretion. Booth sobered up and asked Smailes what he wanted him to do.

Smailes and Van Deusen had agreed to proceed with only the most preliminary checking of Siskin, his family and his story until they knew whether the whole approach was going to backfire. Accordingly, Smailes assigned Booth initially to look into the work of the Disarmament Affairs Department and its players, an area that could be investigated without ringing any bells. Smailes suggested that Booth check through some of the NGOs, the nongovernmental organizations that monitored the UN's work, rather than through the department's own press office. Booth agreed and came back with the suggestion later that morning that he speak with the Quaker Office to the UN and the International Peace Academy, posing as a freelance journalist preparing a magazine piece on arms control. Smailes gave him the green light, with a final reminder about caution.

Three days later, Booth generated a report that he presented to Smailes and Van Deusen in Ralph's office. The work of the disarmament department and the various committees it serviced was fairly closely followed by the two groups Booth had spoken with, and both had described Mikhail Siskin as an important figure. At Van Deusen's registering alarm, Booth insisted that he had shown no greater interest in Siskin than in any other individual; the information had emerged spontaneously as a result of his interviews.

According to Booth, Siskin had won great respect during his term as Soviet representative to the Security and Disarmament Committee, or First Committee, as it was known in UN jargon. In contrast to prevailing practice, Siskin had been a well-informed and independent-minded delegate, and after a three-year tour the undersecretary for disarmament affairs had personally invited him to head up his all-important studies department. During his four years in this capacity, Siskin had sponsored a series of complex studies that had become benchmarks in the multilateral debate. He was regarded as a persuasive and knowledgeable advocate of arms control as a policy instrument, and it was generally agreed that Mikhail Siskin's stature had only grown in recent years, as the Kremlin's agenda had moved closer and closer to his own. There was uniform dismay that the Soviet Union had not yet rescinded its "secondment" practices, whereby its nationals were not appointed to their UN positions for life, as with most nations, but only for the duration of a standard tour. Since Siskin had applied for, and been denied, a waiver of this regulation, he was scheduled to leave his position in the summer.

Smailes listened intently during Booth's presentation, and it only confirmed his apprehension that he was being called upon to bat in the big leagues. Booth asked what he should undertake next, and Ralph told him to prepare a report for his signature, changing the references from Siskin to "Colin" throughout. Ralph would send it through to Curzon Street by the afternoon bag. After that, Booth was told to sit tight, since the Maltese reception would take place the following day.

The British team agreed that Comrade Siskin had roughly a three-day window in which he could credibly protest Smailes' overture to his ambassador. Smailes and Booth were on tenterhooks throughout the whole period. Naturally, Smailes had not told Clea anything about his involvement, and lest she suspect he was preoccupied, he made a big effort to make things appear as normal as possible. He suggested they go to the pictures, or out to dinner, and even one evening invited Graham Booth with them across to the Glades to hear Tyler play.

Actually, this last outing was not his idea. Clea had made one of her rare appearances on the eleventh floor at the close of business, and Smailes returned from the washroom to find her chatting gregariously with Madge Ryan and Graham Booth, and when Madge left, it seemed only courteous to include Graham in their plans. Smailes even restrained himself from criticism after Clea had flirted with Booth quite shamelessly at the bar, although he had to bite his lip more than once. They were in bed later that evening when Clea commented ingenuously that she'd noticed that Madge had been looking nice lately.

"Yeah," said Smailes. "Maybe Ralph's slipping it to her."

"Or maybe Graham," said Clea. "Graham's got such a great body," she added teasingly.

Smailes, who could hardly be described in the same terms, felt goaded, but said nothing, refusing to elevate a punk like Booth to the status of a rival. He reflected that if he felt irritated by Clea's provocation, it was nothing to what she would feel if he were suddenly recalled in disgrace to London. Betrayed would be a better word. Secretly, however, he did not think it would come to that.

The second day after the Siskin contact, Rudy Kabalan called with the news that he had unearthed the information Smailes had requested. Smailes scheduled a meeting at the cabaret bar later in the week, knowing he could cancel if the whole thing fell through. By the end of the third day, Smailes was a nervous wreck, but still there was no ominous summons from Sir Michael, or from anyone else higher up the diplomatic ladder. At 5:25 he stepped into Ralph's office. ·

"Let's go to Stage Two, Ralph," said Smailes.

"Stage Two it is," said Ralph, removing his cigar and giving a conspiratorial grin. After his initial biliousness, Ralph had settled into their working relationship, and Smailes reminded himself to defer wherever possible. If he nursed Ralph's ego carefully enough, Smailes told himself, the whole arrangement might actually work.

The following morning, the three British intelligence officers held a strategy session and agreed to implement the next tier of their verification program, which involved the Siskin family itself. Booth was instructed to apply discreet surveillance to its three members, and to learn as much as he could from co-workers, schoolfriends and the like. Smailes also mentioned that they needed to check on Irina Siskin's medical condition, and when they returned to their office, Booth claimed to know exactly how to do it.

"Go ahead then," said Smailes, curious to know how his new assistant operated.

As Booth got on the phone to the New York Hospital accounting department, it became clear that in addition to his good looks, Booth fancied himself as an actor. Claiming to be a financial officer from the Soviet Mission, he began berating some hapless accounting clerk in a theatrical Russian accent about the incomprehensibility of Irina Siskin's hospital bills. With exasperated courtesy he reviewed the particulars of Irina's tests as far as he knew them, then demanded to know more details. Eventually, the unfortunate billing clerk apparently called up Irina's records on a computer screen and asked him what the problem was.

"So what is the diagnosis, huh?" said Booth. "This bill is not legible. Sorry, you will have to spell that. More slowly please. Start again."

Booth seemed to have the tone of injured sanctimony just right, and Smailes was moderately impressed. Booth held up a notepad to Smailes with Irina's diagnosis and test dates confirmed. But instead of quitting while he was ahead, he kept going, and Smailes began to get alarmed.

"Do not think that we do not know how your elitist system attempts to bleed the resources of the people. In our country, such services are free, the right of every citizen . . ." Booth continued in this bogus, outraged vein for another minute or two, eventually hanging up with a triumphant smirk. Smailes, in contrast, was furious. He strode over to Booth's desk, picked up the telephone and hurled it on the floor. Booth went white.

"Listen to me, you stupid little shit," said Smailes, his voice shaking with rage. "You pull another stunt like that and you're off the case! Don't you realize that's exactly the kind of behavior that's likely to draw a complaint! Then where would we be? The whole operation could collapse thanks to your infantile, stupid behavior. Do you understand?"

"Yes, Derek. I was only—"

"Do you understand?"

"Yes, Derek. Sorry. I wasn't thinking—"

"Damn right you weren't. That's your last warning, Graham," said Smailes, stalking out of the room. Smailes suddenly found himself wishing dearly he still had Kevin Butterworth as backup instead of an immature smartass like Graham Booth. Actually, he doubted there was any real harm done, and he had exaggerated his anger a little, needing to put Booth in his place. And if Smailes' outburst made his assistant think more carefully in the future, so much the better.

Smailes was seated in a booth in the dingy cabaret bar, nursing a gassy, tasteless beer in a greasy glass, waiting for Rudy Kabalan to show up. He was still thinking of Kevin Butterworth, and his guilty, agitated mood had not entirely lifted. He reached down into his raincoat pocket and felt again for the envelope of cash which he had signed out from Madge Ryan an hour earlier. Even in the twilit gloom he could see that the top of his table was dirty. A glass globe encased in orange netting held the guttering remains of a candle. The small stage was deserted, but a speaker above his head gave out muted, frantic crooning. The bar stools were occupied by a row of anonymous fat rumps, although the rest of the room was empty. A television above the bar glowed with eye-punishing rock videos, the volume mercifully extinguished. Smailes looked up to see Kabalan enter the bar and squint around in the penumbra. Eventually, his eyesight adjusting to the light, he spotted Smailes and came over. He was wearing a white polo neck beneath a loud check jacket and an overcoat. Smailes noticed that he had definitely lost weight.

Rudy slid in opposite him. "So you got the goods?" he asked.

Smailes responded quickly. "I dunno, Rudy, it depends on the quality of yours. Is that what your pal Shortstop was complaining about up in White Plains on Saturday? You been supplying inferior stuff, Rudy? He seemed pretty steamed up, I thought, when I saw the two of you through the window. Unless, of course, you still maintain you don't know the guy . . ."

"This is none of your business, Derek," Rudy replied cautiously.

"Maybe not, but if we're going to do business, maybe I'm entitled to know who your associates are. Is that why you go down to Central America so regularly, Rudy? Cocaine one of your little sidelines, is it?"

Kabalan lost his temper and leaned forward across the table.

"Listen, mister, like I say, this is none of your business. But if you want to know, yeah, I tossed Shortstop a bag of flake last month. What am I supposed to do? The contract pilot bringing me in to Homestead has this backhaul arrangement, see, so he gives me half a kilo to keep quiet about it. Now, I can either flush it down the crapper, or I can pass it along and buy myself a whole ton of goodwill. I never took a dime for it."

Here Kabalan paused a moment, his chest heaving, seemingly undecided whether to continue. Eventually he leaned farther forward and said in a low growl, "Look, Derek Smailes, you may not have realized, but I'm the best there is in this business. One big reason is the quality of my contacts—with the feds, on the street, and in the boardroom. I know Shortstop since he was Ricky Simms, wheeling a mail cart around a law firm on Wall Street. He works for me, okay, because he trusts me, and I keep him happy.

"Now, as for you shinin' white Brits, I just got this to say. You people play just as dirty as anyone else in the intelligence game, despite the fact you all got a baseball bat up the ass and despite the snotty dame you got on your bank notes. Don't kid me it's any different."

There was another pause while Kabalan waited for Smailes to reply. He didn't.

Kabalan produced a fiber-tip pen from his jacket and scrawled something on the napkin under Smailes' beer glass. "No go on Malinovsky's actual address, but he plays chess every day of the week in one of these two coffee shops, just off Washington Square. You should be able to find him easy."

Smailes reached into his pocket and laid his envelope down on the table between them. In the same movement, he scooped up the napkin and stuffed it into his coat. He took a final swallow of beer, and rose to leave. There was nothing to say; Rudy's analysis was quite correct, of course.

Concerned with maintaining his poise, Smailes headed for the exit without looking right or left. He thought momentarily of turning back to ask Kabalan for a receipt, but let it go. Focusing on the door, he did not notice Oscar Tufano turn on his barstool at that moment, then pick up a drink and head over toward Kabalan's booth. Neither did he see that Tufano was a dark-complected, balding Latin, about fifty, and the hand that held his glass was missing the last two joints on its middle and ring fingers.

A week passed after Smailes' initial contact with Siskin at the Maltese reception. Booth had watched Siskin and Tatanya board their bus to Riverdale every night outside the Soviet Mission on Sixty-seventh Street, and nothing seemed unusual in their behavior. They came down on the bus each morning also, Tatanya alighting at the mission and Mikhail staying on board until its second stop at the UN itself. Irina herself was a different story. She apparently attended the UN International School twenty blocks down the East River Drive from UN headquarters, and came down from Riverdale on the school's own bus, not the diplomatic shuttle. Booth had had a schoolfriend identify her, then observed her coming and going from school, carrying her violin case. He pronounced her a future stunner—long black hair and dark eyes in a pale, strong-boned face. Watching her innocently pursue her daily life, Booth claimed he could not help but be struck by the tragedy of her condition. She showed no obvious signs of illness apart from an unnatural pallor, he said.

One anomaly had surfaced. Tatanya Siskin was not credited anywhere at the UN as a translator, and having checked further into UN records and also through London's Data Center, Booth had not been able to definitively identify her role. Ominously, he had seen her leave on numerous occasions with the same group of women at lunchtime, a behavior typical of the KGB staff at the Soviet Mission. It was possible she was in fact a low-level employee of the *referentura,* the KGB station, which could complicate things. All Booth's findings were passed along to London, which had not responded to the data so far beyond routine acknowledgments.

Then, in the middle of Friday afternoon, on the eighth day after the initial Siskin contact, the phone in Smailes' and Booth's office rang twice, signifying a direct call from outside. Booth grabbed it, then immediately cupped his hand over the receiver, his eyes widening in excitement.

"It's Colin," he whispered. "He asked for George!"

Smailes fumbled in his drawer for his tape recorder, attached the phone mike to the earpiece, then picked up the receiver. He signaled angrily with his eyes that he wanted Booth out of the room. Booth, crestfallen, complied, and as the door closed behind him, Smailes lifted the receiver to his mouth and said quietly, "George here." He saw the machine's red Record light turn on.

Mikhail Siskin was very agitated. He spoke in an urgent whisper, explaining that he was calling from a pay phone outside the General Assembly hall, and was taking a grave risk in so doing. He said he had not been able to put their brief meeting out of his mind. "You said you could help Irina," he said anxiously. "What exactly did you mean?"

Smailes responded that he would need to meet face to face with him to explain that, but that he had very encouraging news for him.

Siskin's voice grew more fearful. "Who are you? Are you American? I will not work for the CIA!" he said forcefully.

"No. No. I'm British, Mikhail. Listen to my accent. There is no question of your being asked to work for the Americans, believe me."

"I will not betray my government!" he said in an angry whisper.

"No one is asking you to. Some people in my government need your advice, that's all, Mikhail. They believe in arms control as passionately as you do. But we need to meet to discuss this."

"How? Where?" asked Siskin desperately. "I am a Soviet diplomat. I do not have freedom of movement . . ."

"Yes, yes, I understand. Are you planning to attend any more receptions in the near future, preferably outside the UN?"

The red Record light on Smailes' tape recorder went out as Siskin paused for several seconds in thought. Then it came on again as Siskin began speaking.

"Yes. Yes. Next Tuesday evening, at the Plaza Hotel, a reception for the Syrian foreign minister. I wasn't going to go, but I could easily change my mind . . ."

"Next Tuesday?" asked Smailes, flipping the pages of his desk calendar. "The second of February? Fine. I'll book a room, in the name of George Phillips. Come up and talk to me, at your leisure. Complete confidentiality, no commitment required, beyond listening to my proposal."

"Phillips? I'll try. I don't know. I must go now." There was a soft click as Siskin hung up. Smailes snapped off the recorder with a flourish. Fantastic! They had him! Smailes knew all along that they would. He hurried to get out of his chair and cursed as he barked his shin against his desk's metal file drawer. He hopped around his office for several moments, biting his lip against the pain, then hobbled across to Ralph's room and knocked on the door.

Smailes passed through the modest victory arch at the top of Washington Square and headed toward the dry basin of the central fountain. It was a mild, blustery morning and Smailes had to step aside as two burly joggers emerged from beneath the leafless buttonwood trees at the corner of the children's playground. He oriented himself toward the southwest corner, swinging by a red brick public toilet guarded by two surly-looking characters in ski hats. One whistled to him as he passed, but Smailes kept going without turning. In the corner of the park was a small enclosure holding a dozen or so concrete chess pedestals flanked by green wooden benches. A couple of hardy souls had embarked on a match, and were huddled over the pieces, their coats drawn against the wind. Smailes paused briefly to watch, then crossed the road into MacDougal Street.

Greenwich Village reminded Smailes a little of London's Soho—the same narrow streets with their filigree of fire escapes, the same tiny shops and restaurants, the same promise of illicit pleasures. He turned into a café with a striped awning, sat down at the counter and ordered coffee from a dark, unshaven little man in a white apron. Then he swiveled on his stool to check his surroundings.

The clientele seemed to comprise mostly students, who sat around small tables talking and smoking. One chess game was in progress over by the window, but it was clearly an overspill match from the main action in back. Smailes could see through an archway to a rear chess parlor that was full, with seven or eight games in progress between players of all ages. He recognized Vasily Malinovsky almost immediately, seated at the table closest to the doorway.

The most recent photograph he'd seen of Malinovsky had to be fifteen years old, but Smailes had no trouble identifying him. He was now about sixty, a huge bear of a man with long, unkempt gray hair and a face that slanted markedly to the left. The face was more heavily jowled and lined than in the photograph, but otherwise hadn't changed much. Smailes drained his coffee and went across to lean on the arch and watch the progress of his match.

The former KGB man's opponent was a small elderly Slav wearing an old suit that was too big for him and a white shirt buttoned to the neck. He was bald except for a few wisps of white hair pushed back over a skull the color of parchment. He was also apparently giving Malinovsky quite a pasting, since a legion of captured black pieces crowded his end of the board, whereas Malinovsky seemed to have captured only about half as many white ones. Smailes made no sound as he watched the players exchange moves, slapping their twin-dialed clock as they did so, but Malinovsky glanced over his shoulder at one point and looked at Smailes without interest. An ashtray filled with butts was parked next to him, and Smailes watched as he crushed out a Winston and lit another with brown fingers. Malinovsky's elderly opponent paused for a long moment, then shoved a rook onto the back rank and announced a check. Malinovsky pressed his chin into his chest, gave an exasperated shrug, stuck his cigarette in his mouth, and tipped his king over. His opponent betrayed no emotion but reached over to exchange a weak handshake and began setting up the pieces again. Malinovsky said something in Russian to dissuade him, then looked around again at Smailes. He signaled with his eyes that he would meet him outside. Smailes withdrew to the sidewalk.

Vasily Malinovsky emerged two minutes later, wearing a brown raincoat with an iridescent tint and a blue peaked cap. He looked at Smailes with an air of resignation, then touched him on the arm and indicated they should walk down the street. As they set off, he looked across at him neutrally, and said in a thick Russian accent, "Who are you with, my friend?"

"The British," replied Smailes.

Malinovsky brightened markedly, and almost smiled. "Ah, the British. And how is my good friend Simon Montfort?"

Malinovsky was probably referring to his former SIS case officer, a man Smailes had never heard of. "Oh, he's fine," he bluffed.

"And his family?"

"They're fine too."

These responses apparently satisfied Malinovsky, since he lumbered forward and said nothing further. Eventually they turned into another coffee house two blocks away, ordered coffee, and sat down.

Smailes looked across at the famous defector, feeling at a loss how to begin. Malinovsky retained a certain tragic dignity, despite an appearance of neglect. He had apparently shaved carelessly that morning, since patches of silver bristles stood out on his face in the fluorescent light. Malinovsky lit another cigarette and Smailes cleared his throat.

"Seemed like a good player, your opponent," he ventured.

"Efim would have been a grandmaster, if he had not emigrated," Malinovsky replied in a growl. "You play?"

"Barely," said Smailes. "Certainly never against a Russian." Malinovsky gave a faint smile.

"It is still a mystery, why the Bolsheviks chose to encourage such a bourgeois pastime, but you are right, it certainly struck a chord in our soul. I have my own theories. What is your name?"

"O'Connell. Peter O'Connell."

Malinovsky shrugged, as if he knew whatever Smailes told him was an invention. He took another pull on his cigarette then narrowed his eyes slightly above the wide Eurasian cheekbones.

"We are a gloomy and suspicious tribe, Mr. O'Connell, but we are redeemed by our forbearance. That is why we are unbeatable at the game of chess, and also at the game of espionage. We have the ability to wait forever for an opening, and if none appears, to settle for a stalemate and try again. So different from the Americans—so open and eager, yet with so little patience. This is the difference between the pessimistic and optimistic outlooks on life, I suspect."

Smailes shifted uncomfortably in his seat. "What about Bobby Fischer?" he asked, guessing that Malinovsky would not respect his kowtowing.

Malinovsky waved a hand dismissively. "Fischer was a perfect product of the Russian school," he said. "He learned his game by studying the hypermoderns—Alekhine, Tal, Botvinnik. He did not flower until he entered into competition with us." But he stopped and took a sip of his coffee, then drew again on his cigarette, as if partially conceding the point.

"Why is it you wish to see me? Not to debate chess, I should not think."

"No, Vasily, we need your advice," said Smailes. Malinovsky made a gracious gesture with an upturned palm, and Smailes proceeded to give him an outline of the Siskin operation, changing details slightly so the source of the medical information was a British surgeon at New York Hospital.

"What is this diplomat's name?" asked Malinovsky.

Smailes hesitated, then committed himself. "Mikhail Siskin," he said.

"What is he, a Jew?" he asked, incredulous.

"No. Born Karaganda, Kazakhstan. Educated Moscow University Law School, then MGIMO."

"Volga German," Malinovsky muttered. "Never heard of him." He crushed out his cigarette carefully, leaning back in his chair to scrutinize Smailes' face. Then he leaned forward heavily and put his elbows on the table.

"Forget it, my friend. This is a deception. This man is an intelligence agent, and he is trying to trap you. You must decline this pawn gambit, my friend. Tell that to your people in London."

Malinovsky reached for his cup and drained his coffee, as if the discussion was over. Smailes persisted.

"We don't think so, Vasily. We've checked into this character very carefully." He rehearsed for Malinovsky their discoveries about Siskin's background and career, up to his transfer to New York as a disarmament specialist at the UN. The last piece of information seemed to incense Malinovsky, who suddenly interrupted Smailes with a ten-minute diatribe against Western gullibility in the face of Rostov's arms control proposals.

"Ha! And they think their verification arrangements can prevent Soviet cheating!" he concluded, with a scoffing motion of his hand. "Oh, certainly, the Soviets will allow on-site inspection as their engineers destroy tanks and artillery pieces. As much as the West likes! What the West does not appreciate is that the Soviet Army has not destroyed any offensive weaponry since the Patriotic War!

The Stalin-3 is the best battle tank ever made; it changed the course of the war on the Eastern front, and not a single one has ever been decommissioned! They are stored in perfect working condition in vast underground bunkers in the Urals. I have definitive knowledge of this. Along with thousands of T-55s and T-72s that the West does not even know exist!"

Smailes tried to speak, but could think of no adequate reply, and Malinovsky continued in the same indignant tone.

"And, of course, when Rostov gets his arms control agreement, American troops will be brought home and demobilized, whereas Soviet troops will be held as highly trained reserves just hours from the frontier of Western Europe. This man has completely fooled your leaders, my friend. He is the true heir of Lenin and Stalin, and can never renounce the Soviet goal of world domination. It is an article of Communist faith, don't you see, as unthinkable as the Iranians renouncing the Koran! And as for Rostov announcing he is a socialist, no longer a Communist, this is just the wolf putting on the sheep's clothing. He is telling you people exactly what you want to hear, and so you believe him. If you fall for his trap, the world will be at war again within five years!"

Smailes had been prepared for the strength of Malinovsky's opinions, but was taken aback by his almost manic vehemence. "Have you told your contacts at the CIA your views, Vasily?" he asked mildly.

Malinovsky looked up at him painfully from beneath heavy brows and made a gesture of contempt.

" 'Write a memo, Vasily,' is what they say. Write a memo! Writing memos is worthless, so I have given up." He sat there brooding, looking down into his empty cup and Smailes saw his opportunity to steer the discussion back toward Siskin.

"Look, Vasily. There are people in the British government who share precisely your fears. They don't think Rostov can be trusted. That's why they're seeking the cooperation of someone like Siskin. He knows the background to the Soviet negotiating positions, and can help us interpret Rostov's intentions. Our research shows he's remarkably independent."

Malinovsky relented slightly and looked up at Smailes. "Tell me again everything you know about him. Slowly."

Smailes rehearsed from his memory the Siskin file. Then Malinovsky began to cross-examine him.

"What years Moscow University? When in New York? Does he have family with him? Describe them."

After Smailes answered his questions, Malinovsky said, "It might be as you say. He might be clean. I have never heard of KGB going through the foreign ministry after graduating from MGIMO. At least, not in recent years; Gromyko put a stop to it. And GRU would not have that kind of access. Now this is important. Have you seen him face to face?"

"Yes."

"How was he dressed? What kind of wristwatch was he wearing?"

Smailes was a little surprised but described Siskin's somewhat shabby appearance as best he could. He said he could not remember whether or not he was wearing a wristwatch.

"Look for that, my friend," Malinovsky warned. "Intelligence people always give themselves away that way. See, the Soviet UN diplomatic staff have to make a 'donation to the state' of the difference between their UN salaries and the Moscow pay scale. So they save all the hard currency they can to take back consumer goods before they leave. Intelligence officers are well paid, and get to keep all of it. They can never resist expensive things like wristwatches.

"You may in fact be right about this Siskin. The Chekists and the GRU are never posted abroad with families, and certainly not with a teenage daughter. She would be kept behind in Moscow, as insurance. This man Siskin sounds as if he has been highly trusted. What do you want me to tell you?"

Smailes breathed a careful sigh of relief. He had been confident all along that Malinovsky would agree to help, out of combined affection for the British and hatred for his former Soviet masters. He explained that he needed Malinovsky's help with psychological tactics for enlisting Siskin's trust and cooperation. The British wanted him to stay in place, then defect later in the summer as his tour expired, he explained.

Pacified, Malinovsky became a painstaking tutor, explaining patiently how to play down the emotional bribe of the daughter's illness, how to appeal instead to Siskin's conscience as an international civil servant, how to invoke his seemingly genuine commitment to disarmament, and how to reassure him with flawless British fieldcraft. If Siskin were to cooperate, he said, he would need to be sure no British mistake was going to deliver him into the arms of the KGB.

"As for defection, it is a different matter," said Malinovsky sadly. "It depends equally on the feelings of his wife and child. Do not offend his patriotism. Stress the European environment of your country."

He looked up briefly with heavy eyes and Smailes was reminded of the family tragedies he had borne himself. The information Malinovsky had given him was priceless, and he could not think of an adequate way to express his thanks. Malinovsky seemed to sense the interview was winding down, and pushed his chair away from their table. At that point, they were interrupted by a gruff voice from over Smailes' shoulder.

Smailes turned in alarm to see a tall youth in a black studded leather jacket looking down at them. His head was partially shaved, the remaining hair dyed black and cut into a proud Mohican. He had a row of hardware punched into his left ear. Smailes stiffened, but Malinovsky showed no alarm. He grunted something back in Russian.

The youth made an impatient gesture and responded reluctantly, also in Russian. Smailes realized he must be looking at Malinovsky's delinquent son.

Laboriously, Malinovsky went into a back pocket and produced a fat wallet. He removed a couple of twenties and held them up to the youth, who took them unceremoniously, spun on his heel and left. As the door closed behind him, Malinovsky looked across at Smailes and said wanly, "It is Oleg, my son. He is a graphic arts student now."

Smailes managed a smile and nodded. Malinovsky dropped his voice.

"And to think he used to be a Young Pioneer. You don't think he's on drugs, do you? You heard about his sister?"

Smailes indicated that he had. He paused a moment, then said pleasantly, "I dunno, Vasily. Just because he looks like Hiawatha doesn't mean he's a drug addict."

"Who?"

"Hiawatha. You know, red Indian chief."

Malinovsky's lined face was suddenly split by the diagonal crease of his mouth, his shoulders began to shake, and an odd rumbling sound emanated from his chest. Smailes was momentarily nonplussed, but then realized what he was witnessing was Vasily Malcontent, laughing.

Smailes was jumpy. He had been installed in the room at the Plaza since late afternoon, and now it was almost seven. They had run endless checks on the recording equipment, and Van Deusen had finally consented to leave around six-thirty, clearly irked that, although operational head of the mission, he would not be meeting with Siskin face to face. Roger Standiforth, however, had been adamant on that point; all initial contact had to be one on one, a proven strategy. It was also clearly inappropriate for Van Deusen to secrete himself in a bathroom or closet, and he had finally given up and agreed to go home. Smailes had promised to call him as soon as he had any news.

Smailes sat down again in the chair next to the lamp table, and heard his stomach growl—he had been too preoccupied to eat earlier, and now it was too late. He got up again to check the condition of the ice in the bathroom, then fixed himself a weak Scotch. He had taken the precaution of buying several kinds of liquor and mixes to help Siskin feel more at ease—he remembered watching the hungry way he had gulped his cocktail after the first contact at the UN.

He sipped his Scotch and looked at his face in the mirror, reflecting on the bizarre situation in which he found himself. Derek Smailes, the dropout from Cambridge Tech, the lock-and-safe man, was waiting in a room in one of the world's most exclusive hotels to hold a clandestine meeting with a senior Soviet diplomat that might alter the course of East-West relations. Luck, of course, was primarily responsible, as Roger had been at pains to stress. Not that he implied it was not Smailes' investigative prowess that had caused his star to soar in Five's firmament. No, Roger had explained, it was luck that the Cheltenham boffins had finally cracked the new Soviet military codes at such a crucial juncture.

Smailes had listened with rapt attention as Roger had spelled out the background of the British decision to move on Siskin. It seemed that the Soviets, in Geneva, had sought to capitalize on the momentum of the arms control talks by raising the dread issue of linkage. Linkage was the specter that Britain and France, the two European nuclear powers, feared most, since it invoked the prospect of the Soviets' tying further concessions in conventional arms to cuts in the British and French nuclear arsenals. The official NATO position was that cross-referencing weapons systems was impermissible, but London and Paris were deeply concerned that Washington might renege on this commitment in order to secure the further deep conventional cuts it so desperately wanted. Such a move would make Western Europe wholly dependent on the deterrent power of the American nuclear umbrella, a prospect with which none of the European allies was wholly comfortable. And although they might be willing to enter independent, bilateral negotiations with the Soviets at some later stage, the British and the French were both bitterly opposed to some emasculating, preemptive concession forced on them by Washington.

But now, according to Roger, things had gone from bad to worse. GCHQ at Cheltenham, the British government's secret listening station, had apparently broken some higher-grade Soviet military ciphers just three months before. And the eggheads at Cheltenham had learned something that had struck terror into the new government in Whitehall. It transpired that during a routine visit by the U.S. defense secretary to some Ukrainian missile batteries in November, the Soviet chief of staff Sergei Kapalkin had made an unannounced trip to Lvov at the same time. Undoubtedly, secret meetings had been held. What was their agenda? An under-the-table deal on Euromissile linkage? Or worse, some secret agreement that threatened the continuity of the American nuclear umbrella itself? It was certainly true that Rostov and Wilkes had bartered away far more in Geneva than anyone thought they would. Was that the context in which they had sent their emissaries to meet secretly in Lvov? Officially, the Americans were denying everything, including that the meetings had taken place, but the British did not believe them. Which was why Derek Smailes, former policeman and junior security man, was nursing a very weak Scotch in a very expensive hotel in New York, waiting to entice a Soviet disarmament specialist to collaborate with Her Majesty's Government. Smailes gave a sudden, involuntary snort of laughter.

At that moment Smailes heard a weak rapping sound and awoke from his thoughts. He crossed to the door in six long paces and admitted an agitated Mikhail Siskin, who pushed past him quickly into the room.

"I did not decide until the last moment to do this," said Siskin forcefully after Smailes had closed the door. "You must understand, this is very, very difficult for me."

"Sit down, Mikhail," Smailes said quietly. "You have nothing to be afraid of. You want a drink? I've got vodka, Scotch, some gin . . ."

"Thanks. Vodka. I prefer vodka. Straight, no ice."

Smailes went into the bathroom to fix Siskin a drink. When he emerged, Siskin had taken one of the two chairs next to the lamp table. They were the only chairs in the room, so the lamp fixture had been the logical place to conceal the mike. The drawer in the table held the recording equipment itself. Smailes handed him his drink and took the other chair. He looked across at him mildly, noticing he was wearing the same cheap blue suit as before, with a different tie. He was an imposing figure, handsome despite the lack of hair, with a heavy brow, prominent cheekbones and a square jawline. He had an erect bearing, was solidly built without being overweight, and was about average height for a Russian, maybe five eight or nine. Smailes noticed that he chewed the corners of his thick black mustache when under stress. As he raised the glass of vodka to his lips, Smailes saw that he wore a cheap digital wristwatch, the type that cost ten dollars in a department store.

"Thank you for coming," he said.

"Tell me how you know about Irina, and what you can do for her," Siskin replied angrily, almost spitting the words. Then, as an afterthought, "And what I must do to get it."

Patiently, Smailes explained how the British had "overheard" the facts of Irina Siskin's condition, and told of the dramatic breakthroughs of the surgical team at East Grinstead, how their work held most promise for younger patients in the earliest stages of the disease. Smailes said he knew Siskin's waiver petition had been denied and he would be returning to Moscow in the summer, but carefully avoided the issue of the family relocating to Britain. If Siskin wished, he said, they could fly a team of doctors in to examine Irina and prescribe a course of treatment. Siskin gripped his glass and listened painfully to Smailes' account, as if refusing to permit himself hope. As Smailes finished he asked bitterly, "And me? What do you want from me? I do not wish to defect, do you understand?"

Smailes took a swallow of his flavored ice water before responding. This, he knew, was the trickiest part of his pitch. He remembered Malinovsky's instructions to steer clear of the coercive aspect of the relationship.

"The British government has tremendous respect for your work at the UN, Mikhail, both as a Soviet delegate and UN official. They have admired both your expertise and your independence. You don't mind if I call you Mikhail, do you?"

Siskin shrugged.

"As you well know, many members of NATO, the British government included, are concerned about the security situation that will result in Europe at the conclusion of the Geneva arms control talks. Broadly speaking, my government wants to know whether Nikolai Rostov can be trusted. Does he have a secret agenda? Is he negotiating in good faith? Is he conducting clandestine negotiations separately with the Americans, while he negotiates publicly with NATO in Geneva? These are the sort of questions with which we would like you to help us. There is no question about your being asked to defect. Really, we are just seeking your unofficial, professional opinion. Nothing dangerous, no espionage."

Siskin made an exasperated gesture. "This is stupid. Of course Rostov is negotiating seriously. The Soviet economy can no longer support a military establishment even half its current, reduced size. Does Rostov want, at the same time, for the Soviet Union to continue as a world power? Of course! This is not a matter of speculation, surely?"

"And the issue of parallel negotiating strategies?" Smailes had not wanted to broach specifics at this meeting, but Siskin was forcing him.

Siskin made a noise of disgust and appeared about to get up, then thought better of it. "Look, Mr. Phillips, you have the wrong idea about me. I am an international civil servant, see? I deal with treaties, ratification protocols and weapons categories, and more technical things like delivery systems, throw-weight ratios, telemetry, issues like this. I am not a member of the policy establishment. I only learn of Soviet policy positions after they have passed through review, and are almost public. In terms of what you say, I would be guessing, just like you."

"Well, it would be a very well-informed guess, Mikhail," said Smailes. He could tell that Siskin was softening a little, relaxing as he understood what was being asked of him. He decided to push his questioning a little further.

"Tell me about Tatanya," he said.

Siskin stiffened. "What about Tatanya?"

"She is listed as a translator, but we cannot verify that she performs any translation work. What does she really do, Mikhail?"

Siskin did not reply.

"Is she KGB, Mikhail?"

"No!" he replied sharply. "That is, she had no choice. When I accepted the position in the Secretariat and we began a second tour, our security officer got his revenge by convincing the ambassador we needed closer supervision. So Tatanya was told there was no longer translation work available, and she was compelled to work in communications."

"Ciphers? The seventh-floor *referentura?*"

"Yes, but only for the duration of our stay. It is not a permanent assignment."

Smailes thought for a moment. The reassignment probably explained the error in the Sparks manifest he had seen before Christmas. "Who is this security officer?" he asked.

"Semeneyev, the head of the KGB station."

"Why do you say 'revenge'?"

"He never liked me. He always considered me too independent. He is the one who ensured my waiver application would be denied in Moscow. And he made sure when I took the Secretariat position to place informants on my staff."

"How does that affect you?"

"I ignore them. I just do my work, Mr. Phillips."

"And Tatanya? It sounds as if she doesn't like her position."

"She loathes it. Anyone who is not KGB loathes them, believe me. That much has not changed."

Smailes nodded. "Well, perhaps she sees information a little further back in the policy process. Do you ever discuss what she sees at work?"

Siskin looked genuinely frightened. "You said nothing dangerous. No espionage. What you are proposing is an Article Ten offense."

Smailes held up his hand. "She would not need to remove anything, Mikhail, or write anything down. But whatever she could memorize, she could discuss it with you, and you could interpret it and discuss it with us. There are a couple of things in particular—"

"No!" said Siskin forcefully. "That would be treason. My whole family could be sent to prison, or worse . . ."

"Mikhail, be honest with yourself, there would be no risks here. There would be no trail. We will arrange somewhere to meet that is completely safe, that you have a legitimate reason to visit. We only want to pick your brains. And if what you imply is true, that Rostov can be trusted, that he is negotiating in good faith, then it will convince my government to press ahead and endorse the process in Geneva. Which is what you want, in your heart, isn't it?"

Siskin was silent for a long time. He finished the vodka and set the glass down carefully, as if trying to find the right words. Eventually, he raised the great bald dome of his head and looked at Smailes earnestly.

"Listen to me, Mr. Phillips. I ask you to try and put yourself in my position. For years I have done everything I could to lobby for a reduction in this insane arms race. Sometimes behind the scenes, sometimes publicly. I can say, not immodestly, that there have at times been risks to myself. At times I have not been popular in my ministry. Now, finally, a leadership has developed in the Soviet Union that understands the wisdom of putting a stop to this grotesque abuse of resources. In fact, thanks to Gorbachev and Rostov, the Soviet Union is now the major advocate of this process. Finally, I am able to feel proud of my government! This is an extraordinary feeling for me. And now you are asking me to betray it." He met Smailes' eyes pleadingly.

"No. No, I'm not, Mikhail. I'm asking you to help your government attain its goals," Smailes replied quietly. Siskin looked about to respond, but instead looked away, then down at his hands.

Eventually, Siskin said he would talk to Tatanya

about what Smailes had proposed. The two men conducted some small talk about their families, and Smailes made sure to mention that he was a divorced father of a daughter Irina's age. Then he asked Siskin a question that he could not avoid, whether Siskin had ever worked for, or collaborated with, any of the Soviet intelligence agencies. Siskin indignantly replied that he resented the question, but when pressed said firmly, No. Finally, Smailes reluctantly issued the warning to Siskin about independent overtures to the British medical authorities, which Siskin acknowledged with a sad shrug of the shoulders. Finally, Siskin stood and said he ought to get back to the reception downstairs. He said he would try and call within a few days with a decision. Smailes stood also, and the two men faced each other awkwardly, both feeling that a handshake was inappropriate.

"Well then, goodbye, Mr. Phillips," said Siskin stiffly.

"Call me George," said Smailes as warmly as he could. "Goodbye, until the next time." And with that, Siskin was gone.

Smailes flopped into his chair, exhausted. He got up and walked to the bathroom, fixed himself a real Scotch, then returned to the lamp table, rewound the tape, and checked the recording. The quality was excellent. Then he finally permitted himself a large swallow of whiskey.

He felt no sense of triumph, only a quiet satisfaction at a job well done. Siskin was hooked, of course, and they both knew it. They both knew it as soon as he had entered the room. Siskin must have known that the British would run a recording of their meeting, and such evidence was sufficient to destroy his career. Not that Smailes thought blackmail would be necessary, but it was an extremely potent weapon to hold in reserve. Tellingly, once Siskin had learned what the British could offer Irina, he had hardly mentioned her again, as if his mind were made up. His preoccupation with the professional and ethical questions surrounding their meeting told Smailes his decision had probably been taken before he ever stepped into the elevator. Smailes felt no sense of exultation, however, because he knew however Siskin came to justify his actions, he would be violating principles that he had developed over a lifetime. It was not a victory of which he could feel proud.

Smailes finished his drink and realized he was starving. He went to the nightstand between the two double beds and reached for the room service menu. He leafed through it quickly and called down for a sandwich, hoping it would be ready quickly. Then he hung up, took a breath, and called Ralph. He kept the conversation short, explaining only that the meeting had gone well, the recording equipment had worked perfectly, and that they would review it first thing in the morning. When pressed for more details, Smailes would only say, "I think he's on board, Ralph."

He hung up, stretched out on the bed, and closed his eyes. What a day! He felt peculiar—buoyant and sad at the same time. He looked forward to further meetings with Mikhail Siskin, a fascinating, forbidding character, unlike anyone he'd ever met. He started to drift off to sleep.

He awoke to the sound of the room service waiter rapping on the door. He got up to admit a small Oriental man in a starched white uniform, who wheeled a trolley into his room. He signed the bill and the man retreated. He hadn't thought of it before, but he suddenly realized he might as well spend the night—the room was paid for, after all, and he'd just charged his dinner. Then another, illicit thought entered his mind. He wondered what Clea was doing. No one would know, after all, if he had a guest. And she could not fail to be impressed. From an aggregation of motives he did not attempt to analyze, he found himself dialing her number.

An excited Clea arrived an hour later, and happily accepted Smailes' explanation that London had asked him to bug the room that a British businessman was going to be using the following night. She was thrilled by the adventure of spending a night at the Plaza, and was duly impressed by their quarters, despite the modest proportions of the room itself. When Smailes told her where the booze was, she disappeared with her overnight case into the bathroom. She was gone a long time, however, and Smailes was wondering what she was up to, when she emerged wearing an elegant sheer nightgown that he had not seen before. He swallowed hard as she came to embrace him, then caught himself. He went over to the lamp table to check again that the recording gear was switched off before greeting her properly.

"Holy cow," said Graham Booth. "Elevated levels!"

Ralph removed his cigar and gave Booth a baleful stare.

"Yes, well, he was pretty wound up," said Smailes. The three Britons were seated in the secure room in the fort, and Smailes was watching the digital readout and calibrating the sensitivity button on the Voice Stress Analyzer. The operator calibrated the subject's normal speaking voice in the twenty range as a baseline, then watched the readout fluctuate in response to subsequent questions. Any reading fifty percent higher than normal indicated a lie. It was very simple, and completely foolproof.

Ralph, to his credit, had been genuinely delighted by Smailes' handling of the Siskin interview, and shared his conclusion that Siskin had already made up his mind. The confirmation of Tatanya's status was an additional bonus. But Smailes insisted they should make doubly sure of Siskin's bona fides by running the contact tape through the VSA, and Van Deusen agreed. Smailes went to his safe to retrieve the innocuous-looking tan briefcase.

After fixing a reading on Siskin's preliminary remarks on entering the room, Smailes and his two colleagues sat back to listen to the tape again. Predictably, the VSA confirmed that Siskin had been telling the truth throughout, except at one crucial juncture. When Mikhail Siskin asserted forcefully, "I do not wish to defect," the digital gauge jumped to over thirty-five. Smailes stopped the machine, rewound the section and played it again, and the meter again registered in the midthirties. Smailes and

Booth exchanged a grin, and Ralph permitted himself a grunt of pleasure. Equally reassuring was Siskin's response to the question about collaboration with intelligence groups. At Siskin's emphatic No, the meter stayed at twenty-three. Mikhail Siskin was the real thing all right, and the British had him trapped.

"All right," said Ralph. "Let's make a copy of this tape, with a numerical overlay of the questions you put to Siskin. Then do a printout of the VSA readings in response to each. You can do that, can't you, Derek?"

"Sure."

"I'm not sure they use this equipment yet in Curzon Street," he explained. "Then I'll have Madge make a transcript, and hopefully we'll have it all ready in time for the afternoon bag. And I think I'll permit myself a call on the secure line to Roger, to tell him it's on its way." He rose to leave the room.

"And Derek," he said turning at the door.

"Yes?"

"Well done."

Smailes smiled to himself and began rewinding the tape on the VSA recorder. "Graham, I'm going to need another cassette player," he instructed. "Then I think we need to make arrangements about renting an office."

The ground-floor conference room in the defense ministry on Moscow's Frunze Quay was an elegant, high-ceilinged affair with tall windows, ornate sculpted panels, and two enormous crystal chandeliers. A green baize conference table in the shape of a horseshoe stood in the middle of the room, with smaller tables along each side for support staff. Nine men, two in dark suits and seven in military uniforms of various hues, were engaged in animated discussion. It was almost midnight and the special session of the Stavka, the chief military council of the Soviet Union, was already four hours old.

"Okay, okay," said Nikolai Rostov, holding up a hand to placate the commander-in-chief of the National Air Defense Forces, who was arguing bitterly with the commander of the Western Strategic Direction seated across from him. "I think this is enough discussion. I propose that Sergei Andreyevich recapitulate for us, then we move to decisions. Comrade?"

To Rostov's left at the top table sat Leonid Akhmedev, Socialist Party second secretary and Rostov's chief political aide, the only other civilian at the table. To his right sat defense minister General Aleksandr Ermakov, a grizzled old soldier with a vivid pink complexion who also served as supreme commander of the Soviet armed forces, the operational head of the Stavka. To Ermakov's right sat the tall, intellectual figure of Sergei Kapalkin, chief of staff and chief arms control negotiator. Along the legs of the horseshoe sat the five commanders of the five strategic directions of the Soviet Union. Both Ermakov and Kapalkin wore the heavy dress uniform of a full Soviet general.

Kapalkin leaned forward on his elbows to acknowledge Rostov's request, took a drink of water from his glass, then sat back again. Every soldier in the room, whatever his particular fiefdom, had to defer to Kapalkin's mastery of the Geneva labyrinth. Kapalkin was not yet fifty, a young man to hold such twin ranks, and there were some who felt that Rostov had plucked him from the directorship of the Suvorov Military Academy at such a tender age in order to further clip the military's wings. But Kapalkin was an acknowledged master of the arms control process and a respectful silence fell on the room as he brushed back his thin hair and began speaking.

"As I have explained, comrades, the United States is no longer the major obstacle. The Lvov agreements have placated both the advisers on Wilkes' right and the Republican leadership in the Congress. No, it is now the European allies who are squabbling among themselves and preventing us moving forward."

"Let us hear their main objections again," said Rostov, looking down at his notes. "Slowly," he said, without raising his eyes.

Kapalkin straightened the papers on the table in

front of him, but did not look at them. "The British and the French are the biggest single problem, and for the same obvious reason. If we continue to press for a linkage between conventional ceilings and their nuclear capacity, I think they may well withdraw from the whole process. The British government is particularly afraid of seeming soft on this issue, and the French, well, they are impossible. Now, representatives from both countries have approached me in private to say that if the requirement is dropped, they will consent to bilateral negotiations on European nuclear missiles after some decent interval, say, a year. But if we continue—"

"Yes, yes," interrupted Rostov, writing furiously on his white notepad. "What are the other objections?"

"Well, to proceed geographically, the countries of the northern tier—that is, Norway, Denmark, the Benelux countries—are much more concerned about our numerical advantage in amphibious assault craft than about tanks or artillery. The Norwegians also are worried about our helicopter deployment on the Kola Peninsula . . ."

"You think you could get further concessions in dual-capable aircraft in return for withdrawing more helicopters?" asked Rostov.

"Yes," replied Kapalkin quickly. At this point the air defense general in a gray uniform started to splutter something, but was silenced by a glare from Rostov.

Kapalkin continued. "The biggest single issue for the Germans, obviously, is the proposed placement of multi-capacity artillery and short-range missile batteries at the border of the exclusion zone. They still say, 'The shorter the range, the deader the German.' " Here he offered a weak smile, although from the impassive faces around the table no one else seemed to find anything problematic about the prospect of dead Germans.

"For the Greeks and the Turks, the proposed ceiling on amphibious craft is still a difficulty, and the Turks are insisting their forces along the Iraqi border be exempted from per-country troop counts." Kapalkin glanced quickly at his briefing papers. "These are the main issues."

There was an extended silence in the room as Rostov continued writing. He eventually looked up. His eyes were rimmed in red and his face looked gray, but his compact body exuded complete self-control.

"All right, this is what I propose. We will insist publicly on linkage for another month, then drop the requirement in favor of separate talks with the British and French next year. Close a helicopter base on Kola in exchange for the elimination of one air base in Norway and one more American base in England or Italy, if you can get it. Make unilateral concessions of five thousand amphibious craft, divided equally between the northern and southern fronts. Withdraw dual-capable artillery and missile emplacements one hundred kilometers beyond the exclusion zone, if the NATO forces will go another fifty. Forget about the Turkish troops on their southern border. Where would this put us, Sergei Andreyevich?"

Faces around the room were stunned by the rapidity of Rostov's summing-up, but Kapalkin was beaming.

"In Oslo well before Mayday, Nikolai Sergeyevich," he said confidently. "You know, the Western press is already calling it 'the Viking summit.' They will pose you and Wilkes in tin helmets, with horns and pigtails." Kapalkin slapped the table with pleasure and some of the soldiers in the room actually smiled. Rostov's face however, had gone very grave. He gestured to the side of the room and a dark-suited aide approached him for a whispered conference, then left the room.

Rostov acknowledged Kapalkin, then turned to face the room. "Oslo in April, then," said Rostov in a clear voice. "Which is when my enemies in the armed forces will move against me."

There was a shocked intake of breath in the room and an exchange of worried glances. A couple of generals craned in their seats to check the exits. Then the huge double door to the conference room opened and the enormous figure of Grigori Chumak entered, accompanied by an aide carrying a briefcase. All eyes followed him as he lumbered slowly around to the head of the table and stood at Rostov's side. He nodded briefly to his boss, who then addressed the gathering.

"I think you all know Comrade General Chumak, and his position within the GRU. Comrade Chumak has uncovered concrete evidence of a conspiracy among senior military and civilian officials to overthrow the elected government of the Soviet Union. The traitors are awaiting the most opportune time, which will come when I am out of the country at the Oslo summit, I propose."

A number of the senior military men had gone completely white. By contrast, Ermakov on Rostov's right went beet red and sat forward, his hand gripping the edge of the table. There was not a sound in the room.

Methodically, but with sufficient detail to put veracity beyond doubt, Chumak explained how senior members of Krasnaya Zvezdochka, the military officers' club, had used the cover of their organization to foment disloyalty among leaders of nine of the Soviet Union's sixteen military districts. They had also enlisted the collusion of Grishkin and Tumanov, Rostov's main conservative rivals. The ringleaders appeared to be cashiered general staff officer Dolghorukov and Chumak's own GRU deputy, Viktor Kott, although evidence suggested that there was division-level support in all districts west of the Urals, the strategic heart of the country. The aging Stalinist Tumanov had agreed to cosign the military alert in the crucial Moscow military district in order to authorize the capture of the centers of power. Any agreements reached in Oslo would be rescinded, and Rostov and his senior aides would be arrested on trumped-up charges when they returned to the country. Tumanov would then assume the reins of power as deputy leader, leaving Grishkin the real power behind the throne as newly installed chairman of the presidential council. The conspirators would then doubtless cite the "national emergency" as a pretext for canceling the promised general election the year after next. Chumak held up a sheaf of glossy black-and-white photographs which portrayed the conspirators meeting in various locations—in Moscow, Leningrad, the Ukraine.

He passed them directly to Ermakov, who began pawing through them in disbelief.

Eventually Ermakov said in a strangled voice, "Why did the special directorate know nothing of this? What has the KGB been doing?"

Chumak spoke up for his rivals with surprising generosity. "Both the special and political directorates have attempted to infiltrate this group, but without success. The information came to me somewhat by chance, and the traitors have been very careful. Dolghorukov and his allies have been dealing only with divisional and regimental commanders whom they knew in advance to be sympathetic. Only a handful will be told the real reasons for the declaration of the military emergency, but they have enough commanders ready to march without awaiting countervailing KGB orders. They have their command structure very well contained."

"And what is the role of this Kott?" asked Ermakov, attempting to spread the stain of delinquency to the GRU as well.

"We are not entirely sure, except that his cipher traffic has increased lately, and from the rake of the dish during transmission, we know it is being received on the eastern seaboard of the United States."

This last information produced further indignant gasps around the table. The generals were inspecting the photographs one by one as they were passed around the table.

Rostov finally spoke. "I wish to save our discussion of how this disgraceful situation arose for another occasion," he said. "At this juncture, we must consider our options. I propose there are precisely two. We can furnish all this information to the special directorate, and have the traitors rounded up."

The generals around the table collectively stiffened at the prospect of the special directorate, the hated KGB surveillance arm within their ranks, being unleashed against them. The last time it had occurred was in 1937, when Stalin and Beria had beheaded the Soviet officer class on the eve of the Second World War. The country had almost committed suicide in consequence, which no Soviet officer could ever forget.

"Or we can let his conspiracy proceed, allow the traitors to show themselves to the country and the world, and let military justice deal with them. In which case, I need to know the level of your support."

There were sounds of disbelief around the room as the country's military leaders feigned indignation that their commander-in-chief should think to question their loyalty. No one, however, dared speak, until Sergei Kapalkin raised his hand. Kapalkin had said nothing during Chumak's presentation, and it was suddenly clear to everyone in the room that his extraordinary career was about to reach its apogee.

"Comrade general," he said, addressing Chumak in a surprisingly calm voice. "Please tell us again exactly how many divisions these rebels, these traitors, can expect to command."

Chumak slowly rehearsed his exact estimate of the forces at the disposal of the conspiracy.

"So it can be contained easily, wouldn't you say, Aleksandr Petrovich? If you remove the element of surprise?"

"Yes," replied defense minister Ermakov.

At this point, Kapalkin paused dramatically. No one in the room had any idea what he was going to say.

"Well, Nikolai Sergeyevich, I think you have your answer. Of course, you can count on the unswerving loyalty of every commander in this room. We can easily mobilize sufficient strength to neutralize whatever these traitors can muster. But perhaps we should consider, just briefly, the conditions from which this conspiracy has arisen."

At this point, Chumak rocked back on his heels and raised his eyebrows in disbelief. Rostov stiffened but did not look up. No one in the room seemed able to look at Kapalkin.

"Of course, morale in our service has been badly

affected, as we all know, by the necessary changes that have come about in our numerical strength, and in other areas, under your leadership and that of your predecessor. However, we all understand the critical state of our economy and the need for the armed forces to play a leading role in the transformation of society. But in view of this leading role, there have been some changes that have been very hard to understand. In particular, to be led by a defense minister who is not a full member of your presidential council is very difficult for our entire officer class . . ."

Rostov shot Kapalkin an evil glance, outraged that his protégé should be so presumptuous. Ermakov, however, was emboldened by Kapalkin's courage, and saw his chance.

"Perhaps, also, comrade," he said to Rostov, "it is time to consider restoring our peacetime rank of marshal. If the Geneva process is concluded successfully, as it seems it will, I for one would certainly agree that General Kapalkin must be rewarded with this rank. Not to mention the many other deserving officers in this room. This also would go a long way toward restoring morale."

Ermakov looked at Rostov fixedly, daring him to deny him. No one in the room moved a muscle. Rostov scanned the rows of impassive faces on each side of him, assessing the price he was being asked to pay. Decisive as ever, he gathered his papers into a sheaf, dropped them onto the table to straighten them, and said forcefully, "So be it."

Rostov entered his darkened living room noiselessly, tiptoeing across the deep pile of the carpet. A band of light shone from beneath the bedroom door, and he heard his wife call out his name.

"Just a moment, Sonia," he replied. "I'll be in in a moment."

He went to the drinks trolley beneath the window and fixed himself a vodka, fumbling with the bottles in the dark. Then he felt for the controls of the adjacent stereo unit. Lights glowed in the darkness and he punched a button. Billie Holiday's soft voice filled the room.

Rostov crossed to a second door at the opposite end of the apartment and entered his study. He turned on a desklamp and adjusted it quickly so its light was smothered against a pile of documents. Then he picked up one of the four telephones on his desk and dialed a number. When it was answered, he threw a scrambler switch on the black box on which it stood.

"Yes?" said Grigori Chumak's voice.

"You were brilliant tonight, Grigori."

"Get some sleep, Nikolenka. It is very late."

"You are sure you have the bodyguard? This is crucial. I could get killed."

"I told you. He is from Krasnodar. He is our landsman, and he wants to be a Viking."

Rostov laughed. "Perfect. What did you think of Kapalkin?"

"He's got guts." Chumak used the universal term *lapa*—literally, "bear's paws."

"I didn't think so when I picked him."

"I know, Nikolai. You have always been such a terrible judge of character." Chumak laughed his thin, piping laugh.

Rostov hung up, chuckling, and took a swallow of his drink.

13

Dennis Dicenzo and Tyler Dawes lived in a six-story red brick building just off Greenwich Avenue, in the western West Village. Smailes was standing self-consciously in the small living room, waiting for Dennis to return with tea. He looked around sheepishly. The furniture was elegant cordovan leather—a small couch and two armchairs, a glass coffee table. Certainly no room for a piano, except maybe an upright. On the wall facing the windows was a large, original piece of art in vivid crayon and gouache. It was an abstract, but not so abstract that you couldn't make out the figures of two naked men leaning over a rail or a fence or something. Smailes looked away quickly and wandered over to the coffee table to glance at the magazines, feeling uncomfortable with his prejudices. He really didn't mind Dennis and Tyler's being gay, or anyone else's for that matter. He just didn't like being reminded of it at every turn.

"You said sugar, didn't you?" Dennis' voice asked behind him.

"Yes, one, thanks. Look, thanks for agreeing to see me like this. I'm not disturbing you, am I?"

"No, no. Tyler plays the Glades Thursdays, but then, you know that, don't you? No, I had no plans. I was just intrigued you wanted to meet here. When Roz said you were on the line, I thought it must be dental work you wanted."

"Well, it is in a way, Dennis. But not for me. For a friend."

Dennis Dicenzo had in fact been entirely cordial when Smailes had called and asked to see him that evening. Actually, it had been Graham Booth's idea to try to rent an office in the same upper East Side building as Dennis' dental practice. The pair had met once at the Glades, and the connection had somehow stuck. Smailes thought it was a terrific plan, and would give Siskin exactly the sort of cover they had promised. Provided, of course, Dennis Dicenzo agreed to play ball.

Siskin's call to confirm a second meeting had come as almost an anticlimax. The recruitment material had been acknowledged by Roger Standiforth in the next diplomatic bag, with the information that "all systems were go" in London. Clearly, no one expected Siskin to back down at this stage. Smailes had told Siskin they would need another week to prepare an interview room, and arranged for a callback. Then he gave Booth the green light for the office they had located fifteen floors above Dennis Dicenzo's dental suite. After some vacillation, Smailes had resolved to omit from his discussions with Ralph his prospective overture to Dennis. Ralph might get worked up about security issues and try to overrule him. Smailes, on the other hand, felt he knew exactly what he was doing, and took the decision unilaterally.

Dennis indicated one of the armchairs with a hand and Smailes took the tea from him and sat down. He looked across at his host, who was a fair-haired, northern Italian type on the cusp of middle age. He was tall and good-looking, with a high forehead, a wide mouth and a fine web of wrinkles around light brown eyes. Smailes smiled at him and tried to contain his reaction as he sipped the tepid, flavorless liquid. He still had not learned not to ask for tea from Americans.

"Well, it's like this, Dennis. I've got a friend who needs some dentistry. He's a foreign diplomat."

"So are a lot of my patients. That's no problem."

"Yes, well, this is slightly different," said Smailes. "This friend of mine needs an inspection and a cleaning, just routine stuff, and a set of dental records created."

"No problem," said Dicenzo again, slightly suspicious.

"But then, ah, whatever the state of his mouth, ah, we need a set of records created indicating that he needs major work. You know, work that would require several visits over a period of months, like caps—"

"Crowns."

"Yeah, crowns, or, you know, what you do with that deep repair . . ."

"Root canal."

"Right, root canal. Either would be okay, as long as there were real records that indicated the work was being done. You'd even get paid . . ."

"What's going on, Derek?"

Smailes looked across at Dicenzo and realized he had no idea what Dennis was thinking. The two men simply didn't know each other that well. Dennis' eyes regarded him mildly from their beds of creased flesh, without hostility. Smailes cleared his throat and explained that he would be meeting with the diplomat unofficially in another part of the building, and that they needed the dental records created as his pretext for regular visits.

"Why do you need real records, Derek? There must be a dozen dental practices in that building. Your friend could say he's visiting any one of them."

"Because my friend is a cautious type. He would want to come and have a real examination done, so the particulars would be completely accurate. Real appointments would be created, et cetera. Except instead of coming to see you, he'd be visiting me upstairs."

Dennis paused, as if weighing a decision. Eventually, he said in a somewhat pained voice, "Is this a woman, Derek? Because if it is, I'm really fond of Clea, and I don't know whether . . ."

Smailes laughed and held up his hand to correct him,

but at that moment they were interrupted by the sound of a key in the lock, throwing open a heavy deadbolt. A moment later, Tyler Dawes stepped into the living room, his coat half off. When he saw Smailes sitting at his coffee table, his eyebrows rose in mock wonder. Then he lowered them in a comical glower at his lover.

"Dennis, you ol' rascal. You never told me. Am I interrupting something?" The voice was mischievous, but raspy and hoarse.

"God, Tyler," Dicenzo replied, ignoring him and standing to help him off with his coat. "What are you doing here?"

"Told Milo I had to cut out early. Still don't feel so good. What's he doing here?" he asked, addressing Dennis, not Smailes.

"Derek came to ask me a favor about some dental work for a friend," he said. Both Dennis and Tyler saw Smailes' sudden shake of the head.

"No, Derek. I'd never make a decision like this without consulting Tyler. I thought you would have known that."

Despite Smailes' look of anger and alarm, Dicenzo proceeded to give Tyler a condensed version of Smailes' request. Tyler's amusement faded into a look of sour displeasure. When Dicenzo had finished, Tyler gave Dennis a surprisingly accurate description of what Smailes did for a living, and then told Dennis to forget the whole thing, calling Smailes' errand "spook business."

Smailes became angry. "Look, Tyler. You might not like me, and that's fine, that's up to you. But let Dennis make his own decisions, okay? Dennis, think about it . . ."

"I think he's right, Derek," said Dicenzo hesitantly. "Why should I get involved in something like this? It doesn't even sound legal."

Smailes realized his appeal was going to falter unless he made a bigger play. With the words sounding strange to his ears, he told Dicenzo that his participation might be vital to the outcome of events crucial to Western interests.

It sounded like a cliché. Suddenly, it was Tyler's turn to lose his temper, and he wheeled on Smailes, his voice croaking with indignation.

"Listen, mister, can't you listen to the people? People everywhere are sayin' they've had enough of this Cold War crap. It's gone on too long. But you spy people just gotta keep jerkin' off—"

"Tyler!"

"I mean it, Dennis. It makes me sick. Get the hell out, mister."

"Tyler, there's no need to be so rude. Derek, I'm sorry, he hasn't been feeling well . . ." Tyler had retreated into the hall and reappeared carrying Smailes' raincoat. His eyes were narrow and vindictive.

"Well, Dennis?" asked Smailes.

"I don't think so, Derek. Normally, I'd be glad to help. I'll do whatever work your friend needs. But false records, I don't think so."

Smailes felt disgusted. If Tyler had not shown up, he would have landed him. What was it with this guy Dawes, anyway? He took the raincoat from him unceremoniously and left.

New Leninist Party boss Anatoli Grishkin sat in the kitchen of his Leningrad apartment and drummed his fingers anxiously on the yellow Formica tabletop. Russians everywhere preferred to talk in the intimacy of their kitchens, and despite his status, Grishkin was no exception. A dented steel samovar stood in front of him, next to a crowded ashtray and a plate of black bread left over from breakfast. The only indication of privilege was a West German dishwasher that stood next to the sink. He was dressed informally in slacks and an open shirt. His guest was also dressed casually in civilian clothes.

"Tell me again. What are the numbers? How can we be completely sure?"

Lieutenant General Alexei Dolghorukov slowly crushed out his cigarette and patiently rehearsed the rebels' regimental and divisional troop strengths in the eight military districts west of the Urals.

"This is the strategic heart of the country, Anasha. We need not concern ourselves with Central Asia or the East. They will fall into place like ripe fruit, once it is clear we have taken over."

"Kiev, Leningrad, Moscow?"

"I have told you. Palov will take Kiev. I personally will command the Moscow forces after signing the emergency decree with Tumanov. And the Leningrad commander is completely loyal to you. You know that."

"Yes, I know. It's just, I'm aware, we could all be shot."

"Of course we could all be shot!" Dolghorukov yelled back, banging his hand down on the table so the bread plate rattled against the samovar. "Personally, I would rather die in my uniform than suffer this indignity any longer. It is quite clear what Rostov intends to do. He intends to buy the next election by flooding the country with consumer goods. The only way he can do this is on the backs of the military, by cutting us back to nothing. My God, the military-industrial sector is the only part of this damn country that works! We have to act now. There is no other choice. Besides, I now have a way to indict him in the eyes of the world."

"What do you mean?" Grishkin asked. Dolghorukov produced a wallet from his back pocket, removed a small square of yellow paper, and unfolded it with care. He flattened it out on the tabletop, then handed it across to Grishkin.

"What is this?" Grishkin asked.

"A friend on the Syrian general staff sent it to me. Look closely. It is a bill of lading for tractor parts from the port of Novorossiysk on the Black Sea, you see?"

"Yes," said Grishkin doubtfully.

"The Amal militia found it along with many other documents when they overran that Phalange building in Tripoli last month."

"So?"

"This is the disputed matériel from Krasnodar, my friend! See the date? The ministry of agriculture has no knowledge of any such shipment, because in fact it contained the antitank missiles, mortars and landmines that went missing from the Transcaucasus inventory at the same time! Our loyal friends Nikolai Rostov and Grigori Chumak sold arms to the Lebanese Phalange, comrade, disguised as agricultural machinery, and here is the proof! Chumak managed to deflect suspicion at the time, but now the whole world will know Rostov for what he is, a common thief!"

Grishkin held the document a moment longer, and could not suppress a grin as he handed it back. Dolghorukov continued. "Look, it is quite simple. Rostov and his entire mafia, Chumak, Kapalkin, all of them, will be in Oslo for the summit. It will be over before they can even consider a response, and we will arrest them all when they land at Vnukovo. The leadership will be served to you and Tumanov on a silver plate, and the world's leaders will have no choice but to acknowledge a fait accompli." Dolghorukov made a gesture of impatience, rose and walked to the window. He stood there a long moment looking out as Grishkin sat in silence. Eventually, he turned and spoke vehemently.

"You know, Anasha, what sickens me more than anything? It is this Russian inferiority complex of ours, that makes us fawn in the face of our adversaries. It has been the same throughout history. Look at the Crimea! While French warships shelled Sevastopol, our noblemen recruited Parisian governesses for their children. Why, we still conducted our diplomacy in French as we fought against their armies! Now it is the same with the Americans. Their country is spiritually destitute, yet we offer up our heritage in exchange for a handful of electronic trinkets and hamburger restaurants in Red Square. What has glasnost brought us, now that Solzhenitsyn and Brodsky can be read in their own language? Our people clamor for books by this woman Collins, and this man Clancy! Isn't it time we said 'Enough'?"

Grishkin sat deep in thought. "This diplomat. What if he gets cold feet?"

"He won't."

"And this GRU agent. What is the term?"

"Viking."

"This Viking. Is he alone or does he have . . . what do you call them?"

"Borzois."

"Does he have borzois supporting him?"

"Relax, Anatoli. He has two."

"Your dentist friend. He says I only need one filling. Are you sure he will cooperate?"

Mikhail Siskin was sitting opposite Derek Smailes in the sparsely furnished office which Smailes and Graham Booth had finished preparing only that morning. After some disagreement, they had ordered a sign for the door that read CALDWELL MANAGEMENT GROUP, the same name in which they had taken the lease. The set-up costs had pushed him way over budget, but Smailes had had no time to shop around for bargains. The room had the bare minimum necessary to pass muster as a working office—a desk, three chairs, filing cabinets, a phone and a typewriter. Smailes had dispatched Booth to flesh out the environment with office supplies, some posters for the wall, and a coffee machine. He had told Graham to take the rest of the day—Mikhail Siskin was due for his first meeting between three and three-thirty.

"He's quite trustworthy, Mikhail," said Smailes. "I thought at first he would not agree, but after thinking about it he changed his mind, even over the objections of the man he lives with."

Siskin wrinkled his nose at this last information. "Why?" he asked suspiciously.

"He must have guessed that you were Russian—don't worry, I didn't tell him—and he works in a free clinic for Soviet immigrants in Brooklyn. I think he feels sympathetic to the Russian plight, that's all, and that by cooperating with me he might help in a bigger way. But

I'm guessing. He didn't actually say what changed his mind."

Actually, Smailes suspected it was something much more personal that had compelled Dennis to reverse his decision—his need to assert his independence from Tyler's will. Smailes did not doubt that the power dynamics within relationships were universal, regardless of gender structure.

"So, he will make the false records?"

"Yes. Officially, you need a double root canal, plus some crown work. I will make sure he bills your mission at regular intervals."

Siskin seemed to relax a little. He was seated uncomfortably in a chair on the opposite side of the desk from Smailes, and was picking at the flesh of his fingers, like a nervous job candidate. Smailes asked him to recount what had happened since their meeting at the Plaza.

Siskin said that he and Tatanya had spoken at length of the British offer, and Tatanya had been immediately in favor of his complying, for Irina's sake. For herself, she was still angry at being coerced into cipher work and saw no problem providing her husband with information, if she saw anything relevant. Siskin himself had taken longer to come to a decision. He was concerned that Semeneyev and his KGB henchmen seemed particularly agitated of late, and was anxious about attracting their attention. But eventually he agreed, concluding that the risk to Irina if he did not comply outweighed the risks to them all if he did.

"So have you decided? You want the British doctors to come and look at her?"

"No," Siskin responded sharply. "We have not told her yet how sick she is, and this would obviously alarm her. For now, unless her condition gets suddenly worse, I ask you to wait until I tell you how we want to proceed." Smailes inclined his head in acknowledgment.

Smailes next suggested they review ground rules. Meetings were to be on Wednesdays at three. He gave Siskin some telephone numbers and codes, including the code for an emergency meeting. At Siskin's gesture of alarm, he explained that this was merely a routine precaution. Then he asked Siskin whether he had any information for him that day.

"What do you want to know?" asked Siskin, a little belligerently.

"Why don't we start with your assessment of Nikolai Rostov's negotiating strategy in Geneva?"

Smailes scribbled notes furiously as Siskin spoke, if only to disguise the presence of the recording equipment that was hooked up to the mike in the telephone receiver. Siskin's analysis was eloquent and incisive, although hardly revolutionary, in Smailes' layman's view. After speaking for thirty minutes or so, Siskin eventually fell silent. Then he said, almost casually, "Well, I did learn something this week about my own situation that may be of interest to you."

"What?" asked Smailes.

"If the obstacles to a summit meeting are overcome, I am to go to Oslo as part of our Soviet delegation. I am supposed to advise our leaders how to use the UN forum to maximum propaganda advantage," he said with some distaste in his voice.

"Really, Mikhail? And do you think that will happen? Do you think the Oslo summit will go ahead?"

"That is really up to you British and your French allies, my friend. I really think Comrade Rostov is serious about the linkage requirement to your medium-range missiles. After all, we gave up our entire land-based inventory with the INF accord. And he has to placate the right-wingers on the presidential council and in the Supreme Soviet, after all. The other outstanding issues, I do not think they are serious problems. But the linkage issue is a major one, I think."

Smailes felt like he had enough material from Siskin for one day, but before winding up their session, he asked as casually as he was able the major question that he had been drafted to try to have Mikhail Siskin answer.

"Listen, Mikhail. You don't know anything about a

secret meeting in Lvov, do you? Last November, during the American delegation's inspection tour?"

"Secret meeting? Between whom?"

"Kapalkin and the Americans."

Siskin seemed genuinely shocked. "Sergei Kapalkin met with the Americans during the Ukrainian inspection tour? Is this what you are saying? No. I know nothing of this. But it would certainly be most significant if it were true. Why do you think so?"

"I can't say, Mikhail. Will you keep your ears open?"

"Yes, I will. I certainly will. A secret meeting in Lvov? Ah yes, I begin to see why you might be concerned."

This last news rendered Mikhail Siskin almost jaunty, and the two men parted with their first handshake, and a promise to meet again the following week.

Later that afternoon, Smailes had to weather a torrent of invective from Ralph Van Deusen, as the two of them reviewed the tape of the meeting.

"You had absolutely no right, no authority, to approach this dentist without my permission. Do you understand?" Van Deusen spluttered, thrusting his chin at Smailes. The tendons in his neck stood out like umbrella struts, and a distended vein alongside his Adam's apple throbbed alarmingly.

"Calm down, Ralph, okay? It was a snap decision I made to try and allay some of Siskin's fears. If I was out of line, all right, I'm sorry." Smailes was aware the apology did not sound particularly convincing.

"God knows who this man might blab to. What's this reference to 'the man he lives with'?"

"It's the person he shares his apartment with, that's all," said Smailes cautiously. "It's okay. Dennis is a very sensible, mature individual, and he would not have agreed to cooperate had he not understood the need for discretion. And as it is, we have created an ironclad pretext for Mikhail's visits to the building, even if he's checked up on. Siskin's very nervous about the local KGB. I would say that was worth the risk, wouldn't you?"

Ralph changed the subject, lifting Smailes' latest financial report from his desk. "You're way, way over budget, man. Curzon Street's not going to like it."

Smailes began to get angry. "Look, Ralph, Britain's position in the Western alliance may be hanging on this. A few extra thousand for setting up an office is hardly material in that context, is it?" He met Van Deusen's stare for a moment, then looked away. The issue was power, quite simply, and Derek Smailes was damned if he was going to dish up any more than necessary to a desktop surfer like Van Deusen.

"All right, all right, but this breakdown is inadequate," Ralph went on. "It needs to be far more detailed, with supporting documents for everything. What's this 'five hundred, miscellaneous,' anyway?"

"I bought some information, that's all, Ralph."

"What information? From whom?"

"It's confidential."

"Confidential! You have a bloody nerve, laddie." Ralph's color was rising again and he leaned forward across his desk threateningly. Then he thought for a moment and added, "When this next report goes through to Roger, I'm going to request that I be brought in on the Colin interviews from now on. And I'll let Roger know that, in my opinion, you're getting dangerously big for your boots at this early stage. You are not in charge of this operation, remember. I am."

Sure you are, Ralph, Smailes said to himself as he rose to leave the room.

It was a Saturday night in the last week of February and Derek and Clea were eating at a small French restaurant in Dennis and Tyler's neighborhood. It was considerably more expensive than Smailes felt comfortable with, but it was one of Clea's favorites and Smailes had uncharacteristically suggested they make reservations there. Actually, as long as he forgot the prices, Smailes loved the place, since it felt uncannily like the real thing, from the accents of the waiters to the decor and the smell of Gauloises and sauces from the kitchen. For Clea's part, she relished the imaginative menu the chef prepared, and was on first name terms with the maître d' and several of the waiters.

For the past few weeks Smailes had been valiantly trying to maintain normalcy in his relationship with Clea. But his sense of guilt had led to overcompensation, and he knew Clea had guessed he was concealing something from her, if only because of his enhanced attentiveness. A favored weekend pastime for Derek and Clea was to eat inexpensively in lower Manhattan, then see a movie or wander aimlessly, savoring the street theater. But the previous Saturday, Smailes had insisted they see an act and have dinner at the tony Rainbow Room at Rockefeller Center. Clea had been wide-eyed with surprise, but complied readily. She had been yet more puzzled when Smailes arrived for their date bearing flowers, since there was no obviously required act of atonement that explained the gesture.

Clea was due to return to London in less than three weeks for her examinations and training, and Smailes found himself looking forward to the prospect with a perverse relief, since during their two month separation the Siskin operation should be largely concluded. At which point, he presumed, his nervous system and their relationship could return to a somewhat even keel.

The fact was Smailes had to continuously struggle to suppress his intense excitement at the course of the Siskin debriefings. Happily, Roger had overruled Ralph's request to sit in on their meetings, and over the course of the past month Derek and Mikhail, or George and Misha, as they came to address each other, had developed an increasing rapport that lent intimacy and flair to their discussions. Smailes had undergone a crash course in arms control education at Siskin's side, and began to find his counterpart's exposition of the issues—the "dialectic of death," as Siskin liked to call it—entirely fascinating. Siskin had, in fact, considerable insight into the background of the Soviet negotiating positions, and was able to explain forcefully which elements were in earnest and which were mere grandstanding. Smailes also knew from the changing tenor of London's acknowledgment messages that Whitehall was consuming the Siskin intelligence avidly, even requesting that Smailes step up their meetings to twice a week, to which Siskin complied after some initial reservations. On the international level, the standoff between Britain and France on one hand, and the Soviets on the other, with the U.S. prodding anxiously from the sidelines, was consuming a lot of newsprint and broadcast time. February was almost over and still no date for a summit between Wilkes and Rostov had been set.

At some risk to himself, Smailes had at one point dropped a question to Siskin about some of the wilder allegations of Vasily Malinovsky, including the theory that much offensive Soviet weaponry had never been retired but was stored in vast bunkers beneath the Urals. Smailes wondered what his masters in Whitehall would think of their junior operative's posing such a question, but it did not appear to perturb Siskin. He thought for a moment, then said that he had always dismissed such rumors as a product of the "demonologists," but that he had also learned, somewhat to his cost, never to dismiss any rumor of the Kremlin's secret agenda out of hand. For himself, he had no knowledge of such a storage facility.

On the subject of the secret Lvov meetings, Siskin was again of little help. Tatanya had seen nothing pass through her own cipher station that made any reference to such a meeting, and Siskin had heard no mention of the matter in any other forum. He began to suggest that the British were mistaken, that no such meeting had taken place. And he continued to insist that Rostov's linkage requirement was serious, and that the Soviets might very well not back down.

The only real issue that remained between Siskin and the British was the question of his relocation. He had not mentioned medical treatment for Irina again, and Smailes came to believe that, in fact, the family had already made a decision to come across to Britain, since it was, after all, the only feasible way for Irina to receive treatment. Smailes could not believe that Siskin would take his entire family back to Moscow in July, then somehow attempt to have the British fulfill their promise from there. But from Malinovsky's warning, Smailes knew this was the most delicate issue between them, and he was waiting for the right opportunity to bring up the subject again. But it could not wait indefinitely, he was aware.

Derek and Clea had finished their main courses and were drinking coffee when Smailes noticed a slightly pained expression on her face. Smailes was aware he had been preoccupied during much of the meal and that their conversation had been somewhat stilted. He assumed this explained her look of displeasure, and decided to hazard a remark about it.

"What's up, honey? You look a bit fed up. Didn't you enjoy the meal?"

"No, no, it was terrific. You know I love this place. No, I've got something to ask you, but I'm worried about how you'll respond."

Smailes registered internal alarm, but said casually, "What is it, Clea? What's on your mind?"

"Well, you know I leave in, what is it, two and a half weeks?"

"Of course."

"Well, I had a call from Daddy this morning. He's decided to hold a cocktail party next month, for Mummy's sixtieth, and he's asked me to come home a week early."

"Well, that doesn't sound too terrible," he said gamely.

"No, of course not. Except, he asked me to invite you too." Here Clea looked up at him and said with a sudden rush of emotion, "Oh, do come, Derek! Mummy would love to meet you, and my sister will be there, and all my parents' friends. Just for a few days. We could visit your mother too. Admit it, when was the last time you saw her, or your daughter?"

Smailes conceded that it was more than two years, but his spirits were sinking, since he knew he was going to have to decline. Clea also sensed it immediately from the tone of his voice.

"What is it, Derek? Can't you come, just this once? It would mean so much to me," she said in an injured voice.

Smailes hesitated. "Honey, I'm sorry, I just can't. Not now. If it were in just a few more months, I'd love to. Maybe we could go back together this summer . . ."

"Don't be silly. I only come back in May, after two months there. Honestly, what's the matter with you lately? You've been acting so peculiar."

"Peculiar?" said Smailes feebly.

"Yes. You're hiding something from me. I know you are. Half the time, you don't even hear what I say. Then the rest of the time you're being all phony and solicitous. Honestly, last week it was flowers and the Rainbow Room. Then tonight—I didn't even have to badger you to come here, it was your idea. What's going on, Derek? Why can't you come back to England with me? Or why won't you, that's more the question."

"Hey, I like this place too, you know," Smailes protested, sounding even more feeble. Clea was looking down at her coffee cup. She was deeply hurt.

"Listen, okay, you're right. Something's going on that I'm preoccupied with, something at work. It's why I can't leave at the moment . . ."

"Rubbish!" said Clea angrily. "You know what I think? I think you've decided to dump me, and you're being extra nice to me until I leave, then when I'm back in London, you'll write and say I should take a posting somewhere else, because you don't want us to be together anymore. I'm right, aren't I?"

Smailes was mortified. "Clea, my love, no, you're not. I'm telling you the truth. I'm on the biggest assignment of my life. It's absolutely vital to my career that I see it through. I just can't leave New York right now." He reached across the table for her hand. "I would love to come and meet your family, and to take you to meet mine. God knows it's long overdue."

Clea seemed a little mollified.

"Is it to do with that businessman's room you were bugging that night at the Plaza?" she asked.

"Clea, you know I can't tell you," he said gently.

At this point, Clea broke. "Derek, I'm sick of all this secrecy. If you can't bloody well tell me anything that matters to you, what kind of future do we have together?" she shouted, so loud that other diners in the restaurant looked at them and the maître d' appeared anxiously at the end of the bar.

"Clea, please," Smailes said in a lowered voice.

She had regained herself somewhat, and there was a cold anger in her voice. "Are you paying for this?" she asked.

"Of course."

"Good. Because I'm leaving. Alone."

She got up and walked resolutely to the front of the restaurant, drawing a few embarrassed glances from other tables. The maître d' had disappeared and quickly returned with Clea's coat. He held it for her as she put it on, not looking around. As she left, Smailes ran his hands through his hair, then gestured to their waiter.

"A large brandy, please, Alain," he said as the young Frenchman approached.

"*Oui, monsieur. Tout de suite,*" he said, his dark eyes heavy with compassion.

14

The two stocky Russians bustled into their apartment and the man put a leather briefcase down on the black vinyl couch. Then he retreated back into the hallway, removing his topcoat. He returned a moment later, carrying a glass of beer and a handful of crackers. His wife had not removed her own knobbly wool coat but had sat down on the couch and was scribbling furiously on the back of a document, using his case as a writing surface.

"What's the matter with you?" Mikhail Siskin asked his wife irritably, through a mouthful of food. "All the way home, on the bus, you looked fit to burst."

Tatanya Siskin did not reply but held up the message she had completed writing. Her husband set his beer glass down on the littered coffee table and took the document from her. He remained standing, reading in silence. He looked up at her sharply, then strode across to the television set and turned it on. A journalist was interviewing a rock musician who looked like a toilet brush in dark glasses. Siskin turned the volume up loud.

"Are you sure of this?" he asked heatedly.

"That is word for word," Tatanya replied triumphantly, beginning to unbutton her coat.

"'In view of the inviolability of second-strike forces . . .' You are sure those were the exact words?"

"Absolutely," said Tatanya, standing and struggling free of her coat.

"It came through today? For the West European desk?"

"Yes," she said irritably, with a wave of her hand. "As I wrote."

Siskin turned away and looked out of the window, as if weighing the import of the decrypt in his hand. Tatanya interrupted his thoughts.

"I think it is time to talk to Mr. Phillips about our family's future, Misha," she said.

Siskin wheeled angrily. "Don't tell me what to do," he barked.

"It's time to talk to the British," she repeated defiantly.

"Well, you may be right," said Siskin, turning to rest his fingers against the damp security glass of the window.

Mikhail Siskin was usually punctual to within ten minutes of their meeting times, but this particular Monday a half hour had passed, then forty minutes. Smailes got out of his chair to pace around the room and help himself to more stewed coffee. He surveyed the walls with their posters that bore testimony to Booth's overblown attempts at naturalism. In Booth's view, expatriate businessmen had an obsessive interest in expensive cars, hang-gliding and windsurfing; on the back of the door there was even a sign he had found somewhere that read, HE WHO HAS MOST TOYS WHEN HE DIES, WINS. Siskin had objected strenuously to the decor at first sight, but Smailes had merely shrugged and said he thought it lent an atmosphere of authenticity. He was about to sit down again when the door opened and Siskin entered. He seemed agitated and out of breath.

"Sit down, Misha," said Smailes. "You're late. Is everything okay?"

Siskin flopped into his chair, his chest heaving. "I just walked up fifteen flights from our dentist friend's floor. I was nervous about being followed, so I felt I had to get off the elevator at the fourth. Yes, I am late, obviously."

Smailes sat down also, keeping his voice even. "Why the nervousness, Mikhail? You're not being followed. I would know if you were."

"How?"

"Because we have countersurveillance on you, of course," said Smailes, indicating the phone. "Our team would already have called through if they had spotted a tail." Actually, Smailes' "team" comprised Graham Booth, who had proved himself a natural watcher, fetching up twice a week in such disguises for the Siskin detail that on a couple of occasions Smailes had not immediately recognized him.

Siskin seemed duly impressed. "I never thought . . ." he said. "So you're sure?"

"I'm sure," said Smailes. "You can trust us, Mikhail. We're professionals. What's going on?"

"It's that bastard Malik," said Siskin forcefully. "You know the one I mean?"

"That guy on your staff you think is KGB?"

"The one I know is KGB. Yes. He came into my office right at two-thirty and began a completely irrelevant discussion of our arms transfer study, as if, you know, daring me to get up and leave."

"It wasn't a genuine concern?" Smailes asked, relaxing a little.

"No. Not in my opinion. Something about trying to head off Chinese objections in the draft stage. A completely silly argument."

"And what happened?"

"Eventually, about ten to three, I told him we would have to continue our discussion later, since I had a dental appointment."

"And?"

"Well, he just gave this clever, knowing smile and said, 'Certainly, Mikhail Karlovich,' as if I had just confirmed something for him."

"Couldn't you be imagining this, Mikhail?" Smailes

asked carefully. To his relief, Siskin let out a sigh and conceded the point.

"Oh, I suppose so. But, you see, I've been so nervous I feel I'm giving myself away all the time. I told you, our mission is practically under siege, and the whole community is affected. Semeneyev is on the warpath, and I know he's told Malik to watch me especially closely. Last week he reissued the regulation about reporting nonbusiness contacts with foreigners. He assigned a ledger to the receptionist at Sixty-seventh Street, and another one in Riverdale. He has even reinstituted compulsory security lectures in the evenings, and this morning I hear even at Glen Cove on the weekends! Honestly, you'd think we were on the brink of war in Europe, instead of on the brink of eliminating the possibility."

"What do you think's going on?"

"It's coming from Moscow, definitely. The Lubianka must be worried about something. But beyond this, I don't know. I don't think it's coming from the Kremlin or the foreign ministry."

Siskin had settled back into his chair, and Smailes got up again. "You want coffee, Misha? It's a bit old, I'm afraid."

"Yes. Yes, thank you. My throat is quite dry."

Smailes went over to the wall unit that housed the coffee machine, poured some of the charred liquid into a paper cup, then doctored it with various powders. Above the machine a poster of a muscular windsurfer in hot pink trunks beckoned to him. Smailes frowned and turned to see that Siskin had gone over to the window to look down onto the street. He set his paper cup down carefully on the desk and when Siskin turned, he saw his expression was even more animated.

"Sit down, Mikhail. What's the matter with you today?"

"I'm sorry, I can't. I had to get this Malik business off my chest first. I have the most incredible news for you, George."

Smailes stood behind his chair. "Yes?" he asked mildly.

"Friday morning Tatanya decrypted a message for Vorotnikov, the first secretary for Western Europe."

"Well?"

"It was a routine review document, but the content was extraordinary."

Smailes was catching some of his excitement. "Yes?"

"It reported a decision of the presidential council, ratified by the Stavka."

"Who?"

"The Stavka, the chief military council. It said that Kapalkin will continue to press for linkage until the middle of March. Then, if the British and French hold out, they will drop the requirement in favor of separate, bilateral negotiations next year. The wording said 'This concession has been decided in view of the agreement concerning the inviolability of second-strike forces.'"

Smailes was still far from being expert in the field of arms control, but he immediately understood the significance of Siskin's information. The knowledge that the Soviets would soon back off their linkage requirement meant London could continue to stand firm, not lose face with the British electorate, yet not be held responsible by Washington for a collapse in the talks. Smailes actually took a step backward, then felt for his chair with his hand. He sat down carefully, trying to absorb the full impact of the news. Siskin walked around to his chair and sat down also, taking a gulp of his coffee.

"You know what this means, of course?" said Siskin heatedly.

"Yes, that Whitehall can continue to stand firm—"

"No, no, not just that! There has been no agreement on second-strike forces, don't you see! If ICBM systems have been made inviolate, that must be the secret agreement at Lvov that you have been so worried about! It would make perfect sense—Rostov and Wilkes made a secret deal on their strategic weapons first, so they could go ahead and complete the tactical demilitarization of Europe within that context. It explains everything. It was so obvious I never thought of it!"

Smailes was reeling. Had Tatanya Siskin deciphered the significance of the Lvov meeting? Had a deal been struck to guarantee the continuity of the American nuclear umbrella? If so, it would still a lot of anxious hearts in Western European capitals. Particularly London, he realized.

"Mikhail, this is incredible. Is she sure?"

"Yes. She memorized the cable word for word and told it to me Friday night. I've been full of needles-and-pins all weekend. Like you, she thought the major significance was that the Kremlin would back down on linkage. But there can be no other explanation of the reference to second-strike capacity, can there?"

Smailes was prepared to defer to Siskin on that count. He looked down to jot a few notes, if only to provide himself with a breather to gather his thoughts. He had long abandoned the pretense that his hasty scribblings were the only record of their meetings.

"So I suppose I will be going to Oslo after all," said Siskin with a broad smile.

Clearly, Siskin's relationship to his British hosts had reached a turning point, and the atmosphere in the room was sufficiently charged that Smailes was emboldened to broach the last remaining issue between them.

Smailes looked up from his notes. "Mikhail," he began gently, "perhaps it's time to discuss what we're going to do about Irina. It would be simplest, of course, if your family would simply come across to us, in July, when your tour expires. I am empowered to offer you a consultant's position to our Foreign Office, a new identity if you wish, and a settlement that will be large enough for you to buy your own house. Have you given it any thought?"

For a moment, Siskin could not meet his eyes. When he eventually raised them, Smailes saw that they were filled with conflicted emotion. When he began speaking, Smailes realized that the primary emotion was shame.

"George, I have thought of little else since the first

time you approached me at the UN, believe me. You are inviting me to defect. It sounds almost old-fashioned, doesn't it? But in Russian, you see, we have no word for 'defector.' There are only two words for those who choose to leave the motherland—'traitor' and 'emigrant.' And according to my training and background, these words are synonymous."

Here Siskin took in a deep breath and chewed on his mustache before exhaling. "Your approach has made me finally confront my deepest fears and feelings—about my homeland and its political system, about its future and my own career.

"For Tatanya, this is all very straightforward. She saw you approach me that night at the Maltese reception, you see, and immediately guessed why. By the time we were home, she had decided. 'Work with them, Misha, and let us go, before it is too late,' she said. 'Not only for Irina's sake, for all our sakes.'

"Actually, apart from her assignment during this last tour, Tatanya has adored our stay in New York. Her parents are both dead now, and the prospect of returning to Moscow for an indefinite time, even before Irina got sick, was very depressing to her. And for me too, I came to realize.

"You see, George, the founders of our Soviet state thought they were creating the perfect society. But they succeeded only in creating a jail. Oh, certainly, the walls have begun to crumble, but the whole country is still trapped within the mentality of inmate and warder, and will be for generations. And as for Rostov himself, I have grave doubts. Firstly, I doubt whether his commitment to reform is sincere. And secondly, if it is, I doubt that he can prevail, since the forces ranged against him are so powerful. I see no future for my country except anarchy and chaos, perhaps even another civil war, from which some monstrous nationalist state will no doubt arise in the Russian heartland. And I have come to believe passionately in internationalism as the only conceivable future for our species, my friend."

Here Siskin paused to order his thoughts. When he resumed his voice was lighter, but still resolute.

"Where is East Grinstead, exactly?" he asked.

"In Surrey, near London," said Smailes.

"Could we live there, to be near the hospital?"

"Of course."

Siskin paused again, looking down into the waters of his Rubicon.

"Yes, my family will defect, and I accept your conditions, providing you will accept mine. I will consult for your government for a period of three years. After this period, I wish to have British citizenship and to be allowed to return to my position at the UN, as an international civil servant. Is this clear?"

"Perfectly."

"And do you think your government will agree?"

"Misha, I have not the slightest doubt of it," said Smailes, rising to lean over the desk and shake his hand.

The consul general's townhouse was one of those rare Upper East Side brownstones whose four stories had not yet been converted into flats or offices, and were now owned exclusively by foreign governments or the hyper-rich. The CG and his family, in fact, lived only on the top two floors, the parlor floor and service area beneath being reserved solely for entertaining. And during his New York tenure, at least before the latest austerity drive, the CG's lavish and regular receptions had become somewhat legendary.

The particular occasion was a bash for the actors of the Royal Shakespeare Company, which had just concluded a highly acclaimed U.S. tour in New York. It was also something of an unofficial farewell party for Clea, since she had been one of the organizers of the event, and was leaving the following evening for her trip back to Britain. In addition to the actors and actresses, the gathering included sundry hangers-on from the diplomatic, expatriate and artistic communities, and solid representation from Clea's own circle of friends. It was exactly the kind of upscale, prestigious event with which she loved to be associated, and she seemed in fine form. She smiled across at Smailes a couple of times as she circulated determinedly around the large room.

Clea and Derek had made distinct repairs to their relationship since the painful scene in the restaurant, although there was still tension between them. Smailes was fairly sure he had convinced her he had no intention of dumping her at all, and Clea, for her part, had conceded the importance of his career and its strictures regarding confidentiality. She had somewhat qualified the concession, however, by offering her own freelance interpretation of his recent behavior which contained several wild, uncanny accuracies. In Clea's version, Smailes had been acting queer ever since the day he showed up at her apartment looking like a coal miner. She had processed Howard Grundy's travel vouchers for the unexpected return trip from Boston, and guessed that he had been teaching Smailes some dirty tricks in the basement of the Mount Vernon house. Then came the peculiar tape that Smailes said Howard had made, which Felicity had translated. This was obviously significant, because right afterward Smailes found the car bomb, which was obviously meant for him, since the KGB had decided to bump him off because of whatever he and Howard had discovered. Kevin Butterworth was somehow involved in this discovery, since he was killed soon afterward before he and Smailes could discuss their next step. Then came Roger Standiforth's unusual trip to New York. Clea had decided he was Smailes' spymaster, coming to discuss strategy for whatever hugely important mission Smailes was involved with. Which meant finally that Smailes had lured her to the Plaza the previous month as cover for his real activities, which probably involved the bugging of a Russian diplomat, not a British businessman.

At the conclusion of her account, Clea threw her head back and gave a long, low-throated laugh, enjoying the sight of her lover's discomfiture as he hunted for a response. In the end, Smailes would only say, "That's fantastic, honey. You should try your hand at fiction," and Clea pushed his face away with her hand in mock disgust.

Smailes watched her move about the room in her diplomat's suit, and found himself brooding on how their relationship could possibly survive, given this requirement for enforced deception. He had actually been briefly elated after her outburst in the restaurant, since it seemed to betray the depth of her feelings, and suggested she hoped for a future together. But he remembered also her anguished protest about their prospects if they were prohibited from discussing what was really important, and had not yet formulated a satisfactory answer for himself. He wondered what decision he would make if he were faced with a stark choice between Clea and his career in MI5, and could find no immediate answer to that question, either. He raised his glass distractedly to his lips and listened to the babble of voices. He realized how little he had come to appreciate such aggregations of British—the room sounded like an overexcited stable yard.

Ralph Van Deusen was there, unfortunately, stuck over in a corner talking with Lyle Pitkethly. Smailes was not aware they knew each other, but then, the fact that they were chatting at a cocktail party did not necessarily mean that they did. Smailes and Van Deusen had stalked around each other warily of late, and had avoided any further confrontations like the row over the use of Dicenzo's cover. Roger's denial of Ralph's request to sit in on the Siskin meetings had ceded de facto control over the operation to Smailes, and they both knew it. Consequently, Ralph had been largely reduced to communications link man with London, to Smailes' immense relief.

Smailes exchanged a few words with Madge Ryan, whom Clea had thoughtfully invited, as Clea's elegant form caught his eye again, heading over to the doorway. Smailes craned his neck and saw Dennis Dicenzo and Tyler Dawes enter. Dennis was dressed conservatively in a dark sweater and slacks, but Tyler, perhaps in view of the putatively bohemian gathering, was wearing an unusual one-piece outfit with a zipper up the front. Although in subdued gray, it was hardly the kind of thing you saw worn every day at a British diplomatic cocktail party. Smailes heard Clea's voice swell momentarily above the hubbub as she greeted her friends. He smiled into his glass at the incongruity as the formally dressed Clea hugged the outlandish Tyler, then Dennis.

Actually, Smailes was in good spirits, despite the fact that he was going through an awkward period with the woman he loved, and that she was leaving the following day for an extended period. The truth was that his star was in the ascendant with his masters at Curzon Street, and the reason was the peerless quality of the intelligence Mikhail Siskin had furnished. The transmission of the tape and transcript of the pivotal meeting in which Siskin had given his interpretation of Tatanya's crucial decrypt, then had agreed to come across to the British, had been acknowledged within hours by a rare joint cable attributed to both Standiforth and Price-Jones, asking for an affective analysis, meaning that they wanted to know Siskin's mood during the meeting. Smailes filed a lengthy follow-up, which was acknowledged the following day by bag in the usual manner. Almost immediately, Smailes noticed an increased forcefulness in the British prime minister's pronouncements about Moscow's stipulations, as he issued repeated patriotic pledges never to compromise the defense of the British realm. And sure enough, just the previous day, the London and New York papers had screamed with headlines that Moscow had backed down on its requirement. Even the prime minister's enemies had grudgingly conceded his fortitude in the face of relentless superpower pressure. One of the tabloids had even dubbed him "the New Lionheart."

Smailes stood watching Clea as she maneuvered Tyler and Dennis toward him and the drinks station beyond. "She's leaving tomorrow, I understand," said a voice to his right. He turned to confront Van Deusen, who was stoking up a cigar.

"That's right, Ralph," said Smailes.

"Welcome to the bachelor ranks," he said, in a disagreeable attempt at camaraderie.

Clea's path was about to bring her entourage right past them, although she was momentarily distracted in conversation with a woman from her department. Tyler and Dennis halted awkwardly nearby, as if unsure whether to proceed. Smailes had not seen or spoken with Tyler since the night of his outburst at the Greenwich Village apartment, and their eyes met uncomfortably. He wondered what he would say if he knew his lover had defied him and agreed to comply with Smailes' request. At that moment, Clea turned back and saw Smailes standing there with Van Deusen.

"Darling, look who came! I love Tyler's jumpsuit, don't you? Hello, Ralph, let me introduce you. Ralph Van Deusen, this is Dennis Dicenzo."

Dennis held out his hand, and Van Deusen grasped it weakly, his jaw falling open as he recognized the name.

"And Ralph, this is Tyler Dawes. Tyler, Ralph Van Deusen."

Tyler held out a languid hand and Ralph's expression changed from disbelief to something approaching horror as he stared at Tyler's outstretched hand, to his face, and back again. The moment lengthened, then Ralph made a bizarre gesture of dismissal, spun on his heel, and plunged back into the crowd. Tyler lowered his hand slowly, his jaw set in anger.

"Tyler, honestly, ignore him, he's . . ." Clea began, mortified.

"Who is that asshole?" Dennis asked.

"Listen, ignore him. He's just stupid. He's Derek's boss."

Tyler had still not spoken. He presented an ostentatious shoulder to Smailes, as if to move past him toward the bar.

"Birds of a feather," he said quite distinctly as he moved by, and Smailes' face burned. Dennis Dicenzo gave him a look of mute appeal, and Clea halted in her tracks. "Look, it's back over there, you two," she said, stopping at Smailes' side.

"Honestly, that man Van Deusen. He's contemptible," she said forcefully. "Whatever did Tyler mean?"

"You tell me," said Smailes, his feelings still smarting. "He's your friend, not mine."

Clea did not stay parked beside him for long, and soon left him to hobnob with a group of handsome young actors. Smailes replenished his drink and wandered out into the hallway where the crowd was thinner, and began inspecting the collection of Hockney prints that the British government had acquired in more expansive times. In truth, he was still angry at Tyler's gratuitous insult, and didn't want to be anywhere near him.

"Hello there, old man. Thought it was you," said a familiar, fruity voice. Smailes turned to see Alan Sparks approaching him unsteadily, a full tumbler in his fist. The unruly hair stood up in a crest from his skull, and Smailes could make out the beginnings of a posy of gin blossoms across his nose and cheeks.

"Alan. How are you?" he asked pleasantly.

"Oh, fairly well, fairly well. Never miss a chance to hoist one on the consulate, you know. Sorry I never got back to you earlier, but then, nothing to report. No trace of that chap Solovyov. Your friend must have been misinformed."

Smailes felt a moment of panic, since for a second he had no idea what the SIS deskman was talking about. Then it came to him in a rush. "Oh right. That's what I had decided. Like I said, it wasn't his specialty. Probably a crossed wire."

Sparks moved toward him and put a hand on his sleeve conspiratorially. "Listen, can we have a word in private, old man?" From the smell of liquor on his breath, Smailes knew the cocktail he was holding was not his first.

"Of course, Alan. What's on your mind?"

Sparks did not reply, but steered Smailes out through a small staging area where a dumbwaiter shaft emerged from the kitchen below, and out through a back door onto a small wrought-iron balcony. The evening was brisk and Smailes drew his suit jacket around him. Sparks seemed oblivious as he followed him, the metal plates on his heels clanging against the steel grid of the balcony. As he began speaking clouds of white vapor shrouded his face.

"Listen, I just wondered if you knew whether Ralph was up to anything unusual at the moment."

"Whatever do you mean?"

"Look, between you and me, Quentin has been getting terrific flak from London. Apparently Five has a tame diplomat somewhere who's feeding the most sensational intelligence on the Geneva positions. The JIC is going ape, but Five won't release particulars and the Old Man is climbing the walls. It's got to be somewhere Five has a station, and the Old Man thinks Moscow, but it could be any of them, couldn't it? What are there, seven or eight?"

"Something like that," said Smailes, enthralled.

"Naturally, Quentin is pretty steamed up that Ralph might be pulling off something right under his nose. Since I'm Soviet colony man, he thinks I should be able to tell him if anything's up. I don't know, but you don't seem to pay too much attention to all this silly divisional rivalry stuff, and I thought you might tell me if you knew of anything."

Smailes' face showed alarm. "Honestly, Alan, I haven't heard a thing. But listen, if I do, I'll let you know. It would have to be strictly confidential, of course."

"Would you, old man? I'd really be grateful. Here, let's go back in. Bit parky out here, isn't it?"

Smailes held the back door open for Sparks as he maneuvered unsteadily back into the warmth and light. Of course, it would destroy Sparks' career when Mikhail Siskin finally came in from the cold, and Smailes well knew it.

"So have you forgiven me?" he asked quietly.

"What do you think?" she replied, reaching for his fingertips in the darkness. It was their last night together, and they were lying face to face, finally still. Actually, the generosity of her lovemaking had told him more than any avowal ever could. Taken together with her revelations in the bistro, it made Smailes' heart sing with hope. Perhaps it was really true, improbably, that she loved him as intensely as he loved her, that she, too, wished for a long-term future together. Smailes compressed his elation into a tight ball and jammed it into the strongbox where he kept all his keenest hopes and fears. When the Colin operation was concluded, when Clea had her new posting, he told himself, they could talk about their future together. Not before; it would be imprudent. Still, he wished he could simply drop his guard and say, "I love you." After all, people in the movies did it all the time. Finally, he found some words.

"Listen, when all this is over, by the time you're back, I'll explain it all to you. As much as I'm able."

"Wouldn't that be unprofessional?" she asked, but not accusingly.

"Some things have to take priority, ultimately," he said, and Clea squeezed his fingers again.

"Are you in danger?" she asked.

"No," he said, hoping it was true. "What time's the plane?"

"Seven."

"I could come to the airport."

"No, don't," said Clea, reaching down the bed for her discarded nightgown. "This was the nicest goodbye."

He smiled in the darkness and reached out to touch the soft flesh of her back, realizing he was going to miss her terribly.

When Smailes entered the British offices the next day, he was relieved to find a workman in overalls removing the digital pad at the front door to their suite. The recommendation for its removal had finally been signed by all the principals, reviewed and approved by the management committee, then relayed to Whitehall and back again. The process had taken a mere three months. The workman was being babysat by Reg Dwyer, one of the remaining employees in the foreign office's own security department, whose work the Five station had largely supplanted. Understandably, the FO security men loathed the upstarts from Five, who had usurped their most important functions and relegated them to the status of glorified messengers. Most of them were former NCOs in the British Army, men who knew their station in the imperial scheme of things, and who were generally much more deferential to their diplomatic overlords than MI5 people. Reg Dwyer, a former regimental sergeant who had served in Malaya and Cyprus, was no exception.

"Morning, Reg," said Smailes brightly as he squeezed past him through the open door.

"Morning," said Dwyer reluctantly, turning away.

Smailes spent the next hour in his office, reviewing the British press accounts of the preparations for Oslo. Booth was bantering somewhere on the edge of his consciousness, when the door opened and Hugo Brook, the senior comm, stuck in his head.

"Eyes-only for you, Derek," he said, and Smailes swung out of his chair, ignoring Booth's importunate stare. He padded down the corridor behind Hugo's broad back toward the fort, trying to contain his curiosity. He had never received an eyes-only cable before, which, according to civil service regulations, could only be read in a secure area. He followed Hugo into the cipher station's antechamber, and waited while Hugo disappeared for the decrypt and the ledger book in which it was recorded. When he returned, Smailes signed where Hugo instructed him, and accepted the flimsy printout. Hugo stood over him as he read it. The cable was from Roger Standiforth, naturally, ignoring his own proscription on cipher traffic. The message was laconic. It read simply, MONDAY, MARCH 20. 1 PM, LUNCH, OXFORD AND CAMBRIDGE CLUB, 71 PALL MALL. COLIN IMPREST.

Smailes handed the sheet back to Hugo and returned slowly to his office. He was highly intrigued. Why on earth did Roger want to see him? And at such short notice? He had specified the Siskin imprest fund for the expenses, suggesting a direct relation, but that could easily be a cover. He looked at his watch and realized he had better get on the phone right away. Weekend flights were often full.

Suddenly, Smailes was aware that if he could find a seat that night, he might be able to attend Clea's family gathering after all. Maybe they could even drive up to Cambridge together and see his mother. He would have to skip Monday's meeting with Siskin, which was a problem. And he would have to tell Ralph that he was leaving, which was an even bigger problem.

Back in his office, Smailes would only tell Booth, "I've got to go back to London for a flying visit," and began making phone calls. He called Clea's department to find out which flight she was taking, then immediately called the airline to check on seats. There were five left. Smailes hurriedly made a reservation, with a return on Tuesday, then grabbed Booth and headed across the hall.

Madge looked up reproachfully as Smailes and Booth entered. Smailes gave her a hurried explanation and handed over his notes with the flight and fare details, and asked her to arrange payment through the mission's travel agent, using the Colin imprest. Then he asked her to buzz Ralph, and a moment later Smailes and Booth took their seats at the opposite side of Van Deusen's desk.

Ralph was not about to be hurried, and spent some amount of time fiddling with a tiny guillotine with which he trimmed the ends of his cigars. He twirled the next victim in his fingers for a moment, then circumcised it with relish. He lit it with a fan of flame from an old petrol lighter, then looked across at Smailes and Booth. He nodded, and Smailes went ahead and rehearsed the latest development in full.

"What?" Ralph said with a pained expression, pretending he hadn't heard. "Whaddya mean? I don't understand."

Smailes was compelled to repeat the whole story. An eyes-only cable from Standiforth, a Monday lunchtime meeting in London, Colin imprest. Smailes had reservations that night, returning Tuesday.

Clearly, Ralph was furious that Smailes had been summoned back to London, not he. And just as clearly, he was not going to admit it.

"What's it about?" Van Deusen asked eventually.

"Ralph, I've no idea."

"Have you any idea, Graham?" Van Deusen asked improbably.

"No," said Booth, surprised.

Van Deusen changed tack. "What about Monday's meeting with Colin?"

"We can either cancel, or you'll have to take it, Ralph. Can't just not show up, it might panic him. I imagine I could get a message to him through—"

"I'll take it," interrupted Ralph. "It's what Roger would want."

Smailes already knew this would be Van Deusen's decision, and saw no point challenging him. "Well, he's going to be spooked, no matter what, since he's never met you before," said Smailes, as uncontentiously as possible. "But I agree, it's better than not showing at all. You'll need to do a lot of pacifying, I think, although I've referred to you, to Bruce, that is, once or twice. Graham can review how the recording system works, if you like. He can take the watcher detail as usual . . ."

"Don't worry. I can tell Graham what to do. I'm in charge of this operation. Had you forgotten?" asked Van Deusen, all his envy and spite restored.

"No, of course not, Ralph. Let me just review the emergency procedures I set up, in case anything happens while I'm gone, okay? Then I'm going to have to go home and pack."

Clea actually sounded a little disappointed when she heard his voice. "Darling, it's really sweet of you, but we've already said our goodbyes—"

"What should I get your mother for her birthday?" he interrupted.

"Whatever do you mean?"

"What time are you checking in?"

"Half past five. Why?"

"Meet you there. I'm booked on the same plane." Hurriedly, he explained his sudden recall to London for a Monday meeting. Clea was overjoyed.

"Oh, Derek, this is wonderful news! Can we go up to Cambridge too?"

"I don't see why not, on the Sunday. Can we borrow a car?"

"Of course," said Clea, laughing. "Do you want to come over here? I've ordered a taxi for half past four."

"No, no, I've got some things to take care of, then I need to pick up the ticket and pack. I'll meet you at the check-in."

He hung up, then sat for a moment lost in thought. The meeting might be a routine review, of course. But then why had Roger scheduled the meeting in the privacy of his club, and not at his office in Five's Curzon Street headquarters?

15

The first thing Smailes noticed as they stumbled out from the customs hall into the waiting corridor of faces was how dainty and improbable things seemed. The policemen standing over by the information booth were wearing their peculiar shorty raincoats and ludicrous helmets that looked like something out of Gilbert and Sullivan, and the cheeky billboards with their claims to "Royal this" and "Royal that" made Britain seem an unlikely caricature of itself. Perhaps it was only the lack of sleep, but the effect on Smailes was overwhelmingly poignant. He had been away less than three years, but already his native land had grown quaint and unfamiliar to him.

Anthea Lynch met them over by the bank counter and Smailes could tell immediately where Clea derived her looks and build from. Her mother was an exceedingly well-preserved woman in late middle age, with long, straight, steel gray hair and a knowing, intelligent smile. She was the same height as Clea, and as the two women embraced they looked like the youthful and elder versions of the same person. Anthea Lynch turned and greeted Smailes graciously, then led them to the parking garage and a large maroon Peugeot station wagon. Smailes was momentarily nonplussed as Mrs. Lynch climbed into the wrong side before opening the doors for them.

The Lynches lived in an enormous, mock Tudor house set back behind a semicircular driveway in Purley, in the stockbroker belt south of London. Smailes and Clea were ushered into a large, modern kitchen where Anthea Lynch seated them in a breakfast nook and plied them with limp sandwiches and magnificent tea. Peter Lynch appeared at some point, and Smailes made a weary attempt at small talk. Neither Derek nor Clea had really slept during the flight, and it was now six in the morning, their time. Eventually, Clea pointed Smailes up the stairs with his overnight case and showed him to the guest room.

"Get some sleep," she said. "Mummy will wake us at four. The bathroom's across the hall."

"Where are you going?" he said.

"My room's at the end of the hall, round the corner," she said. Smailes made a half-serious attempt to follow her, but retreated back into his room, took off his boots, and closed the curtains. He remembered listening to some unfamiliar birdsong for a moment, then fell asleep.

Clea woke him in late afternoon, and after he had washed and shaved and changed his shirt, he felt almost human. He went down the back stairs to the kitchen and found Clea in her candlewick dressing gown, seated at the breakfast table talking with an arresting-looking blonde. Clea looked up immediately as he entered the room.

"Hello, darling. You're looking a lot better. This is my sister, Julie."

Julie Lynch got up from the table and offered Smailes a small, warm hand. He had to fight to contain his reaction, for if Clea Lynch was a good-looking woman, her sister Julie was an absolute stunner. She was a little taller than Clea, with delicate, even features, thick, ash blond hair and a dramatic hourglass figure. She was wearing a ribbed navy turtleneck, a tight check skirt and suede boots.

"Hello, Derek," she said, in the same pedigree accent as her sister's. "We were all so thrilled you could come. Honestly, I've heard so much about you, I wanted to know if you're really everything Clea says."

"Oh yeah? What's that, then?" asked Smailes, leaning on his proletarian vowels a little.

"Well, according to Clea, you're the last of the real men," she said, looking at him archly. "Have you recovered from the flight?"

"Well, I'm still a bit groggy," said Smailes. "It must be culture shock," he added with a smile.

"I know just the thing," she said, spinning on her heel. When she left the room, Clea leaned across the table, took his hand and said, "Now you see what I mean about being a little competitive with my sister. Isn't she gorgeous?"

"Not as gorgeous as you, honey," he said, and in that moment, meaning it. She gave him a scoffing look with her eyes but squeezed his hand in appreciation of the compliment. Julie came back into the kitchen swinging what looked like a bottle of brandy.

"It's Daddy's Benedictine. He hides it in his study. Costs a hundred pounds a bottle or something. Here, do this."

Julie stood between them, tossed her hair back, then uncorked the bottle and hoisted it to her lips. She took a tiny amount into her mouth, made a rivulet of her tongue, then sucked air sharply across it. Her eyes smarted and she swallowed quickly, then gave out a guffaw.

"Honestly, try it. It's the best thing for jet lag. Gives you a huge rush, then your head's completely clear."

Clea laughed. "Honestly, Jules, you don't change. You'd better put that stuff back before Daddy gets in."

"He's out buying the plonk, and Mummy's getting a face lift or something. They'll be hours. Here, Derek."

Smailes accepted the bottle and took a quick swig. It certainly was magnificent stuff. He offered it to Clea, but she declined.

"So, tell me again. Why isn't Alf coming?" Clea asked.

"Oh, he's in training for a fight next week, and his

trainer insists he be in bed by ten. I don't think he would have enjoyed it anyway, do you?"

"Really? I would have thought Daddy was dying to meet him." The two sisters looked at each other solemnly for a moment, then burst out laughing. Clea turned to Derek to explain.

"Julie's going out with this chap Alf, who's a boxer from Hackney—"

"Stepney," Julie corrected.

"Stepney. He's a contender for the middleweight title, or something, isn't he?"

"Well, he will be if he wins his next fight. I don't know, I couldn't quite see him here, could you?"

"Derek came, didn't he?" said Clea provocatively.

"Darling, Derek's a civil servant, not a boxer," said Julie.

Clea was about to respond when the kitchen door opened and Anthea Lynch staggered in, her face barely visible behind two huge bunches of flowers.

"Julie, my love. How are you?" she asked, setting her parcels down and offering her daughter her cheek. "You lot are going to have to clear out," she said, addressing the gathering. "The caterer's van just arrived."

"Right, well, I have to get dressed," said Clea. "Are you going to change, Julie?"

"Oh, I brought a dress, if I can still get into it," she said.

Smailes considered offering her help with the zippers, but thought better of it. "Is there a phone I can use? I should call my mother," he said.

"In the living room," said Anthea Lynch. "The morning papers are in there too, if you want something to look at."

Anthea Lynch's birthday party was a protracted and tiresome affair for Smailes, since he knew hardly anyone apart from Clea and did not feel entirely at ease in the clubby, upper middle-class atmosphere of Peter Lynch's drawing room. Clea had been fairly protective of him at first, and Smailes had felt self-consciously proud as she introduced him to a succession of family friends and relatives. She had chosen a blue floral drop-waist dress that was one of Smailes' favorites, which together with her hairstyle made her look like a twenties filmstar. Julie, in contrast, was wearing a simple black evening dress with a scoop neck and pearls, and looked ravishing. Smailes was careful not to stare at her, but once or twice she met his casual glances and gave him sudden, heart-stopping smiles. At some point Smailes found himself alone with Anthea Lynch, and was impressed by her wise reflections about her daughters, and about life in general, and the ease with which she expressed herself. He found it a little odd that she'd had such a long, apparently successful marriage to an oafish man like Peter Lynch, but dismissed the thought as uncharitable.

Clea rescued him for a while, until she became distracted by her duties again, and Smailes eventually parked himself by the buffet table with some business cronies of her father's. In response to queries about his livelihood, Smailes unrolled his standard response about being transportation supervisor for the New York Mission, then settled back to listen to their conversation. It was all about the international situation and preparations for Oslo. Most people seemed to agree that world affairs were approaching an extraordinary climax, and several voices expressed disbelief that they were witnessing the demilitarization of Europe in their lifetime.

"Well, we've won, of course," said a fat banker with a lisp. "Although we're damn lucky the Russians never found a credible hard-liner in place of Rostov. If they had, I doubt their army would have ever accepted such a capitulation."

"I don't know if you can call it such a victory, Horace, when you've got eighty million reunified Germans rattling around with only a partial allegiance to NATO. Do you consider fifty thousand American troops a tight enough leash?" asked a gloomy commodities broker in a loud suit.

"Oh, I don't count German nationalism much of a threat anymore, do you?" countered Horace. "Not without a sense of injustice to fan it. After all, they got what they wanted. They're one of the richest, most respected nations in the world, after all. Did you see the statistics in the FT on Friday?"

"Well, you may both be premature," interjected a lanky neighbor, a man with a bulbous nose and prominent nostril hairs. "My sister's boy Gilbert is with the Foreign Office, and he says there's apparently some last-minute, high-level hitch between London and Washington. Something to do with verification . . ."

"You don't say?" said the banker. "Have you heard anything about this, Derek? It was Derek, wasn't it?"

"Yes, that's right," said Smailes. "No, I haven't. I don't pay much attention to politics, I'm afraid," he added, looking at the three men wanly over the rim of his glass. In fact, he remembered seeing a short piece in the paper that afternoon about a high-level Foreign Office delegation having left unexpectedly for Washington, and wondered if there was a connection to this latest development. But he merely blinked and made an expression that suggested he was out of his depth.

Actually, Smailes felt intensely pleased with himself. He imagined the same conversation being repeated in living rooms all over the Western world at that moment, and knew he had played no insignificant role behind the scenes. For now, he was quite prepared to play the supplementary part of Clea Lynch's reticent and somewhat slow-witted companion.

Eventually, Smailes treated himself to the luxury of a private conversation with Julie, and found her overprivileged nonconformity to be an exaggerated and somewhat immature version of her sister's. She lived with flatmates in South Kensington, and as she told him of her succession of boyfriends and jobs and her estrangement from her father, he realized that she was in fact desperately unhappy, and probably contrived much of her behavior as a means to gain attention, *pour épater la famille*.

As Anthea Lynch had hinted to him, Julie obviously envied her elder sister's grace and success, and Smailes felt acutely sorry for her. He realized also that in her quest for acceptance, her looks were merely a curse, and that his own attitude to her had been unavoidably colored by her sexual allure. Throughout their conversation he kept his gaze studiously above her collarbone, and he could tell she was intensely grateful for the seriousness with which he listened to her.

Finally, the last guests left around midnight and Smailes began helping Clea and her mother carry plates and glasses out to the kitchen. Anthea Lynch stopped him as he headed back for a second load. "No, Derek, we can manage this. You should go and have a nightcap with Peter in his study." Smailes caught Clea's amused look over her mother's shoulder and hesitated. "No, no, go on. He's expecting you. It's sort of an initiation rite, I'm afraid," she added with a look of sympathy.

As Smailes stepped into the hallway, Clea followed him, found his arm and reached up to whisper in his ear. "Come into my room later, when everyone's asleep," she said. "End of the hall, last door on the left. Don't go to the right, that's Julie's room." Smailes made a careful mental note. It was not, after all, a mistake he would want to make.

As his wife had predicted, Peter Lynch was seated in a leather armchair in front of the hearth in his study, waiting for Smailes to arrive. Fake coal glowed above the bars of a gas fire, and the priceless Benedictine and two snifters stood on a coffee table in front of him. Smailes maneuvered past a small writing desk and took the wing chair that Lynch indicated. He accepted the liqueur and declined a cigar, omitting to mention he'd already sampled the former earlier. As Lynch began speaking, Smailes realized that Clea's father was in fact quite drunk.

Peter Lynch began with a bumptious speech about how delighted he and Anthea were that Clea was finally associating with someone appropriate, with someone of her own caliber. Smailes noted that Lynch did not say "of her own class."

"Really, what with those layabouts she hung around with at university, and afterward, we were beginning to despair. Of course, her sister's much worse. You hear she's been seeing a boxer?" Lynch made the description sound like the breed of dog.

"No, really?" said Smailes. He realized with alarm that Peter Lynch was offering him tacit approval should he seek his daughter's hand in marriage, and didn't know quite what to say. He changed the subject.

"Well, I was just glad I was able to come at the last minute," he said.

"Ralph gave you the time off, did he?" Lynch asked, and Smailes stiffened, not wishing to be led into territory he'd already declared off limits during their meeting in New York.

"It was owed to me," he said carefully.

"Bloody awful character," said Lynch forcefully. "Known him since Teddy Hall, but I never liked him, even though I stood behind him when he got himself into the soup, whenever it was, must be nearly twenty years ago."

Smailes' curiosity was piqued. "When he was transferred internally, you mean? What exactly happened there?"

"Bloody fool got caught with his trousers down in the wrong company, didn't he? You don't know the story? God, it must have been well covered up."

"No, I don't."

"Well, you see, I knew Van Deusen at Oxford, we were at St. Edmund Hall together, then my firm had some business dealings with his family once he went back to Rhodesia. Then, when he and Grace bailed out, whenever it was, in the seventies, I acted as one of his referees when he joined MI5. I was on the select committee on defense at the time, so it must have had some weight.

"Anyway, they'd only been in London a couple of years when the marriage began to come apart. Ralph started frequenting a Mayfair prostitute, who, it turned out, counted several Eastern European diplomats among her clientele. Terrible error in judgment. Well, the watchers spotted him, didn't they, and he got in a terrible stew. Profumo affair still fresh in people's minds, you see, and, if you ask me, he was damn lucky to escape with a divorce and a demotion. I stood by him, of course, because the fellow doesn't have the imagination to be disloyal, but I felt I had egg on my face, I'll tell you. Bastard never thanked me either. But there you are, that's typical of him."

"Yes, well, he can be a difficult bloke to work for," said Smailes. "No question about that. But I'm surprised, I had no idea." The fact was, the story of Ralph's lapse seemed entirely in character.

Smailes drained the liquid in the snifter and set it down on the coffee table as a prelude to leaving. He realized some sort of testimonial was expected of him.

"Well, I'm very pleased to visit your home, Mr. Lynch, and feel privileged to be associated with Clea, believe me," he said, starting to stand. "But I really must be . . ."

"Call me Peter. Peter, for Christ's sake. Won't you have another?"

"No really, I'm very tired," he said. He crossed to the door but stopped and turned as Lynch said something behind him. He rested his hand on the edge of the writing desk, where a sheaf of correspondence held down by a brass paperweight caught his eye. In the light provided by a green-shaded banker's lamp Smailes thought he saw a name he recognized on a letter protruding from the pile. He looked more closely, and saw the elegant, copperplate signature of Lyle Pitkethly.

"I'm sorry, what?" said Smailes, looking up, disoriented.

"Nothing, nothing," said Lynch, waving his hand. Smailes thought he had heard him say, "I bet Clea's terrific," but did not want to believe it was true.

He waited twenty minutes, then half an hour, after

he heard Peter Lynch enter his bedroom and after the sounds of the plumbing finally died away. Then, slowly, he tiptoed down the hall and around the corner, the creaking of the boards sounding deafening in his ears. He entered the last door on the left quietly, without knocking.

His eyes were adjusted to the darkness, and he could see Clea sitting up in bed, breathing lightly.

"Derek, honestly. You took forever. You don't know how many schoolgirl fantasies I've had in this bed. Hurry up and get in."

Smailes sat on the edge of the bed and started to undress as Clea held back the covers. "There's not much room," he said. "Boy, you're warm."

"Warm? I'm on fire," she said, sitting up to pull her nightdress over her head. "We'll have to be awfully quiet."

The bed was so small and creaky they were compelled to make love extremely slowly, side by side. Their union seemed to last forever, and Clea had obviously been in a state of intense anticipation, for she reached her climax almost immediately, then almost a second time before he reached his. As they lay still he cradled her head in his hands and felt overwhelmed with his love for her. As usual, he could think of nothing to say. Eventually, he said quietly, "Hey, does your dad know Lyle Pitkethly?"

Clea raised herself slightly on an elbow. "Lyle? Good Lord, I don't think so. Why?"

"Thought I saw a letter from him just now in his study, after our little climb-up-on-my-knee session."

Clea laughed softly. "How was that?"

"Oh, I think I reassured him my intentions were honorable."

Clea relaxed again, and ran her hand from his shoulder to his hip. "God, Derek, that was fantastic, but you're going to have to go. We can't possibly both sleep here." She adjusted her position uncomfortably.

"Okay, just another minute. What are you going to do about the sheets?"

"Oh, throw them in the wash before we go. Mummy's a woman of the world."

"You're very much like her," he said, sitting up.

"You think so? That's a wonderful compliment."

"Get some sleep," he said. He rose and left the room, striding confidently back down the hall, oblivious to the sound of his footfalls, feeling invincible.

Smailes insisted that Clea drive the following day, not wishing to be immediately entrusted with an expensive car like the Peugeot, which had its steering wheel on the wrong side. They got a late start and stopped en route for a pub lunch north of London. After his first taste of a premium draught beer, Smailes' happiness was practically complete.

Smailes' mother was expecting them and greeted her expatriate son in her own characteristic way—she burst into tears. Flustered and embarrassed, she ushered them both into the tiny living room of her flat, holding on to Smailes' arm and trying to excuse herself to Clea. Smailes was touched to see that Clea had to brush aside a tear herself.

"Let me put the kettle on, Mrs. Smailes," she said, walking into the kitchen. "You sit down with Derek."

His mother, to Smailes' surprise, complied, and as they sat down on the worn chintz couch, she whispered in his ear, "Derek, she's very nice."

His mother's one-bedroom council flat, in which she had lived since her husband's death when Derek was a teenager, could not have stood in greater contrast to the Lynch mansion in Purley. Clea, however, was completely at ease, and soon the three of them were drinking tea and chatting away freely. Mrs. Smailes brought her son up to date on all manner of family news and gossip. She chided him for putting on weight, and Smailes told her not to embarrass him. For his part, he was heartened to see his mother in such robust health and spirits. She had not aged significantly in the three years since he had last seen her, except that her hair was now pure white.

"You mustn't let him get away with anything, love," she warned Clea. "He's very stubborn."

"Oh, I know, Mrs. Smailes," Clea replied, her eyes round with amusement.

"Call me Elsie, love. Everybody does. Now tell me what you're doing while you're here. I've barely got you twenty-four hours, you said, Derek."

"Right, well, I thought I'd give George Dearnley a call, see if he's up for visitors."

At the name of Smailes' former boss from the Cambridge police force, Derek's mother became grave.

"You heard about his stroke, didn't you?"

"Yes, you wrote."

"Well, give a call. I hear he's home from the hospital."

"Then I'm supposed to see Tracy at three. I dunno, I thought I'd take her into town, buy her some new clothes, have tea . . ."

"What are you going to do, love?" Mrs. Smailes asked Clea.

"Well, I think I'll go with Derek to meet George. He talks about him so much. But I think I'll leave father and daughter to themselves. I don't know, I'll probably look around the shops myself. Are they open on Sunday?"

"Oh, a few, probably. Then you're here for dinner?"

"Right," said Smailes.

"Neil and Denise are coming at six."

Smailes groaned. He had never gotten along well with his sister, and her husband drove him up the wall. "Not with the kids, I hope," he said.

"No, just the two of them. Isn't really the room here, I told her. Did you hear the younger one took up the trombone?"

"No!"

"Making Denise's life a misery. Honestly, I said to her . . ."

Smailes held up his hand. "Hold it, Mum. Let me call George's house."

"And you can't stay longer?"

"No, I've got a lunchtime meeting in London, and Clea has to prepare for an examination next week."

"We're talking about coming over for a longer visit in the summer, Mrs. Smailes," said Clea, meeting Smailes' surprised look evenly.

George Dearnley and his wife, Jill Wilde, lived in a big house off Grange Road, over in don country. Smailes pulled into the driveway and switched off the engine of the Peugeot, hesitating to get out. He had been acutely affected when he had learned of George's stroke just before Christmas. George Dearnley had been both boss and surrogate father to him during his time on the force, a man whom he trusted and respected like no other. Jill had explained moments earlier on the phone that the stroke had been only partially paralyzing, and the prospects for a significant recovery were encouraging. George, who had been head of Cambridge CID for fifteen years, was on indefinite medical leave from the force. But the problem, Jill explained, was George's mood. His incapacity had left him deeply depressed, and he did not really believe he would be well enough to walk again or resume his duties at the station. The main obstacle to George's recovery was psychological, in Jill's view. She strongly encouraged them both to come and visit. The afternoon was one of George's better times, and would probably do him the world of good, she said.

When Jill Wilde answered the door Smailes was immediately struck by how much she had aged. It was a second marriage for them both, and Jill was a good twenty years younger than George. She had to be about forty now, Smailes guessed, and although she still wore her brown hair long and loose, it was streaked with gray and her face was deeply lined. He wondered how she felt, having compromised her career as a crime reporter to marry George, and now finding herself housekeeper to an invalid. She greeted Smailes and Clea warmly, and showed them into the kitchen. A frisky spaniel leapt at

Smailes' hands; George's children were grown and married, and he and Jill had had none of their own.

"Just push him away, Derek. He's such a pest. Here, let me take your coats. George is waiting for you in the conservatory. It's so kind of you to come—he's been so excited. Through that way," she said, pointing.

Derek and Clea maneuvered around the furniture in the living room toward a solarium that Jill and George had built onto the back of their house. They stepped through French doors onto a red terra cotta tile floor. George was seated in a wheelchair just inside the door, a tartan travel rug across his knees.

Clea sat down on a white wicker settee next to a profusion of potted shrubs as Derek bent down and took George's right hand. The handshake was warm and firm. "How are you, George?" he asked.

Smailes squatted back on his haunches as Dearnley replied. His heart was torn to see his former boss. He had lost a lot of weight, and the features on the left of his face were canted downward where the paralysis had struck him. He still spoke clearly, although the words came slowly and had a nasal twang. He raised his right hand and made a poignant, shrugging gesture. Smailes could see that his eyes were moist.

"Oh, I dunno, Derek, can't really complain. I survived in one piece, and the physio says I should get most of my strength back along the left side. I can already walk with a stick, a bit. No need for built-up shoes, or anything like that, she says."

"You wait, you'll be back on the tennis court in no time," said Smailes, a little too heartily.

"Sit down, sit down. You can't squat there all day. And who's this you've brought to meet me?"

Smailes introduced Clea, who wisely complimented George on the beauty of his home and began asking questions about the addition of the conservatory. George warmed to the theme and was still explaining where they had picked out the floor tile when Jill came in carrying a tray, with yet more tea.

"George, are you boring your guests?" she chided him.

"George was just telling me how you designed your sun room. It's gorgeous," said Clea, springing to his defense.

Jill poured tea for them all, setting George's cup down on a wicker side table so he could reach it easily with his right hand. The conversation moved to New York, Clea's latest career move, and then the international situation. Dearnley had been instrumental in Smailes' recruitment into MI5 and knew better than to ask direct questions about his work.

Time passed easily and George showed no signs of depression or fatigue. Eventually Smailes looked at his watch and saw it was time to leave. Jill saw the gesture and began gathering the crockery onto the tray. Later, Smailes was unsure whether his sudden impulse to confide in his former boss was from compassion or some less noble motive, but he turned to Clea at that moment and said, "Will you give George and me a moment alone, honey?"

Clea rose immediately and said to Jill, "Here, let me help you." It was clear from her tone that she understood, and was not offended.

As Clea closed the glass door behind her, Smailes squatted forward again and took Dearnley's hand.

"I'll be all right, Derek," said Dearnley. "Jill's worried though. She thinks I'm depressed."

"Are you?"

"Derek, you can't imagine how hard this is," was all he would reply, and fell silent. "She's a beauty," he said eventually, meaning Clea.

"I know she is. George, do you remember Howard Grundy?" he asked.

George Dearnley listened with rapt attention as Smailes gave him a condensed history of the Colin operation, starting with the discovery of the bugging gear, through Howard's Riverdale intercept to Smailes' enticement and debriefing of the Soviet diplomat. Smailes was well aware that Dearnley knew Grundy from CID training school days, and thought the story would impress him. At first he seemed to be right. Dearnley's eyes widened as Smailes' story gathered momentum up to the present. Smailes knew that George could hardly have envisaged such possibilities for him when he acquiesced in Roger Standiforth's recruitment of him into MI5. But to his dismay, Dearnley exhibited no particular surprise. He merely sat silently for a long moment, then pulled his trademark expression of skepticism and annoyance, a pursing of the lips together with a vigorous shake of the jowls. With George's deformed mouth and shrunken cheeks, the gesture was almost unbearably poignant.

"How well do you know Howard Grundy?" he asked eventually.

"Quite well. Met him at Hendon, then again at the listening station outside St. Albans. He's swept our building in New York two, three times."

"That thing at the block of flats," said Dearnley. "Doesn't sound like Howard."

Smailes felt slightly foolish. Perhaps George disapproved of his protégé's divulging such sensitive information. He stood up awkwardly.

"Well, George, got to get going. Any idea what you buy for a fifteen-year-old these days?"

Dearnley held up his hand. "Look after yourself, Derek. Hang on to Clea."

"I will George. Keep your spirits up."

Derek Smailes and his daughter Tracy got along about as well as a teenage girl and an expatriate father could be expected to. Smailes dropped Clea at Lion Yard and drove out to his ex-wife's house in Histon, hardly recognizing her when she answered the door. It seemed another lifetime when they had met and fallen in love as sixth formers, lost their virginity together, then had their brief, unsuccessful marriage.

"Hello, Yvonne, how's life?" he said, stepping onto a

nylon shag carpet. Tracy bounded down the stairs, tossing a lock of orange hair out of her eyes.

"Hullo, Dad," she said, reaching up to kiss his cheek. She was wearing a shrill perfume and had a row of studs and pins punched into her left ear.

"My, my, Tracy. You look interesting."

"Don't start, Dad, okay? Did you get my Christmas present?"

"Yeah. Loved it."

"You could've written. Where are we going?"

"Sorry. It's up to you. I guess not to the swimming pool."

"Honestly, you sound more American than ever. Doesn't he, Mum?"

"Bring her back by half past five, Derek," said Yvonne tartly, retreating down the hall.

Tracy was already halfway out the door. "Boy, fancy car," she said, with a whistle of appreciation.

Smailes was not sure he could physically drink more tea, so the two of them toured the town center shops and record stores. To his relief they did not bump into Clea, which would have presented a collision of worlds he was unsure how to handle. Smailes bought his daughter a pair of jeans and a top, and a couple of cassettes of juvenile performers who looked like career criminals. Tracy teased him mercilessly about the kind of music he liked.

"Look, I just like to hear the words, Tracy," is all he would say in his own defense. But he knew she was enjoying herself when they ran into some boys she knew in a record store and introduced him proudly as "my dad from America." Smailes found himself distracted throughout the afternoon as he tried to decipher the import of George Dearnley's last remark about Grundy. Was he really suggesting that Howard would not have undertaken such a stunt? Could Kevin Butterworth have come to the same conclusion, and was that why Kevin had tried to see him in New York, in order to warn him? The question continued to gnaw at him through the banter with his daughter, and on a couple of occasions he missed remarks she made because of his preoccupation.

Eventually, they ended up in a crowded burger joint which in Smailes' day had been a quaint café that served cakes and tea in individual pots. Tracy had a diet soda and an order of chips and Smailes had a plastic cup of dreadful coffee. He still had not learned the inverse rule—never order coffee from the British.

Tracy wanted to know whether she would meet his new girlfriend, but Smailes said not on this trip, since he wasn't picking Clea up till six, and her mother wanted her back by five-thirty. They chatted more about her step-brothers, her friends, and what she did at school, and they were both disappointed when it was time to leave. As Smailes pulled up outside her house, however, he said he wanted to come in.

"Good. Are you going to stay to tea?"

"No, love. I just need to use the phone, if your mother will let me."

After a frown from Yvonne, Smailes got Howard Grundy's number from information and called through to his home outside St. Albans. Howard's mother answered.

"No, he's not here," she explained, after Smailes introduced himself. "He's at some conference in London all weekend. Won't be back till tonight." Smailes inquired whether he could ring the next day, or better, stop in and visit. He was driving down to London from Cambridge, he explained, and it would only involve a slight detour.

"Well, I don't see why not. He's on the afternoon shift at the center, and doesn't go in until half past one." The "center" she referred to was the Sandridge listening post, Howard's permanent assignment. "Can I tell him what it's about?"

"Just say it's Derek Smailes, and I'll be there about half past ten," he said.

"Do you need directions?"

"No, I've been there a couple of times before," said Smailes.

* * *

"So how did it go with Tracy?" said Clea, settling back into the passenger seat.

"It actually went very well," said Smailes. "We bought some clothes and tapes, had some tea. What did you do?"

"Oh, I looked around the shops a bit, but I decided to save the main action for tomorrow, when Mummy and I go to Knightsbridge. So I took a long walk along the Backs. It's so beautiful. Much nicer than Oxford."

"Oh yeah, change of plan there, honey," said Smailes, accelerating down Trumpington Street. "You remember Howard Grundy?"

"Of course. Your technical wizard friend."

"Right. I need to drive by St. Albans tomorrow to see him. Might take a while. Would you mind taking the train down? I can meet you somewhere with the car after you've finished your shopping trip. What are we doing, anyway?"

"Mummy's taking us out to dinner. Is something wrong?"

"No, no," said Smailes nonchalantly. "I just gave him a call on impulse, and he wants to have a chat about a couple of things. Only take an hour or so, but I don't want you to have to hang around."

"Of course, darling," said Clea dutifully. "Are you confident driving Mummy's car now?"

"Oh, Christ," said Smailes, pulling into the lot in front of his mother's flat and recognizing a blue Vauxhall. "My sister and her husband are already here. Prepare yourself."

Denise and Neil finally left and Clea helped Mrs. Smailes clear the table and wash the dishes. Smailes was aware he'd observed her minutely around his mother, and had detected not a trace of condescension in Clea's behavior toward her. He wasn't surprised, but subconsciously he knew she'd passed a big test. She'd even responded graciously to his sister's nosy inquiries and her husband's predictably asinine remarks. When his mother served steak pie for dinner and pronounced it Derek's favorite, Clea had even gamely taken a couple of bites and called it delicious. What more could a man ask of her?

At around nine o'clock the three of them were watching television when Mrs. Smailes got up to go to the bathroom. As she left the room, Clea asked in a whisper whether Derek had thought to pick anything up for his mother that afternoon, as a gift for putting them up. Smailes responded defensively that he hadn't even thought of it; it wasn't the kind of thing he did.

"Honestly, Derek, you're hopeless. Is there a shop open somewhere? At least I could get her a box of chocolates."

Smailes thought for a moment, annoyed at being made to feel delinquent. "Yes, there's a Pakistani grocery, I think, over on Histon Road. They're always open. But do you really think . . . ?"

"Give me the keys, Derek," she said, and was gone before his mother came back into the room.

16_____

The tall Russian dug the feet of the crowbar in next to the lock and leaned against the jamb with all his force. There was the sound of splintering wood and buckling metal, and then he stood back a pace and kicked viciously at the handle. The door did not give. After another couple of attempts, the Russian spun the crowbar in his hand and stove in the frosted glass panel with its heel, ignoring the sudden shriek of the alarm. He used a leather-clad elbow to punch out the remaining glass, then reached in and threw back the deadbolt. He stepped into the reception area and flipped on the lights.

Behind a desk that held a computer terminal stood a bank of filing cabinets, which held an array of potted plants and some toothpaste company ads. The Russian quickly scanned the drawer labels, then dug the crowbar in next to a top-drawer lock. It burst quickly, and he pawed through the files in the third drawer. He pulled out a file and opened it on the desk, photographing its pages quickly with a tiny, oblong camera. Then he tossed the file on the floor.

Working quickly and systematically, the Russian broke the locks in the remaining cabinets and dumped their drawer contents onto the floor at his feet. Then he smashed in the screen of the computer terminal with a backhand swipe of the crowbar and pushed it off the desk. Stepping carefully around the wreckage, he left by the broken door, leaving the lights on.

Smailes consulted Anthea Lynch's road atlas and resolved to take the A1 toward London rather than the motorway. After some trouble with a primitive manual choke, he finally got the car started, then went back up to the flat to make final arrangements with Clea; she would take a taxi to the station later that morning and meet up with him at six at a Knightsbridge restaurant that sounded vaguely famous. He headed west out of town and joined the A1 at St. Neots; he had begun to appreciate the big Peugeot and was well ahead of schedule by the time he hit the roundabout just above Hatfield where the minor road cut across toward St. Albans and the village of Sandridge.

The road curved gently through the placid spring landscape, yellow expanses of oil-seed rape alternating with cow pasture and ploughed fields. Presently he spotted the Sandridge church spire ahead above the hedgerows, and instinctively looked over his right shoulder. He found he could easily make out the upper gantry of the Sandridge station radio mast on the near horizon. Smailes had completed a four-month tour at the facility during his probationary year, and well remembered his shock on first driving up to the place back in the eighties. The listening post was approached via a single-lane road that wound through high banks of hawthorn and sycamore, past a farm and a riding stable; suddenly the hedgerows gave way and there it was, squatting like an ugly, bristling wart on the bucolic complexion of southern Hertfordshire. Low red brick buildings flanked a massive radio pylon that soared from behind a double chain-link perimeter fence like some mad inventor's folly. Originally built for the interception of German signals during the war, it was now operated by Five's radio technology directorate, scanning the airwaves for illicit domestic traffic, for the "fists" of illegals. It was unsignposted and unidentified, and the locals had come to ignore its presence, accepting that some vague, Home Office research was conducted there. Smailes had served in its security department, where he had renewed his acquaintance with Howard Grundy, one of its more talented, if eccentric listeners.

Smailes reached the roundabout at the main St. Albans road and swung right toward Sandridge, passing a prim cluster of maisonettes at the edge of the village. A road sign told him to slow to thirty, and he braked the Peugeot past a school and a mobile library trailer. He thought he saw Howard's street on his right but kept driving into the village center, where he turned around in the car park of the Green Man pub, which stood opposite the gray, pebble-fronted church. Proceeding carefully back down the St. Albans road he slowed and turned left into Hastings Crescent, the connections in his memory finally meshing. Howard was in fact a local man, and had returned to live with his widowed mother in their council home after he won the Sandridge posting. It was something of a joke that a well-paid technician like Grundy lived in subsidized housing, but it was a sensitive subject that Smailes had learned to avoid around him.

Hastings Crescent was a steep cul-de-sac of council houses that rose sharply from the main road, and Smailes stayed in second as he drove up to the turning circle to park. From the medley of front-door styles, bold emblems of Britain's new, enterprise culture, Smailes could tell the houses were now mostly owned by their former tenants. He remembered that Howard lived in number seventeen, but even if his memory had failed him the Grundy residence would have been self-evident; the thicket of radio antennas and the satellite dish on its roof gave it away immediately. Smailes stepped out of the car and drew his coat and scarf around him against the wind. The modest semidetached house with its stucco facing was like hundreds of thousands throughout Britain. At the end of an alley that ran alongside the house Smailes could see an island of garages, and a sign prohibiting ball games. He looked over his shoulder and saw a raked terrace of old people's bungalows directly opposite, whose lace-curtained windows showed no signs of life.

Smailes knew something was wrong as soon as he strode up the path and saw the front door standing ajar. He rapped on it forcefully and called out, hesitating only a second before pushing the door open with a foot and feeling it swing open freely. He stepped quickly into the dim hallway and caught his breath, fighting an instinct to vomit. At the bottom of the stairs the body of Howard's mother lay facedown in a dark lake of blood, a huge exit wound in the middle of her back. Her flowered housecoat was bunched obscenely around her thighs; the force of the bullet in her chest must have literally lifted her off her feet and spun her backward. Smailes stood transfixed for a moment in horror, then leapt over the body and bounded up the stairs two at a time, yelling Howard's name as he did so.

He was too late, of course. He had known it as soon as he had stepped into the hall. He headed straight at the top of the landing, to the back of the house where he remembered Howard kept his workshop. The room was a grotesque tableau. The bullet had caught Howard somewhere above the right temple, and he lay sprawled on his back beneath his computer table in a riot of wires and extension cords, with most of the roof of his head blown away. His office chair had tipped over and lolled stupidly against his knees. His spectacles had flown off but, absurdly, he still wore his headphones, held by their concertina cord into the front of his radio set. Of course, he had heard nothing of the silenced bullet that killed his mother, turning only when his murderer burst into the room. Smailes looked around. Darkening blood and pink cerebral tissue was sprayed everywhere across walls, the ham radio equipment, both computers and their banks of printers. There was still a faint smell of cordite in the room—Smailes estimated the Grundys had not been dead an hour. He looked again at Howard's mutilated skull; he remembered the size of the exit wound in Mrs. Grundy's back, and realized the killer had used soft ammunition, leaving nothing to chance. The radio set on the table below the window gave out a sudden squawk, and Smailes' heart leapt in terror. Then he understood that Howard had been interrupted in the middle of one of his morning chats with a fellow ham somewhere, murdered in cold blood while gassing about the weather with some other Howard, crouched over his equipment in Queens or São Paulo. Smailes wondered momentarily what the other man had thought when his connection had gone so suddenly and dramatically dead.

Smailes moved unsteadily across the landing to examine the chaos in the bedrooms. The murderer was a professional, that much was evident. Both dressers stood with all their drawers open, showing that the killer had gone at them from the bottom drawer up, the way a professional burglar always attacked that particular piece of furniture. The mattresses had been scored and gutted, and their innards cast onto the floor. In what Smailes assumed was Mrs. Grundy's room, the carpet had been pulled aside and some floorboards lifted. Since there was no sign of the use of force, he assumed the killer had found a secret hiding place. Smailes peered in and could see where the floor joists and plaster had been worn smooth by friction. By what object, Smailes wondered. A cash box? A one-time cipher kit?

He turned on his heel and started back down the stairs, wiping the banister with his scarf as he did so. At the bottom he turned and briefly contemplated the telephone on the hall stand, just beyond the body of the dead woman. But he quickly changed his mind, moving instead to the front door and opening it with his scarf wrapped around his hand. The door was not on the latch and locked behind him as he closed it. He hesitated a moment, adjusting to the light, then wound the scarf around his neck and moved quickly to the car. As he opened the driver's door he looked across to the bungalows and saw a curtain move as he ducked into the seat. Cursing under his breath, he backed up quickly and drove down to the main road, his mouth dry and his heart thudding against his chest.

The burglary was camouflage, obviously. Someone had silenced Howard Grundy to prevent Smailes speaking with him, just as Kevin Butterworth had been killed for the same reason, and the killer had been forced to include the mother in the hit. The murderer, or murderers, were pros, which suggested a contract job. Could that have been arranged in the handful of hours since Smailes had spoken with Grundy's mother? Possibly. But more likely the hit had been set up on his arrival in Britain. So had Howard been killed on the off chance Smailes would try and contact him? Unlikely. Neither could he believe that his visit and Grundy's murder were a coincidence. Everything pointed to the probability that, somehow, his call to Howard's mother from Cambridge had been intercepted, then a prearranged hit had been called.

Smailes gripped the steering wheel, the muscles of his jaw working angrily. He passed a road sign announcing the Town of Verulamium and glanced distractedly around at the large houses set back from the road behind bushes of lilac and laburnum. He had been spotted, that was the worst of it. The curtain in the bungalow window had moved, unmistakably. On the outskirts of the town he saw a call box and slowed to turn into a pub car park. He had to wait to pull in as a woman in a headscarf pedaled slowly by on a bicycle with a basket of groceries in front. Smailes entered the booth and lifted the receiver, his hands shaking slightly as he fished in his pockets for change. Roger's secretary Glenys answered the private line, then suddenly Standiforth's own voice came through urgently.

"Derek. Where the hell have you been? I've been phoning—"

"Roger, Howard Grundy's dead. And his mother. They were murdered about an hour ago. I've just found them."

There was a pause, then Standiforth said more calmly, "Where are you?"

"Just outside St. Albans."

"Be at the club in an hour. What does it look like?"

"Professional hit. Faked-up burglary. Listen, Roger. Someone saw me drive away."

Smailes heard a muttered curse, then Standiforth said, "I'll try and take care of it."

"I don't know if I can make it to the West End in an hour, Roger."

"I'll be waiting," Standiforth said, and hung up.

Smailes swung around the huge traffic island of Trafalgar Square and entered Pall Mall in a stream of taxis and government limousines. He drove past a towering statue of Clive of India, craning his neck for the numbers on the south side of the street. After several expensive travel agencies and exotic banks interspersed with government buildings, he suddenly saw a brass number plate next to a large, columned entrance, above a plaque with twin university crests. Improbably, in the heart of imperial London, there was a vacant meter directly outside the double front doors, to which was clamped an expensive-looking racing bicycle. Smailes parked and began clumsily feeding coins into the meter's mouth, when a voice behind him suddenly said, "Yo, mon!" He turned to confront a muscular young Rastafarian wearing a striped jersey and spandex racing pants, with a messenger pouch slung over his shoulder. Smailes stood aside as the man unlocked his bicycle, tossed the clamp into his pouch, then embarked recklessly into the tide of traffic, waxed locks streaming behind him. Smailes mounted the steps, crossed an acre of coconut mat, and entered the lobby.

Immediately on his left was a replica of a Cambridge porter's lodge, complete with a polished mahogany counter, a bank of wooden pigeonholes and a young uniformed porter waiting to greet him.

"Yes, sir?" the porter asked, in a distinct Ulster accent. He wore a formal jacket with a satin shawl collar.

"I'm here to meet Roger Standiforth," said Smailes. "I think he's a member."

The porter made a production of examining one of the leather-bound ledgers on the counter. Somewhere Smailes could hear a teleprinter chattering. The man looked up. "Mr. Smailes?"

"Right."

"Yes, Mr. Standiforth has booked the North Library. I'll show you up."

The man ducked into the doorway behind him and said something to a colleague. Then he emerged around the side of the counter and directed Smailes toward a marble staircase with brass stair-rods and a royal purple runner as wide as a goalmouth. Smailes padded obediently behind, his footsteps deadened by the thick shag. The two men passed one landing, which held an enormous portrait of Arthur Wellesley, the Duke of Wellington, past the doorways to a bar and a restaurant, and mounted to a second landing, where the porter opened a door and gestured for Smailes to enter. "This is the South Library, sir. The North Library is through that door," he said, pointing to its far end. Then he retreated, closing the door behind him.

Smailes found himself in a large, sunlit room which was carpeted with a huge Oriental rug. Glass-fronted bookshelves of dark wood rose from floor to ceiling around the walls, and maroon leather furniture stood in clusters around low coffee tables. He walked to the far door and opened it without knocking. The North Library was a smaller replica of its counterpart, except the bookshelves were of lighter wood and the furniture of green leather. Roger Standiforth stood in front of a tall window at the end of the room, his profile wreathed in cigarette smoke.

Smailes advanced without speaking. Standiforth turned and gestured to a coffee table that held a tray with an empty glass, a bottle of whiskey, a pitcher of water and a small tub of ice. The empty glass stood next to a silver cigarette case and lighter and a heavy glass ashtray which contained a single crushed butt. Standiforth had not been there long, Smailes reflected, pouring equal measures of whiskey and water into the glass. His next move was almost reflexive. With an interrogative lift of his eyebrows he picked up Roger's case and lighter, removed and lit a cigarette, then inhaled deeply. He had been quit for almost three years and the nicotine made his head spin. A swallow of Scotch restored his balance.

"Messy?" said Roger.

"Head shot, soft bullet. No way it wasn't going to be messy. He never knew what hit him, thank God."

Standiforth walked over to the window and looked down from his perch at the traffic below. "The woman who saw you leave the scene called the police," he said, without turning around. "Thought you looked suspicious. She gave them a pretty good description of you and your car and two digits from the number plate. The police have an all-points bulletin out for you. You're lucky you weren't picked up on the way here."

"Jesus Christ," said Smailes, pulling on his cigarette.

"I've got a call in to Waddington, but he's in a meeting till noon."

"Who's Waddington?"

"The commander of Special Branch. It's the only way I can handle it. But I think you can relax. We can eliminate you as a suspect, at least. Leaving the scene, failure to report, they'll accept that under the circumstances. Preventing them from questioning you might be a little more difficult."

"I don't mind talking to them, Roger. I've got nothing to hide."

"In the circumstances, it's out of the question. When you hear what I have to say, you'll understand. You say it had been made to look like a robbery?"

Smailes felt fortified by the drugs in his bloodstream. "Roger, that was no robbery," he said forcefully. "Even an armed burglar doesn't carry custom ammunition. I called Howard yesterday evening, and was on my way to see him. That's why he was murdered."

"I know you did," said Standiforth, finally turning to face him. Smailes had difficulty making out the expression on his face because of the intensity of the sunlight behind him. "The intercept report was on my desk first thing this morning."

Smailes shook his head in disbelief, and took another swallow of Scotch. "For Christ's sake, Roger. Please tell me what's going on."

Standiforth indicated that they should both take seats. Smailes felt like standing, but complied. He reached forward to stab out his cigarette in the tray. Roger sat down carefully, hoisting his pants by the crease above the knee, then adjusting his cuffs. Smailes saw he was wearing a dark blue suit, with a wide pinstripe, and a red tie. The shirt was pale blue with a white starched collar.

"A yellow file was opened on Howard last week. Nothing I could do about it," he began.

"A yellow file?" Smailes protested, well aware that such a step required strong prima facie evidence of treason. "On Howard? Whatever the hell for?"

"This is why I summoned you here at such short notice," Standiforth said. "What I am about to tell you is not top secret. It is ultra secret. Do you understand?"

"Yes," said Smailes without hesitation.

"The British and French are nearing completion of a joint satellite project, code-named Phoebus. Do you understand what that means?"

Smailes thought he might, but considered it wise to defer. "No," he said.

"If successfully deployed, it will give London and Paris independent verification capability of any European arms control agreement. Independent of Washington, that means. Now do you understand?"

Smailes saw the implications immediately. "Pretty high card to play in any new European security order?"

"Exactly. It would alter the balance of power within the Atlantic Alliance and allow us to stop kowtowing to those polysyllabic louts in Virginia. The CIA might finally stop treating us like a querulous and indigent relative," said Roger, jerking his chin back and forth in indignation. Smailes had rarely seen him exhibit such passion.

"So when was Washington going to learn about all this?" asked Smailes.

"After Oslo was the plan, after it was too late to change positions. But the existence of the damn thing has leaked. Washington is furious. And Howard Grundy had become the leading suspect."

Smailes suddenly recalled the news piece he'd read about the unscheduled Foreign Office mission to Washington, the talk at the Lynch party of unspecified "verification problems."

"Howard, disloyal?" Smailes responded. "Impossible."

"Percy and I happen to agree with you, at least that Howard could have been disloyal wittingly. But it may well be that Howard was led into an indiscretion without his knowledge. You know the Dufleur Company of Welwyn Garden City?"

"Yes, I've heard of them."

"They're the major contractor. Howard was called in as a consultant on some of the destination systems at the end of last year. With all his contacts at NSA, it's possible he let something slip on his last trip without realizing it, which has backfired in a big way. You know the sort of esoteric clubs these chaps tend to form."

Actually, as Smailes thought about it, it added up. He could quite imagine Howard letting some telltale detail slip in an innocent fit of braggadocio. Or being manipulated into such a slip, more probably.

Standiforth lit another cigarette and offered the open case to Smailes. Smailes shook his head and Roger continued.

"So anyway, Grundy's phone was tapped ten days ago. The DG personally ordered it and Percy got the Home Secretary's approval. He was due to face a committee of inquiry on Wednesday, which I felt at the time was quite unnecessary. But it may well explain the timing of his murder, rather than your visit, if Grundy was indeed a double."

"Howard Grundy a double agent? Roger, that's an outrageous idea."

"I agree, I agree, but the DG has got a bee in his bonnet about it. You see, we had to indoctrinate Pawson of A Branch because of the legal questions surrounding Colin's coming across to us, and he and Percy are bitter rivals, unfortunately. Pawson has latched on to this suspicion about Grundy to cast a pall over the whole Colin operation. He has even tried to persuade the DG that if Howard Grundy was a CIA recruit he may have planted that bugging equipment in the mission, the first time he swept the building. It might have been operational during that whole period, and God knows what else the Americans might have learned. And he's claiming this may explain Butterworth's murder, if Butterworth had in fact discovered Grundy's treachery and was trying to warn you."

Smailes thought for a moment. "Roger, Howard found that damned bug. No way could he have planted it. Kevin and I were with him the whole time, both times, remember? And Roger, Howard Grundy was not a CIA agent. I'd stake my career on it."

"Yes, yes, but he was due to appear before the high priests on Wednesday, and now he won't be able to testify. Convenient, don't you think?"

Smailes was trying to digest all this information. "I thought the Gaffer was practically retired," he said eventually, referring to the DG.

"So did we," Standiforth snapped back. "But he seems to regard the Colin operation as the swan song of his career. He's been getting more and more involved."

"To the annoyance of you and Price-Jones."

Standiforth glared at him, as if weighing a reprimand for impertinence, but did not contradict him. "We just want a step-by-step account of how that damn equipment was found. In your report it's unclear who spotted the irregularity on the video screen that led you to it. It was you, wasn't it? Or was it Butterworth?"

Smailes suddenly realized why he was meeting Roger in the seclusion of his club. "And you didn't want any of Pawson's or the DG's people seeing me around headquarters, right, in case they suspected something?"

Again, Standiforth did not reply, but Smailes could tell from the slightly injured look on the tapered features that he was correct. Smailes searched his memory carefully. "No," he asserted finally, "it was Howard himself who spotted it. I merely waved at the bank of screens and complained that we didn't have them hooked up to recorders. Kevin was standing with Howard, examining the harmonica bugs. Then Howard spotted the discrepancy in the resolution of the camera that had been fiddled with. Hardly reasonable behavior if he'd planted it himself, is it? And remember, there had definitely been a break-in. No question about that."

Standiforth looked visibly relieved and reached forward to replenish his Scotch. He dropped a couple of ice cubes into the amber liquor and rose again to look out of the window. Smailes changed his mind and extracted another of Roger's cigarettes. After all, he told himself, there were mitigating circumstances for his lapse.

Standiforth turned again to look at him. The feeling in the room was oddly intimate. "It could not have been simple burglary, could it? You know the rumor that Grundy and his mother didn't trust banks, that they kept money hidden around the house?"

Smailes had not heard the rumor, but it didn't sound out of character for Howard or his mother, from what he remembered of her. He thought of the smooth cavity underneath the floorboards in Mrs. Grundy's bedroom, and told Roger of it.

"So perhaps some cash was stolen?" said Roger hopefully. "Perhaps that was the motive."

"No way," said Smailes forcefully. "Professional villains like these know enough to wait until a house is empty. Easy enough to find out. No, these guys were experienced burglars, all right, maybe they did get a cash box or something, but that was bonus money. Howard and his mother were murdered in cold blood by a contract killer. The robbery part is just camouflage. And like I said, I don't mind explaining what I saw to the St. Albans police. If they're any good, they'll reach the same conclusion as me, anyway. It's pretty obvious."

Standiforth glanced down at his watch. "Look, I've got to call in, see what's developed, and see if I can get hold of Waddington. Stay here. We have more matters to discuss. You have your bag with you?"

Smailes nodded, puzzled by the question, but before he could respond Standiforth rose and strode quickly to the door. Smailes got up and paced round the room during Roger's absence. The volumes in the North Library seemed to comprise everything written about Oxford and Cambridge Universities since the invention of print. Smailes examined the leather spines, then the massive marble fireplace, next to which was inset an old-fashioned bellpull. A feeling of terrible foreboding was building in his chest. After what seemed an eternity, Standiforth returned.

"Well, you were right about one thing, this murder was carefully planned," he said, advancing to their table and picking up the remains of his drink. "It seems the woman who spotted you is a pensioner who lives alone with a bedridden husband. She spends every morning from about half past eight sitting at the front window, listening to the radio. At about nine-twenty this morning she took a call from someone claiming to represent a tour agent connected with the local Derby and Joan club. He gave her a long description of a Caribbean cruise they were offering to club members, and she was away from the window for about ten minutes, which must be when the murder was committed. As far as the local police can tell, the call was entirely spurious, designed only to get her away from the window. You're still a major suspect, of course, since she actually saw you leaving the house in a suspicious manner. But I've managed to give Waddington the full story and he's going to get straight on to the local superintendent, hopefully before the press is briefed. The police are working on robbery as the motive, thank goodness. Apparently the story of the two of them keeping money about the house was well known locally."

"Did Howard have a cover?"

"Computer programmer, Home Office statistical department," Standiforth replied. "It might even hold. Of course, Special Branch would love to speak to you too, but I've told them you're unavailable."

"What's going on, Roger? What's the problem with me telling them what I found?"

Standiforth paused and seemed to be searching carefully for the right words. "A hitch has arisen in the Colin operation, at the New York end. You have to return immediately, this afternoon."

Smailes was stunned. "Hitch? What kind of hitch? What are you talking about, Roger? Why didn't you tell me right away?"

"If you had listened to me this morning when you called through you would have heard me say I had been trying to locate you. I spoke to your mother this morning, but she said you'd already left. Then when you arrived I thought it prudent to dispatch our other business first." Standiforth seemed considerably calmer than half an hour earlier. He sat down again and leaned forward to drop fresh ice into his drink before continuing.

"Van Deusen cabled early this morning. You've been using some dentist's office as cover? Apparently it was broken into last night, around midnight, New York time. The dentist called the duty officer with his emergency code as soon as the police informed him. The duty officer called Ralph, who went into the cipher room and cabled."

Smailes was horrified. Dennis Dicenzo's dental office had been broken into? He had to be in a state of panic if he'd invoked emergency procedures. What the hell was going on? And was the New York break-in somehow linked to the murder of Howard Grundy?

"Roger, Jesus Christ, couldn't you have told me

straightaway? Can I get back by tonight? Colin has a regularly scheduled meeting at three that Ralph was going to handle. If Colin learns of the break-in, he'll be terrified."

"As I said, we had more pressing matters to discuss, I'm sure you'll agree. Yes, you can get back by this evening, so it happens, thanks to the time difference. The two o'clock and four o'clock flights are both full, unfortunately, and standby is far too risky. But we were able to get you on the Concorde. It leaves at five, and lands before it takes off, if you will, at half past four New York time." At this last piece of information Standiforth gave a slight pout of distaste.

"Roger, I dunno if I've got the cash or room on a credit card for that . . ."

"A courier is on his way over with the ticket, and will drive you to the airport. I think we should keep you and that maroon estate car quite separate for now, don't you? What is it, by the way? A hire car?"

"No, it belongs to Anthea Lynch."

"Good Lord, of course, I had forgotten all about you and Miss Lynch. Well, that complicates things a little. What were your arrangements for returning it?"

Smailes told Standiforth of the proposed rendezvous at the Knightsbridge restaurant. Standiforth took the information in his stride.

"The courier is Tennant," he said, "one of my more able assistants. He will drive you to Heathrow in a department vehicle, then return and take the other car to Knightsbridge for you. We should have him convey some pretext for your sudden departure. What should we say?"

"Roger, Clea knew I was on my way to visit Howard Grundy this morning, and she'll probably hear about the murder on the news tonight. I can't just tell her nothing."

"Well, write a note if you must, but keep it short and don't go into details, of course. She knows nothing of the Colin operation, does she?"

At this Smailes glared at Standiforth, angry at the imputation. "No. No, of course not, Roger. She knows nothing about it."

Standiforth rose and grabbed the bellpull. "I'll have the porter send up stationery. Tennant should be here shortly, and I suggest you leave immediately. You'll have plenty of time to get some lunch out there. We'll dine at the club some other time," he added with a weak smile.

The young Irish porter appeared in due course and Standiforth asked him for writing paper and envelopes. Smailes' expression clouded during their exchange, and as the porter withdrew he went back over some of the extraordinary information Standiforth had presented him with.

"So your interpretation is that Howard was silenced by the Americans, because he was due to face the high priests on Wednesday? That would be quite an overreaction, don't you think? And that my visit this morning was coincidence?"

"Well, that's my reluctant conclusion," said Standiforth uncomfortably.

"Look, Roger, maybe that's not it. Maybe that's not it at all. You see, I was going to visit Howard to check on how he first made that Riverdale intercept. Something I heard in Cambridge made me think twice about it. Now, Howard claimed he'd seen the building was under renovation while driving by on his way to a friend's on the West Side of Manhattan, but who knows? That could have been a cover. Maybe that's why Kev Butterworth was trying to see me in New York—maybe he'd come to the same conclusion. After all, isn't a bit of a long shot that Howard could have captured such a crystal-clear recording at the first attempt? Maybe we're being set up, Roger. If you were tapping Howard's phone, maybe someone else was, too, and called the hit to prevent me from finding this out, the same reason Kevin was killed. Maybe what all this means is that Colin is a dud, Roger. Maybe Colin has been a dangle from the beginning—"

"Nonsense!" Standiforth snapped back. "The JIC regards Colin as the best HUMINT source since Penkovsky," he said vehemently. "The quality of the Colin material has been literally beyond value. The prime minister wants to give him a bloody knighthood, for heaven's sake, and I think—"

"There are those who think Penkovsky was a dud, Roger," Smailes said quietly.

"Well they're bloody well wrong!" Standiforth shouted. "He helped avert nuclear war over Cuba, that's all! The people who say Penkovsky was a plant are crackpots, believe me." Standiforth glared across at him for a moment, then continued. "We've run every test we could on those initial recordings, and Colin has been telling the truth throughout, with a couple of irrelevant exceptions. Grundy insisted that intercept was completely random. You said you'd stake your career on the fact that Howard Grundy was not a CIA spy? Well, I'd stake mine on Mikhail Siskin's bona fides," said Standiforth, momentarily embarrassed that his anger had made him lapse from code.

"We will go ahead and bring him across," he said, regaining his composure, "with one exception. You need to evaluate what kind of trouble he is in. If it is clear that he has been blown by the KGB, we may have to drop him. He has served his major purpose, after all, and we can't risk an international incident at this stage. Find out what happened at this meeting and let me know exactly what's going on. The final decision will be the JIC's, but I'm sure that's what they'll say." Smailes thought momentarily of the commitment the British had made to Siskin's daughter, and was considering saying something when they were interrupted by a knock on the door. "Come in," Standiforth called, and a well-groomed young man in a dark blue suit entered the room.

"Ah, Tennant," said Standiforth. "Meet Smailes."

Smailes wondered whether they were to be further enlightened by Christian names, when Roger added, "Peter Tennant, meet Derek Smailes."

Smailes grasped a cold, firm hand. Tennant was a poker-faced fellow in his midtwenties who looked like he was not yet shaving regularly, but whose heavy jaw and lids gave the appearance of a perpetual scowl. "How do you do? The porter asked me to give you these," he said in an accent with a northern twang, handing over paper and envelopes. Peter Tennant gave the impression he had been groomed from infancy to be Roger Standiforth's dogsbody.

"Heathrow, isn't it?" he asked.

"That's right," Standiforth replied, then turned to Smailes. "Where is your car parked?"

"Right out front."

"Let me have the keys." Smailes complied. "Tennant, remove Mr. Smailes' bag from the car. And put something in the windscreen to prevent it getting a parking ticket. You're going to deliver it to Knightsbridge when you get back."

Tennant complied wordlessly and Smailes and Standiforth were left alone again. "Well, write your note," Standiforth instructed, and Smailes retreated to a writing table that stood next to the fireplace.

Smailes found the letter exceedingly difficult to write, and not only because Roger was standing in the room with him. After a couple of drafts he offered Clea the explanation that the fellow delivering the note had driven him to the airport, since he was needed back in New York immediately. He had had the shock of discovering Howard Grundy murdered that morning, but his superiors had explained his involvement to the police and he was under no suspicion nor in any personal danger. Neither should there be any repercussions for Clea or her family, he said. Knowing this was not enough, he said he hoped to be able to explain more fully, someday soon. And then, sensing the inadequacy of what he'd written, ended simply with "I love you." It was the first time he had pronounced it, even on paper. He signed, then added a postscript that Clea should not attempt to call him on an open transatlantic line. She should write and send the letter by diplomatic pouch, if she chose.

"Okay," said Smailes, swiveling as he licked and sealed the envelope. Standiforth was looking at him thoughtfully. As Smailes got up, Roger asked, "You haven't been talking to Vasily Malinovsky, have you?"

Smailes knew better than to pretend ignorance of Malinovsky's existence. "Of course not. Whatever gave you that idea?" he replied evenly.

"He's exactly the sort of nut case who thinks Penkovsky was a fake," he said. "And then that question you asked Colin, about the Ural bunkers. Malinovsky has been trying to peddle that theory around London and Washington for years."

Smailes thought quickly. "No, it was an ex-CIA contact who gave me that idea."

"And who is that, may I ask?"

"Rudy Kabalan," said Smailes, without hesitation. He could see Standiforth making a mental note to crunch the name through Data Center, to check the story.

"Well, goodbye," Standiforth said, holding out his hand. "Despite these violent developments, your visit has been worthwhile, for me at least. I know now that Grundy didn't plant that bugging equipment, which should cool off Pawson and the DG a bit."

Smailes shook his hand and turned to leave, but stopped and turned to face Standiforth again.

"Listen, Roger, if Howard's loyalty was in question, how about mine? Am I under some kind of suspicion too?"

Standiforth paused. "I will confess, when I saw the report this morning that you had telephoned him, a trace of doubt crossed my mind. But that's all it was, a trace. No, Derek, you have no motive for disloyalty that I can discern, and you're far too clever to be manipulated. I have the same confidence in you as I have in Colin," he added with a smile. It seemed a curious compliment.

The trip to Heathrow was completely wordless. Tennant drove skillfully at just under the speed limit. At Terminal Three the car pulled over and Smailes exchanged his letter for a ticket folder, then hoisted his bag from the back seat. "See you later," he said, and got out.

He checked in but didn't enter the special departure lounge immediately. He wandered over to the buffet for a beer and a sandwich, preoccupied by Standiforth's news, and still in shock from the grisly murder of his friend and colleague. He knew the murders of Grundy and Butterworth had to be connected, that both were professional hits, and felt a direct responsibility for both of their deaths. After completing his lunch, he walked over to a bank of telephones and called George Dearnley's house. Jill Wilde answered on the third ring. Smailes identified himself and asked to speak with George.

"He's napping, Derek," she said. "Can you call back later?"

"Wake him up, will you, Jill? It's urgent." She was clearly taken aback, but complied. After a long interval, Dearnley's voice came gruffly on the line.

"Derek. What's up?" he said. Quickly, Smailes explained his discovery of the Grundy murder, and asked Dearnley to explain his remarks to him the previous day.

"Like I said. Howard Grundy would always follow orders to a T, but not much personal initiative, I always thought. That thing at the block of flats, it didn't sound like him, that's all, unless he'd changed a lot."

Smailes asked Dearnley how good his contacts were in Chigwell and Brentwood these days. In his day, George had run a couple of the best underworld informants in East Anglia.

"I dunno, Derek," Dearnley responded suspiciously. "Harry the Fish still owes me a few. But he won't talk on the phone, and I don't know if I can get over there."

"Check him out, will you, George? See if he heard anything about a contract on a computer programmer in St. Albans? I know this was a paid job."

"Well, I suppose Jill could drive me across . . ."

"Please, George. I feel I owe it to Howard."

There was only a momentary hesitation. "What's your number in America?"

Smailes gave it immediately, ignoring the proscription he had given Clea. "I'll see what I can find, ring you in a few days," said Dearnley.

Smailes thanked him and hung up.

17

Ralph Van Deusen's office was filled with cigar smoke and venom. Ralph himself twitched angrily back and forth in his swivel chair, a cigar butt jammed between his lips. He was indignant on several counts. First, the setbacks in the Colin mission were clearly attributable to Smailes' delinquency, particularly his stupid trip to England. Second, he was incensed that Colin had bailed out of his regular Monday afternoon meeting, thereby denying Ralph the opportunity to definitively assume the reins of the operation. And third, and most galling, Smailes had arrived back in New York in time to attend the fallback, which Colin had invoked by calling through with an emergency code that afternoon.

Smailes was working on betraying no emotion whatsoever, listening in silence as Booth and Van Deusen brought him up to date on the dramatic developments of the last twenty-four hours. He had called the office from Kennedy as soon as he landed, and Booth had taken his call with astonishment that he had made it back with such speed. Smailes had offered something vague about tailwinds, not wishing to ignite Booth's envy or Van Deusen's wrath by reference to the mythic, unattainable machine in which he had traveled.

"I've never seen him so jumpy," Booth was saying.

"He kept looking back over his shoulder, and seemed to panic as he approached the building, then just kept going. He took a circular route back to the UN, stopping only once to buy a newspaper at the kiosk at Fifty-second and Third. I waited ten minutes then called through to Ralph, but when we got back here we found he had called in with the fallback code. Something has really scared him, Derek."

"Maybe he knows about the break-in at the dentist's," said Smailes.

"That's highly unlikely," Van Deusen growled.

"Well, maybe you're right," he responded. "Even assuming it was KGB, those records are solid. That can't have blown him." Smailes glanced down at his watch. It was six-thirty in New York, eleven-thirty London time.

"Could be a leak," Van Deusen continued. "I was against using that bloody dentist from the beginning." His face clouded, as if he was weighing some unpalatable truth. "Listen, that was the man I met, wasn't it, at that reception at the CG's place for the theater people?"

"Yes," said Smailes, unsure what was coming.

"So that means he's a queer and lives with that nignog, right?"

Smailes felt his face go scarlet. The obscenity hung in the room between them, poisoning the air like fecal gas. He could not look at Booth. Eventually, with some difficulty, Smailes said, "That's not quite how I'd put it, Ralph."

"Put it how you like, it's true," Van Deusen declared. "Wonderful material for indoctrination into the most sensitive intelligence operation we've ever attempted. There's your leak, if you ask me."

"I doubt it. I really doubt it. How did he sound when you spoke with him?"

"He sounded terrified," said Van Deusen, "particularly when I told him you were out of the country."

"And it was just the dental records that were ransacked?"

"That's right, and a computer smashed. Raw gold in the laboratory was untouched."

Smailes had to concede it looked bad, flawless records or not. "And so the fallback is at eight?" he asked rhetorically.

"Yes, and I'll be with you. Roger called this morning on the secure line to say you were on your way, and to authorize its use after we've met Colin. He and I agreed I should take part from now on. Seniority may be needed," he added tartly. Smailes doubted that was quite how the exchange had gone, but could easily visualize Standiforth's finally caving in to Ralph's indignant demands for inclusion. He winced inwardly, but thought it wise to comply. "Okay. I think I'll get coffee and something to eat. You free, Graham?"

"Of course," said Graham. "You want a watcher detail tonight too?"

"No," said Van Deusen.

"Yes," said Smailes simultaneously.

Van Deusen glared at Smailes and seized the opportunity to pull rank. "Damn it, man," he said, "we don't even know what direction he's coming from, how can we give Graham a watcher detail? I'm running this operation, and I say no."

Smailes had to concede the point, although in his view it might still have been worthwhile to monitor the building entrance. Again, he decided against confrontation, shrugged and rose to leave. Booth had remained seated, but suddenly Van Deusen dismissed him and asked Smailes to stay. "So what did Roger want?" he asked after Booth had left the room.

Smailes had been expecting the question. "I'm not really at liberty to say," he replied, which was technically correct. "It didn't relate directly to the Colin operation, if that's what you're wondering. Internal stuff," he offered.

Van Deusen was clearly angered by the defiance, but knew he had no means of prying the information out of him. Smailes had decided much earlier that day to omit any knowledge of the Grundy murder. He would have to feign shock and surprise when the account reached New York via memo or the London press, but preferred that option. As far as he was concerned, the less Ralph Van Deusen knew about anything, the better.

Darkness had fallen over Manhattan by the time Mikhail Siskin arrived for the fallback, and Smailes, glassy from jet lag, was on his third cup of sour coffee. Ralph, after some barbed comments about the imbecility of the office decor, had fallen silent, and the two men had sat for almost an hour with only the occasional awkward exchange. Ralph had taken Smailes' customary seat behind the desk to emphasize his station, and Smailes sat to his left. Both men straightened as their quarry came into the room. Siskin closed the door and moved wordlessly to his usual chair. Then he lifted his eyes and looked at the two men. He looked truly terrible.

"Who the hell is *he?*" he asked, indicating Van Deusen with his head.

"This is Bruce, Misha. My superior officer. You have heard me mention him, I believe. How are you?"

"There is a leak," said Siskin in anguish. "My career is destroyed."

"Why do you say that?" Smailes asked evenly.

Siskin glared at him with red-rimmed eyes. "I say that because I know that. On Friday, I come back to my office and find Malik going through the papers in my desk. Completely brazenly."

"Malik is the KGB officer on your staff?" asked Smailes mildly, largely for Ralph's benefit.

"Yes, yes, of course. How many times do I have to tell you? Then this weekend, we go to Glen Cove as usual, and this new man, Kirilenko he said was his name, would not leave Tatanya or me alone. Said he was a new appointee to the trade mission and wanted advice about life in New York, but he kept asking us all kinds of questions about our past, and our present work. Again, completely, totally blatant."

"Could just be routine," Smailes volunteered.

"You've said yourself, the KGB station has been excessively jumpy lately."

"Shut up!" Siskin shouted. "Let me finish, can you? So today, this morning, I am summoned by the ambassador to the mission, and I'm told quite casually I am being recalled directly to Moscow after the Oslo summit, 'for consultations.' Ha! I know the kind of consultations that means. Consultations in the basement of the Lubianka, that means. God, was I a fool to ever cooperate with you." He raised his eyes again briefly to the two men, then looked away in anguish. Smailes' earlier doubts about Siskin were evaporating; if Siskin was acting, he was certainly doing a superb job.

Ralph spoke up for the first time. "How did the ambassador give you the news, Mikhail? Could it perhaps be a legitimate request?"

Siskin ignored him, turning on Smailes with a look of loathing. "Let us stop this stupid pretense, George," said Siskin, in a voice thick with sarcasm. "You see, I now know who you are. You are Mr. Derek Smailes, junior security officer at the British Mission. So who is this man you have brought with you? The custodian?"

Smailes was stunned, and could find no immediate reply.

Siskin continued. "You see, after I told Tatanya what had happened this lunchtime, she took the risk of examining the photographic files in the *referentura*. She remembered clearly what you looked like from the reception at the UN. It was dangerous, but we needed to know with whom we were really dealing. And so it seems you are not even an intelligence officer. Why does your government send me such an amateur? Or does your government even know of our meetings?"

Smailes tried to respond, but found his capacity for artifice had suddenly failed him. Van Deusen intervened again. "You're quite right, Mikhail. George is indeed of junior rank, and you are correct about his real name. But I am head of station here, and have monitored all his activities, and he has acted throughout with the full approval and authority of the British government. You can rest assured on that score."

"Rest assured!" Siskin retorted derisively. "Rest assured! There is a leak, I am blown, and I know who is responsible. It is that shit-eater girlfriend of yours, Mr. Smailes. She knows of our collaboration and has betrayed me to the KGB."

"Who?" asked Smailes, astonished.

"Miss Clea Lynch, I think is her name, isn't it? She is listed in your file, along with some rather telling details. Did you know, for instance, that she belonged to the Socialist Society at Oxford University, and that her last lover was an exiled Argentinian terrorist? She is exactly the kind of ideological recruit the KGB has by the dozen. Shit-eaters, we call them. You see, we regard any Westerner who works without pay for Soviet intelligence as beneath contempt."

Smailes' grip upon reality was slackening. The KGB kept a file on him that included details of his relationship with Clea? But so what if she had joined a left-wing club at Oxford? And Raul, the steakhouse waiter, an Argentine terrorist? It was a ridiculous notion.

Ralph took advantage of Smailes' confusion to continue to take the initiative. "Why did you not turn up this afternoon?" he asked.

"I have been in a state of panic all day. I could not be sure I was not being followed. I have often been working late recently. It was safer for me to come here by taxi after all my staff had left. I cannot stay long. You must help me. You have done this to me. You have made me risk my career and my family's safety."

"Relax, Mikhail," said Ralph unctuously, "we won't let you down. I will communicate with London immediately. Perhaps I can gain authorization for an exit from Oslo. Your family could seek asylum in New York and be brought across directly from here. How soon do you leave?"

"It is the end of next week. Can we not do something before then, from New York?"

"I doubt my government would allow it, although I will ask them for you," said Ralph. Smailes had regained himself somewhat, and now felt threatened by Ralph's usurping his role. By mutual consent, the British had agreed to omit any details of the dental office break-in, if it appeared Siskin knew nothing of it, and Smailes hoped the bravado in his voice masked his deception.

"Listen, Mikhail, none of these developments means you're blown. Okay, so perhaps you're under suspicion, but given the level of tension in your colony at the moment, many diplomats probably are. You have a reputation for nonconformism, after all. It's probably just routine surveillance activities that have been focused on you. There is no leak at our end, believe me, and particularly not from Miss Lynch. She knows nothing, I repeat, nothing, about this operation. If you can sit tight, as Bruce says, we will simply bring forward your exit to Oslo itself."

Siskin looked from Smailes to Van Deusen, then back again, as if weighing whether either of them could be trusted. Then he said moodily, "All right. I suppose I have no choice. How will you inform me of the plan? I do not wish to risk any more meetings."

"We'll need to meet just one more time, Mikhail," said Van Deusen, "to confirm details. Let's say the usual time, one week from today. Do you have any further questions? You know how to contact us in an emergency."

Siskin sat silently for a long moment, as if pondering his predicament. Smailes was sure he was well aware the British could simply drop him at this point, cut him loose, and he would have absolutely no recourse. What had been Standiforth's phrase? He had served his purpose, after all.

"It's all going to work out fine, Misha," Smailes offered weakly.

Siskin rose slowly from his chair. "I wish I could believe you. Now I must go."

As he turned to leave, Van Deusen spoke up again. "One more meeting, Mikhail, is all we will need. Next

Monday, same fallback. As George says, just sit tight, and everything can still go smoothly."

Siskin looked down at Van Deusen, then across at Smailes again. He had a wounded look that told Smailes he held him personally responsible for the danger he and his family were in. It was a responsibility Smailes could hardly deny. As the door closed and the footsteps receded, Ralph reached inside the desk drawer to switch off the recording gear, then said to Smailes, "This doesn't look good, Derek. And that was a peculiar accusation against the Lynch girl."

Smailes did not immediately respond, because he had just remembered something that had made his stomach lurch with fear.

"Peculiar, don't you think?" Ralph repeated. "Of course, London will have to hear of it. It's all on tape."

Smailes emerged from his reverie and mustered a reply. "Ridiculous, Ralph. Absolutely bloody ridiculous," he said, with an odd lack of conviction in his voice.

Smailes had one more trip to make that night before he could finally return to Brooklyn and collapse. He had called both Dennis Dicenzo's office and home numbers before leaving for the Colin fallback, and had gotten no reply at either. But at the home number he had left a message on an answering machine that he would try and stop by before ten-thirty. He hoped Dennis had retrieved the message and would be there to receive him.

As his taxi bounced south toward Greenwich Village, Smailes speculated a little about Dennis' frame of mind. Doubtless, it could hardly be good, since the very things he had feared and about which Smailes had so confidently reassured him, had in fact come to pass. There was also the unknown factor of whether Tyler had learned of his lover's reversal of his earlier decision, and what his reaction had been. As he paid off the driver and headed for the bank of doorbells beside the building entrance, Smailes found himself hoping that Dennis was alone and that his acerbic companion was out for the evening.

Dennis' voice came over the intercom. "Yes?" he asked.

"It's me. Derek."

"Goddamn it, Derek. If I'd been in to take your call, I would have told you not to bother. I don't want to have anything more to do with you."

"Please, Dennis. Just a couple of minutes. I heard what happened. I'm really sorry."

"Sorry?" Then a pause. "I thought you were out of the country."

"I got back this evening."

There was another pause, then the rasp of the release buzzer. Smailes pushed the door open and headed for the elevators.

Dicenzo answered his door without looking at Smailes. As usual, he was dressed immaculately in gray gabardine slacks and a fawn cardigan. He retreated back into his living room, and Smailes followed him.

"You want a drink?" he asked. Smailes noticed a glass of Scotch on the coffee table.

"Sure. Whiskey would be great. A little water," he said. "What happened?" he asked, after accepting his glass from Dicenzo.

Dennis looked at him directly for the first time. "Last night, about one-thirty, the police called. They'd responded to a call from my alarm company after those . . . whoever it was . . . broke into the office. Of course, I got up and started to dress immediately, but Tyler had woken up, obviously, and asked me what was going on. I told him there'd been a break-in, and he just came straight out and asked me whether I'd cooperated with you after all. I couldn't deceive him any longer, you see, so I admitted it. When I came out of the bathroom he wouldn't even speak to me. I think he felt betrayed. Then when I got back, around three, he had left. He's even taken an overnight bag with him, and I've no idea where he's gone. Honestly, I think he may have left for good."

Here Dicenzo's voice broke slightly, and he reached down for his drink. "So you can hardly be surprised that I didn't want to see you, can you?" He looked across at Smailes despairingly.

"What was the scene at your office?"

"An incredible mess. They had broken into the filing cabinets in Roz's office and thrown the records around the room. Smashed her computer. I don't think they had even been into the other rooms. I've got seven or eight ounces of gold and all kinds of drugs in the lab, thousands of dollars worth of equipment in the operatory, but none of it had been touched. The police said the burglars must have hidden in the stairwell during the day, then broken in after the cleaning staff left."

"What kind of questions did they ask? The police. What did you tell them?"

"Well, after it became obvious that nothing of value had been taken, they asked me whether I could think of a motive for the burglary."

"And?"

"I lied. I said I couldn't think of anything. I went in early this morning and gave the staff the day off. I've been there alone, trying to clean up, most of the day."

Smailes breathed an inward sigh of relief. "Dennis, those records for Mikhail Siskin. Were they up to date?"

"Yes, we updated them every week, like we agreed."

"We?"

"Yes, Alison and I. Alison is my hygienist, my assistant. She actually makes up the charts. I wanted them to be completely authentic, like you said."

"Did she think it was weird?"

"At first. Then she stopped asking about it."

"Could she have told someone, if she was asked about it casually, in a bar or somewhere?"

"No. I don't think so. She'd have told me. She's very reliable."

"How about Tyler? You think he might have learned of what you were doing earlier than you know?"

Dicenzo's anger rose. "Honestly, Derek, you've got a damn nerve asking such a question . . ."

Smailes was about to apologize, but both men were

distracted by the sound of a key in the lock. The door swung open and Tyler Dawes entered, wearing a black leather coat, dark glasses, and a black pillbox cap. He was carrying a shoulder bag. He said nothing, but dropped the bag on the floor and advanced toward Dicenzo. Dennis walked toward him, and then the two men embraced silently. Tyler's hands clenched across Dennis' back as their embrace extended, and then Dennis broke away and said, "I'm sorry," in a voice thick with emotion.

"It's okay," said Tyler. "You're a crazy fool and that's one of the reasons I love you." It was clear from his voice that he had been drinking. Then he looked over at Smailes, who had begun feeling very uncomfortable.

"Well, if it ain't our spooky British friend," said Tyler sarcastically. "I keep interrupting the two of you."

"I was just telling Derek what happened," Dennis explained.

"Tell him to get his racist ass out of our apartment," Tyler said in a voice knife-edged with bitterness.

"Tyler!" Dicenzo said, remonstrating.

"No, Dennis, you wouldn't notice," said Dawes, rounding on Smailes unsteadily. "But I do, see? I notice the hate in his voice when he tells his stories about black hoods on the subway. I notice the way he treats me."

Smailes face was burning. "How do I treat you, Tyler?" he asked.

"You treat me like I'm a freak, that's what. You treat me like you can't quite believe I'm as smart as I am, because of the color of my face, right? You try a little too hard, see, because you want me to like you, to placate your conscience about the bigot you really are. But I see right through you. And I see a two-faced white man who thinks he rejects racism, then holds his breath when he passes us on the street."

Again, Dicenzo tried to intervene. "Tyler, that's not fair," he said quietly.

"Oh, it's fair, all right, and if Mr. Smailes here looks inside himself, he might even admit it. See, Derek, it's almost easier for me to handle the kind of prejudice that's out front, like that jerk you work with, who couldn't even shake my hand. I'm real familiar with that. It's the phony liberals like you I can't take."

Smailes was fighting something inside that was approaching panic. There was too much truth in what Dawes was saying for him to issue a flat denial.

"Now, there's another reason Mr. Smailes is friendly with me," Dawes continued, turning back to address Dicenzo. "You see, I'm what he would accept as a nonthreatening black, because my face looks almost white, right? But how would he feel if I had a nose like a cauliflower, and lips like two salamis? Pretty uncomfortable, I would say. Always been the same for white folks. Someone like me would have fetched a higher price back in the good old days of the slave auctions, see." Tyler turned back to face Smailes angrily. "You know what this face means, Mr. Smailes? It means that somewhere in my past, Ol' Whitey got his leg across Mother Africa, that's what it means."

Tyler Dawes turned away from Smailes in disgust, picked up his shoulder bag, and went into the bedroom. Smailes stood rooted to his spot, struggling against a riot of emotions. Eventually, he said quietly, "I think I'd better leave."

"Don't take it to heart, Derek," said Dennis. "He gets like this sometimes, when he's been drinking. Even with me."

"Tell him I'm sorry he feels that way, and that I think some of it's true," he offered, feeling an overwhelming sense of shame. He walked slowly toward the door, then realized his business with Dicenzo was not quite finished.

"Dennis," he asked, "did you bill the Soviets for the work you were supposedly doing on Siskin?"

"No, of course not. I didn't want to get paid for work I wasn't actually doing. That would have been fraud."

Smailes was furious with himself for the stupid oversight. "Listen, do me a favor and send in a bill, will you?"

"I think I've done you enough favors," said Dicenzo firmly. "Goodnight, Derek," he said, opening the door.

Smailes finally found a cab driver who claimed to know where Brooklyn was, and collapsed into the back seat, dizzy with fatigue. He could hardly believe that the same morning he had woken in the living room of his mother's flat, given the day's developments. He felt an unfamiliar tug in his bloodstream, and realized that he needed a cigarette. He considered telling the driver to stop so he could buy some, then admonished himself angrily.

He reviewed the accomplishments of his day. Howard Grundy was dead, and Smailes knew he was in some way responsible. Mikhail Siskin was very probably blown, and Smailes did not doubt he was partly responsible there also. Dennis Dicenzo's office had been wrecked and his life disrupted, and there Smailes was very definitely responsible. And Tyler Dawes had forced him to confront some of his most shameful prejudices, prejudices he had not even realized were there. He was responsible for those, too. Then, remembering events before Christmas, Smailes had to conclude he was also responsible for the murder of his talented young friend, Butterworth. But as the taxi lurched up the ramp to the Brooklyn Bridge, Smailes' mind lingered on none of these troubling particulars. Smailes' mind was dwelling on what, to him, was the most extraordinary revelation of that extraordinary day, that the KGB kept a file on him, and that in that file were listed details of his relationship with Clea Lynch. And while he tried to dismiss any notion that Clea might be disloyal as preposterous, his thoughts kept returning to the previous evening, when Clea had left the apartment, after she had learned of his switch of plan to visit Howard Grundy. She had said she was going to buy chocolates, as a gift for his mother.

Grigori Chumak entered the Soviet president's official dacha at Barvikha with the proprietorial air of one who knew his privileged access could not be challenged. The contrast with the hunting lodge at Zavidovo could not have been greater. A large security and communications station formed the only public access, and Chumak endured the light frisking of the Ninth Directorate guards with an air of taxed patience. Rostov's personal bodyguard, Prokhanov, even asked to see the unmarked envelope he was holding, but Chumak defied him, telling him its contents were for the president's eyes only. With a shrug Prokhanov let him through, opening the door to the sitting room for him.

Nikolai Rostov put down the briefing papers he had been studying and rose to meet his military intelligence chief. Chumak advanced across the thick pile of the white woolen carpet, noticing that, as usual, American jazz was emanating from the West German stereo on the Danish wall unit in the corner. The white brocade furniture had been imported from Hong Kong, as had the table lamps and their rosewood stands; the only domestic touches were the Uzbek rug beneath the huge coffee table and the nineteenth-century landscape above the fireplace. Chumak offered a broad smile to counter his boss's concerned expression.

"I had rather we not meet here, Grigori," said Rostov.

"I have it, Nikolenka," said Chumak, tossing his envelope onto the coffee table in front of him. "The evidence of Kott's link man in the West. I knew if I spent long enough in the archives, something would turn up. I didn't think you would want this to wait until Monday."

Rostov picked up the packet and removed two eight-by-six black-and-white photographs, and one more recent color photograph. The quality of the older photographs was poor, so Rostov moved over to the huge picture window to look at them more closely. After examining them both and comparing them to the third, he said slowly, "Yes, I see. And who is this person?"

Chumak gave a name and an affiliation.

"And where is he now?"

"New York."

"So the transmissions to the Eastern United States . . . ?"

"Exactly."

"I agree, these are highly compromising. The question is, what should we do with them?"

"You want my advice, Nikolai? Let's ignore them. We don't want anything to upset momentum at this stage—Oslo is less than two weeks away."

Rostov thought for a long moment. "No," he said eventually. "Let us send a good-faith warning to our new British friends. It will pay off in the long run. Send a courier, someone completely reliable."

Chumak plainly did not like the decision, but knew better than to challenge Rostov, who was still staring out of the window.

"Maybe Palov?" Chumak offered.

"Who is Palov again? Our man in the Carpathian command?" responded Rostov, without turning around.

"Yes."

"What do you think, Grigori?" asked Rostov, indicating the bare limbs of the birch trees. "You think spring will be late this year?"

18

Smailes woke late and lingered over his ablutions, needing time to gather his thoughts. He ate a slow breakfast, then left the flat and crossed Adams Street, strolling past the gray Brooklyn courthouses into the enchanted ghetto of Brooklyn Heights, heading for his garage. By the time he emerged into the midmorning traffic, the questions arising from the previous day were largely in focus, although the answers remained cloudy in his mind.

The major likelihood was that Colin was indeed blown, although that did not mean that the British could not still bring him across, if they chose. It was a definite possibility that the combination of stepped-up security together with Smailes' oversight regarding dental bills had called attention to him, and that the KGB now had a strong circumstantial case against him. But the possibility also remained of a leak, in which case the KGB was holding concrete evidence and was indeed planning an arrest and interrogation back in Moscow.

But where could the leak be? On the Russian end? With Tatanya, or perhaps even Irina herself, in some unwitting way? Or what about Dennis Dicenzo? Had the reconciliation scene Smailes had witnessed the previous evening been stage-managed for his benefit? Had Tyler discovered Dicenzo's deception earlier and insisted upon blowing a whistle to teach both Smailes and Dennis a lesson? Such a stunt would be well within Tyler's capability, he felt. And what about the British end? What about the skeletons in Ralph Van Deusen's closet, which Peter Lynch had drunkenly revealed over brandies in Purley? Had Van Deusen been entrapped by the Soviets all that time ago, and been blackmailed by them ever since? The possibility could not be ruled out. Yet whatever explanation his mind entertained, his private thoughts always came full circle and sank into the same deepening trough of doubt. Was Clea, as Siskin himself had protested, really the leak? Had her naïveté and idealism led her into a relationship with the Soviets from which she could not now extricate herself? Had she learned much more about the Colin mission than she had allowed? Or perhaps Smailes' evaluation of her was fatally flawed. Perhaps she was as cynical and ruthless as he did not doubt her father could be. Perhaps her whole relationship with Derek Smailes was an exercise, designed to test her commitment to her real masters. This train of thought opened a raw vein of insecurity within him, since he had always secretly feared she was unattainable, in some ineluctable, British way. Could she really be as in love with him as she appeared? Some voice inside warned him it had always been too good to be true.

It was well after eleven when Smailes walked distractedly into his office, and Booth greeted him with a silent grimace and a theatrical gesture toward Van Deusen's office. Smailes hung up his coat without speaking and walked across to the outer office. Madge looked up from her typewriter with her typical expression of martyred annoyance.

"He's been here since I don't know when, Derek. Asked to see you as soon as you came in. He even had me call you half an hour ago, to see whether you were taking a day off, but you must have been on your way."

"Thanks for the warning," said Smailes, rapping on the inner door and opening it at Ralph's gruff response.

"Morning, Ralph," Smailes ventured, moving to sit

down. Van Deusen removed his cigar very slowly and glared at him. Smailes could tell he was very angry.

"Why didn't you inform me of Howard Grundy's murder?" he asked.

"That wasn't my place, Ralph. I didn't know what kind of spin Curzon Street was going to put on it, whether anyone was supposed to learn of my involvement. Roger told you?"

"Of course. And please don't use such terms. MI5 offers interpretations, it doesn't 'put spin' on things." Ralph jutted his chin forward in irritation and rotated his neck to free its wattle from his collar. "I came in at six to speak to the Director D at midmorning, London time. He wants you to call him on the secure link as soon as you arrive." At this point, Van Deusen made a production of examining his watch, as if to underscore the sheer scale of Smailes' lateness. It was typical of Ralph to refer to Standiforth as Director D, a title rarely used since reorganization in the seventies. "I suppose he'll still be there."

Smailes said nothing and Ralph gave his cigar a couple of violent puffs. "He seemed to assume I would know of the Grundy murder, since, as he had to explain, my own assistant had found the body. He said he thinks they've contained the story, at least so far."

Smailes was relieved to hear it. "What did you tell him of last night's meeting?"

"A fairly detailed summary, including Colin's own conjectures. Plus my own evaluation, that he's blown and we should play it very safe from now on. I had Madge send the tape in this morning's bag."

"And?"

"Roger says there's a meeting of the JIC tomorrow morning, that the issue will probably be decided there. Either way, we'll have a ruling before next Monday's meeting."

Smailes decided he owed Van Deusen something further. "Look, Ralph, I'm sorry you had to learn of Howard's murder from Roger. But he'd given me no instructions, so what could I do?"

Van Deusen seemed somewhat mollified. "Who do we think is responsible?"

Smailes let out a sigh. "There's a faction thinks Howard was working for the Americans. That's why Roger wanted to see me, to ask whether I had any inkling of it. Howard was due to face the high priests on Wednesday and Roger thinks that's why he was killed. The faction also thinks Butterworth was killed because he'd found it out."

Van Deusen's eyes widened and he rocked way back in his chair. "Good Lord, Derek. What do you think?"

"That Howard was working for the Americans? I think it's a ridiculous idea. But frankly, I never believed Kev Butterworth was a mugging victim, did you?"

Ralph was still weighing the news, and ignored Smailes' question. "The Americans?" he repeated in disbelief.

"Look," said Smailes, "I'd better go call London. Anything else?"

"No. Not yet."

Smailes knew that Ralph's feelings were still smarting from his omission over Howard's murder. For such a bellicose character, he had a remarkably thin skin. "Look, Ralph, I'm glad you're in on the Colin operation now, however it turns out," he lied.

"So am I," Van Deusen replied, looking up. "You recovered from your trip?"

"I feel fine," said Smailes, which was also a lie.

The secure link to London was a piece of MI5 equipment in the fort which represented the Rolls-Royce of the British Mission's voice encryption systems. Many of the senior diplomats' phones had simple but effective scramblers that could defeat most eavesdropping efforts, but the secure link, which had entailed the installation of parallel equipment around the globe in Five's several outposts, was ironclad. Smailes picked up the receiver that stood on top of its innocuous-looking, briefcase-size tan box, and punched in the numbers for Five's reciprocal machine in

Curzon Street. When it was answered by an operator, Smailes called out "Seven" off the top of his head and pressed the digit, listening for the beep at the other end as the operator followed suit. Then he said "Secure" and flipped the On switch on the encryption unit. He listened to the whooping and shrieking as the two units searched through their vast algorithmic loop for the first common point at which to communicate, then heard the yodel as the two units "shook hands," as Howard Grundy had always called it. The sound somehow made him think of an electronic orgasm. When the operator's voice came back to him, it was metallic and choppy, as if the person were talking into a tin cup through an electric fan. The distortion, a minor inconvenience at worst, reflected what was lost as the analog signal of the speaker's voice was converted to a digital approximation several thousand times a second, then bounced off a communications satellite and retranslated into analog sound waves by the encryption unit at the other end.

"This is George in New York. I'd like to speak with Nigel," said Smailes, observing code conventions despite the miraculous wreckage of the telephone signal. He paused while the operator fell silent as he scanned his printout of code names, then summoned Roger Standiforth on another line. Presently Standiforth came through, his perfect vowels barely damaged by the violence of the encryption.

"George. How are you?" he asked.

"I'm fine. What's new at your end?"

"The St. Albans police will take our word on the innocence of your involvement, and we got to them before they said anything official to the press."

"Good."

"They are treating it as a botched armed robbery, and so far the newspapers are going along with it, we think."

"Great."

"What was your impression of Colin last night?"

Smailes paused as he composed his answer, realizing

this question was probably the real reason for his call, in order to provide counterpoint to Van Deusen's version. He took a deep breath and said he thought Colin was in trouble, even though the records the KGB had probably found at the dental office were both up to date and authentic. He left out any reference to the absence of bills which may have alerted them. Roger wanted to know more of Colin's demeanor, and Smailes reported that he seemed both angry and scared, although given the circumstances he was bearing up all right. There was a pause, then Roger confirmed that Bruce had told him much the same thing.

"Which way will it go in the JIC, then?" asked Smailes.

"We'll know tomorrow," came the laconic reply. "Look, the St. Albans police are being a little more testy about calling you back for questioning, and I can't really blame them, but I think I can stall them until after the Colin issue is resolved. I'll try to call or cable tomorrow."

"Okay," said Smailes, relieved that Roger had not brought up the wild theory of Clea Lynch's involvement. But he grimaced anyway as he hung up the phone, since the last thing he needed was another transatlantic trip.

Smailes took Booth out to lunch and brought him up to speed on most of the developments in New York and London. He reasoned that Booth would read of Grundy's murder in the British press, and Smailes could not face the thought of another dissimulation exercise. Graham also needed to know that the Colin exit was in jeopardy and that they might be dropping him fast. Predictably, Booth was depressed by the notion.

"After all we've done with him, the risks he's taken? Doesn't seem fair, Derek," he said.

"I agree, but the Oslo summit is only two weeks away. Whitehall isn't going to risk throwing a spanner into those works, are they?"

"Should I keep watching him?" Booth asked. "I know he wasn't followed yesterday afternoon. He was clear."

"I'm going to have to run that one by Ralph, Graham," Smailes replied, and Booth cast his eyes to the ceiling in dismay. "Yes, well, between you and me I feel the same way, but London wants him included and I've got to keep his feathers smooth. Let's hope he agrees. It would be really helpful to all of us to know whether Colin's being tailed."

Booth was silent for a few moments, then said, "Derek, when this is all over, and you write up your report, give me a good recommendation, will you? I'd love to end up in A Branch," he said, referring to the MI5 department that ran the London-based watcher service.

Smailes broke into a grin. "Graham Booth, master of disguise," he said.

"Well . . ." Booth protested.

"Sure, Graham," Smailes replied, scanning his menu for dessert. "I agree. You're a natural."

The afternoon bag brought the London papers and most of them ran some account of the shocking double murder outside St. Albans. Predictably, the tabloids treated the event with great relish, and one of them ran a sidebar under the headline THE MISERS OF SANDRIDGE, which listed a lot of village tittle-tattle about how the thrifty Grundys were thought to be extremely wealthy and how they were suspected of hoarding cash around the house. According to local people, Howard Grundy and his mother owned several properties in Sandridge from which they drew rents, which was news to Smailes. Most of the accounts described how a vigilant neighbor had been called away from her window by a phone call, which turned out later to be a hoax and which was likely made by an accomplice of the brutal killer. The police had also issued details of the ransacking of the top floor of the house, and their discovery of an empty hiding place beneath the floorboards. Howard was variously described as a "bachelor civil servant" and a "government computer programmer." Smailes was vastly relieved that the whole cover story was holding, and the news actually took his mind off its other preoccupations.

As the day drew to a close, Smailes remembered something that he had meant to check on his return. He put in a call to his friend Bob Lustig in the New York field office of the FBI, and within minutes the agent returned his call. The two men spent some minutes chatting, since they had not spoken since the car bomb incident. Smailes was aware he was still in Lustig's debt over that, but had another favor to ask of him.

"What's up?" Lustig asked eventually.

"Listen, Bob, you fellas do the background checks for appointments to the executive branch, right?"

"Yeah, up to a certain level. Judicial branch too, even though we're part of it."

"What level?"

"Executive branch? Cabinet level and the two ranks immediately below. Sometimes others, in special circumstances. Why?"

"Would you have done a background check on a State Department diplomat who's now a big cheese at the UN?"

"Could be. What's his name?"

"Lyle Pitkethly."

"Spell it."

Smailes complied.

"I'll check. Whaddya want to know?"

"Just general features of his background. What his area was at State."

"Why?"

Smailes hesitated. "He seems to have some connection with my girlfriend's father that neither of us knew about. I'm just curious, that's all."

"Clea's father? Hey, how're you two doin', anyway?"

"Fine," Smailes lied, unsure whether he sounded convincing. "She's in London for two months, taking the training to be upgraded to diplomatic rank."

"No kidding. That's fantastic. But I was going to say, you two should come out one weekend, have dinner."

"We'd love to, Bob. Maybe later in the summer."

"Okay. Say, what's going on over there with you guys? Everyone getting fired up about this Oslo meeting?"

"Not in security we're not," said Smailes, injecting a note of regret into his voice. "Business as usual here."

"Okay, well, I'll get back to you, Derek."

"So long, Bob," said Smailes, hanging up. As he put down the receiver he turned to look at the street map on his wall, and reflected how typical Lustig was of the Americans he'd encountered in federal law enforcement —courteous, helpful, open-minded—and how far this simple truth was from the liberal stereotype of the boneheaded sadist with a gun. He wondered if he would have received the same kind of courtesy and cooperation from a call to the American Civil Liberties Union. Then he shook his head sadly at the thought. Here he was, not yet forty, and he was starting to sound just like his father.

The diplomatic bag the following day brought troubling material for Smailes. First, two of the London tabloid papers had done further digging into the Grundy murder, and one had run a story arising from an interview with the nosy-parker neighbor in which she described seeing a man leave the Grundy house around ten-thirty, wiping his hands on a scarf and driving off hurriedly in a maroon estate car. Smailes found himself described as a tall, heavily built man in his early forties, wearing a tan raincoat. The St. Albans police had been forced to respond to this information, and had described Smailes as a colleague of the dead man whom they had eliminated from their inquiries. Smailes found himself sucking in his gut involuntarily at this unflattering description of himself, and experiencing alarm that this story might get out of hand and lead to a summons back to Britain to give the police his full account. A second newspaper had run a different story under the headline DOUBLE MURDER VICTIM WAS SPY STATION EXPERT, in which it ran information wheedled out of local people about the real location and nature of Howard's work, which a few of them had obviously guessed. The Home Office had issued a flat "No comment" to this account.

In the same bag was another item that affected Smailes more directly and personally. Clea had written a letter in response to his, obeying his instructions about unprotected lines of communication. She was, predictably, anxious and alarmed at Monday's developments, and wanted to be reassured that Smailes himself was in no danger. She reported that her mother had been particularly upset by the unexpected arrival of the courier at the restaurant (he was also apparently bearing, in addition to Smailes' letter, a very expensive parking ticket) and by the explanation that Clea had been obliged to give of Smailes' absence. Things, however, had gotten worse the following day when a policeman had followed her mother home from the supermarket and then had demanded to know the whereabouts of her car the previous day. Anthea Lynch had apparently gotten quite flustered and refused to speak to the policeman without the presence of her solicitor, at which point she had been compelled to go down to the local police station. Calls to the family solicitor and to Peter Lynch had eventually cleared the whole thing up, since it appeared the St. Albans police were no longer searching for such a car, but her mother had been quite shaken by the incident. Her father had tried to explain it away that evening by revealing to her that Smailes in fact worked for MI5, but that had only succeeded in making Anthea Lynch question whether he was an appropriate suitor for her daughter after all. Clea had gamely refrained in her letter from criticizing Smailes directly for his involvement of her family in such an upheaval, but he could detect a sense of injury behind her hurried prose.

In a more personal closing paragraph, Clea had asked him to wish her luck in her examinations at the end of the week, professing that it was very hard to be separated from him at such a time. She closed with the simple declaration, "I love you too, Clea." The letter was direct and straightforward, and he wondered why he kept reading and rereading it. Then he realized he was scanning its every word for sign of artifice or duplicity. He read its closing declaration also, again and again, pierced through the heart by his knowledge that he could not now believe her. Could he ever? He thought back to the uncharacteristic obscenity Siskin had used to describe her—"shiteater." The word repeated and repeated in his mind as he made the weary journey back to Brooklyn, like a needle stuck on a damaged record.

Smailes spent a restless night. During his several periods of wakefulness his mind would return to the scene three nights earlier in his mother's council flat, when Clea had obdurately insisted on taking the car keys in search of a box of chocolates for Mrs. Smailes. But had she made a parallel gift to her own mother? Yes, he remembered the presentation in Purley of an expensive bottle of perfume, but it was Anthea Lynch's sixtieth birthday, after all, and the two events could hardly be compared. At the time, her action in Cambridge had seemed just a typical thoughtful gesture, with the additional motive, perhaps, of currying further favor with Mrs. Smailes. Now Smailes could visualize her scurrying to a phone box, to place the fatal call that propelled Howard Grundy's murderers to Sandridge the following day. The contract had obviously been bought and established earlier—the killers' research about the nosy neighbor proved that—but something had provoked its authors to call it for the following day, an hour before Smailes' projected arrival. If such a phone call had indeed been made from Cambridge, then Smailes felt doubly responsible for the death of his amiable, eccentric friend. It was a thought that turned his face clammy and his stomach into a bunched knot.

He rose early and was at the office soon after eight, determined in part to silence Ralph's carping at his timekeeping. He was pleased with his action, however, since Roger Standiforth called on the secure link minutes before nine, asking to speak with both Smailes and Van Deusen. The diplomatic bag had now been all but abandoned as too slow.

Since there was only one handset to the equipment and no extension, Smailes had to wait impotently by Ralph's side as Van Deusen got on the line first. Ralph's end of the conversation consisted mostly of affirmative grunts of "Yes," "Okay," and "I see." But Smailes could tell from the general mood of the exchange that the mission was on. He felt relieved. Then he heard Van Deusen ask Standiforth something about an earlier inquiry, about operational control. Ralph broke into one of his rare smiles as he listened to the lengthy response. Then Ralph said, "Yes, okay, he's right here," and handed the receiver triumphantly across to Smailes, his hand cupped over the mouthpiece. "The word is Go," said Ralph. "From Oslo. Let's meet in my office as soon as you're finished, and bring Graham in with you." Then he left the room with a smirk, the heavy steel door clanging shut behind him.

Smailes got on the line and introduced himself. Roger's reply came through in its choppy, metallic way.

"I don't want to repeat myself entirely," he said, "but the JIC gave the green light on Colin, and the PM, after thinking about it overnight, agreed."

"What's the thinking?"

"Our friends in SIS played the decisive role, I'm afraid. We were in favor of cutting him loose, but the top people in Six are so upset by our success, they want to bring him across in order to get their turn. Sir Humphrey agreed and I think his decision held sway at Number Ten."

"Who's Sir Humphrey?"

"The chair, the cabinet secretary," said Standiforth, a little impatiently.

"What's the plan?"

"A waltz."

"When?"

"After the talks have been completed, but before the final signing ceremony. Moscow will have some ruffled feathers, but probably minimal. The treaty will give them most of what they could have hoped for, after all, and Colin's switching sides probably won't even be made public."

"What was the last part of your conversation with Bruce?"

There was a pause at the other end of the line. "He just wanted it confirmed that he's in operational control of the mission from now on. Of course, I could not withhold that from him."

"Yeah, right," said Smailes, his voice doubtless conveying his dismay.

"George, you've done a marvelous job. You'll be in on the operation in Oslo. I'll also be there at the embassy, unofficially, for consultation. But Bruce has to be put in control from now on."

"Yes," said Smailes.

"You meet with Colin Monday and he leaves the following Friday?"

"That's right."

"Right. Operational plan filed by Wednesday, 0700 GMT. Got it?"

"Yes. Look, Nigel, before you go, did you hear of Colin's theory regarding a certain junior British diplomat?"

"Yes."

It was Smailes' turn to pause, to hear whether Roger would add anything voluntarily. He didn't. "What did you think?" Smailes asked eventually.

"Probably the wild conjecture of a frightened man. But the diplomat has to face PV if she passes the competition, and I've been on to the FO people to take extra care. Why, what did you think?"

The reference to positive vetting reassured Smailes in an odd way. If there were secrets in Clea's past, the PV investigation would probably uncover them, and he wanted to be on record as having raised the question himself. "I agree with you, but he was right about the existence of an Argentine boyfriend, and I think it should be checked out."

There was an element of surprise in Roger's response, which the electronic distortion could not entirely mask. "All right. It will be, of course," he said.

"Anything new in the Grundy murder?" asked Smailes.

"A little. The call to the neighbor was traced to a phone box in St. Albans, but no one was seen making it. Some prints not belonging to the Grundys have been taken from the house, but they're not identified yet." Smailes winced inwardly, imagining they were probably his.

"The press got hold of the neighbor, you know, and she blabbed about seeing me."

"I know. We've spoken to her, and I think she understands the need for restraint in the future."

"Can you count on it?"

"I went myself, and I think she was impressed by the chauffeur-driven Bentley I arrived in. Yes, I think we can count on her. But I've had to make a deal with the superintendent in St. Albans. You have to make a full written statement of everything that happened from the time of your decision to visit Grundy to the time you called me the next day after discovering the body. Do it right away and send it through by bag. Then I had to assure them that you would come back to Britain directly after the meeting concludes in Oslo to answer any of their questions. Understood?"

"Yes. I'll write it up this morning."

"Anything else?"

"No."

"Good. Well, let's not use this line further, except in emergencies. Goodbye."

"All right, I'll tell Bruce," he said, hanging up.

Smailes and Booth found Ralph barely able to contain his glee at his assumption of the reins of the Colin mission. He told Booth brusquely that his services would no longer be needed. He didn't want to take the risk of further countersurveillance on Colin, and Booth would not be needed in Oslo. He dismissed him without even thanking him for the work he had done to date. Smailes could see that, as he left the room, Graham Booth was crushed.

"Now, this is the way we're going to handle it . . ." said Van Deusen, rocking back into his chair and putting his feet up on the desk.

Alone in his apartment that night, Smailes found himself in lower spirits than he had felt for years. Booth had been inconsolable about his exclusion from further duties, and Ralph had been insufferable the entire day as he began planning the logistics for the exit from Oslo. He had Madge conducting all the research on hotels and airlines, telling Smailes he didn't want to "tie him up" on trivia. He had announced a plan for the Colin waltz which entailed taking him out of the back entrance of a restaurant the night before the signing ceremony, which Smailes thought was asinine, but his opinions were now largely academic, since Ralph chose to ignore them. He had managed to complete his report for the St. Albans police in time for the morning bag, and his heart had felt like lead as he recounted the circumstances of Clea's departure from his mother's flat on a mission to buy chocolates. He kept the account as mechanical as possible, his police training proving invaluable, although his hand shook slightly as he was forced to recall the grisly scene at the Grundy house.

Smailes had finished some leftovers from his refrigerator and was just rinsing his plate when the phone rang. He dried his hands hurriedly and caught it on the third ring; his answering machine took the call automatically after the fourth. From the howl of static as he raised the receiver to his ear, he could tell immediately it was a long-distance call.

"Derek? Derek, this is George," said Dearnley's voice.

"Yeah, George, how are you?" he said, sitting down and pressing the handset into his face. "I'd know your voice anywhere."

"What time is it over there?"

Smailes looked at his watch. "Just after seven."

"Right, I thought so. Midnight here. We just got in from Enfield, wanted to give you a call right away."

"You find out anything?" he asked, his pulse quickening.

"Well, maybe, maybe not. I'll let you decide."

"Go on."

"Monday night, after you phoned, Jill drove us over to Chingford."

"Harry Fisher's turf?"

"Right. Well, we had to go into three pubs before we found him. I got up on my stick, didn't want to be too conspicuous. Jill stayed in the car."

"Yes, of course," said Smailes, imagining his former boss, a semi-invalid, hobbling across dark car parks into shady Essex pubs.

"Well, Harry pretended as though he didn't remember me at first, but I told him to come off it and he came out to the car to talk. Asked him if he knew about the St. Albans murder, whether he heard who pulled it."

"Yeah?"

"He says no, but tells me to drive over to another pub in Enfield, and wait in the car park. He comes across about an hour later, says he doesn't know anything positive, except the landlord of the Bull, which is the pub we're sittin' outside of, tells him that around Christmastime he remembers this bloke, a Cypriot he calls him, comes in the pub asking him where he can find Nicky the Greek."

"Nicky the Greek?"

"Nicky Draconis. Actually, he's from Cyprus. He's fairly big in scrubbers and drugs around Waltham Forest and Redbridge. Very nasty. The Yard's never been able to touch him."

"And?"

"Well, the landlord tells this bloke to bugger off, like, then he lets one of Nicky's soldiers know about the incident. Thinks no more of it."

"So?"

"Well, I'm getting to it, aren't I?" said Dearnley, his voice betraying an uncharacteristic excitement. "So, Harry says for a consideration, he'll dig further."

"You had to give him money, George?"

"Fifty quid. Forget it, Derek."

"George, I'll get it to you—"

"I said forget it, all right? So we go back down there tonight, and Harry tells me that this same Cypriot bloke went around a lot of pubs trying to find Nicky, and told someone on Nicky's payroll that it was about a hit, a contract job. That's all. Now, just this week, Harry says that a couple of real nasty characters he knows, who live in Woodford and he thinks work for Nicky, he says these villains are suddenly spending a lot of money round the local boozers. Really flush, they are. Now usually, that points to a big robbery somewhere, but nobody's heard anything, so Harry's guess is they've been paid off for something else. Made a point of saying they're real scum, these two, he wouldn't dare go near 'em."

"He give you their names?"

"After a bit of prying, yes. I never heard of 'em."

Smailes' brain had been working feverishly during Dearnley's account. "George, this Cypriot fella, this guy making the inquiries, could he have been a Latin, you know, of Hispanic origin?"

"Derek, you know villains. Anyone with a dark skin and a funny accent is a Cypriot, unless they're told better."

"Yeah, you have a point. Listen, did you hear anything about this guy having any fingers missing?"

George sounded puzzled. "Missing fingers? No, no one said anything about that. Why?"

"Just a hunch. Let it go, George."

"All right. Look, Derek, I'd like to ferry this info across to the St. Albans police, if that's all right with you."

"Absolutely. Just leave my name out of it, will you?"

Dearnley hesitated. "All right. I'll tell them I was

seeing Harry on my own. Listen, the kettle's boiling. I'd better go."

"George, I can't thank you enough . . ."

"Just a minute, Jill's coming in from walking the dog. What? Hang on a minute. Jill wants a word. I'll ring you if there's more developments, Derek, all right?"

Smailes tried to get Dearnley to stay on the line, but he had obviously handed the receiver over, since Jill Wilde's voice came through. "Just a minute, Derek, I want to close this door." There was a pause during which all Smailes could hear was the rush of static, then Jill came back on the line.

"Listen, Derek, I can't thank you enough for what you've done."

"What? What do you mean?"

"I don't know whether that was a real mission or not that you invented for George, but whatever it was, it seems to have done the trick."

"What?"

"He hasn't got back into that wheelchair since you called him. His leg is getting stronger all the time, he's walking with his stick quite well, and his spirits are completely transformed. I think you've convinced him he can work again, Derek, which no one else had been able to. I just can't thank you enough."

"Well, honestly, that's great news, but I—"

"No, tea for me, George," she yelled. "I've got to go. Come and see us again soon. And thanks again."

"Absolutely. Definitely," said Smailes, hanging up, his own spirits, like George's, suddenly soaring.

19

Viktor Kott had barely finished inspecting the overnight cables when Borya bustled into his office, holding a fistful of flimsies. His uniform was rumpled, his hair stood up comically from his head and a black stubble darkened his chin. Quite clearly, he had been working all night.

"Yes, Borya?" asked Kott indulgently.

Borya could barely contain his excitement. "I've cracked them! The Navigator's codes! I knew that clown he chose would get lazy sooner or later!"

"Really?" asked Kott, catching some of his enthusiasm. "Let me see."

Borya handed over the sheaf of decrypts and took a skip backward, not attempting to conceal his glee.

"When?" asked Kott.

"Yesterday. I've been here all night, going back over what I've been able to steal, as a test. There is not much in this first batch, unless you count some Ukrainian general being sent to New York," said Borya buoyantly. "You want me to keep going?"

Kott reviewed one of the documents several times, then his expression hardened, and he reached into his desk for a transmission sheet.

"No," he said, scribbling furiously. "Send this

through to New York immediately. Immediately, you understand?"

Borya's smile drained from his face, acknowledging Kott's sudden mood change. He accepted the document and left quickly, not waiting for congratulation.

The improvement in Smailes' mood proved temporary. By the weekend he found himself with an uncomfortable stretch of time on his hands, which he was unsure how to fill. He had not replied to Clea's letter, and had decided he would not communicate with her further until after the conclusion of the Colin mission, and until some of its unanswered questions were resolved. But he could not prevent himself from thinking about her, no matter what he chose to do, and the preoccupation was beginning to wear on him.

On Saturday afternoon he decided to take a long walk, since the New York weather had finally turned springlike. Uncharacteristically, he headed for the paved chaos of the Fulton Mall as a route toward Flatbush Avenue and the distant goal of Prospect Park. Downtown Brooklyn was a predominantly black turf, and he had always felt conspicuous there on his few earlier visits.

He turned left at a bank and entered the bedlam of the downtown pedestrian precinct. The street was an unappetizing medley of fast-food parlors, discount clothing stores and boom box outlets, which assaulted the senses simultaneously on several fronts. Floor managers perched in front of sidewalk clothing racks, sobbing their prices into bullhorns, their voices competing with the jagged rhythms of the rap music which pulsed from giant speakers outside the electronic appliance stores. The predominant odor was that of boiling beef fat, in which the food emporia cooked their chicken legs and French fries. Outside A&S, the mall's lone department store, a group of Jehovah's Witnesses in formal suits and dresses was selling Bibles and magazines, as one of their number harangued indifferent passersby through a portable PA system. Droves of black teenagers, separated into packs by gender, roamed back and forth. Smailes stayed in the middle of the street, walking as quickly as the crowds allowed him.

Long before he reached the end of the mall, Smailes realized he had chosen this route in order to test himself. He'd been deeply affected by Tyler Dawes' accusations of racism, although he could not deny that the criticism was partially true. And certainly he felt self-conscious, even uneasy, as he strode hurriedly down the mall toward Flatbush Avenue. In particular, the gangs of young men made him apprehensive; everything about their style, from their loud voices to their bizarre sculpted hair and swaggering gait, seemed hostile to him and warned him to be on his guard. Only the sporadic Muslims, wearing skullcaps and African robes at corner stalls where they sold tincture and incense, seemed at all nonthreatening. Not that he particularly blamed young blacks for their anger, their most palpable emanation; their ancestors had, after all, been forcibly enslaved by the white race and they, their descendants, were relegated to second-class status in a society that crowed about equality of opportunity. But Smailes was also aware that his fear and guilt probably extended toward all black people, so that he treated them differently, holding them to a subtly different standard. That, he assumed, was what Tyler had meant, and he could not, in all conscience, deny it.

Smailes leaned forward into the long, steep hill of Flatbush Avenue as it rose toward Grand Army Plaza. The sidewalks were less crowded and his mind quickly returned to its familiar groove. He found himself rehearsing scenarios which largely exonerated Clea for any presumed collaboration with the Soviets. They went something like this: first, an approach while at university to work "for peace," or whatever the KGB tacticians deemed most effective in those days before communism had begun its public death throes. Then, the suggestion of entering the civil service and the casual, friendly meetings with a case officer that followed, in which she gossiped about traffic in her section. Clea might not even realize with whom she was dealing, he argued; he could see her divulging a seemingly innocent detail like her overnight stay at the Plaza, by which the KGB had then been able to isolate Siskin as the likely British target. She probably did not even realize the destructiveness of what she had done . . .

But then he would snap out of his reverie, his thoughts returning to the telling disappearance from his mother's flat, and any such mitigating interpretation would evaporate. He thought of her European travels after Oxford, which had included several East-bloc capitals, which at that date were all under effective control of KGB surrogates. Was this where she had taken further training? The greater part of Smailes' mind simply could not believe it; it refused to credit Clea with the cynicism or determination necessary to perform such a dual role. But a smaller, equally insistent voice warned him that he had once been very wrong about a woman before, and the error had almost cost him his life. Nowhere was it decreed that he could not make the same mistake again.

Prospect Park was filled with people enjoying the blustery sunshine. Smailes watched a lithe and noisy group of West Indians as they played a frantic game of soccer, then walked on to watch a group of mentally handicapped youngsters playing softball. Their coach would perch the giant ball on a large plastic tee, then each batter would take a swipe at it. Most managed to avoid strike-outs. At the fenced baseball fields at the park's perimeter he stopped to watch a pick-up game between a black and a Hispanic team. The Hispanic team, wearing uniforms supplied by a local dairy, were batting and Smailes stopped behind the cage at home plate for the best view of the action. He flinched, unable to believe how hard and fast the pitcher threw the ball. The skinny batter missed the first pitch, fouled off the second, but then caught the third with a full swing of his aluminum bat and the ball sailed away with a clang out of the field and into a distant stand of maples. As the hitter began his leisurely trot around the bases, Smailes turned to a sad-eyed man standing nearby, who looked like he might be a father of one of the black players, and asked him the score.

"Can't be that close," said the man, with a hopeless gesture of his heavy lids.

Smailes swung around into the yuppie enclave of Park Slope and walked down the main Seventh Avenue drag back toward Flatbush. He stopped at a bookstore and bought a couple of paperbacks, finally arriving home shortly before six. He felt weary, but not particularly any less tense.

On Sunday he toyed with the idea of calling Bob Lustig at his home in Teaneck or Tenafly, or wherever it was in New Jersey that he lived, and asking whether he could drive out for a visit, but felt he was not giving enough notice. Instead he chose to take himself across to Manhattan for a movie and dinner, time continuing to weigh heavily on his hands. Then he spent another fitful night, wondering if Clea had passed her exams that week, or whether she had faced the positive vetting panel yet.

The final meeting with Mikhail Siskin turned out to be an anticlimax. Ralph completely took over its conduct, and Siskin barely addressed Smailes, as if he sensed that control had slipped away from him. Siskin seemed surly and dejected, but considerably less frightened than before, since it seemed his new "friends" were now leaving him alone. Malik, the stool pigeon on his staff, had done nothing further that could be construed as provocative, and Siskin and his wife had seen nothing more of the supposed neophyte trade delegate. Siskin almost seemed tempted to credit Ralph's bluster that the KGB were not on to him, and that his recall therefore had no sinister overtones. He listened without comment to Ralph's outline of their planned waltz, asking only a few questions about sanctuary arrangements for Tatanya and Irina after he arrived in London. He had one final requirement; he told Van Deusen quite forcefully that he wanted no use of military aircraft or airfields. He wanted no one ever to claim that coercion had been a factor in his decision.

"Absolutely, Mikhail," Ralph told him. "We have reservations on the nine o'clock British Airways flight from Fornebu Airport, Oslo. The flight is just under two hours."

"All right," said Siskin distractedly. "Let us go over it all, once again." He looked across briefly at Smailes, but Smailes did not acknowledge the look. He was preoccupied, and chose to keep his features impassive.

On Tuesday evening Smailes was alone in his apartment, trying to focus on one of the paperbacks he'd bought, an expatriate novel about two horny Cuban musicians in New York. His attention kept wandering and he had to force it back to the page. He and Ralph were booked onto a Thursday morning flight to Heathrow with a weekend stopover in London, before traveling on to Oslo the following Monday. He had had nothing to do with the operational plan, which Ralph had gleefully filed immediately after the final Siskin meeting. Smailes presumed it would work, since the KGB could not keep a physical leash on Siskin during the Oslo stay, even if they knew of his collaboration. He just felt the use of a restaurant back entrance was melodramatic and unnecessary. Why couldn't the British just pick him up one afternoon at the conference hall? He had known better, however, than to communicate these doubts to Van Deusen.

Suddenly, Smailes nearly leapt out of his skin at the sound of a vicious hammering at his door. Who the hell could it be? Outside visitors, who were extremely rare, always buzzed up on the intercom, and no neighbor had ever used such a frantic summons before. Thinking there must be an emergency on his floor, he rushed to the door and threw it open. Ralph Van Deusen was standing there, his face purple with suppressed emotion, and Graham Booth was standing behind him. Graham was holding a gun.

"Ralph, what the hell . . . ? Graham, what are you . . . ?"

"Shut up, Smailes," said Ralph, actually pushing him

in the chest. "Shut up and sit down. Keep the gun on him, Graham, and use it if he tries anything."

Smailes felt giddy with disbelief. "Honestly, Ralph, what's all this about? Graham, put your peashooter away. You look ridiculous."

Smailes had backed into his living room and Booth kicked the door shut behind him. Van Deusen repeated his command for Smailes to sit down. Realizing he was not going to learn more unless he complied, Smailes sat down on the couch and put his feet on the coffee table. "Okay, I sat down. Now please tell me what's going on."

Ralph had gone into the breast pocket of his suit jacket and had produced a piece of paper which he unfolded with a flourish, then handed across to Smailes. It was a fax copy of a bank form issued by the federal government.

"Right," said Van Deusen. "Tell me you don't recognize that."

Smailes looked more closely. The form was filled out in his handwriting, and seemed to report the cash deposit of thirty thousand dollars into a Manhattan Liberty Bank account, the day after his return from England. The form described his nationality, reported his correct address in Brooklyn and was signed with his signature. It was an exquisite forgery.

"Ralph, this is a dud. It's forged. I've never seen it before in my life, and I don't have any accounts at Manhattan Liberty." He handed the paper back.

"Oh, it's a forgery, is it? I don't happen to think so. Neither does Roger Standiforth. We both agree it's probably your fee for the murder of Howard Grundy."

The penny started to drop for Smailes. "Oh come on, Ralph. You can't believe this is for real. If I'd taken a cash payoff from someone, you think I would have been so stupid as to deposit it into an account under my own name?"

"Apparently you were. You see, it used to be that cash deposits over ten thousand were only reported to the IRS. But now there's a regulation that requires banks to report big cash deposits the same day with both the DEA and the FBI as well. Now, the IRS would have had no interest in you, would they, but the FBI in Quantico sent a routine copy to the embassy in Washington, and the embassy identified you and faxed it through to us at the end of business today. I managed to reach Roger Standiforth at home, and he agreed you should be placed under arrest until you can be returned to Britain to give a full account of yourself."

Smailes looked over at Booth, who looked distinctly uncomfortable as he stood in the center of the room, gripping the heavy gun close to his belt. The pistol looked like a Smith & Wesson, and Smailes momentarily wondered where the hell they had gotten hold of it. Smailes was unaware of the presence of any firearms in the whole British Mission.

Ralph had walked over toward his bedroom door, and resumed his gloating tone. "I intend to search your apartment while I have the opportunity. Graham, if he moves a muscle, shoot him in the leg. Graham, did you hear me?"

"Yes," Booth croaked, his face red with the exertion of keeping the big revolver trained at Smailes' chest. Smailes shook his head in disbelief, then craned his neck to see Ralph enter his bedroom. Van Deusen checked quickly beneath the mattress, then went into the drawer of the nightstand and removed a stash of mildly aphrodisiacal literature that Derek and Clea had once bought for a lark. Smailes found this exercise deeply humiliating, and his face went crimson with embarrassment as Ralph flicked through the magazines, then tossed them down on the bed. He poked around in Smailes' closet, then emerged again into the living room.

"Look, Ralph. Be reasonable," Smailes said. "This is obviously a setup. Someone doesn't want me in Oslo, do they? It must have to do with Colin's exit. Just let me speak with Roger."

"I don't think that's a good idea. Roger agreed you are to be held in Mount Vernon until a team can be

318

brought over from Bovingdon to take you in. You'll have plenty of opportunity to present your version to the interview team there, and to Roger himself, in due course."

Van Deusen had begun pawing through the titles in Smailes' bookcase, tapping the panels at either end to check whether they were hollow. Then he moved to the desk and opened its drawer. He rummaged briefly through its contents and removed Smailes' passport, which he put in his breast pocket. "You won't be needing this, now, will you?" he asked, without turning around.

The panicked rush of Smailes' thoughts had begun to ebb. If the British were thinking of holding him in Mount Vernon, things were not as bad as they seemed. He had stayed in the Mount Vernon "hard room" for the first two months of his tour, and if his speculation was correct, the room was still about as hard as an eighty-year-old man after a bottle of whiskey. He might yet have the chance to find out what was really going on.

Ralph had dumped the contents of his desk drawer onto its top and inverted it to check beneath. He removed a slim plastic sachet that was taped to its underside, then carefully slid the drawer back into its aperture.

"Now then, what have we here?" he asked rhetorically, brandishing the small envelope, then removing an oddly shaped key. "Looks like the key to a safe-deposit box, I would guess. Where is it, Smailes, at the same branch where you keep your secret account?"

"Ralph, as you must well know, I don't have a clue. That key is a plant, just as the bank deposit is a plant. Don't you see? We're being set up."

Ralph grinned his idiotic, tobacco-stained grin. "I don't think 'we' is quite the right word to use in this context, do you? I'm sure we can find the box this key fits in a day or so. Now, are you going to come quietly, or do I have to get Reg Dwyer up here for reinforcement?"

"You've got Reg downstairs? Honestly, Ralph, this feels more and more like the 'Keystone Kops.' " Smailes, however, had already made up his mind that cooperation was his smartest ploy. "What do you want me to do?" he asked.

"Graham, give me the gun," Ralph ordered. Booth seemed tremendously relieved to hand it over. "Okay, now cuff him," Ralph said.

"All right," said Smailes, thinking rapidly. "Just let me see that bank form again, okay? I want to see if there's anything that proves it's a forgery."

Van Deusen produced the form again carefully. "Put the cuffs on him first, Graham," he ordered again.

"Wait, let me put a bloody coat on first," said Smailes, retrieving his jacket from the hall closet. He could not help smiling as he held his hands behind his back and Booth snapped the handcuffs in place, the situation was so absurd. Ralph stowed the gun in a coat pocket, then produced the bank form again and held it up so Smailes could review it; Smailes quickly memorized the branch address and account number. "No, it's perfect," he said, a note of regret in his voice.

Van Deusen asked for Smailes' keys and wallet, and Smailes indicated the right front and back pockets of his pants. Ralph fished for the keys, then removed the bulging wallet with some difficulty.

"I get to sign off on these, right?" asked Smailes.

"Don't be clever," said Van Deusen. "All right, Graham, let's go."

The three men headed out to the elevator, Van Deusen locking the apartment door behind them. Outside the front door of the building Reg Dwyer sat double-parked in a British government sedan.

"Evening, Reg," said Smailes, as Graham Booth held his head down as he ducked into the back seat, then climbed in beside him. Van Deusen got in next to the driver and the car pulled away. Smailes decided to drop the banter; Reg Dwyer didn't appear to be in a talkative mood.

Graham Booth was Smailes' reluctant jailer, and he seemed determined at first to avoid any fraternization, as he had obviously been ordered. Smailes had been installed in the hard room, actually a bedroom and bathroom suite on the third floor of the Mount Vernon house, which had barred windows and a steel door with a food hatch. It had been designed as a kind of deluxe detention cell for use by MI5 and SIS, although to Smailes' knowledge it had never been used for that purpose until now. The room had been hurriedly prepared for Smailes' arrival, and had the stale, dusty smell of a motel room that had not been occupied in weeks. Booth, Smailes surmised, had taken one of the second-floor guest rooms and had been assigned baby-sitting duty until the Bovingdon team arrived to take him back to Britain.

An hour or so after Smailes had been locked up, the hatch opened and Booth appeared with some toiletries that he had apparently just returned from buying.

"Here's a toothbrush, toothpaste and soap, Derek. There should be towels beneath the sink," he said awkwardly.

"Yeah, thanks, I've already checked," said Smailes, advancing to the door to take the brown paper bag that Booth dangled in front of him. "How about a razor?"

"Sorry, Derek, Ralph said definitely not. He told me to get your belt, too."

"Oh Jesus, come on. What does Ralph think, I'm going to commit suicide?"

"I've just got to follow orders," said Booth disconsolately, standing aside deliberately so Smailes could not see his face. "The belt, please." Smailes shook his head sadly as he complied and held the belt through the hatch. Booth took it quickly. "Look, good night. I'm not supposed to be talking to you."

Smailes thought quickly. "Hey, is there anything to eat in this place? You blokes interrupted me before dinner, and I'm starved," he lied.

"Well, I just bought a few things. What do you want?"

"How about a ham sandwich and a cup of tea?"

"All right. Give me a few minutes."

Fifteen minutes later Booth reappeared at the hatch and passed the tray of food through. As Smailes took it from him he asked casually, "So you're replacing me on the Oslo trip?"

Smailes had guessed right, that Booth would not be able to hold back. "No," he replied hotly. "Ralph says reinforcements are going from London. Besides, I have to stay here until Friday."

"When the Bovingdon goon squad arrives?"

"Right."

"Graham, this is a setup, you realize?" he added quickly, changing the subject. "You don't believe I killed Howard Grundy, or took a payoff, do you?"

"I don't know, Derek. It looks bad from where I sit. But I don't know. Look, I'm not supposed to be talking to you. I'll see you in the morning," he concluded quickly, closing the steel hatch. Smailes sat down with the tray of food and smiled. So he had about forty-eight hours to kill, he reasoned, if he waited until after Ralph's departure but before the arrival of the baby-sitters. He would have to get Graham to go buy him some novels, he thought, looking round and realizing for the first time that the television set had been removed. At that moment, he heard the distant signature music of a local news program, as Booth settled in for the night on the floor below. Smailes shrugged and picked up his sandwich, forcing himself to eat it.

Smailes' spirits remained quite good for the next two days, although he tried to appear depressed and anxious for Booth's benefit. Booth, at his request, had bought him a handful of crime novels, although he had drawn the line at newspapers. Smailes read fitfully, spending hours lying on his bed, trying to figure who wanted him off the Oslo job so badly as to set him up so elaborately. The KGB? The CIA? His own team? Absurd as it seemed, this last possibility at first seemed the most likely, since someone had provided considerable access to his handwriting and signature samples, not to mention his apartment. But then he thought about Van Deusen's theatrical behavior in the flat, how he had seemed to go straight to the concealed key, as if he knew where to find it. But who was Ralph really working for? The likelihood that he was a KGB double was getting stronger and stronger, in which case Siskin was definitely blown and the Soviets were planning some diabolical exercise in Oslo to plaster egg all over British faces. Why? To teach the British a lesson that the KGB, and by extension the Soviet government, could not yet be counted out? It was a definite possibility, one that Smailes began to consider more and more likely as time passed.

Rewinding the whole sequence of events to its beginning, Smailes wondered whether the "Cypriot" whom Dearnley had tagged shopping for a murder contract in Essex was the same man as the middle-aged Hispanic who had led the break-in into the British Mission, and who had followed up with the murder of Roberts, the security guard. That was also possible. But what had Howard known that had provoked his murder? Could Howard really have been working for the Americans? Smailes still could not quite credit that version. Smailes also speculated about the possible involvement of Lyle Pitkethly, who seemed to know Clea Lynch's father and had had a brief affair with Clea herself on her first arrival in New York. Then he remembered that party at the consul general's house before Clea left, seeing Ralph and Lyle speaking together as if they were acquainted. Did Ralph, in fact, work with the Americans as well? The implications of that ramification defeated him.

One conclusion Smailes reached was that Kevin Butterworth's murder was incontestably linked to these events, and was not a random crime. So had Kevin's killer been this same Latino hit man? Quite possibly. Smailes thought back to Kevin's phone call announcing his change in plan, which Smailes had taken in Ralph's office for convenience. Was that the crucial coincidence that had led to Kevin's death? Smailes could much more easily entertain Van Deusen's passing along such information, and understanding its consequences, than Howard Grundy's doing so.

One train of thought ended up leaving Smailes genuinely depressed. He was aware that one person with plenty of access to both his handwriting and his apartment was Clea herself. Memos and notes passed between their two departments continuously, and since accommodation had been one of Clea's JAO responsibilities, her office kept duplicate keys to all the units in the British inventory. Not that she would have needed them—there were plenty of opportunities when Clea was in his apartment alone when she could have planted whatever she liked. Smailes also realized with a sickening feeling that Clea probably processed Kevin's change in travel plans, and could easily have been the source of that leak. But were Ralph Van Deusen and Clea Lynch therefore in cahoots, traitors together? It seemed an absurd proposition. Clea seemed to genuinely loathe Ralph, unless, again, he had drastically underestimated her powers of dissimulation. What was certain was that Derek Smailes did not intend to stay cooped up in Mount Vernon until the Bovingdon debriefing team arrived to escort him home. Risky though his escape might be, it was less of a risk than if he allowed this botched mission to play itself out, and at the same time allowed MI5 to walk into a Soviet trap to humiliate them internationally. No one's career would be worth a damn in that eventuality. He had no money, no identification and no passport, but he needed somehow to get to Oslo to present all this evidence to Roger Standiforth, who could not fail to come to the obvious conclusion and would cancel Siskin's exit, he reasoned.

On Thursday evening Smailes finished his supper and consulted his watch, rubbing the three-day stubble on his chin. He wished again that Ralph and Graham had left him the television, since he had a long stretch of time to kill. He distractedly finished his third whodunit and finally, around eleven, heard distant sounds of water running through the plumbing and, minutes later, heard Graham Booth moving about in his bedroom below. He did not hear the television turn on and concluded that Graham was reading, so he killed his lights and took up his position next to the ornate, padlocked gate that was the exit to the fire escape. He had formulated a plan for how to get back to his apartment, if he could persuade a taxi driver to give him a somewhat unorthodox ride, reasoning that the gypsy cabs that hung out near the Mount Vernon station would do almost anything for a fare. Standing at the window, Smailes was able to see the subtle dimming of reflected light as Booth turned out his reading lamp. Smailes guessed it was nearly eleven-thirty.

He waited with bated breath for twenty more minutes, then padded gently into the bathroom and opened the cabinet door beneath the sink. There, tucked in to the right on the hook where he had installed it was the spare key to the window gate padlock. When he had moved into the Mount Vernon suite more than two years earlier, Madge Ryan had insisted on supplying it. Since the window gate was technically the only third-floor exit to the fire escape, the British were in violation of the building code by keeping it locked, and Madge refused to take responsibility for a British diplomat's being trapped up there in the event of a fire, and had therefore supplied Smailes with the key. He had concealed the key himself, and the only other person who definitely knew of its existence had been Howard Grundy, since Smailes had pointed it out to him the first time he stayed in the refurbished suite. Smailes retracted the key, unlocked the gate soundlessly, removed his shoes and hitched up his beltless pants. He pushed open the aluminum window on its noiseless vinyl track and climbed out onto the metal landing, waiting until his eyes grew accustomed to the darkness. Then he made his way cautiously down the stairway, holding his breath as he passed in front of Booth's window. Pausing at the lower landing, he did not kick loose the drop ladder from its anchor, but put his shoes in his pockets and climbed over the railing, swinging silently into the darkness, then dropping four feet to the ground. He stifled a cry as he landed unevenly on the concrete surface, then hoisted his beltless pants again, put on his shoes and walked briskly off toward the center of town.

Smailes waited until the ancient Plymouth Volare had lurched southbound onto the FDR Drive before telling the driver of his two destinations in Brooklyn.

"Adams Street, then Court Street, what you mean, man?" asked the driver, glancing up into his rearview mirror to look at Smailes' face.

"Had my wallet stolen, so I need to go get my spare bank card, then go over to the machine on Court Street to pay you. I'll walk back from there," Smailes explained.

The driver was a large man wearing a knitted cap and a combat jacket. He hesitated, and the cab slowed a little. "You jivin' me, man, I'm gonna be upset," he said.

Smailes held up his watch so the driver could see it. "Look, I'll leave you my watch as collateral," he said. The driver glanced up, then back again at the road. "Okay, thirty dollars," he said, revising his fare upward.

"Okay," said Smailes, and the rest of the journey proceeded in silence.

It took him a good five minutes on the doorbell to rouse Mrs. Ortiz, the building superintendent, and give her his explanation through the intercom of the theft of his keys. She checked his name and buzzed him through. He went straight to her apartment on the first floor behind the elevator banks, and she came to the door in an old bathrobe and a foul temper.

"Two new keys is ten dollars," she said, holding out the replacements to him.

"Great, Mrs. Ortiz," he said. "I'll give it to you tomorrow. Had my wallet stolen too, see?"

She frowned at his unlikely story, but handed the keys over and slammed her door. Smailes hurried back to the lobby.

His apartment was just as they had left it, with the mountain of drawer contents piled on top of his writing desk. He rummaged through it, and to his immense relief quickly turned up the second automated teller card to the account that he had opened with Madge Ryan's permission. Like all diplomatic personnel, Smailes was paid in sterling into his London account, and wrote checks to the mission cashier for personal funds in dollars. The mission provided a generous exchange rate without fees, so he lived largely on a cash economy. But with the commencement of the Siskin mission, he had lobbied successfully for the opening of a New York account in dollars, so he and Graham could have access to cash whenever it was needed. Madge had concurred, with the warning that his record-keeping had to be flawless. Smailes, to his immense relief, had also never given Booth the second card. He also found in the pile an old Home Office lapel badge, a laminated card on a clip with a picture on it that he had used during his probationary year and had never turned in. He pocketed that also, then went hurriedly to the bathroom to pack a toilet kit. In the bedroom, he stuffed two clean pairs of underpants into his jacket pocket, then hurried back to the door. He wondered briefly what else might be planted there, what else the Bovingdon team might turn up, but was in no mood to stay and look further himself. He gave a quick, final glance around the apartment, then saw that the message light on his answering machine over by the couch was blinking. Stepping back into his apartment, he strode across to the machine and hit the Play button. The machine rewound itself, hummed and beeped, then produced the familiar voice of Special Agent Bob Lustig. Smailes cocked his ear to listen.

"Hi, Derek, this is Bob, Bob Lustig, Thursday evening, six P.M. Say, where the hell are you guys, anyway? The secretary says you're all 'unavailable.' Anyway, if you get this message, give me a call, will you? I think one of the John Does from the Staten Island murders last night might be a Brit. Seems like the other might be an Ivan Doe, if you get my meaning. Look, call me tomorrow morning before ten and I'll have you see if you can ID the guy. Otherwise, I'll have to go through the consulate, I guess. You know the number, right? Okay, over and out. Talk to you later. Bye."

Smailes, who had not seen or heard any news in two days, wondered what Lustig could be referring to. He rewound the tape again, then pressed Play and Record to erase the message, then rewound it again to the beginning. The message light had gone out, but he didn't want his friends from Bovingdon finding any such information. He walked back to the door, left the lights on, then locked up. Within minutes he was back at the battered Volare, which stood idling hoarsely down the block from the building.

"Okay, Court Street," said Smailes, pointing. "It's just over there."

20

Smailes hit the call bell outside his Brooklyn Heights garage and waited as the lot attendant peered out through his reinforced window at him. As the overhead door shuddered and began to retract, Smailes stepped in and gave the guy the number and description of the government Ford he had garaged there. He would leave his own car behind, he reasoned; the Ford's diplomatic plates might come in useful.

The newspaper kiosk at Grand Army Plaza stayed open all night, and Smailes bought copies of the three main New York dailies. He was almost tempted to buy cigarettes, but again fought off the impulse. Then he drove to an all-night coffee shop he knew on Seventh Avenue, which stood opposite an imposing fortified building that was in fact a New York City high school. He parked down a side street and entered the restaurant carrying his newspapers and toilet kit. It was a little after one, but the place was crowded. Two city cops sat in the window booth, talking out of the sides of their mouths as they feasted on eggs and hash browns, their squashed-pie hats sitting on the table beside them. They ignored him. Smailes took a booth and ordered coffee and a muffin, then headed for the rest room to shave.

The early pages of each paper were taken up with

news of the Oslo summit, and in their different ways they trumpeted the arrival of the heads of state and their entourages in the Norwegian capital. YALTA TWO! blared the banner in *Newsday,* which struck Smailes as particularly silly. There were no prominent accounts of any murders on Staten Island. Inside the Metropolitan section of the *Times,* however, Smailes eventually found a long piece on the double murder. Two men had been found shot dead in a remote section of the island near a golf course on Tuesday night. One body had been found in a car, and the second on a sidewalk some hundred yards away. No one had been seen leaving the scene, although area residents had reported hearing shots and the squeal of tires just after midnight. A search of the area had not turned up a weapon, but an abandoned motorcycle had been found in a wooded area nearby. Neither victim had been carrying a wallet or any identification, which led the police to think the killing was linked to drugs and organized crime, since the remoter sections of the island had become a preferred meeting site for couriers and their contacts. No drugs, however, had been found in the car or on either victim.

The New York *Post,* which had obviously been printed later, carried an updated report on an inside page under the headline SI SLAY VICTIM MAY BE FROM EAST BLOC— FEDS. The story reported unspecified autopsy findings that indicated the dead man found on the sidewalk may have been an Eastern European. The car which contained the body of the second victim had been rented to an unknown executive with a fictitious Manhattan company. Both victims were still to be identified, the FBI claimed. Smailes conjectured that if the FBI rather than the DEA was involved, it was possible the murders had political rather than drug-related overtones.

Smailes went back to the *Times* and brought himself up to date on the major news stories he had missed during his confinement. Remaining obstacles to a historic accord in Oslo had seemingly been cleared away, and all that remained was fine tuning by the teams of bureaucrats before a signing ceremony at the end of the following week. The *Times* ran an Op-Ed column under the head-line END OF AN ERA which heralded the last gasp of the Cold War and the dawning of a new transatlantic "com-munity of nations." Perhaps it was his training, but Smailes could not help feeling skeptical that all accumu-lated East-West tensions had been so neatly and finally resolved.

Smailes finished his second cup of coffee after paging through the two tabloids. He looked around and saw that the crowd of night owls had thinned and that the cops had left. The graveyard chef, a stocky Greek with dark blue jowls, was scraping his griddle with a heavy spatula which he then tossed into a bin with a crash. He exchanged words with the lone waitress, who was seated at the counter, smoking a cigarette. From somewhere in the ceil-ing above them, Frank Sinatra crooned about his kind of town. Smailes saw that it was one-forty, and knew he could not sit in his booth all night nursing cups of coffee. He rose slowly and left, but out on the sidewalk he hesi-tated; he had literally nowhere to go. A strand of melody —*Oh, that magic feeling*—came into his mind. He tossed the newspapers into an overflowing bin and headed back to his car. In the driver's seat he adjusted the back as low as it would go, zipped up his jacket to the chin, hugged himself around the waist, and closed his eyes. He won-dered momentarily where Ralph Van Deusen and Mikhail Siskin were at that moment, and then his thoughts began to drift. He wondered about Graham Booth, whether Clea had really ever been attracted to him. He wondered what it would be like to go to bed with Julie Lynch, Clea's sister. And soon he was dreaming about England, a far-off place where the grass grew green and the birdsong was sweet.

He was woken by the cacophony of the sanitation department's morning concerto. A garbage truck double-parked alongside him whined and strained as its packer unit crushed Brooklyn's rubbish into a dense bale. Voices hollered and whooped above the sound of crashing, bouncing plastic as the workers flung the empty galvanized bins over the parked cars and strode up the street. Two men in overalls grabbed handles on the rear of the truck and jumped up on a step, then one removed a glove and whistled through his fingers. With a roar and a belch of exhaust, the truck pulled into Seventh Avenue and was gone.

Smailes rubbed his eyes and reached for the lever on the side of his seat to pull himself upright. He checked his watch and saw it was six-twenty. Then he fished for the toothbrush and paste in his toilet kit and headed back into the coffee shop. The day was going to be a busy one, he told himself.

Soon after seven he was on the public telephone in the corridor outside the washroom, pawing through his date book for Lustig's New Jersey number. To his relief Lustig himself picked up the phone on the second ring.

"Derek, you're up and about early. Get my message?"

"Yeah, late last night. Hope you don't mind me calling you at home, but I've been out of town. What have you got on these Staten Island murders?"

"Let's not talk about it on the phone, okay? Meet me at the morgue at about quarter till nine. I'm pretty sure one of them's yours."

"Why?"

"He had taps on his shoes. I'll tell you more when I see you. You know the place?"

"Give me the address again," said Smailes, memorizing a location in midtown. He told Lustig he would be there, and hung up. Then he walked back to his booth, aware of a sinking feeling in the pit of his stomach.

First Avenue and Thirtieth Street was not the easiest location at which to find parking at eight-thirty on a Friday morning, but Smailes hoped his blue and red diplomatic license plate would keep him out of trouble as he eased the Ford into a spot a little too close to a fire hydrant. He glanced at his watch again as he locked the car door, wondering whether Graham Booth had tried to bring him his morning tea yet, or whether he had begun his panicked journey in to the mission twenty blocks away to call Curzon Street on the secure link. The Bovingdon team was doubtless already en route, Smailes reasoned, and there could be nothing the hapless Booth could do to head it off. Poor Graham, Smailes told himself a little unconvincingly, he must devise some way to make it up to him.

Special Agent Robert Lustig was waiting for him in the building lobby, and had the jaunty air that law enforcement people affect around death when the victim was not one of their own.

"Derek," he said, holding out his hand. "It's been a long time."

"Bob," replied Smailes, returning the firm handshake. He registered a momentary pulse of alarm that Lustig might know of his troubles at the mission, but quickly dismissed the notion. Ralph, after all, had claimed the bank form had been sent directly from FBI headquarters at Quantico, and Lustig seemed his usual friendly self. If he thought Smailes' casual dress was peculiar, his eyes did not betray it. Lustig was a man six or seven years older than Smailes, short in stature with a head of prematurely gray, wavy hair. He had wrinkles of amusement around his eyes, and seemed to genuinely revel in his work. Smailes had found him unflaggingly helpful during his tour in New York. "What do we have, Bob?" he asked.

Lustig checked the directory for the individual offices of the chief medical examiner of the City of New York, then led Smailes to the elevator bank, where a group of office workers stood waiting. Two cars arrived almost simultaneously; Lustig directed Smailes to the one that was empty, and pressed the button for the sixth floor before answering.

"Looked like a drug hit at first. Like the papers said, no ID on either party. Then when it became clear the party in the car was wearing clothes with all the labels removed, and the second party had on a jacket bought in Budapest, we were brought in. Then yesterday, they do the autopsies, and tell us the second guy, the guy on the sidewalk, has gutta-percha for fillings in his teeth. That's an East-bloc thing, right? I inspected the clothing, and the second party's is definitely all East European, and I would swear the first party's shoes are English, they're wingtips with these little steel plates set in the heels."

The elevator stopped and Lustig directed Smailes to a set of double doors, stopping before the two men reached them.

"So, the clothing, I'm thinking operational rules, right?" Lustig was right, Smailes was thinking exactly the same thing. "Some kind of contact, some kind of drop is taking place, which is interrupted by the perp. Then, the car." At this point, Lustig went into his suit pocket and withdrew a small notebook. "It's rented to an executive with this nonexistent company, South Audley Exports, with the only address a box at the Murray Hill station." Smailes stood transfixed, waiting for the next information.

"So the registration card identifies the people authorized to receive mail there as someone called Roger Bolton, the proprietor of this fake company, and one Nigel Allsop, of the Devon and Cornwall Development Bureau, and his address is the same as yours, the British Mission. So I called you as soon as I found out. You know the guy?"

"I think I might," said Smailes, passing through the swing door as Lustig held it open for him.

Lustig hooked up with an orderly he obviously knew, a young Hispanic wearing hospital scrubs, and the three men headed off toward the refrigerated end of the floor. They entered an enormous room with a couple of metal tables and a bank of drawer fronts occupying a whole wall. Without speaking, the orderly scanned the labels on the drawers, then unlatched one in the third row and pulled it open silently on its heavy rails. When the drawer was fully retracted he stepped up to the head and pulled back the top of a white sheet. Derek Smailes looked down and saw the gray, lifeless face of Alan Sparks, lying there with all the grim authority of death. A sewn, horizontal incision circled the cranium, where the surgeons had sawed open the top of his skull to examine the brain, but Smailes could make out that Sparks had taken at least one bullet wound to the head. He stood motionless for a moment, then nodded.

"The other?" he asked.

The orderly closed the drawer, then released the latch immediately below it. Smailes saw the face of a middle-aged man with dark curly hair cut very short, and an olive complexion noticeable even through the pallor of death. Smailes frowned and shook his head, and the orderly drew the sheet back farther, down to the ankles. Smailes noticed without reaction that the corpse really did have a label tied to its big toe. The lithe, athletic body had a small wound to its shoulder, which Smailes could make out despite the crude repair of the Y-incision which had been made by the autopsy surgeon across the whole torso, from each shoulder to sternum to pubic bone. The young orderly then rolled the upper torso by its shoulder to display the two fatal wounds in the central upper back. Smailes nodded and the orderly closed the drawer.

In the corridor outside the cold room the orderly left the two investigators to themselves. After he had disappeared around a corner, Smailes said, "The first body is Alan Sparks. He's our SIS man in charge of the Soviet colony. The Devon and Cornwall bureau is its operational cover."

Lustig gave a low whistle. "No kidding. So that would suggest that the other guy—"

"Is a Soviet, yes."

"Well, frankly, that's the first thing I thought, even though the guy doesn't look like a Russian, does he? But I called them in yesterday, and brought a couple of heavies up here late afternoon. They looked at him for a few moments, then said, 'He's not KGB,' just like that. They took his prints, dental chart and mug shot and said they'd try and identify him. We've faxed the prints through to Quantico and Langley too, but no news yet. So what was your guy up to? Did you know him well? Was he a friend?"

"Not really. Nice guy, drank a bit too much. No, I've got no idea what he was doing there," said Smailes, which wasn't entirely true. "Wasn't there something about a motorcycle?"

"Yeah," said Lustig. "Ten-year-old Harley, dumped under the trees fifty yards off. No plate, and the serial number's been punched out. We figure the perp has arrived early on the bike, then stakes out the place. He waits for them to get into one car, then offs the first guy, but only wings the second. The second guy takes off and gets a hundred yards or so up the nearest street before the killer catches him and drops him with two shots in the back. Then he fleeces him, takes whatever ID he's been carrying, and steals whatever car he showed up in. He's already ditched the bike and blanked out its traces."

"How did the second guy get a hundred yards away with a wounded shoulder?" asked Smailes.

"Very good question. I asked that one myself. You notice that your guy had taken a couple of head shots?"

"Yes, looked like it."

"Okay, the first one is in the side of the head, above the left ear. No way he's going to survive that, right? The second wound is weird. The perp must have squeezed off his first shot through the driver's side window, which is shattered like you'd expect, then opened the door and fired again, but only winged the second guy. Then, instead of finishing off the passenger, he leans in and plugs the first guy again, who's already dead, in the mouth. The bullet exited the back of the jaw, making quite a mess. The autopsy confirmed the sequence of the shots. So, as he's foolin' around in there, our friend Ivan has taken off up the block, and the trigger man has to chase after him. Catches him, bang, bang, that's the end. What do you make of that?"

Smailes had gone ashen white. He remembered the grisly tale of the interrogation Sparks had undergone in East Berlin, when the revolver was taped into his mouth. He shuddered and said, "I really don't know, Bob. Sounds kind of peculiar. Ritualistic, almost."

"Unless our man genuinely wasn't sure he'd got him with the first shot. But I've got to doubt that."

"I would too," said Smailes. "Look, let's get going."

Out in the street, Smailes asked Lustig to give him the exact location of the murder, then lied and told him he would go straight into the mission and report Sparks' death to the head of station. The British would then make the arrangements for the removal of the body and its shipment back to Britain.

"Look, if you get any confirmation on the Russian, let me know, will you? It could be crucial to finding out why Sparks was out there."

"No problem. The KGB said they'd let us know immediately, and I don't see why they wouldn't. I'll call you."

"Listen, Bob, I don't know how much I'm going to be in the office today. Leave a message on my answering machine at home, will you? It's the safest way."

Lustig hesitated a fraction before assenting, as if he was beginning to sense something of Smailes' unorthodox situation. But he kept his tone neutral, then shook hands and was about to head off on foot when he caught himself.

"Hey, I nearly forgot completely. I found out something about your guy at the UN."

"Who?"

"You know, that bureaucrat, Pit-something."

"Right, right," said Smailes eagerly, suddenly remembering. "Lyle Pitkethly. What was his background?"

"Well, I didn't think I was going to turn up anything, because we hadn't done a check on him here or in Washington, the two logical places. So I went back through a few Federal Registers to see if I could find where and when he worked at State."

"And?"

"He wasn't listed anywhere. So I think, Either he's a nobody, which is unlikely, or he worked somewhere else. So I begin checking other agencies. Bingo. Your man never worked at State. He's DIA."

Smailes was stunned. "Lyle Pitkethly worked for the Company?"

"No, no, DIA, not CIA. Defense Intelligence Agency —the Pentagon spooks. Kennedy set them up after the Bay of Pigs when he was trying to shorten his leash on the CIA. Generally more hawkish than the Company, if you can believe that. They report to the same oversight boards. And it's probably 'works' rather than 'worked.' "

"No kidding."

"Yeah, all the major intelligence groups take turns rotating their people through the UN, you know that. The Register reported his last position three years ago as deputy director of Arlington Hall in Virginia, which is one of Fort Meade's outposts. So, does that solve anything for you?"

Smailes thought for a moment. "Maybe. I don't know. Listen, Bob, thanks for everything."

"Yeah, I'll be in touch," he said, turning and heading across the street toward Second Avenue. Smailes himself walked distractedly a couple of blocks up First toward the mission, then stopped at a curbside phone booth.

Quentin Smith's voice came through crisply, despite the mild distortion of his scrambler. "Derek, old chap. Where are you? You know, I heard a funny story about you."

"Quentin, listen. One of the double murders out on Staten Island Tuesday was Alan Sparks. I just identified him at the city morgue."

"Good Lord! Sparks? He's been out a couple of days, but I thought nothing of it. Listen, Derek, where the hell are you . . . ?"

Smith's protest was the last thing he heard as he hung up and headed back toward his car. Unable to assess its import, he put the Pitkethly news out of his mind, and returned to his thoughts about his murdered colleague. He found a complex knot of emotions, the most prominent of which appeared to be guilt. He felt guilty because his first thought on seeing Alan Sparks, and the thought that kept returning to him as he unlocked the car and fished under the passenger seat for his street atlas, was that he was glad it was Sparks lying there, and not him. Smailes knew intuitively that Sparks' fateful meeting must be linked to the mission from which he had just been so cleverly dumped, which meant it could have been Derek Smailes lying in that refrigerated drawer, shot point blank through the temple. But it had been Alan Sparks, not him, sitting in that rented car on Staten Island, and Derek Smailes felt an overwhelming sense of relief.

Smailes was not exactly sure where Staten Island was, let alone how to get there. But by consulting the large map of the city in the front of the atlas he saw that by catching the expressway right off the Brooklyn Bridge he could drive all the way out to the Verrazano Bridge, which provided direct access to the island by car. Now, as Smailes rode the elevated highway past the deserted warehouses and asphalt rooftops of Italian Brooklyn, he wondered why Sparks had chosen such an inaccessible venue for his contact. It must have been the virtue of its very remoteness, he reasoned. But somehow his intention had leaked, if Lustig's version of the murder was correct, and the meeting site had been staked out. Or one or the other of the parties had been tailed, Smailes told himself, slowing as he hit the magnificent span of the Verrazano to look out over his right shoulder at New York Harbor and the soaring optimism of southern Manhattan beyond. A tanker was steaming toward the straits and the open sea, and just in front of Liberty Island two yellow ferry boats crossed paths. Then the cars in front of him slowed to a crawl, anticipating the permanent fixture of nearly all New York's bridges and tunnels, a toll booth.

He took the Todt Hill exit off the highway that bisected the island toward New Jersey, then began winding through streets of modest tract homes that had vinyl awnings and the occasional plaster Madonna in the yard. He was soon thoroughly lost, and stopped to inspect his atlas. Unenlightened, he drove to the end of the block, parked at a convenience store, and went in to get directions for

La Tourette Golf Course and Park. Repeating them over and over in his mind, he took his third right and next two lefts, then found himself climbing into a grander neighborhood where large houses hid behind hedges and driveways. Passing an old people's home, he began a descent toward the park, in the geographic center of the island. The houses grew smaller once more, and then he found himself at the junction of a winding, almost rustic road that skirted a dense wood. Applying the hand brake momentarily, Smailes checked the atlas again and turned left. A hundred yards farther he saw a dirt shoulder that answered Lustig's description, and pulled over. He got out of the car and looked around.

On the ground in front of him were fresh windshield shards and a dark stain that might have been oil, but wasn't. Away in the direction from which he had come an angular stretch of gray-and-white condos flanked a clearing which Smailes presumed was a fairway. In front of him, streets rose in perpendicular succession from the wooded road, the nearest house about fifty yards away. It was hardly deserted, but probably about as private a spot as you could find within the physical limits of the city. The occasional car swept by at speed, unimpeded by traffic lights or stop signs.

Smailes pushed the glass shards about with his toe, then glanced up to try and discern the direction in which the dead Russian, Sparks' contact, had fled. It was probably up the first street on his left, he reasoned, and began slowly walking the route he thought the dead man might have taken. There was a cement sidewalk on the opposite side of the road and Smailes spotted a couple of small stains that might have been blood. He turned up the first street, but saw no further stains on the ground, or anything to indicate the victim had taken the same turn. Retracing his steps, he continued along the perimeter road to the next street and turned left, spying another small stain just at the turn. He looked up and saw an elderly man walk a black poodle up his driveway and enter a house about halfway up the block. Smailes walked up the street, past a mailbox, and then, almost opposite the poodle house, saw the fading chalk outline where the homicide team had traced the position of the fallen body. Here there was a much larger stain where the victim had obviously expired. Smailes looked up, scanned the street in both directions, then began a slow walk back to his car. Back in position, he began to walk the route again, very slowly this time, his eyes fixed to the ground. He spotted bloodstains about every ten feet. So the victim was badly wounded, but running hard. He thought back to the small, athletic frame in the refrigerated drawer. The guy had ducked the first street, maybe hoping in the darkness to throw his pursuer. He hadn't, and as he turned into the second street, maybe he knew he hadn't and had only seconds to live. There, at the turn, Smailes saw the small stain again. The man's last desperate dash had taken him thirty yards up the street. Smailes saw for the first time another, larger stain near the blue metal foot of the mailbox. Curious, he looked more closely, and saw what might have been a smudged stain on the rounded corner of the box itself. So the victim had stopped to steady himself, Smailes reasoned. No way! The man was in flight for his life! Heart racing, Smailes opened the hinged metal drawer of the box itself. There, on the white label that reported collection times, was a distinct, dark red spot. Had the victim stopped to dump something in the box? Of course! Then he had continued his futile lurch up the street, until he was overtaken and felled by two shots in the back. My God, had the killer seen him ditch whatever it was? Smailes asked himself, his head reeling from the implications. In Lustig's version, the body had been fleeced, its pockets emptied. Had the killer in fact found what he wanted? Smailes looked up and saw that the old-timer, minus poodle, had come out to fuss with the trunk lock of his car. What he was really doing was keeping tabs on him, Smailes realized. He advanced a few paces and yelled out, "Excuse me!"

The old man took fright and retreated toward his front door, so Smailes yelled again. This time the man turned and Smailes called out for the location of the nearest post office. The man made a vague gesture up the street.

"What address?" Smailes called.

"Manor Road," the man responded, ducking back into his home.

The main Staten Island post office at Victory Boulevard and Manor Road was a sleek, glass-fronted building from the sixties, with a bank of mailboxes and a flagpole out front. Smailes drew into the lot and parked, looking down to check his location on the street atlas again. Then he walked quickly to the entrance, his hands stuffed into the pockets of his jacket. It was late morning, and he wondered what kind of pandemonium had broken loose at SIS; their top Soviet man was murdered, and the crime had been called in by a fugitive from their derided sister service, who stood accused of disloyalty. Smailes could barely imagine the impact on the studied calm of the ninth floor; Quentin Smith had to be positively dyspeptic.

Smailes joined the queue of patrons inside the roped gangway that funneled them toward the three clerk stations actually operating. He rehearsed his story over and over, and when his turn eventually came, he walked with deliberate ease over to the counter. A bilious-looking postal clerk, an enormous man wearing a short-sleeved blue shirt and a haircut from the fifties, was leaning on his counter with one elbow, regarding him indifferently. He had the face of a disgruntled bison. A name badge pinned to his shirt identified him simply as "Maglio."

"Yeah?" Maglio asked.

"I think my wife mailed some papers from my desk by mistake, Wednesday morning. You know, she picked up some bills I'd left, and took the stuff underneath. It wasn't stamped or anything. You'd have held it here, right, if you'd found it?"

"Which mailbox?"

Smailes gave him the location of the blood-smeared box.

"What's your address?" he asked suspiciously. Smailes hesitated briefly, then gave the address of the poodle house.

"Name?"

"There wouldn't be a name on there."

"Name?" he repeated, more forcefully.

"Peter O'Connell," replied Smailes, equally forcefully.

"What am I checking for? Papers, you say? In an envelope?"

"Yes, I think so," said Smailes, aware he was sounding unconvincing. The clerk began to leave, and Smailes added, "Some papers may be written in Russian. I teach Russian, you see, in the city . . ."

Maglio paused to frown at him, then disappeared behind a partition. He was gone for what seemed like an age. Eventually, he sauntered back to his station, having discovered a toothpick somewhere in the depths of the mailroom. He removed it carefully as he leaned again on the counter.

"Nope," he said, craning his neck past Smailes, about to yell "Next" to the head of the line.

"Wait a minute," said Smailes hurriedly. "There may be photographs. I'm missing photographs, too."

The clerk put both hands on the counter. "Why didn't you say so the first time?" he asked in exasperation. "Wait there."

Smailes held his breath as the clerk disappeared and returned again, holding a medium-sized envelope of gray shiny paper, very un-American in size and appearance. He tossed it on the counter and asked, "These them?"

Smailes removed the contents quickly and saw about half-a-dozen black-and-white photographs, approximately eight by six.

"Yes, absolutely, fantastic. I'm so relieved."

"They were taken out of that box Wednesday morning. Wasn't that right near where those two drug guys got shot?"

"Right down the block," said Smailes, stuffing the

photos back in their envelope, and noticing for the first time a dark stain on its top right-hand corner. "The shots woke us up. My wife was half scared to death. That's probably why she grabbed this envelope without looking. Look, thanks a million," he said, turning to leave.

"Not so fast," said the clerk, and Smailes hesitated, his bowels turning to water. The clerk had ducked beneath his counter, then resurfaced. "You gotta sign the Unintentional Mailed Object release," he said, scribbling some data onto a form. He turned it around to Smailes and indicated where his signature was needed. Smailes obliged with a flourish, thanked the clerk again, then walked slowly out to his car, his heart racing. Taking his seat, he removed the photographs carefully, and saw that there were in fact seven. He examined each one at length.

The first was a picture shot through a car's rear side window of a stout military man, about sixty, talking animatedly with a sour-faced civilian. Then a grainy picture of this same officer, addressing a group of other military men in a paneled office somewhere, obviously taken with a telephoto lens from outdoors, or maybe a nearby building. Then the same military man again, who wore what looked like a Soviet general's uniform, leaving a building via an ornate columned doorway. Then a second man, a heavyset, gray-haired civilian, leaving the same building. Then a grainy shot of this second man, walking in a park with a third, older man, deep in conversation. Then two other, older prints, which from their faded, worn condition were clearly at least a dozen years old. The first was of a group of ten or so soldiers in light gray uniforms, seated on a tank. The second showed a classroom somewhere, where a man in civilian clothes was addressing a room of other, younger civilians seated at desks. It was clearly summer since the men were all in shirtsleeves and the windows of the room stood open behind drapes that looked like fishnets. The photographs meant nothing to Smailes, although the heavyset man in the third and fourth prints looked vaguely familiar, as if he might be a politician. He had no sense of their significance, although clearly the fleeing Russian had succeeded in a last desperate bid to keep them out of the hands of his pursuer, which meant they were highly significant, in some way.

Smailes considered his options. He could drive into the mission and surrender to Reg Dwyer, then present this evidence to the Bovingdon team when they arrived, and hope they made the right calls. Or he could try and arrange a clandestine meeting with Quentin Smith, enticing him with further evidence in the Sparks murder. At least the British could not suspect him of complicity in that, he reasoned, since he had already been installed in the Mount Vernon hard room when Sparks and his contact had been killed. Perhaps Smith could identify the characters in the photographs, he argued to himself, and thereby evaluate their significance. But Smailes could also easily see Smith panicking at the prospect of a meeting with an MI5 fugitive, and setting him up. So who could evaluate the import of the material he'd uncovered for him? Lustig? No way. Kabalan? A possibility, although Rudy would probably need to take them elsewhere for evaluation, and might even be tempted to sell them to the highest bidder. Then Smailes remembered Vasily Malinovsky, émigré chess master and embittered defector. Of course Malinovsky was the perfect source, if he could find him, and provided he could conceal the circumstances of their discovery from him. Smailes looked at his watch and saw it was almost noon. He started up the Ford and maneuvered it out of the parking lot, then pointed it back toward the distant spires of Manhattan.

21 _____

"Have you seen the big Russian guy, the one who plays chess here most days?" asked Smailes, sliding onto a stool. The shift boss was preoccupied with a sink somewhere below counter level, and dried off his hands on his apron before responding.

"Which Russian? We get plenty Russians in here."

"Tall, heavy, gray hair. Chain-smokes Winstons."

"Yuri? Naw, he no been here today."

"Where can I find him? I already tried the other place round the corner."

The old waiter cast a weary glance out of the front window then rubbed his knuckles across the stubble on his chin. "Nice day today. Maybe he play in the park."

"Washington Square Park?"

"Yeah, top of street."

"I know it. Thanks," said Smailes, turning on his heel, and checking once again for the packet of photographs through the lining of his pocket.

Smailes discovered Vasily Malinovsky seated at a chess pedestal, engrossed in a match against a young black man whose free hand rested on a copy of the New Testament. The inspiration appeared of little avail, however, since the older man was winning easily. Smailes eased onto the concrete bench nearby and watched quietly. Malinovsky, who was wearing his iridescent brown raincoat and blue cap, pushed his pieces around quickly and with confidence. His younger opponent, a man in a white turtleneck and a green corduroy jacket, responded diffidently, pirouetting his fingers on the tops of his pieces before he could bear to commit them. At one point Malinovsky swung his huge head around to Smailes and registered his presence without response. Then he crushed out a cigarette beneath his foot and initiated a flurry of piece-taking, at the end of which Malinovsky thrust his queen through his opponent's denuded defenses and announced a check. The young man riffled the pages of his Bible anxiously, then pushed his king sideways a square, at which point Malinovsky landed his queen firmly beside it and called, "Mate, I think." The young man studied the board, then laughed a little in embarrassment and asked whether Malinovsky wanted a rematch.

"Another time, I think," said the Russian, standing and shaking his hand. "Thank you for the game." He turned to Smailes. "Mr. O'Connell, yes? You want to take a walk?"

Smailes stood also and the two intelligence men walked slowly back toward MacDougal Street. Smailes noticed they were almost of identical build, although Malinovsky now had a pronounced stoop. They were seated with coffee in the front bay of the chess parlor before the big Russian chose to speak again.

"So what happened with our diplomat, my friend? Did you have success?"

Smailes tried to look rueful, and glanced out of the window before responding. "Not really. Looked promising at first, but he got cold feet after the KGB began to heat things up at his mission. It was worth the try, though, and your advice was very helpful."

"Security was increased? Did he say why?"

"The delicacy of the international situation, he guessed. It was enough to scare him off, anyway."

Malinovsky looked skeptical and stared away over Smailes' shoulder, a sour look on his face. " 'Ridiculous' is the word I would choose, my friend, not 'delicate.' The West is going to step straight into Rostov's trap. Anyway, why did you want to see me?"

Smailes produced his envelope and passed it across the table. "We just received these photographs, but they make no sense to us. Could you help us with them?"

Malinovsky tried to look scornful, but his curiosity got the better of him. He took the packet from Smailes, immediately spotting its small blood smear on the top corner.

"This is a Russian envelope. Only in the Soviet Union can we make such a lousy product from such vast resources. How did this arrive?"

"In the mail, anonymously."

Malinovsky raised his eyes sharply. "And you cut yourself shaving, which is how the envelope comes to be stained with blood. Do not play games with me, Mr. O'Connell."

Smailes hesitated. "It was brought by courier. The courier was murdered two nights ago, along with our Soviet desk man, and is not identified yet. This packet was found near the scene." Smailes caught his breath, unsure of the wisdom of this revelation. But he desperately needed Malinovsky's cooperation, and could not think of any other plausible explanation.

Malinovsky removed his Winstons and a dog-eared matchbook from his raincoat, lit one and parked it in the corner of his mouth, then removed the photographs with his thumb and forefinger. He examined each one quickly, without betraying emotion. Then he looked at the last two again more closely, knitting his brow before their meaning became clear to him. Then he shrugged his shoulders and nodded his head sadly a few times. Eventually, he looked up at Smailes.

"What do you want to know?"

"Who are these people? What do the pictures signify?"

Malinovsky responded in a rapid, dismissive tone. "The first one, in the car, it is Alexei Dolghorukov talking with Viktor Kott. Dolghorukov is the fat one in uniform. You know who he is?"

Smailes shook his head.

"He was first deputy chief of staff until Rostov supposedly sacked him last year. Now he has some honorary title, I think. A general and a well-known conservative. Viktor Kott is also a general, and is still first deputy chief of the GRU, I think."

"The what?"

Smailes immediately remembered the acronym for Soviet military intelligence, but was unable to recover himself in time to prevent Malinovsky's launching into a withering diatribe against the ignorance and complacency of Western intelligence services in the face of their twin Soviet adversaries. Smailes interrupted him. "Yeah, yeah, I know what the GRU is, Vasily. I just didn't hear you properly. You can get down off your high horse."

Malinovsky wagged a finger at him. "Just never forget, my friend, that if KGB is the world's biggest intelligence agency, then GRU is second biggest, and, if anything, more . . . what you say . . . like the Frenchman, de Sade."

"Sadistic."

"Yes, sadistic. Kott is its number two, or was. I have not heard he has been fired. Now the next one, this is Dolghorukov holding some meeting, I think in his office at the defense ministry. I do not recognize any of the men in the room, but I can see from their uniforms they are all senior officers. There are some illuminated pictures in this recess on the wall." At this Malinovsky held up the second photograph to Smailes, and pointed to its left-hand corner. "I do not know the significance of this."

Malinovsky paused to draw on his cigarette. "The next two are interesting. This is the entrance of the Sandunov *banya,* our famous Czarist bathhouse, in Moscow. Here is Dolghorukov leaving, and in the next one . . ." Malinovsky held it up to him. "Don't tell me you don't know who this is?"

Suddenly, Smailes did. "Anatoli Grishkin?" he ventured.

"Yes, yes, very good. Anatoli Grishkin leaving the same building, as we see. Grishkin is supposedly Rostov's most serious rival. He is party boss of the New Leninists in Leningrad, and head of VPK, the Military-Industrial Commission. Popular with the army, very powerful. You understand the implication, that these two have held a secret meeting in the baths, yes?"

"Right," said Smailes. "Obviously."

"This last of the recent ones. It is in a park, probably Gorky Park, central Moscow. Grishkin is walking with Georgi Tumanov, and they are conversing. You know who is Tumanov?"

"Vice President?"

"Very good. Vice President, supposedly very powerful also, deputy to Rostov. In this case, just a rubber stamp, a token appointment to keep the *apparatchiks* happy. He is old and feeble. And so these men walk and talk together. Very ordinary, yes?"

"I don't know, Vasily, is it?"

"No, in Moscow, it is not. Where are their aides? Where are their bodyguards? Why do they not talk in his office? Very suspicious, you see," said Malinovsky, his voice thick with sarcasm.

"Now these last two are old, I have some difficulty at first. Then I see what I am meant to see. Look, the first one, these men in the light gray uniforms sitting on the tank. Look closely at the officer, a lieutenant colonel, yes? It is Viktor Kott, perhaps fifteen, twenty years ago. Now, in the Soviet Union, it is airborne troops who wear light gray uniforms. So why do airborne troops sit on a tank? Funny, isn't it? Because this is a Spetsnaz squad, my friend, our elite, special forces who wear this camouflage uniform on Soviet territory. They are like your best commandos, your SAS, yes? All senior GRU men are recruited from the ranks of Spetsnaz, so this photograph must have been taken shortly before Kott began his career in GRU.

"Now, this last one, this is a prize. This is very rare. This is again Viktor Kott, see, some years later, now in civilian clothes. He is teaching in a classroom, and you see the nets before the windows? This must be the Military-Diplomatic Academy in Moscow, the highest GRU training school, very secret. I do not even know where it is, just that it exists. But you see it is summer, and the nets are there to prevent even a scrap of paper being blown out of a window. Crude, but effective, yes? Just like the Soviet Army itself, I would say!"

At this point, Malinovsky actually chortled with glee. He was clearly delighted with his performance so far, and paused for effect before pronouncing further judgment.

"So, your next question, what do these photographs signify? Why did some poor KGB courier take such risks to bring them to you? Why did he, and your own man, meet such unfortunate ends? Listen closely, my friend." Malinovsky paused again to drain his coffee cup.

"If there was a conspiracy to overthrow Rostov, these would be its logical members. You see, count them. Dolghorukov, the bitter general fired from the general staff; Kott, his GRU protégé; then Grishkin, the politician closest to the military leadership; and finally Tumanov, the feeble old Stalinist, Rostov's deputy, to be installed as puppet leader. Then a picture of a secret meeting in Dolghorukov's office, just to make sure we get the point, that this conspiracy has a broad base. What danger Rostov is in! You must communicate this news immediately to your political leadership, so they will urge acceptance of whatever last-minute conditions Rostov demands in Oslo! Because you know what he doesn't, that he is in mortal danger from his military, plotting against him with the right wing! So he needs all the help you can give him!"

Malinovsky's eyes had widened in mock horror, and he delivered his lines with melodramatic relish.

"Obviously, you think the whole thing is a fake," said Smailes woodenly.

"I know the whole thing is a fake, Mr. O'Connell. Do you know who said this: 'When organized, pretend disorder; if weak, pretend to be strong; when strong, pretend to be weak, so your enemy grows arrogant'?"

"Lenin?" said Smailes, guessing.

Malinovsky smiled and shook his head patronizingly. "No, no, a good guess, but wrong. No, it was Sun-tzu, my friend, a Chinese general who wrote a wonderful intelligence manual, *The Art of War*, two thousand years ago. He makes Machiavelli seem an innocent. But you are right, these have been the Kremlin's tactics ever since the founding of the Soviet state. These photographs are simple but clever disinformation, my friend. The courier and his contact were murdered to make them seem more authentic, that is all. Nikolai Rostov wants you to believe he is in danger, so that if the West wants to keep a so-called sympathetic leader in the Kremlin, they had better do what he says. When the Soviet leadership pretends disunity, that is when it is most unified. This conspiracy is a false flag, my friend. You know what is a false flag?"

Smailes nodded, and repeated obediently, "A front organization created and controlled by an intelligence service, designed to spread false information."

"Very good, very good. Yes, this terrible conspiracy is a false flag, orchestrated by Rostov himself to make you believe he is in big trouble. It is a trick that has been successfully used against the West countless times."

Had Smailes not possessed direct knowledge of the photographs' unlikely discovery, he might still have thought Malinovsky's interpretation farfetched. But since he was convinced there was no way he was meant to find the envelope or its contents, he had to reject the old defector's analysis. He was tempted to believe there was indeed a military conspiracy against Rostov, and that the British were for some reason being warned of it. Malinovsky was looking across at him defiantly, a strange, angry glitter in his eye. It gave a glimpse into the chasm of suffering that was his life, a suffering for which he undoubtedly held the Soviet leadership, and the Communist creed, directly responsible. Smailes realized that Malinovsky saw everything through this prism of compressed hatred, that consequently he could never take anything about Nikolai Rostov at face value.

"What about the other two, the older prints?" Smailes asked.

"I am not sure. Perhaps to establish the credentials of the courier, to prove he has access to such an archive."

Smailes nodded slowly, as if weighing the sheer bulk of Malinovsky's revelations.

"So what will you do with them, my friend?" asked Malinovsky.

"Send them through to London, probably, along with your interpretation. I don't know really. It's not my decision."

"I suggest you destroy them, Mr. O'Connell. Or give them to me. I know one or two people in Langley who might appreciate this joke."

"I'm sorry, Vasily, I can't do that," said Smailes, gathering the prints into their envelope a little hurriedly. "I'd get into all kinds of trouble."

Malinovsky shrugged and looked out onto the street. He looked back and asked, "So, what do you think of this rubbish in Oslo?"

Smailes stood, took some bills from his wallet and dropped them on the table. "Look, I'd love to stay and talk, Vasily, but I've really got to get back to the office. I'll look you up in a week or so, and we can chat at more length. And Vasily, I can't thank you enough for your help. I'll tell our station chief exactly what you've said."

Malinovsky looked up at him painfully, and Smailes knew he did not believe him. Vasily Malinovsky had long since ceased to believe that anyone in Western intelligence would ever credit his description of their folly.

"Goodbye," he said, looking away as he lit another Winston.

Smailes was almost at the door when he doubled back to ask Malinovsky one more question. "Listen, Vasily," he said, "maybe you can help me with one more thing."

"Perhaps."

"What's the significance of shooting someone in the mouth?"

"What is its significance in the Soviet Union, you mean?"

"Yes."

Malinovsky shrugged. "It is a GRU signature, that's all. The KGB, they like to dispatch their victims like this." Malinovsky stuck his index finger into the back of his neck, and pulled an imaginary trigger. "With GRU, it is like this," he said, repeating the gesture with his finger in the roof of his mouth. "Or they throw them in an oven. Like I told you, more sadistic," he said wearily.

Smailes headed back across the park to the Eighth Street garage where he'd left the government Ford. He kept going down the block and turned in to a clothing store, where he finally bought himself a belt. Hitching his trousers and actually feeling them stay, he reached for change and found a pay phone on the corner of Broadway. It was a curious anomaly, he realized, that for all the violence of New York City life, the street phones almost always worked, which was more than you could say about London.

Smailes punched in his home number, trusting it was too early yet for the Bovingdon team to have visited his apartment. After the machine answered with his announcement, he punched in the three digits to access his messages. The machine clicked and whirred, indicating some inches of tape had been used. He was in luck, for Bob Lustig's voice came across immediately.

"Listen, Derek, hi. It's Bob here, just about an hour after I left you over at the morgue. The KGB claim they've identified their guy, and it's kind of a weird one. Apparently he's Major General Anton Palov, and his position was deputy commander of the Carpathian military district, in the Ukraine. He's apparently of mixed Russian and Azerbaijani background, which is why he looked a bit different. That's all they're telling us, and if they know why he was over here, or why he was meeting with your guy, they're not saying.

"Listen, since it's bound to come out in the press, I gave them the identity of your guy, too. Sort of reciprocal good faith. And look, since I don't know when and if you'll pick up this message, I'll go ahead and call it through to your mission, too. Wouldn't want them to find out from a newspaper, would we? So call me when you get this. Okay, so long."

The machine beeped and squawked and Smailes hesitated a moment, weighing whether Lustig sounded suspicious, or whether he was imagining it. But if Lustig didn't yet know of Smailes' problems, he might well find out when he called through to the mission and was put through to Quentin Smith. Only then did he stop to consider Lustig's information. The courier was a senior military man? What the hell did that mean? Smailes was so engrossed in his thoughts that he almost failed to notice his machine had begun to deliver a second message. He suddenly stiffened, all his attention focusing on the gravelly voice speaking to him through the tiny speaker. The message was delivered in low, measured tones, and the accent was unmistakably Russian.

"Mr. Smailes. We trust you will receive this message. We understand you are in a little trouble. We think we can help, and have a proposition to make to you. Meet me in the restaurant next to your apartment building at one o'clock today. If you cannot make that, one o'clock tomorrow, Saturday. Come alone, and do not try anything foolish. I repeat, come alone."

The machine beeped the conclusion of the message, and Smailes stood transfixed, his heart racing. He announced a marker message onto the tape, and hung up. Then he called again, and listened to both Lustig's and the Russian message again. His first thought had been that it was a trap, that the great thespian Graham Booth was affecting his Russian accent so Smailes could be enticed into the arms of his frustrated colleagues from Bovingdon. He listened intently the second time, however, and was convinced the accent was authentic, and that anyway, Booth would be unable to force his voice down into so a low register. He glanced at his watch and saw that it was almost two-thirty. If he was going to attempt the fallback, he had almost twenty-four hours to kill. Then he heard his marker message and cursed as he racked his brain for the code to tell his machine to rewind itself and erase all its messages. It took three more attempts before Smailes got the sequence right, and he breathed a sigh of relief when his final call elicited nothing but static from the equipment. If he was going to keep his appointment, he hardly wanted the Bovingdon boys to learn of it too, did he?

Smailes hung up and stood aside to let an aggrieved, androgynous-looking couple use the phone. So who the hell was calling him to offer him deals? The KGB? Or the GRU? Had Palov maybe been a GRU officer? No, not possible, unless his command in the Ukraine was fake, which would be simple to check. But the message confirmed for him what he had believed all along, that he had been set up by some arm of Soviet intelligence, which therefore knew everything it needed to know about the British plan to waltz Mikhail Siskin out of Oslo. He had his photographs and Vasily Malinovsky's wild interpretation of them, but that was really all he had with which to try and convince his team to drop the good Comrade Siskin before it was too late. So he had no real alternative but to try and meet his mysterious Soviet counterpart the following day, Saturday. He looked anxiously again at his watch, and wondered where the hell he could go to lie low for almost a day. His own apartment was obviously out, and for the same reason, so was Clea and Felicity's place. In other circumstances, he might have asked Bob Lustig for a room for the night, but he had the definite feeling that if Lustig had not yet learned of his detention and escape, he soon would, and such a proposition would compromise him badly. That only left people on the periphery of his acquaintance, like Lyle Pitkethly, or Dennis and Tyler in the West Village. He gave an inward, derisory hoot at both prospects. Which was why, when the phone became vacant again, he found himself checking through his date book for Rudy Kabalan's home number, and discovering himself very relieved when Rudy himself answered the phone.

Smailes watched the second hand on the clock above the coffee machine sweep around again to its apex, signifying exactly two o'clock. He took a sip of water and ate a bite of his tuna fish sandwich, but had no appetite. He wondered if his contact was going to show, or whether the whole thing was an elaborate hoax. A couple of promising characters had arrived—a Slavic-looking type in a raincoat and dark glasses, then an overweight, bald-headed man in a cheap business suit—but they had both ignored him and ordered lunches at the counter. Realizing his mouth was dry, he finished off his water and headed off to the bathroom, hating to leave his table for even a moment.

Rudy Kabalan had been genuinely nonplussed by Smailes' request on the phone, as if such an appeal for help from a friend was completely outside his experience. But he had told Smailes it was fine for him to come and spend the weekend, if he really needed somewhere to stay. Rudy had warned him it might be a little noisy, since it was his weekend with his kids, but Smailes had said that was fine with him. In fact, although Smailes did not completely trust him, Kabalan was the perfect resource for the kind of jam he was in, and Smailes was immensely pleased that he was around and willing to help.

Smailes drove out to Rudy's modest ranch-style house in Port Chester, one of the last Westchester communities on Long Island Sound before the Connecticut line. Rudy had welcomed him warmly and had shown him straight to the room in the basement where he said he could stay. The room had a musty, unused smell, but came with its own bathroom, so Smailes thanked him profusely and said he needed to take a shower.

"Sure," said Rudy, "take your time. Then we can talk

—I don't go for the kids until tomorrow morning. Hey, you hungry? I was just going to fix something."

"Well, actually, I haven't eaten since seven o'clock this morning."

"Okay. How about a burger?"

"Fine," said Smailes, wondering if Rudy had broken his diet.

Seated at Rudy's dinette table with the remains of their enormous lunch in front of them, Smailes stalled for time by asking Rudy about his family.

"Well, Rudy Junior's ten, and Marcella's nearly seven," replied Kabalan, wiping grease from his mouth with a paper napkin.

"Where do they live?"

"Fishkill, with their mother. Way up the goddamn Hudson near the Newburgh-Beacon Bridge."

"You two still get along?"

Rudy gave him a theatrical grimace. "Not really. The bitch is suing me for more alimony, and I'm countersuing for more custody. I want more quality time as they get older, and all I get's two weekends a month."

"I know what you mean. That's all I used to get with my daughter in Cambridge."

Kabalan lifted some plates across to the sink, then stowed condiment jars in the enormous refrigerator. "Hey, anything you want, just take it," said Rudy, indicating its groaning shelves. Smailes saw jumbo bottles of soda, gallons of milk, loaves of bread, fruit and several fat packets of cold meat. Smailes even thought he caught sight of a bag of potatoes. Americans, Smailes told himself, they put everything in their bloody refrigerators.

"Thanks, Rudy. Say, you still on your diet?"

"Nah," said Rudy. "That OA thing got too trippy for me. Besides, gotta have some food in the house when the kids come over. Hey, bring your coffee into the living room. You haven't told me what's going on yet."

Smailes padded obediently behind Rudy into the sitting room and parked himself on a brown Herculon couch that crackled when he sat on it. The house was furnished in a combination of the spartan and the gruesome, the sort of environment you'd expect a bachelor Lebanese-Venezuelan spy with an eating disorder to inhabit.

"So what's the poop?" asked Kabalan, taking an armchair. "You said you were in a jam."

Smailes gave Kabalan an edited description of the Siskin operation, from the discovery of the mission bugging gear to the enticement of the diplomat and the plans to waltz him out of Oslo. But somewhere, he explained, the wheels had come off, the operation had leaked, and Smailes himself had been framed as the culprit. The British had hauled him off to detention, but he had escaped and now he was on the lam from his own team. He gave Rudy the details of the Staten Island murders, leaving out his discovery of the photographs, and told him of the message on his machine from an unnamed Soviet to meet the following day, at one o'clock. He said he felt he had to go, since he was trying to compile enough evidence to get through to Oslo and convince his superiors to call the whole thing off.

Kabalan said nothing during Smailes' account, but leaned forward with his elbows on his huge hams, listening intently. When Smailes had finished, he asked, "You want me to back you up? I got the photographic gear, the long-range mikes."

He indicated with a nod an aluminum equipment case stowed behind the television set. Smailes suddenly froze in terror, remembering a similar case that the killer of Roberts, the mission security guard, had been described carrying. Could Rudy be described as a middle-aged Hispanic of medium build? Then Smailes breathed an inward sigh of relief. Rudy Kabalan, after all, was a fat Arab, no matter how bad the light.

"Say, you want me to back you up?" he repeated. "I'll call Felice and cancel the kids."

"No, thanks, but I don't think so. I'm running solo on this, Rudy, and anyway, the place will be staked out."

"Hey, I could bill you later, and only if the job's a success, okay?" said Rudy, misinterpreting him.

"No, thanks anyway. But listen, maybe I could wear a wire."

"Forget it," said Kabalan. "If they're any good, it's the first thing they'll check for."

Smailes hesitated, knowing he was right.

"One o'clock tomorrow?" Rudy repeated rhetorically. "What are you gonna do till then? I gotta go do more grocery shopping and stock up on videos."

"Right now, Rudy, I think I'll take a nap. I got about four hours sleep last night, in my car."

"You bet," said Rudy. "Make yourself at home."

Now, as Smailes turned back to his booth, he had the sinking feeling that his prospective interlocutor had scratched, that the meeting was a bust. At that moment, a tall punk sat down opposite him, and Smailes, in his irritation, told him the seat was taken.

"Yes, by me, I think, Mr. Smailes," said Oleg Malinovsky.

Smailes was speechless for a long moment. Then he saw again the studded leather jacket, the cockscomb haircut and the black fingernails, the kind that came from tinkering with an old motorcycle, and he knew instinctively he was sitting opposite Alan Sparks' murderer.

"Hello, Oleg," he said, as casually as he was able. "I didn't recognize your voice on the tape."

"Not surprising," said Malinovsky, passing his wrist back and forth in front of Smailes' chest, then checking a small, Walkman-sized object in an inside pocket. Kabalan had been right; a wire was the first thing they checked for.

Smailes looked at Malinovsky more closely. The Russian was maybe twenty-three or -four, had a prominent Adam's apple, a long beak of a nose, a white complexion and high cheekbones beneath cold, gray-blue eyes. Smailes noticed that his shaved patches of hair were beginning to grow out, and that while he was a little taller than his father, he was of much lighter build. He struck Smailes as very young to be handling such a weighty job.

"You said you had a proposition?" Smailes asked.

"Yes, we do. Take a look at this," said Malinovsky,

going into an inside pocket and producing a passport. He held it out reversed so Smailes could inspect it. It was a small, slightly worn blue booklet with SUOMI—FINLAND printed above a heraldic lion. Malinovsky flipped it open to the second page, and Smailes saw his official MI5 mugshot crimped by an embossed seal, above another of his cleverly forged signatures. This time he saw that he was described as Lars Tulku, businessman, and that he had been born in 1953 in Ino, Karelia, Finland. Suddenly, it all made sense to him. Oleg Malinovsky, former Young Pioneer turned Soviet agent, the graphic arts student turned master forger.

"You do excellent work, Oleg," said Smailes, without sarcasm. "This is almost as good as the bank form."

"Your colleagues will find some of my earlier efforts in your safe-deposit box," said Malinovsky in his deep growl. "Along with a lot of money in foreign currencies. If they search your apartment properly, they will find more things. Some encryption equipment, a pistol and some ammunition. You see, Mr. Smailes, you really do have some big problems."

"I don't think so, Oleg. I think your attempts to set me up are pretty clumsy, and I'll be able to talk my way out of this fairly easily. Why did I deposit cash in a bank account if I keep currency in a safe-deposit box? I think it's you who has the problems."

Malinovsky responded in a slow, insolent voice. "Obviously, you got lazy and overconfident. And I would not have such faith in your powers of persuasion. When the defection of your little tame diplomat goes so badly wrong, I think there will be some unhappy people in London, don't you? And you will be an obvious candidate for traitor. You see, anyone in your Section K will know that this passport identifies you as a KGB agent. The village of Ino has been inside the Soviet Union since the war, you see, and a Finnish passport from Karelia is a common KGB travel document. And don't forget, you are on the run. This is hardly the behavior of an innocent man, is it?

Whatever happens, your career will be over. Surely you can see this."

The sneer in Malinovsky's voice had begun to rile him, and Smailes felt like grabbing him by the knob of his Adam's Apple, mashing it against his windpipe, and forcing him to confess to the murders of Sparks and Palov. Instead, he turned to a passing waitress and held up his empty water glass. He waited until she had refilled it before replying. The waitress tried to put a menu down in front of Malinovsky, but he waved it away.

"What do you have in mind, Oleg?" he asked casually.

"A simple trip to meet with one of my superiors, and one debriefing session, maybe two. Nothing clever, no force, no kidnapping, nothing like that. No one need ever know the trip was made. Then we will find a way to let your service know that you were framed, an innocent victim, as you say."

"Why should I trust you?"

"You have no choice."

"Why don't I simply walk into the FBI office in midtown and spill everything I know about you? You would be the one arrested, Oleg, not me."

"Unlikely. I think by now the FBI has been asked to help find you. They would hand you straight over to your investigators. And anyway, I am finished here. I am going home, and have fifteen, twenty ways to leave the country."

Smailes thought he would try a different tack. "What's with you, Oleg? Don't you appreciate the sacrifices your father made, the risks he took for you?"

The question incensed Malinovsky, who leaned forward with a snarl. "Don't mention my father to me. Look what his stupidity has brought! My sister is dead from drugs. My mother is a drunk. And my father, he is a standing joke on both sides of the Atlantic, as you well know. And this is what he calls the freedom of the West."

Malinovsky paused to gather himself, his chest heaving. "I at least have the opportunity to repair some of the

shame and destruction my father brought to our family,"
he said, looking down, a fierce determination in his voice.
Smailes looked away also. In fact, Malinovsky's outburst
had given him the germ of an idea, and he did not want it
to show on his face.

"This meeting, debriefing, why can't it happen
here?" he asked.

"This is not your concern. It must take place out of
the country. I am holding reservations to a Carribean destination, on Monday afternoon. You can travel on your
new documents. We return the next day, Tuesday. Then
we will make some 'mistakes,' to prove to your anxious
colleagues that you have been loyal all along, as you
claim."

Smailes took a swallow of water and pursed his lips,
as if struggling with a decision. "All right," he said eventually. "What are the arrangements?"

"Meet at noon, Monday, outside this restaurant. Wait
here until you are picked up by a yellow taxi. If you try
anything, anything at all, we will abort, understand? Very
simply. Do not think I am alone in this."

"Who's working with you, Oleg?" asked Smailes angrily. "Who's on the inside, supplying my mugshot and
writing samples, the keys to my apartment? Who do you
have in your clutches?"

Malinovsky stood and looked down on him. "Monday
at noon," he said as he turned on his heel, and was gone.

22

Clea Lynch dabbed absently at her nose with a tissue and looked about her at the cramped office. There was barely room for its cluttered desk and bank of ancient filing cabinets, which held a stack of gray files and a dusty spider plant. She shifted uncomfortably in the interview chair, concerned that in the small, shabby room she might appear overdressed, or that her cologne was too strong. Above her weak sunlight filtered through the bars of a small, high window. She could see occasional shadows as pedestrians passed by on the Whitehall pavement above.

This basement security office could not have stood in greater contrast to the high-ceilinged, paneled room in which she had had her final meeting with the Three Wise Men the week before. Their interview had been the culmination of the entrance procedure, and Clea felt she had risen appropriately to the occasion. Their questioning had been gracious but tough, and while Clea had struggled initially with a response on the merits of Sunday trading, she felt she had done much better with the Falklands War and the future of diplomatic relations with Argentina. More importantly, she felt she had demonstrated confidence and ease, and that by the conclusion of the interview the Wise Men had tacitly acknowledged her right to membership in their club.

Positive vetting was, she assumed, a formality. However, she was less certain of any such rapport with Alan Barrowclough, deputy head of Foreign Office security, who now reentered his tiny office carrying a file and sat down opposite her. He had greeted her at the guard station with a cold handshake, but had said nothing further as he led her down to his office and indicated a chair. As they now exchanged pleasantries, Clea noticed that the elbows of his suit were shiny and that his vowels had the telltale twang of state education. Barrowclough was a small, wiry man with a ruddy complexion who looked like he might be more at home in an anorak and gumboots than in pinstripes. He opened a file flap and extracted a document, then tapped a row of small, uneven teeth with the end of a pencil. He leaned back and studied it for a moment, his face collapsing in on itself. Eventually he looked up.

"Sorry it took us so long," he said affably. "We were waiting for the response from your old tutor at Oxford. He seems to have been quite fond of you," he added with an unconvincing smile.

"Well, we disagreed on absolutely everything, but yes, I think he was," said Clea.

"He had no comment on your political views beyond 'strong-minded,' I see."

Clea smiled, and Barrowclough went to another document in the file. "You declared your membership in the Oxford University Socialist Society, we noted," he said.

"Yes," said Clea. "I also belonged to the Conservative Association and the Liberal Club, I think I put down," she added, craning forward to try and read her application.

"Well, quite," said Barrowclough, without looking up. "Although our enquiries have suggested you hardly ever attended either of these two groups, although you were quite a regular at the Socialist Society, it seems."

"No, that's not true," said Clea quickly. "I wasn't a regular at any of them. I just joined them all in my first term because I thought—"

"Well, yes, that's what someone of your views might have done, we thought."

"What do you mean, 'my views'?" Clea asked pleasantly.

"Someone of your extreme left-wing views, I mean," said Barrowclough. "They might have joined all the political clubs, for the sake of camouflage."

Clea maintained her poise. "I don't have extreme left-wing views," she said carefully. "That characterization is not accurate."

Barrowclough paused for a long moment as he hunted for another document in the file. He still did not look up at her. Clea was aware she had reddened slightly.

"Did you ever meet Adolfo Stevens?" he asked eventually.

Clea had not the slightest idea about whom he was talking. "Who?" she asked.

"Adolfo Stevens, elder brother of Raul Stevens. Both from Buenos Aires, I gather."

Clea's face was still a blank. "I believe you were romantically involved with Raul Stevens, two years ago, in New York. He was a waiter, I think," Barrowclough added helpfully, finally looking up.

The realization struck Clea like a blow in the chest. "How on earth do you know about Raul?" she asked, despite herself.

"Ah, Miss Lynch, it's our job to know about these things," said Barrowclough contentedly.

Clea had regained herself. "No. No, of course not. I never met Adolfo. Raul said his brother was disappeared in the early eighties. That's why Raul got out."

"According to some accounts, Adolfo Stevens escaped arrest and joined the Tupamaro underground in Montevideo. Did you have any knowledge of that?"

Clea was now feeling seriously disoriented. "No, no, I did not. Raul hardly ever spoke about him. I had completely forgotten his name was Adolfo, if I ever knew . . ."

"Did Raul Stevens have contacts with any terrorist organizations himself?"

"Of course not," said Clea sharply. "Raul was an innocent. He was completely apolitical."

"If he was apolitical, why did he leave Argentina?" asked Barrowclough mildly.

"Because his brother had been disappeared by the army, that's why," she said heatedly, immediately regretting her tone. "Anyway, I only went out with Raul for a few months. This line of questioning seems—"

"He did not share your left-wing views?" suggested Barrowclough reasonably. Clea was about to respond sharply, but caught herself and took a long, slow breath. Her face was flushed and her heart was pounding, but with patience, she would put this silly little man in his place. She sat up very straight in her chair. She just needed to guard against being overly rude, she told herself.

"Shall we start again at the beginning?" Clea suggested helpfully.

Smailes knew he had no choice but to put his trust in Rudy Kabalan. When he arrived back at the Port Chester house he found no one home at first, although Rudy's big powder blue Cadillac Fleetwood was parked in the driveway. Then he heard shouts out back and saw through the kitchen window Rudy and his kids out in the yard. His daughter pumped vigorously on a beltlike swing that hung from a rusted metal frame, and Rudy and his son were flinging a ball back and forth and catching it in baseball mitts. Smailes went out the back door to join them.

"Hi, Rudy," he said, thrusting his hands into his pockets and glancing up at the gray sky.

"Hey, Derek, what's happening?" responded Kabalan, with the forced jocularity that adults affect around children. "Hey, you guys, this is my friend Derek, the guy I told you about."

Marcella stopped her swing with an expert drag of her feet and came over to say hello, her eyes averted. She was a pretty, slight girl with frizzy hair caught in a braid, wearing overalls and a sky blue jacket.

"Hi," she said.

"Hi, mister," said Rudy Junior distrustfully in his turn, slapping a fist into his mitt. Young Rudy was indeed a cut-down version of his dad, with tight wiry hair, a Giants sweatshirt, and a double chin. He was a good twenty pounds overweight and waddled slightly as he walked. Sharing his father with a stranger on their weekend together was clearly a new and unwelcome experience for him.

"Hi," said Smailes awkwardly. "Hey, Rudy, can we talk?"

Kabalan saw the anxiety on Smailes' face and understood immediately. "Sure. Let's go inside. Hey kids, wanna watch a video?"

"Whaddya got?" asked his son reluctantly.

"I got *Star Trek Seven* and *Superman Five.*"

"Yeah, *Star Trek*," said Rudy Junior, brightening.

"Okay," said Marcella, obviously interested but affecting an air of injury anyway. Rudy took the mitt and ball from his son and guided both children toward the back door.

Smailes ducked down to his room, then came back up to discover Rudy seated at a desk in his dark den at the back of the house. Smailes tossed his packet of photographs down in front of him, took a seat, and looked around. The study was lined with fake walnut paneling, and around the walls was shelving which held a collection of bowling trophies and a profusion of artifacts and mementos from Rudy's trips around the world. One wall held photographs of his children at various ages, and a faded sepia print of a couple in wedding clothes that Smailes presumed was Rudy's parents. The only picture of Rudy himself was an incongruous black-and-white print of a much younger and lighter Rudy shaking hands with Jimmy Carter, which was signed and dedicated by Carter himself. Smailes looked at Rudy across his desk and smiled. Kabalan had never particularly struck him as a political liberal.

Smailes could hear the volume on the television turned particularly loud, and watched Rudy as he struggled out of his swivel chair to check the door was firmly closed.

"Hey, you want a drink or something?" he asked nervously, as if still unsure of his performance as host.

"No thanks," said Smailes.

"Okay," Rudy asked. "What happened?"

Smailes recounted in full detail his meeting with Vasily Malinovsky's son, pausing only when Kabalan interrupted with operational questions. Then he rewound the Siskin mission to its inception, filling in all the details he had left out in his earlier account. He described how a middle-aged Hispanic with two missing fingers had led the mission break-in, and how a man answering the same description was suspected of murdering the security guard in Newburgh a few nights later. Just a week later, one of Smailes' colleagues had been shot outside his apartment, perhaps by the same man. He explained the intercept and subsequent enticement of Mikhail Siskin, his increasing nervousness about KGB surveillance, and how the dental office they had used as cover had been raided while Smailes was back in England. Then he told of his attempt to meet with Grundy back in England and how he had discovered both Grundy and his mother brutally murdered. He detailed the circumstances of his frame-up and detention, and how his boss Van Deusen seemed to know exactly where to go to find the hidden safe-deposit key. Then he recounted his escape from Mount Vernon and his identification of the victims of the Staten Island murders, and finally, hesitantly, produced the photographs he had retrieved from the post office. As Rudy flipped through them, Smailes gave him Vasily Malinovsky's interpretation, then his own opinion. The last thing Smailes told him was his belief that Malinovsky Junior was the killer of Alan Sparks and the Russian courier, and his hunch that Malinovsky was dissembling his real allegiance. He was claiming to be KGB, whereas it was more likely he was GRU. He had finished off Sparks in a particularly distinctive fashion, and if he was linked in any way to the action back home, the implication was again GRU. What Smailes couldn't fathom was how the pieces fit together, but if he could somehow fleece Oleg of the false travel documents, he had a chance of getting through to Oslo before the British made asses of themselves. The only thing he omitted from his account was any suspicion that his lover Clea had been the leak on the British end, since he found the implications too painful and embarrassing.

Kabalan had listened to the bulk of Smailes' account in silence, but now he asked a bizarre question. He asked if Smailes was aware whether the bomb he had found in the diplomatic Lincoln was designed to go off or not. Smailes, never having made any connection between this event and the Siskin operation, was momentarily nonplussed.

"What?" he asked. Rudy repeated the question.

"Well, I don't know. There was a defective wire, I think, which suggests it might not have gone off. Although the police took it out to their range in the Bronx and detonated it, so the explosives were real enough. Why on earth—"

Kabalan, who was examining the last two photographs again, had suddenly held up his hand and shouted for him to be quiet.

"Sure, Rudy, but what—?"

"Look, look," he said excitedly. "These two old ones, this is the same guy in both. Look!"

"I know that, Rudy. Malinovsky said—"

"No, not him. *Him*," said Kabalan, training his desk lamp onto the prints, and turning them around so Smailes could view them.

Smailes caught his breath, his mind suddenly empty of all thought as a cataclysmic revelation struck him. "You're quite right, Rudy," he said quietly. "And I've just realized who the hell it is."

The discussion over the next two hours was interrupted only twice; once, when Rudy Junior came in to say the movie was over and could they watch *Superman* now, and the second time when Rudy Senior had to go to the door to pay the delivery man for the pizzas he had called in for the children's dinner. He came back with two slices each for Smailes and himself, a jumbo bottle of Coke and glasses, and a handful of paper napkins.

"Incredible," said Rudy, through a mouthful of dough and cheese. "Absolutely incredible. But it might work."

"How much would you want for a job like this?" Smailes asked.

Without hesitation, Kabalan replied, "Twenty grand, plus expenses."

Smailes smiled. "Well, that happens to be exactly what I can offer you," he replied. "You're hired."

"Listen, Derek, we're gonna need a third hand, I think. I dunno if we could pull this off just ourselves."

"I'm already ahead of you, Rudy," said Smailes, pulling a slab of pizza away from his face until the strands of cheese snapped. "I've got just the candidate."

Graham Booth, predictably, had eschewed the British housing inventory and had taken his allowance downtown in search of an apartment in the trendiest part of town. Consequently, he occupied a fifth-floor walk-up just off Bleecker Street in the West Village which was about the size of a shower stall. Smailes had stationed himself in a fast-food bar down the block which offered an oblique view of Booth's front window. It was already dark when Smailes arrived, but he was not surprised the studio apartment was still unlit. Graham was probably off at the mission, or maybe still in Mount Vernon, being barbecued by the investigating team from Bovingdon. He doubted very much that Graham could have been recalled as yet, although that had to be a firm prospect down the road a little.

Smailes left his perch at the high Formica counter a

couple of times to walk down the block and check how frequently people entered and left the building. Perhaps Graham was out with friends somewhere, he reasoned, drowning his sorrows, in which case Smailes was in for a long wait. But it was an unlikely prospect, he argued to himself. In his position Booth would behave exactly like most people—he would sit at home and mope.

It was after ten when the dark sedan with its diplomatic plates pulled off Bleecker and stopped in front of Booth's building. Booth emerged from the back seat with his head down, and did not turn back. The car drove off as Booth fiddled with his keys and entered his building. Smailes stationed himself directly opposite and watched as Graham's fifth-floor light came on. He waited another twenty minutes to make sure Booth was not going anywhere, then saw what he wanted—a couple descending the staircase to the hallway, about to leave.

Smailes walked up to the front door as the couple pushed through it. They ignored him as he grabbed the handle before the door swung shut, and headed up the stairs. At Booth's door he paused to regain his breath, then knocked twice, hesitantly.

"Who is it?" called Booth's voice.

"Itsa you neighbor. Downstairs. You gotta light boolb I can use?" said Smailes, in his best mock Italian.

Graham Booth threw the bolts on his door and opened it a crack. Smailes barreled through it, knocking Booth backward to the floor. Then he kicked the door shut and locked it again.

"Hullo, Graham," he said pleasantly.

Booth cowered on the floor, horrified. "Look, leave me alone, Derek, for God's sake. What do you want? Don't hurt me, okay?"

"Don't be silly, Graham. Come on, get up," he said, offering a hand. "No one's going to hurt you. Listen, have you got a beer you can spare?"

Graham Booth got to his feet without help and looked at him woundedly, rubbing a forearm. "Look, just get out, just leave, and I won't say I saw you, okay? Just go now. Don't get me into any more trouble than I'm already in."

"That's why I'm here, Graham. I can offer you a way to redeem yourself, by using some of your favorite skills. Listen, get those beers, and I'll explain the whole thing."

"You must be crazy. You think I'd believe anything you say? Those two blokes from A Branch are still not persuaded I'm not in league with you. The only hope for my career is to convince them I'm not."

"The Bovingdon team? They giving you a hard time?"

Graham Booth had taken a seat at the tiny table near his galley kitchen, beneath a poster of a Matisse still life. "What do you think? They're pretty upset. We just had another session in Mount Vernon, after they got back from going over your place. How the hell did you get out of there anyway? You have a key up your arse?"

Smailes laughed. "No. I used to live up there, didn't you know? Madge Ryan gave me a key so I could get out in case of fire. It was hidden beneath the sink."

"That cow. She could at least have told them, and spared me the grilling I've taken. I think they suspect I unlocked that bloody gate for you myself."

"Maybe she's forgotten all about it. I'll tell them, if you like, Graham. What else did they pull out of my place, anyway?" asked Smailes.

"Why should I tell you?"

"Let me take a guess. A one-time cipher pad and a gun. I met the guy today who planted them."

Booth looked at him suspiciously. "No, just the one-time pad. Hidden in a waterproof bag in the toilet tank. Look, what are you talking about, anyway, you met the guy?"

Smailes brought out the photographs from his jacket. "Look, offer me something to drink, there's a good chap, then we'll look at some snaps together," he said patronizingly, tossing the packet down in front of Booth and taking the seat opposite.

Booth listened in silence for the most part, taking

anxious pulls on his beer and occasionally having Smailes back up and go over a detail again. But his forehead was still furrowed with doubt by the time Smailes finished his pitch.

"Okay, it might be like you say. But how can I be sure? How can I be sure that Ralph doesn't have it right, that you're a Soviet agent after all? How do I know you're not trying to trap me into cooperating? I like this job, Derek. I don't want to do anything even more stupid than I already have and blow it completely. I just don't know if I can believe you."

Smailes shook his head in exasperation. "For Christ's sake, Graham. Look, who at the mission knows I'm in the soup?"

"What do you mean?"

"Who besides you, Madge, Reg Dwyer and these Bovingdon blokes knows I was arrested and then escaped? Do the comms know? Does Oral Yates?"

Booth was unsure what Smailes was driving at. "No, I don't think so. The ninth floor definitely knows, Smith's people, and the A-list diplomats, probably, but that's it, I think. Others have been told you're on leave, that's all. Some may have guessed something's up. But I don't see why Mr. Yates would know."

"Where are those cuffs you had on me the other day?"

"They're in the safe. What's that got to do with anything?"

"You agree the Voice Stress Analyzer is foolproof, if the operator's in control?"

"Yes, the VSA is foolproof, supposedly," said Booth, a little doubtfully.

"Okay. I've got my car here. Let's drive to the mission, go into the office, and you can handcuff me to my desk. Then run my story through the VSA. If I'm lying, you can simply call the Bovingdon boys in, and there I am, a stuffed duck, and you're a hero. If I'm telling the truth, then what do you have to lose by coming with me?

We're all screwed if we let Standiforth and Price-Jones walk into this shit storm, aren't we?"

Booth grudgingly acknowledged Smailes' logic. "What's to stop me cuffing you, then just calling Mount Vernon?" asked Booth.

"Nothing. But unlike you, I'm a trusting person," said Smailes sarcastically. "Well?"

"I'll get my coat," said Booth.

Booth flipped the switches on the VSA, then parked it on the desk between them, tipping it slightly so Smailes couldn't see the dials. Smailes glanced down at the wrist that was not handcuffed and saw that it was almost eleven-thirty.

"Ready?" asked Graham.

"Ready when you are," responded Smailes jauntily.

"Okay. Is your name Derek Smailes?"

"Yes."

"Did you formerly work for the Cambridgeshire police force?"

"Yes."

"Is your daughter's name Annie?"

"No."

As Smailes responded, Booth carefully calibrated the digital readout in the normative range. Satisfied he had the control levels right, he took a breath and launched into the real questions.

"Have you ever accepted money from a foreign government or intelligence service?"

"No."

"Did you murder Howard Grundy?"

"No."

"Do you know who did murder Howard Grundy?" A pause. "No."

"Did you conceal a safe-deposit key in your apartment?"

"No."

"Was Van Deusen's discovery of it the first time you'd seen it?"

"Yes."

"Did you betray the Colin operation?"

"No."

"Do you know who has betrayed it?"

Smailes hesitated. "No," he said eventually.

"Do you know who murdered Alan Sparks?"

"Yes," said Smailes, hesitating again. Booth was still tilting the equipment so Smailes could not see the readings, but he could see that Booth was brightening, and knew he was passing the test. Booth asked several more questions about the Colin mission and Smailes' plans for Oslo, and relaxed further. Then he asked, "Do you think Clea Lynch has the hots for me?"

"No," Smailes responded angrily.

"That's the only one you lied on, Derek," said Booth with a smirk, reaching to unlock Smailes' wrist. Smailes rubbed his freed hand then faked a cuff at the little smart aleck.

With his studious professionalism, Oral Yates had not acknowledged the two men earlier, preoccupied as they were as they hurried through the sign-in formalities on their way up to the mission. Now, as they signed out, Smailes tarried.

"Mr. Yates, can I ask you a question?"

Oral Yates removed his librarian's spectacles and stood regarding him mildly. His shirt collar was starched and his blue uniform, as always, was immaculate.

"Yes, sir, Mr. Smailes. What's on your mind?"

"Would you call me a racist?"

Oral Yates blinked twice, then cleared his throat. "No, sir, Mr. Smailes. I don't believe that's a word I would have cause to use about you, no." He hesitated slightly, as if unsure whether to continue. "Mind you, I would not say the same about everyone in your office, and I don't mean young Mr. Booth here."

Smailes nodded, weighing the degree of offense Ralph Van Deusen must have given for Yates to speak so boldly. "Well, thank you," he said, turning to leave.

"Someone been calling you names, Mr. Smailes?" Yates asked quietly.

"Well, someone I know used that word to describe me, yes."

"Let me tell you something, Mr. Smailes. The way some of the black folks behave in this town, *I'm* a racist," he said, leaning forward and gripping his podium. "Now, some people, they say all the problems we got are on account of white folks. Now, I'm not saying that any black person in this city is not goin' to face racial prejudice every single day of his life. I'm not sayin' that. What I'm sayin' is that the problems we got, that black folks have got, is mostly because the family and the church got no authority in our community anymore. And I don't see as you can lay all that at white folks' door, is what I'm saying. No sir, you never been anything but a fair-minded person with me, Mr. Smailes. And it's something I notice, believe me."

Smailes was both embarrassed and heartened by Yates' testimonial. But before he could respond, Yates spoke again. "But some people like to call names, you see, Mr. Smailes. This person you know, called you racist? He's got a name for me too, you can bet. Uncle Tom is what I get called, see, and that's something I don't like either," he said sadly, putting his spectacles back on the bridge of his nose, and pressing them home with his index finger. "You gentlemen have a good evening now," he said, returning to his ledger.

The yellow cab made three passes in front of the restaurant before it pulled over. Smailes was standing on the sidewalk dressed in his windbreaker jacket and cowboy boots, carrying an overnight bag that he had hurriedly packed in the wreckage of his apartment upstairs. The bank transaction had been considerably more risky, with Graham Booth providing some valuable countersurveillance as Smailes hurriedly closed his slush fund account. Then he had consigned his younger colleague to the cavernous Fleetwood and taken a taxi across to Brooklyn.

Malinovsky unfolded his long limbs from the back seat and climbed out, and Smailes saw that the prow of his hair had been clipped much shorter, so that it was now almost of equal length all over, and that he was wearing a sober jacket and jeans. He leaned in and paid off the driver, then came over to Smailes, a small bag over his right shoulder.

"Change of plan," he said, guiding Smailes down Tillary Street then turning right into Jay. He stopped in front of a light blue, late model sedan. The car the luckless Palov had rented for the Staten Island drop, Smailes told himself.

"Put your bag here," said Malinovsky, indicating the trunk lid. Smailes complied and Malinovsky waved his wrist in front of Smailes' body, then across the bag. Smailes heard a faint whine, and then Malinovsky checked his jacket pocket.

"What do you have in there, with batteries? A tape recorder?" he asked angrily.

Smailes frowned, genuinely puzzled. "Nothing, as far as I know."

"Do not try and play tricks with me, Mr. Smailes," said Malinovsky, unzipping the bag and rummaging inside it.

"Oh yeah, a travel clock," said Smailes, remembering, but Malinovsky had already retrieved it from his toilet kit. "What else?" asked Malinovsky.

"Nothing. Just clothes, Oleg. Check if you like."

Malinovsky felt around inside the bag further, discovered his fringed buckskin coat and began going through its pockets. It was all Smailes could do to prevent himself from felling the skinny runt and stomping a boot into his gut. Malinovsky looked up and saw Smailes regarding him pleasantly. Then he dropped the tiny black clock to the sidewalk and crushed it with his heel.

"Let's go," he said, producing keys. "Kennedy Airport. You drive."

Smailes started the car and emerged slowly into Tillary, pointing the car down the hill toward the expressway ramp. He purposely did not look in his rearview mirror. Malinovsky sat stone-faced, occasionally looking across at Smailes as he drove the looping route out toward the airport in the deeper recesses of Queens. As they forked off the highway, Smailes asked matter-of-factly, "Which airline?"

"British Airways."

"Where we going?"

"Kingston, Jamaica. Now, no more questions." Smailes gripped the wheel a little more tightly, looking up for the signs for their terminal. Eventually, they found their exit and Smailes followed a hotel shuttle bus around toward the long-term parking lot.

"You could have taken short term," said Malinovsky.

"You want me to turn back, Oleg?"

"No, it is not significant," he said, as Smailes drew the car to a halt.

"Let me have the passport and ticket, Oleg," he said.

"Not until we are inside the terminal," Malinovsky replied, reaching into the back seat for his bag. Smailes handed him the parking lot ticket and reached back also, locking his door as he climbed out.

Malinovsky came around to his side of the car. "Okay, I think we can walk," he said.

Smailes had been waiting for this moment, having rehearsed the moves in his mind a dozen times. He'd resolved on the hot shin and the dead knee, not wanting to leave anything to chance. Poor Oleg, he told himself. Altogether a little out of his depth.

As Malinovsky approached, Smailes stepped forward and grabbed his lapels, then stamped his cowboy boot down the tall youth's shin, from knee to ankle. It was a move his father had taught him years before, long before he ever joined the police or used it on football hooligans. Malinovsky howled in pain and buckled forward. Smailes grabbed him by a tuft of hair in front and jerked his head down as he brought his knee up with all its force. There was a crumpling sound of collapsing bone and cartilage, and Malinovsky shrieked and fell to the ground, his body twisted in agony. Blood poured from the wreckage of the front of his face. As he squirmed, Smailes kicked him very hard, once, behind the kidneys. As he aimed another kick, firm hands gripped his shoulders.

"Steady, Derek," said Rudy Kabalan. Graham Booth was climbing out of the other side of the blue Fleetwood, which had drawn up in the next bay.

"He killed a colleague of mine," Smailes explained, gathering himself, but not taking his eyes off the prostrate, writhing figure of Oleg Malinovsky. A frothy, whimpering sound came from where his mouth ought to be. Smailes reached down and retrieved passports and tickets from Malinovsky's inside pocket. He tossed Malinovsky's Finnish passport and the tickets aside, pocketing the Lars Tulku document.

"Cuff him to the wheel," Smailes told Booth in a tone of contempt. "I'll call Lustig from the terminal. You spot the switch okay, Rudy?"

"No problema," said Kabalan suavely.

A woman and her daughter had emerged from a car nearby and walked anxiously by them, appalled by the horrific scene. Graham Booth pulled a bloodstained hand away from Malinovsky's face and slapped a handcuff on it, then tugged the limp form toward the open car door and lifted the arm until he was able to hook the second cuff onto the steering wheel. Malinovsky's eyes were screwed tight against the pain, but he was still conscious. His mashed lips moved soundlessly. He had a broken nose, teeth, and maybe jaw, but he would live, Smailes told himself disgustedly.

He turned and only then noticed Kabalan manipulating an enormous suitcase from the trunk of the Fleetwood. His mood brightened. "What the hell have you got there, Rudy?" he asked.

"Couldn't be a hundred percent on the uniform," Kabalan explained. "Wanted some choice."

23

Oslo was a stolid and comely city of placid northern European burghers, built around the most beautiful harbor Smailes had ever seen. The Oslo fjord was dominated in its turn by the turreted Akershus Castle, the Viking-era fortress in which Rudy informed him the celebrated traitor Quisling had been shot. In fact, it was difficult for Smailes to conceive that this same city and its idyllic harbor, now studded with pleasure boats and yachts, had once broadcast the Vikings upon the world, sending them howling across the seas for plunder and ruin. Modern Oslo seemed to epitomize civilization itself—prosperous, clean and tolerant. It was also, for this brief interval, the center of the Western world, and flags of the thirty-five nations represented at the summit fluttered everywhere from hotels and public buildings.

Security at Oslo's Fornebu airport had been both subtle and tight when they landed after the long, all-night flight, and Smailes found his palms sweating when he presented his forged passport to the expressionless immigration officer. Oleg's work was apparently first rate, however, since it was handed back to him without comment. The customs inspector, to his relief, addressed him in English, the Scandinavian lingua franca, and failed to find anything unusual in the fact that a Finnish businessman on a supposed sales trip was carrying little besides a buckskin jacket, some underwear and a toilet bag. The summit had gotten under way without incident and the airport officials seemed relatively relaxed, although there were still plenty of uniformed security people about, together with a number of well-dressed civilians with miniature receivers in their ears.

Booth and Kabalan passed through to the concourse unimpeded and the three travelers met up at the information booth. Predictably, there were no vacant hotel rooms within twenty kilometers of Oslo, so they accepted the recommendation of a guest house at Sandvika, a resort community to the west of the city. They visited three car rental agencies before finding exactly the vehicles they wanted, and after completing formalities with Rudy's American Express card, they drove both cars out to the Hotel Bergen in Sandvika, thirty minutes away. Booth and Smailes checked into a double room, and Kabalan took a single. Within twenty minutes they had set off again, to complete their reconnaissance before allowing themselves to recuperate from the jet lag. Rudy again drove the rented Volvo, the larger car.

Kabalan had obviously studied local maps, for after they passed the airport exit and entered the western outskirts of the city, he forked right off route E18 down Drammens Veien, an elegant, tree-lined street of impressive buildings that stood behind high walls and security gates. From the variety of flags and uniformed guards about, Smailes realized they were driving along Oslo's Embassy Row and wondered aloud what kind of head count of world leaders the street currently boasted.

As they passed in front of the Brazilian and Israeli embassies on their right, the ground suddenly gave way to wooded parkland that sloped dramatically down toward the sea and gave a partially obscured view of the harbor and the promontory of land beyond. A couple of distinctive buildings dominated the far shore, the first a very Scandinavian affair of multiple gables and roofs, and the second a sleek glass pyramid. Rudy pointed them out and explained casually they were museums of Viking culture and polar expeditions, respectively.

Below their car on the near shore was a nondescript three-story building of white stucco with barred windows and a high fence, from the top of which fluttered a red flag. To its side was a squat concrete construction that looked like an air raid shelter. Kabalan jerked his thumb toward the buildings. "Soviet Embassy," he said knowledgeably. "That's where Rostov and the Soviet leadership are staying."

"What's that thing beside it?" asked Smailes.

"It's a World War Two pillbox the KGB uses as a guardhouse."

"I thought you'd never been here before," said Smailes.

"I haven't. I just do my research," replied Kabalan pointedly. He turned to look up the hill, away from the harbor. Indicating an elegant Victorian mansion with a modern extension and a large car park out back, Kabalan said, "British Embassy. That's where your team is staying."

"And Roger Standiforth too, if he was telling me the truth," said Smailes. "You know for sure, Graham?"

"No," said Booth from the back seat. "I just know where you and Ralph were supposed to stay."

"Hotel Scandinavia, right?" said Smailes.

"Right," said Booth.

"Let's go take a look," said Kabalan. "Dumb move, if you ask me," he added as they drove off. "It's where all the goddamn media is staying."

Kabalan steered the big Volvo expertly through dense traffic to the fringe of the commercial district, then took a left in front of a manicured park at the end of which stood the columned facade of the Royal Palace. Then, maneuvering around a traffic island, he pulled up in front of the huge glass box of the SAS Hotel Scandinavia. The car was illegally parked, so Kabalan did not linger. "Largest hotel in Norway," he offered. "Twenty-one stories, a thousand beds. Now let's take a look at the Vista."

Through the simple expedient of checking news stories in the *Times* before leaving, Kabalan had learned that the Soviets had brought the largest single delegation to Norway, a team of almost three hundred diplomats and staff, and that they had commandeered an entire downtown hotel to house them. The Vista Hotel stood on Storgata, a busy commercial street just blocks from the Oslo Plaza Hotel and its Spektrum conference center where the talks were actually being held. Kabalan drove slowly past its steel-and-glass entrance, which was barricaded behind Day-Glo traffic cones and wooden railings. The Vista was less than half the size of the Scandinavia, but of the same generic, boxy construction.

"There, look," said Kabalan as they drove by. "It's got an underground lot. There's the entrance. See the guard station down there?"

Smailes craned backward. "That's perfect, Rudy. Perfect. Let's make another pass. Hey, Graham, look over there."

The two Britons peered out of the back window as Kabalan drove slowly on. A handful of demonstrators paraded on the opposite sidewalk, outnumbered by a phalanx of Oslo policemen. Kabalan made a big wheeling turn at the end of the street and drove by again, and this time each man paid particular interest to a different aspect of the scene. Booth looked carefully at the dress and behavior of the demonstrators, while Smailes peered down the parking garage ramp at the guard post below, and Kabalan seemed intently interested in the police themselves. In fact, as they drove through into the huge plaza in front of the central railway station, Kabalan pulled over briefly to scribble notes. Then he looked across at Smailes.

"Okay, *finito?*" he asked.

"Let's just check out the main police station, then home," said Smailes.

Kabalan went into the glove box for his Oslo street map. "Okay, other end of town," he said, jabbing a fat finger at the map. "Let's get this over with."

Back at the Hotel Bergen, the three travelers forced themselves to stay awake for an early dinner, then dragged themselves back upstairs.

"See you tomorrow, Rudy," said Smailes at their door. "Could be a busy day."

Smailes was watching the evening news broadcast, which, although delivered in singsong Norwegian, allowed him to pick up sufficient details to learn that everything at the Oslo summit was proceeding according to plan. The formal talks would be concluded the following day, Thursday, then a banquet and signing ceremony would be held Friday at the Akershus Castle, with King Harald of Norway presiding. The news program showed tables and graphs of troop and armaments levels in Europe before and after the signing of the accord, and a map showing the broad swath of the proposed demilitarized zone. Smailes had to concur, it really was an extraordinary diplomatic accomplishment, if ever properly consummated.

Graham Booth was seated at the mirror of the dressing table wearing a shabby secondhand raincoat, manipulating a bald wig over his newly shorn hair. A tube of rubber cement and sticks of makeup were scattered in front of him. Smailes looked again at his watch when the door rattled and he got up to admit an excited Rudy Kabalan, who was carrying an armful of parcels, which he tipped over onto Smailes' bed.

"Hey, look at this, you guys," he said, going into a paper bag and producing a bizarre-looking, boat-shaped paper hat with flattened sides.

"Got it in a joke shop. No good, right?" he said, tossing it aside. "Now, look at this."

He went into another parcel and produced a similar hat, but this time made from heavy blue wool with yellow piping around the edges. "Now, this is the real thing," he announced proudly, planting it on his head. He looked absurd. "Found it at a theatrical costumer's outside the city." Then he retrieved a small heraldic badge of a gold lion rampant from a different parcel. "Just have to sew this on the front."

"Terrific, Rudy," said Smailes. "You fix up the Volvo?"

"Naw. Let's wait till dark. I got the decals and the paint. We all set?"

"All set," said Booth, swiveling on his chair and presenting his bald, bedraggled appearance.

"All set," said Smailes, laughing despite himself.

It was just after five-thirty and Smailes was guiding the blue Saab awkwardly through Oslo's rush hour traffic. He was wearing his buckskin jacket, jeans and cowboy boots, and the percussion of his heartbeat in his inner ear blocked out all other noise. He had almost called the whole thing off at lunchtime, wondering aloud whether the safest bet wasn't simply to hunt down Standiforth and present him with all their evidence. But even Graham Booth had demurred. He didn't think anything Smailes could produce at this point would hold any sway at all with the British, and they would simply get themselves shipped home.

Smailes turned left at Oslo Cathedral into Storgata, soon seeing ahead of him the small posse of demonstrators with their police escort across from the Soviet hotel. As he passed in front of the barricades he swung left down the parking ramp, slowing as the plainclothes guard stepped out of his cubicle and held up his hand. Smailes wound down the driver's window as the man said something to him in Russian. Smailes responded simply by producing his passport from his inside pocket and handing it over. Now came the real test of Oleg's handiwork, he told himself.

The guard backed off into his cubicle and produced a walkie-talkie from a bracket on his hip. There then followed an extended exchange as the guard read out the details of Smailes' travel document to an unseen superior. Eventually he returned to the car.

"Please report to the colonel in Room 311, comrade,"

he said in English, then stood back as Smailes pulled the Saab into the void of the underground garage. He parked as close as he could to the elevator bank and left the car unlocked. He was beginning to feel considerably more calm as he waited for the elevator car to arrive. Then he stepped in and punched the button for the lobby.

Smailes was aware he cut an unusual figure as he swaggered across the plush carpet to the reception desk, and asked in a loud voice for the room number of Mikhail Siskin. As the clerk consulted his computer screen, Smailes glanced around to see two expensively dressed men with bulges around their jacket vents, watching him intently from behind a large tree that stood in a brushed steel planter. Smailes was given a room number on the seventh floor, then sauntered back to the elevator bank as casually as he was able.

Mikhail Siskin answered the door himself in his socks and shirtsleeves, holding what looked like a glass of Scotch. He was clearly aghast at the apparition in front of him, and actually took two steps backward. But he regained himself quickly, and said in a loud voice, "George, what a wonderful surprise! I didn't expect to see you here in Oslo, of all places! Vladimir, we have a visitor, my old friend George Phillips."

He stood aside to admit Smailes, who was fighting his own surge of panic at the news Siskin had a roommate. He saw an older, heavyset man, also in shirtsleeves, lying on a bed watching television. The Russian got up on one elbow as Smailes entered the room.

"This is Vladimir, a colleague from the disarmament conference in Geneva. Vladimir Butanov, George Phillips."

The older man frowned and made no attempt to get up to greet Smailes. Siskin kept talking urgently in English. "George is a friend from the UN. Listen, Vladimir, let us have a few moments in private, will you? This is an unexpected visit."

Butanov swung his feet off the bed and glared across at Siskin, then responded angrily in Russian. Smailes stood aside awkwardly as the older man thrust his feet into slip-on shoes and retrieved his jacket from the back of a chair. Then he leaned forward, turned off the television and headed toward the door.

"Remember, Mikhail Karlovich, the bus leaves in thirty minutes," he said in English, closing the door behind him.

As soon as he was gone, Siskin spat in an angry whisper, "What the hell are you doing here? How did you get into the hotel? What on earth is going on?"

"Plan's changed, Mikhail," Smailes said quickly. "We identified the leak, and we've got to take you directly to the airport."

Siskin hesitated. "What do you mean? Don't you realize that Butanov is my KGB escort? Don't you realize he has gone straight to the KGB commander to report that you are here?"

"Okay, I'm sorry, it was a risk. So let's get going. Just get your passport and jacket."

"What do you mean? Who is the leak?" asked Siskin, sitting down to tie his shoes.

"Bruce. Ralph Van Deusen, my head of station. He was recruited in a KGB honeytrap eighteen years ago. He has betrayed us all along. The KGB would have arrested all of us if we tried to waltz you out of that restaurant tonight. A big, nasty scene."

Smailes watched as disbelief, fear, anger, then resignation passed across Siskin's face. He saw he had no choice.

"How do we get out of this place? You have a car?"

"In the underground lot."

"We are still taking nine o'clock flight?"

"No, we're booked on the SAS seven o'clock flight to Heathrow. Are you ready? Let's go."

Siskin retrieved his blue UN passport from a bureau drawer and allowed Smailes to escort him out of the room to the elevator. The car arrived quickly and the two men stood side by side in silence, watching the panel as the lights descended through the floors. They bypassed the lobby and went straight to the first basement level. Smailes checked his watch. "The blue Saab," he said. "Hurry."

Siskin climbed into the passenger side and hooked on his seat belt. He had gone gray, and licked his lips nervously. Smailes wound down his window and backed up the car sharply. Gratefully, he could hear a ruckus coming from the area of the guard station.

Smailes drove around to the exit and waited. Graham Booth, wearing his downtrodden Soviet exile costume, was giving the KGB guard a terrible time, waving a heavy placard that read FREE IOSEF LEVIN, and yelling at the top of his lungs in an incomprehensible tongue. The guard was trying to reason with him, but as Booth spied the Saab he suddenly bolted toward the elevators, the guard taking after him and flooring him with a flying tackle. The heavy sign went spinning across the floor as the guard immobilized Booth with a hammerlock, pinning him with his knee as he struggled with his two-way radio. He did not even seem to notice as Smailes accelerated past them up the ramp and into the bright Norwegian sunshine.

Siskin seemed to relax slightly as Smailes steered him across the bridge from the multistory car park into the departures building and across to the SAS check-in counters. Smailes produced their tickets and passports for inspection and collected boarding passes, the clerk telling them to hurry to Gate 34 since the plane had already begun boarding. They rounded the Pan Am and British Airways desks and followed signs to their right for Gate 34. After a clerk checked their boarding cards, they passed through the security checkpoint and through automatic doors into the departures lounge.

"We need to hurry, Mikhail," said Smailes, grabbing him by the elbow and steering him past the duty-free emporium. The two men mounted an escalator, then continued straight toward their gate, which was just to the right of the bar area. Siskin kept looking all about him, but did not resist Smailes' grip as they walked briskly along. For Smailes' part, he showed no interest in his surroundings. He was quite confident they were being closely watched.

The male clerk smiled brightly as the two men approached his podium at the entrance to the jetway. He looked down to inspect their boarding cards and waved them through pleasantly. Smailes slowed his pace deliberately, staying half a step behind Siskin and hearing their footsteps echo from the walls of the telescopic metal ramp. The entrance to the plane itself seemed about a mile away.

Smailes had once seen a television drama about an eighteenth-century Scottish sheep-stealer, who was hanged at Edinburgh Castle after a celebrated trial. The behavior of the hangman in the execution scene had fascinated and appalled him long afterward, for the man treated his charge with utmost care and gentleness as he guided him backward up the scaffold, then caressed the masked head in its fat noose one last time before thrusting him off the ladder into violent oblivion. It was a similarly perverted solicitude that Smailes now practiced upon Mikhail Siskin, he thought afterward.

As the cabin stewardess smiled and prepared to take their boarding cards, Smailes tapped Siskin gently on the shoulder. He wheeled, a puzzled look on his face, at which Smailes slipped a careful arm around his shoulder and brought his knee with all its force into his groin. Siskin buckled forward in agony and the stewardess cried out in alarm, but Smailes produced his Home Office pass from his pocket and yelled, "Interpol!" and simultaneously barged through the panic door of the emergency exit. He thrust the disabled Siskin in front of him down the metal stairway, their footsteps clattering above the deafening whine of jet engines. An airline employee in overalls and orange ear baffles looked up at them quizzically, but at that moment a white Oslo police car drove up at speed and screeched to a halt under the wing of the big jet. The driver reached back and pushed open the back door of the red-and-blue-striped Volvo, which had the word POLITI printed on it. A blue magnetic light flashed on the roof. Smailes thrust Siskin into the back seat and climbed in after him.

Rudy Kabalan leaned over from the driver's seat in his Oslo policeman's uniform, complete with its distinctive hat. "Time to go?" he asked.

Smailes looked up at the stewardess and her crew chief who were standing anxiously on the metal landing of the emergency stairs. Then he saw them exchange shrugs and go back inside.

"Time to go, Rudy," said Smailes, settling back into his seat next to the doubled-over figure of Mikhail Siskin, who was breathing with difficulty through his teeth.

Kabalan guided the big Volvo expertly around the airport's internal traffic lanes, saluting a colleague as they passed through the mesh gates by the catering area into the airport frontage road. He looked up in the rearview mirror and gave Smailes a thumbs-up, then returned his attention to the road.

As instructed, Kabalan had stashed half bottles of Scotch and vodka in the pouch behind his seat. Siskin, still ghostly pale, was beginning to straighten up, and Smailes held up both bottles in front of him. Siskin grabbed the Scotch hungrily, removed the cap, and took a large swallow. Then he gasped and leaned backward against the headrest, his eyes closed tight as his other hand still grasped his wounded testicles.

"You got greedy, Mikhail," said Smailes eventually. "If you hadn't tried to recruit me, you would have gotten away with the whole thing. But Oleg wasn't up to it. He made too many mistakes."

Siskin rolled his head around on its support and opened one eye. "Oleg tried to recruit you?" he croaked. Then, although the movement seemed to cause him pain, he shook his head sadly several times.

"Yes, I think it would have worked," Smailes went on. "First, set me up like some counterintelligence hero, feed us the bait of Irina's phony illness, then string us along with some haute cuisine intelligence. Then get me dumped from the endgame in Oslo, since I was the only

391

one with field experience and might have finally begun to get suspicious. Then waltz out of your restaurant with the New York station chief and the head of K Branch on your arm, while a signal goes through to London and the world's press assembles at Heathrow, since the Soviet Embassy is claiming the British have kidnapped a diplomat from Oslo. Then you, Standiforth and Van Deusen march out into a bank of klieg lights and microphones, you fall into the arms of your military attaché and hold an impromptu press conference about the brutality of the British intelligence service and its violation of international law. That was why you insisted on a commercial flight, wasn't it, Mikhail? All this would have provided the pretext for the army brass to declare a military emergency back home, right, in the unfortunate absence of the political leadership. Only then it would have become a full-fledged coup, wouldn't it? But it was never going to work, Mikhail. You see, the government is on to you. They sent a courier to New York with surveillance pictures of the ringleaders, along with a couple of really prize, older ones. Show him, Rudy."

Kabalan went into the glove box and held up the sheaf of photographs over his shoulder. Smailes took them.

"Look now, here we've got Dolghorukov, Kott, Grishkin and Tumanov, right? Then these last two," said Smailes, fanning through them. "Didn't catch it at first, but you're in both of them, aren't you, Mikhail? Oh, a lot younger, much more hair and no mustache yet, but it's you all right, lolling against the tank next to your protector Kott, and there in the front pew of the Military-Diplomatic Academy. Which made you Spetsnaz and GRU, didn't it, Mikhail, instead of Moscow Law School and the Institute of International Relations? You're a military spy, aren't you, Mikhail? And a pretty good one too, I would say."

Siskin was still leaning back against his headrest and now half closed his eyes. "Very clever, Mr. Smailes," he said, without looking at him. "Why don't you tell him who you really work for, Mr. Kabalan?"

Smailes froze. How the hell did Siskin know Rudy's name? Kabalan looked up slowly into the rearview, searching for Siskin's eyes. Smailes was fighting panic, wondering if he wasn't the victim of some outrageous triple bluff, but Rudy held Siskin's gaze with a look of contempt.

"Chew my fat one, Boris," Rudy said, returning his attention to the road. Siskin closed his eyes again, a slight smile playing on his lips, then brought the whiskey bottle to his mouth once more. Smailes continued.

"Now, I notice you happen to prefer Scotch, Mikhail, which doesn't come as a big surprise. After we identified you in the prints, we had to rewind the whole operation to figure how you'd done it. At first, the one thing I couldn't figure was how you defeated the lie detection we ran on the tapes of the contact meeting. Then I remembered that as soon as you came into the hotel room, you made a couple of ordinary remarks in a loud voice which didn't seem significant at the time. You said you had only just decided to come up and meet me, and that you preferred vodka to whiskey. Both lies, right? You knew what kind of system we used, that we would calibrate control levels from your initial remarks. Then none of your subsequent lies stood out, did they? Pretty clever. Which meant all the rest of it was bogus. The deliberate mistake in the sign-in sheets so we would sweep the mission again and find the bugging gear, the phony conversation we intercepted, even the bomb in the Lincoln. It was all just bait, wasn't it, Mikhail?"

Siskin decided to break his silence, rolling the bald dome of his head around on its headrest to look across at Smailes. He was apparently recovering, since he moved his hand from his crotch to wipe his mouth and mustache. "Ah, Mr. Smailes, you are indeed a Viking," he said slowly. "We knew it all along. We just had to convince your employers."

"What do you mean?"

" 'Viking' is the term the GRU gives its senior officers. We are the elite, the ones trusted with the most hazardous missions. We are supported by the 'borzois,' officers and agents of lower rank. Oleg was just a foot soldier, you see, a borzoi, but he wanted to be a Viking. That must have been why he tried to recruit you. Recruiting new agents is the quickest way to upgrade your rank. You think I would have authorized Malinovsky to try and recruit you? Give me more credit, my friend. I have considerably more respect for your abilities than that. Oleg was a simple shit-eater. They are the worst, the least dependable kind of agent. Give me someone who works for money, any day."

"Was the car bomb really necessary, Mikhail?" Smailes asked.

"I thought so," Siskin replied evenly. "The discovery of the bug could easily have been credited to your technician. This was an unusual opportunity we were offering your people. We needed to make you look like James Bond."

Kabalan was driving the Volvo west on the motorway out of Oslo, but at Drammen he took the exit for Kongsberg, then headed into the mountains.

"Where are we going?" asked Siskin.

"Anywhere you like," said Smailes, "as long as we kill a few hours. What do you think's going on back in Moscow at this moment?"

"Your guess is as good as mine," said Siskin resignedly.

Smailes resumed his reconstruction of the intricate trap into which the British had so nearly fallen. "Now I understand why the security guard had to be murdered, Mikhail, since he was instructed to make the mistake on the original sign-in sheet, so I would know there had been a penetration, right? He was killed to preserve the original deception. Am I right, Mikhail?"

Siskin had closed his eyes again and his face was impassive. He did not respond.

"You knew we'd find the burst-transmitter bug even-

tually, and somehow you managed to tip off Howard
Grundy about the leaky security glass in your apartment,
so he pulled off an intercept that seemed completely random, didn't it? Actually, I slipped up there. There was no
background noise on that original recording, and I should
have known that Russians never discuss anything serious
without at least a radio or a television playing, usually
both, in the background. But you wanted to be sure we
heard every word, didn't you? Somehow, Kevin Butterworth worked this out, didn't he? He knew Howard had
been set up to make that intercept, maybe he realized the
lack of interference meant it had to be a dud, so when he
tried to warn me, you had him killed. Then you had to
murder Grundy too, when I went back to England, for the
same reason. You had to make sure I didn't shake it out of
him, how he really came to be in Riverdale that evening. I
don't believe he could ever have been consciously working for you. Am I right, Mikhail? And, tell me, are you
really married to Tatanya? Do you even have a daughter?"

Siskin smiled again and opened his eyes. He looked
across at Smailes with a puzzled look, as if noticing for the
first time the incongruous cowboy gear he was wearing.
"We got so tired, night after night, repeating those same
lines, the same story," he said slowly, as if he was struggling against an enormous lassitude. "No, Tatanya, she is
not my type, candidly speaking. She is my cipher clerk,
one of our agents inside the *referentura*. No, we have no
children, of course. We got the idea when we read about
the work of your clever neurosurgeons. There is a Jewish
émigré musician, Erik Susskind, who has a daughter at
the UN school. It seemed close enough, if you ever
checked. We fed the information of her existence to your
Soviet man through the cook at Riverdale who keeps your
files up to date. It was not difficult. Neither was creating
the hospital records. But, believe me, I know nothing of
the murder of this man Grundy. Neither this Butterworth.
Who is he? The security guard, I accept, was unfortunate,
but necessary. That was the only murder I have autho-

rized. Now tell me something. Who was this courier who brought you photographs?"

"Major General Anton Palov, deputy commander of the Carpathian military district," said Smailes. "He was killed by Oleg on Staten Island just before you left, along with our Soviet man, as you call him. Don't tell me you didn't know about that either?"

Siskin ignored the question. "Palov? Never heard of him," he said. He closed his eyes again and creased his brow for a moment, finally relaxing as a realization struck him. "Palov? Shot by Oleg, you say? He must have been Rostov's man inside the conspiracy. Of course, it was infiltrated. I was never told the larger purpose of this mission, you see, but I knew it had to be something like a coup, or we would never spend my cover. Kott must have found out why Palov was being dispatched, and notified Oleg directly. He tried to recruit you? Ah, Oleg."

"Did you control Oleg?" Smailes asked.

"Not really. He was Kott's agent. He felt he needed an additional radio man in New York. Tatanya trained him."

"And you communicated with him through that drop at the newsagent's booth by the UN?"

"You saw me that day? I could not be sure. Your watcher, he has to be good at disguises. That was him again, the dissident at the hotel?"

"Yes."

"Ah, very clever. You see, my borzois were only the caliber of Oleg. Inadequate, really."

"Yes," Smailes agreed, "he made several mistakes. He claimed to be KGB, but finished off our man with the bullet-in-the-mouth signature, you see? Then he showed me a forged passport that would guarantee my entry into any KGB-controlled facility in the world. If I needed any encouragement to try to get to Oslo myself, that was sufficient. You must have got quite a shock when you saw me standing there. What did you think, Mikhail?"

"I really wasn't sure. I thought maybe I was blown,

but I had no choice, did I? That really was a KGB escort I had."

"Were they ever as vigilant as you claimed? Were they really on to you?"

"I don't think so. Malik in my office is certainly a plant, but he is a fool. No, I don't think the KGB has ever had the slightest suspicion who I really am. The roommate at the hotel is just routine. There was no recall, of course."

"The break-in at the dentist's office?"

"That was Oleg. To make sure you understood the urgency of my situation."

"Now, that was another mistake of yours, Mikhail. You needed to provide cover for your agent on the inside, so you decided to point the finger at Clea Lynch. With her university background, maybe it seemed plausible. But you'll never be able to understand a woman like Clea, Mikhail. She's into designer socialism, you see. She'd faint at the first sight of polyester."

Kabalan in the front seat rocked with laughter at this remark, the big uniformed shoulders shaking beneath the preposterous hat. Smailes persisted.

"So who was really helping you, Mikhail? You had to have someone on the inside, a feedback agent to tell you how it was all playing in New York and London, to provide my handwriting samples, mugshots and apartment keys, the same person who told you of my plans to grill the guard, of Kevin's unscheduled trip to see me. Now Ralph Van Deusen is no shit-eater, that's for sure, but he's still not much use as an agent. He went straight to the concealed key in my apartment, after pretending to look for it elsewhere. That was a GRU honeytrap you caught him in, wasn't it? He's been blackmailed into working for you since then, hasn't he?"

Siskin thought for a long moment before replying, staring out at the spectacular scenery as Kabalan guided the Volvo around the majestic escarpment of the Norsjo fjord toward Larvik. "I think I have probably said enough, my friend. Now I would like to meet with your Mr.

Standiforth, or with this man Price-Jones, if he is here. There is much I can offer in return for asylum in your country. Very much. You see, I told one lie that was bigger than all the rest, the night we met at the Plaza. I said I would never defect. Well, there is nothing left for me now in the Soviet Union. I am sure it is as you say, that Rostov has known of the plot against him all along and has taken steps to neutralize it. No doubt the ringleaders will be shot. Myself, I am probably heading for some rocket station in Siberia, if I escape court-martial. Viktor Kott is finished, too, that is for sure, so in that sense I am free. I would like to discuss our original bargain, that I will come to your country for three years, then return to the UN. You may be surprised, but I have quite enjoyed my time there. I have been wondering if there was some way to shed this cover and become a legitimate diplomat."

"Not a chance, Mikhail. Six people are dead, by my count. I don't see why I should give you any chance to make a deal and beat the rap."

"Be reasonable, Mr. Smailes. Look at my situation, if you will. I am Volga German, born in Kazakhstan after the war when Stalin exiled my family there. You know what it is to be Volga German, in the Soviet Union? It is like being Irish in your country, only worse. Just the lowest jobs are available to us, no matter how clever or able we are. So I do well at the technical institute, but I see no future for myself in Karaganda. So I join the army, and again I do well. I am tank commander by the time I am twenty-four. So I come to the attention of Viktor Kott, a bigshot in Spetsnaz. He observes me for a while without my knowledge, then arranges for me to get into big trouble with my commanding officer. I am headed for prison, but he intercedes, rescues me, and offers me a transfer into Spetsnaz. This is something you do not refuse, my friend. Kott tells me our careers will be linked forever, and as long as he rises, so do I. Then Kott is promoted to GRU, and I am taken with him. He trains me as a weapons specialist. Yes, I did enroll at MGIMO, but that was all part of his plan. At the same time I study at the GRU higher school, as your photograph shows. But no one, none of my classmates at MGIMO, know this. So I graduate as a legitimate diplomat, and become a disarmament specialist. All the time, I am working for Kott, for military intelligence. I work in the foreign ministry, then the Disarmament Commission, then the Secretariat itself. There can be no better place for a military spy, can there? But that career is now over. I no longer have any debt to pay to Viktor Kott, since he will undoubtedly be one of those who will be shot. So I can be of many uses to your counterintelligence agency, I think, Mr. Smailes. Let us just have a discussion, the two of us, with Standiforth. I think it could be quite instructive."

Smailes listened with careful attention as Siskin described his offer. He also knew, intuitively, that Standiforth and Price-Jones would buy it, as a means of saving some face from the botched operation. But just as intuitively, he knew he could not live with himself if he went along with it. Butterworth, Grundy and Sparks had been three of the less tarnished souls of the intelligence world, and their deaths should not go unpunished.

"I said forget it, Mikhail," said Smailes in as hard a voice as he could muster. "We've got a date, you and me, with some of those chimps back at the Vista."

Siskin looked at him in mute appeal for a moment, but saw that further argument was useless. He took another pull from his bottle, rested his head against the window, and appeared to fall asleep.

Kabalan had reached the Oslo fjord coastline and steered the car north out of Larvik back toward Sandefjord and Oslo. After listening to Siskin's rhythmic breathing for several minutes, he glanced at Smailes in the mirror and said, "He's fakin' it, right?"

"I don't think so, Rudy," said Smailes. "Seen it before, when I was a cop. We caught a serial sex killer once, and as soon as he was booked he slept for the better part of two days. The pretending's gone, see, and they can finally relax. He's asleep all right," he added, looking across at Siskin.

"That was quite a deal he was offering," said Kabalan, nonchalantly.

"I don't want to get into it, Rudy."

"Okay, okay," said Kabalan, holding up a hand. "Only passing the time."

By the time the car pulled up outside the Vista Hotel it was after nine o'clock and quite dark. Smailes went into his inside jacket pocket and handed Kabalan an envelope.

"Here you go, Rudy. Second installment, courtesy of Soviet military intelligence. Thanks for everything."

Kabalan thrust the envelope into his uniform and looked at Smailes again in the rearview. "You bet," he said. "It was fun."

"Where are you headed now?"

"I'll take this boat through the car wash, then get it back to the airport. My bag's in the trunk. There's a flight at eleven I think I can make. You'll book the Saab back in?"

"No problem," said Smailes. "But hey, I just thought of something." He produced his Home Office card, passport and the sheaf of photographs and handed them over to Kabalan. "Don't want the KGB to get hold of these. Leave them in an envelope at the airport information booth, okay, and I'll get them tomorrow."

"Which name?" asked Kabalan.

"Better use Tulku," said Smailes.

"Got it," said Rudy. "Say, when are you back in New York?"

"I dunno. A week or so, I would guess."

"Give me a call, okay? I think I've got a lead could wrap this whole thing up."

Smailes was intrigued by the remark and was tempted to question Kabalan further, but he could see their police car was beginning to attract attention from the security men just inside the hotel.

Siskin was stirring, and Smailes shook him by the elbow. "Come on, Mikhail, it's time to go," he said.

Siskin blinked twice and rubbed his eyes, and saw they were back at the hotel. Smailes uncapped the bottle of vodka and took a swallow. Then he upended it over his head and let about half of it soak his hair, jacket and shirt. Then he grabbed Siskin roughly by the sleeve and poured the rest of the liquor over him, despite his spluttering protests. He opened his door and kicked it wide, pulling Siskin out onto the sidewalk beside him. Smailes maneuvered unsteadily around the wooden barricade, then lunged into the revolving door, dragging Siskin behind him. As the door spewed them both into the lobby, Smailes and Siskin fell over into a reeking pile on the carpet. They were quickly surrounded by men in suits, waving radios.

Smailes kept repeating his same drunken protests, and eventually the KGB commander stood before him. He had been dragged into a room off the reception area, which the KGB were using as a communications post. He had been thoroughly frisked and manhandled, but was otherwise unhurt.

"You the boss?" asked Smailes belligerently. "Tell these charlies to get their mitts off me. I been for a drink with a pal from New York. No crime in that, is there? Hey, let me talk to my ambassador. Or the prime minister. I wanna talk to my prime minister." He tried to get up and one of his escorts pushed him back into his chair.

"Bugger off, Ivan," Smailes said drunkenly. "Get me a phone. I wanna call the British prime minister."

The KGB chief, a small man with a cherubic face and cold eyes, looked down at him with disgust.

"Call the police," he said, turning away.

24 _____

"Well, it's a little difficult to know where to start," Smailes was saying. "Has anything been on television yet?"

Ralph Van Deusen's face was purple with fury, and the wounded beast of his ego stalked the tiny room. "Just wait till we get you into British jurisdiction, laddie," he spat. "You're going away for a long, long time."

"Just a minute, Ralph," said Standiforth, exercising an icy control. "You'd better try and explain, Derek. You'd better try. We can have the Oslo police drop the trespass charges, but we'll need a better explanation than you've given them. Where the hell are they, anyway?" he added, looking around at the door.

Van Deusen had been leaning across the table at Smailes, but now straightened and pointed at him. "It's just as I told you, Roger. He's been recruited by the Soviets. He managed to escape from Mount Vernon and get to Oslo, and took Siskin on a drunken joyride to prevent us from bringing him across. We still have the death penalty for treason, don't we?"

Van Deusen's self-righteousness was too much for Smailes. He leaned back in his chair and pointed also. "You'd better hope not," he retorted. "Here's your traitor, Roger. Siskin was a dangle from the beginning, and Ralph knew it. He's worked for the GRU since he was recruited in that Mayfair honeytrap, eighteen years ago. I'm not supposed to know about that, am I, Ralph? Well, your old friend Peter Lynch told me all about it."

Van Deusen looked ready to explode with rage, but Smailes silenced him with a yell. "You want me to spell it out? Okay. First, palming the Janowitz memo so I wouldn't know there was a relief guard scheduled, then supplying the keypad codes so the burglary team could break in. Second, the warning to Siskin that I was going to interview the guard, which set up his murder. Then, agreeing to run the original intercept through the VSA, knowing Siskin had devised a way to beat it. Third, the information about the limo job at the Long Island shop, which you must have arranged somehow, when I was being set up to look like James Bond. Next, you guessed Kevin Butterworth had rumbled something and was trying to get back to New York to warn me, so you arranged his murder to prevent the whole thing unraveling. You were sitting right there when I took his call, remember? Then, the tip-off to Grundy's killers that I was traveling back to England. And last, the handwriting samples and apartment keys so I could be stitched up, and the convenient way you went straight to the planted evidence in my apartment. Maybe even the tip to Malinovsky about Sparks' meeting with the Soviet courier, which makes you directly responsible for six murders—"

"You bastard, Smailes," interrupted Van Deusen. "That's a pack of goddamn lies, Roger. He's guilty as all hell."

"Wait a minute, wait a minute, both of you. What do you mean, Siskin was a dangle? What evidence do you have? Are you trying to say Vasily Malinovsky shot Alan Sparks and that Soviet general? What on earth are you getting at?"

"Not Vasily. Oleg, his son," said Smailes. "The FBI arrested him at Kennedy—"

Smailes was interrupted by a knock at the door, and the three men turned to see a uniformed police officer enter, carrying a sheaf of papers. "Very sorry for the delay," he said in lilting English. "I couldn't find the chief inspector anywhere. You see, there has been an attempted coup in the Soviet Union, and Nikolai Rostov is speaking live on television from the Soviet Embassy. Everyone is in the recreation room watching him."

The three Britons and their uniformed escort squeezed into the back of the recreation room, in which a sea of uniformed and plainclothes policemen had taken every available seat and windowsill space. Others stood around the walls and sat on the floor. There was not a sound as all eyes focused on the television screen suspended from its elbow bracket high on the far wall. Nikolai Rostov was speaking into a bank of microphones, flanked by Defense Minister Ermakov and Chief of Staff Kapalkin, both wearing full dress uniform.

As Rostov spoke, a television interpreter translated into Norwegian. "What the hell's he saying?" Standiforth asked their escort, who began translating into English in a low voice for the Britons.

" 'Let me ask Defense Minister Ermakov to elaborate on the current military situation,' he is saying.

" 'Thank you, Nikolai Sergeyevich,' says the old general. 'Rebel units have now surrendered unconditionally in Moscow and Leningrad. There is still some sporadic fighting in Kiev, at the television station and near the Ukrainian Soviet building, and in the Odessa military district. In the Baltic, Byelorussian and North Caucasian districts, rebel units have been forced to surrender by the overwhelming superiority of the forces loyal to the government.' "

At this point Ermakov stopped speaking as he took a document from an unseen aide off camera. He showed it to Rostov, who resumed control of the briefing.

"Now Rostov is saying, 'Here is the latest casualty count. The rebellion has sustained two hundred and seventy-five fatalities so far in the seven districts where fighting has taken place. The Soviet Army has sustained eight casualties and twenty-two wounded. Among the fatalities in Moscow is Prime Minister Georgi Tumanov, who has been discovered in his office in the parliament building, having taken his own life. It is now clear that Tumanov was a part of this plot, since he cosigned the initial military alert earlier this evening. The pretext for this so-called emergency was the supposed abduction of a Soviet diplomat from Oslo, a claim which turns out to be entirely false. Loyal forces have also arrested deputy Anatoli Grishkin, another conspirator, whom a rebel unit was shielding in the Leningrad council building.'

" 'The military ringleaders are yet to be fully identified, but a central role was played by General Viktor Kott, first deputy chief of military intelligence, who has fled the country.' "

Here Rostov paused and was interrupted by a barrage of questions from the reporters in the room. Smailes leaned over to Standiforth. "Kott is in Kingston, Jamaica," he whispered, and Standiforth turned and looked at him in disbelief. On the television screen, Rostov was holding up his hand for order. He began speaking again and their escort resumed his simultaneous translation.

" 'I will recapitulate for you, and then make a final statement. Tonight, reactionary political and military forces attempted a coup d'état in the Soviet Union. This coup has failed, since the general staff learned of this plot some time ago, and has contained it with ease. The traitors, driven by misguided patriotism, wished to install a reactionary political leadership in the Soviet Union, which would then rescind our historic Oslo agreement and plunge our continent back into the hostility and mistrust of the Cold War. However, the force of historical progress is unstoppable, these rebels who cherished the past have been vanquished, and tomorrow our ceremony and celebration must proceed as planned.

" 'I salute the loyalty and courage, and the invincible might of the Soviet armed forces, which will guarantee the safety of our citizens in the new era of peace and cooperation that is dawning. The traitors who sought to subvert democracy will be arrested and punished. Rank-

and-file soldiers who misguidedly followed treasonous orders will be returned to their units, or will be allowed to reenter civilian life. The Soviet Union tonight belongs irrevocably to the community of European nations—humane, democratic and free. Thank you all, and good night.' "

Pandemonium broke out in the briefing room as Rostov and his two cohorts rose to leave. The television screen flickered, then cut to a news announcer.

"He says they are now going straight to their correspondent in Moscow," their escort explained.

The policemen in the room began to stream out of the door, returning to their posts and duties. The three Britons stood to one side. Ralph and Roger were both completely speechless. Their uniformed escort tore off a sheet from the papers he was holding and handed it to Standiforth.

"All right, you are free to go," he said, as a burly inspector with a red face came toward them.

"Ah, our British friends," he said warmly, as if appreciating a huge joke. He took a sniff of the alcohol fumes emanating from Smailes and smiled more broadly. "I think you and your Russian friend jump the gun with your celebrations, yes? Just like you jump the gun at your London airport tonight, I think?"

"What do you mean?" asked Standiforth, with great restraint.

"You did not see the news earlier? There was a hundred press people at your Heathrow airport, because the Soviet Embassy claims you have kidnapped one of their diplomats on the seven o'clock flight from Fornebu. But there was no one, and now the Soviet Embassy is denying everything, saying it was all a British hoax! What do you think of that?" He laughed again, then jerked a thumb over his shoulder.

"That Rostov. Quite a performer, eh?" he said, still chortling as he swept out of the room.

Out on the sidewalk, Smailes could barely contain himself. "There's your proof, Roger. Siskin was Viktor

Kott's sleeper all along, he was the bait for the trap waiting for us at Heathrow. His supposed defection was the trigger for the whole thing back home, so the new government could claim some vindication for its actions. Don't you see, we had bought the whole package!"

Van Deusen craned his neck nervously in the cool night air, suddenly looking quite old. Standiforth, with some difficulty, was attempting to reassert control. "I think we'll take a taxi, shall we, back to the embassy? Then let's sit down and see if we can straighten this whole thing out." He stepped out into the traffic and began waving. Smailes noticed for the first time that his shirt was sticky and that it reeked of vodka.

The British Embassy was in an uproar. From the number of limousines choking the driveway, it seemed half the cabinet and their aides had arrived. British television crews were attempting to set up equipment in the grounds and in the lobby, and the harassed protocol and security people were completely frantic. Standiforth managed to steer the three of them around to the residential wing where he had a room that was doubling as an office, but as soon as they sat down they were interrupted by a knock and the youthful Tennant, Standiforth's factotum, entered the room.

"Ah, there you are, sir. Head of station would like you to attend a security briefing, sir. It's already begun. And Mr. Price-Jones has been on the line from London. Wants you to call him as soon as you're in. And—"

"Just a moment, Tennant," said Standiforth, holding up his hand. "I can see we may have to postpone this debriefing for a while, gentlemen. Where are you staying, Derek?"

"A guest house about fifteen miles out."

"That's no good. Ralph, is there a spare bed in your room at the Scandinavia?"

Van Deusen began to splutter a protest, but Roger silenced him. "No, I agree, that's not a good idea. Look, Derek, you can bunk with Tennant here. He can probably turn up a camp bed from somewhere. Go back to your hotel, Ralph, and come back first thing tomorrow, when the chaos has died down, all right?"

"He might try and escape, Roger," said Smailes.

Van Deusen was incensed, but Roger cut him off by saying, "I'll take that risk, I think."

Van Deusen shot back his own charge. "You're crazy, Roger," he said. "This man's dangerous," and Roger rejoined, "I'll take that risk too."

The baffled Tennant was still pinned in the doorway. "All right, let's go, Peter," said Standiforth, turning toward him.

"Hey, Roger, can I wash up and get a change of shirt, do you think?" asked Smailes.

Standiforth suddenly became aware of Smailes' condition. "Of course. Look, fix him up, Peter, will you?"

Smailes was dozing on Tennant's bed when the young man came in hours later, struggling with a military-looking camp bed.

"What's new, Tennant?" asked Smailes pleasantly. He was wearing only his underwear and Tennant's dressing gown, which was far too small for him.

The monosyllabic Tennant had turned unexpectedly loquacious. "Hey, is it true?" he asked excitedly.

"What?" asked Smailes.

"That Roger and Van Deusen were going to escort a false defector through to Heathrow, which is why all the press was there, but that you headed him off and took him on a drunken spree?"

"That sounds a bit farfetched, Peter," Smailes offered. "Who's spreading that rumor?"

"It's all around the place," said Tennant. "Go on, tell me."

"Now, you know our official secrets policy, don't you, Peter?" he responded condescendingly. "Am I supposed to sleep on that thing?"

"No, it looks rickety. I'll take it," he said, according Smailes a newfound respect.

"Need the dressing gown back?"

"No, no, that's all right," he said. "Keep it as long as you like."

It was quite late the following day by the time Standiforth had corroborated the key elements of Smailes' story. Quentin Smith in New York confirmed that the younger Malinovsky had been discovered at Kennedy Airport handcuffed to a car linked to the Staten Island murders, and that the FBI had arrested him and expected to charge him with the Sparks and Palov murders. A shortwave radio and encryption gear had also been recovered from his apartment on the Lower East Side. Tennant had made the trip out to Fornebu and recovered the Tulku package that Kabalan had left there, containing the photographs and false passport, together with Smailes' old Home Office pass. Smailes summoned Graham Booth by phone and told him to check them both out of the guest house and bring him a change of clothing. Booth appeared sheepishly in the early afternoon to confirm the details of the sting at the Vista Hotel, by which stage Standiforth had accepted the broad outline of Smailes' account. For Van Deusen's part, he remained glowering and silent, and continued to vehemently deny any complicity in the trap that the British had almost bought hook, line and sinker. Finally, Roger suggested that they break off their meeting and resume back in England, when they could take a nice, comfortable break at Bovingdon and get to the bottom of the whole thing. Percy Price-Jones was particularly interested in attending the debriefing, he noted. Then he arranged for Smailes to be issued a temporary passport and had Tennant make reservations for them all on Saturday, the following day. Eventually, Smailes secured permission to travel out to the airport to turn in his rented Saab, languishing on Rudy's credit card in the parking lot since his drive there with Siskin Thursday evening. And since he was apparently now cleared of all suspicion, he was not even required by Standiforth to take along the worthy Tennant as chaperon.

Finally alone on the airport bus, Smailes had the first inklings of an explanation for why Howard Grundy had allowed himself to be manipulated so easily in the Soviet plot, and what Kevin Butterworth might have discovered that led to his death. He thought back to Howard's larger agenda for his U.S. trip at Christmas, and matched it with some earlier information that he had stored, without recognizing its import. As soon as he did, gears meshed and the whole intricate mechanism began to come clear to him: how Howard had been tricked into making the original intercept; how he had been duped into betraying the Anglo-French satellite project; how the burglars had known to target the Long Island telephone shop; and why both Howard and Kevin had lost their lives to protect the information. By the time he stood at the car rental counter signing off on the paperwork, he was completely convinced. Which was why, instead of heading back to Oslo on the next bus, he took his temporary passport and his remaining roll of dollars up to the Pan Am counter, and bought a standby ticket on the next plane to New York.

It was after two A.M. when Smailes got back to the Brooklyn apartment, but he made no attempt to sleep. Even had he been so inclined, it would have been impossible given the wreckage the Bovingdon team had made of his bedroom. He restored the cushions to the sofa, righted the coffee table and turned on the television, hunting for the twenty-four-hour news channel. The big stories were still the mopping-up after the failed putsch in Moscow, and the festivities in Oslo following the treaty signing earlier that night. Smailes kept consulting his watch, which he had set back six hours on landing at Kennedy. He reckoned he could call Lustig as early as six-thirty, but in all conscience had to allow him to sleep until then.

But he was blazing mad, and could not stay seated for long. He was furious at his newly revealed adversary, and furious with himself for having overlooked the obvious for so long. The reason, he knew, was his own insecurity over Clea, which made him even more angry. By three-thirty he was pacing about through the chaos of his apartment, wishing he had cigarettes.

On a trip to the bathroom he picked up and replaced the porcelain lid of the toilet tank, from which Booth had told him the British investigators had pulled a pistol in a waterproof bag. No, that was wrong, wasn't it? It was a one-time cipher kit they'd pulled from the tank, Graham had said. Hadn't Malinovsky said there was a pistol and ammunition concealed somewhere in the flat? Perhaps Smailes could find what the British team had missed, which would give him the kind of firepower he needed to bring in his man on his own. Feverishly, he began to search the apartment, starting with the obvious places in the bedroom. But he could tell that other hands had been there before him, looking for false-backed drawers or loose parquet tiles. It was not a large apartment, and after forty-five minutes he decided to give up, and wait for a rendezvous with Lustig. It was then that he looked across the living room and thought to try the combination heating and cooling vents. They were such an unfamiliar appendage to a Briton, maybe the Bovingdon team had overlooked them.

He went over to the window and inspected the screws on the waist-high, horizontal registers. He could see where paint seals had been broken on the brass screw heads of the second grille. Excitedly, he got a screwdriver from the utility drawer in the kitchen, removed the register quickly, and reached down into the darkness. At the base of the duct, where it turned a right angle into the wall, Smailes' fingers felt a heavy plastic bag. Reaching in as far as he could until his face was flush with the grating, he gripped a corner and pulled the heavy package up into the light. Inside the plastic Ziploc bag was a greased rag, and inside the rag was a cheap, small-caliber revolver and a box of bullets. Without further deliberation, Smailes spun the magazine and loaded it. Twenty minutes later he was standing outside the door of his all-night garage in Brooklyn, leaning hard on its bell.

* * *

Lyle Pitkethly's apartment was in one of the giant lime-stone cubes that marched up the canyon of West End Avenue. Smailes cruised slowly past the building in a futile quest for parking. Even at five in the morning, there was none. In fact, he saw a number of expensive cars double-parked opposite the entrance—two Mercedeses, a Jaguar, a BMW. Smailes doubled back and pulled into the No Parking zone right outside the front entrance, reasoning again that his diplomatic license plate would keep him out of trouble during the short business he had upstairs.

He leaned on Pitkethly's bell for a long time before drawing any answer.

"Yeah, who is it?" came Pitkethly's groggy voice, eventually.

"It's Derek Smailes, Lyle. Let me come up. I'm in a real jam."

"What kind of jam?"

"Look, let me up, will you? I'll explain."

There was a pause of fully five minutes before the door release buzzer sounded and Smailes marched into the lobby. Minutes later he was at Pitkethly's door, twisting its old-fashioned, mechanical doorbell.

Pitkethly opened the door and Smailes went through it with his shoulder, catching Pitkethly in the sternum and sending him backward to the floor. He was dressed in chinos and a blue shirt, with his oxblood loafers over bare feet. He looked up angrily as Smailes drew the revolver and held it on him.

"Stay right there, Lyle. Stay right there, you fucking murderer."

Pitkethly got up to a sitting position and rubbed his chest. "Derek, what the hell . . . ?" he began.

"You killed Howard Grundy, after setting him up with the laser mike and giving him the tip about the leaky glass up in Riverdale, didn't you, Lyle? You killed Kevin Butterworth for the same reason, after he saw you at Mount Vernon getting your equipment back, after he decided to warn me."

"I don't know what the hell you're talking about, Derek. Look—"

"Just shut up, Lyle," Smailes spat back. "You see, now I know you and your pals from the McLean Cartel were part of the Soviet conspiracy from the beginning, weren't you? Let's wind back the watch on the Cold War, and keep the profits rolling, right? You see, Lyle, I discovered that you're DIA some time ago, only the significance didn't dawn on me until last evening, as I was taking a little trip out to the airport in Oslo. You knew Howard Grundy, didn't you, from his tours of NSA facilities? You were the DIA point man at that listening post in Virginia, right, before you came to the UN? That was where you met Howard, and when he came through New York, you'd make sure to maintain contact with him. Maybe you even shared some of his high-tech enthusiasms, which is why he was so thrilled when you gave him the loan of that laser mike. He showed it to me too, you know, but was vague about where he'd got it. Then he claimed to have noticed the construction at the Soviet facility in Riverdale on his way to a friend's on the Upper West Side. Who the hell did Howard know in New York, Lyle, except for me and his ham radio pal, Harvey, who lives in Queens? It had to be you he was visiting."

Pitkethly scooted backward on his rear to lean against a couch, his arms folded. He glanced over at the bedroom door, through which Smailes could see a section of unmade bed.

"Now, Howard Grundy was a simple man, but he was no fool. He would never have taken such a tip from an impeachable source, but you were his friend, a colleague from U.S. intelligence working under cover at the UN, right? Howard knew how to keep a secret, and he assumed you did, too, which is why he shared the information about the Anglo-French satellite project he was working on, right?

"Howard didn't have the slightest suspicion where your allegiances really lay, with those clanking arms barons you work for, did he? But you've been involved with the McLean Cartel from its inception, I would guess. I know for sure you were hooked up with that spin-off, Friends of the Western Alliance, because I happened to see the letter you'd written to Clea's father, in his study. You were the one who invited him to that Washington bash in the New Year, weren't you? Which is why you ducked out of the Glades that night before he came over for drinks, right? Peter Lynch would have recognized your name and the cat would have been out of the bag. I might have even become more suspicious about why the Lincoln dealership was suddenly overloaded with a rush UN order, and had to sub out the phone job to that low-security outfit on Long Island. Official transportation is one of your areas, isn't it, Lyle? But you arranged to plant that bomb and then sat back while I drew all the applause for finding it. Tell me, Lyle, why were you interested in Clea in the first place? As an introduction to her father? How come you're not saying anything, Lyle?"

Pitkethly looked at Smailes without expression, then got to his haunches and squatted on his long legs, his back still resting against the couch.

"See, I couldn't quite resist the opportunity of a face-to-face meeting before we give the FBI a call. Call it a special personal interest. You see, I had made a kind of pledge to myself to get to the bottom of Kevin Butterworth's murder. He must have seen you with Howard when you picked up your gear in Mount Vernon, maybe even overheard Howard thanking you for the tip, or something, and you realized he was a big threat to your whole scheme. That's why you called his murder when he made plans to visit me.

"I also happened to like Howard Grundy, and I've been feeling responsible for his death, too, since I had called his house the day before. I was sure my call had been intercepted, which is why he and his mother got shot. But that's not the case, is it? You arranged the contract on Howard during that trip you took last winter, as insurance. Then, when it seemed the summit was unstoppable, you played the card of the Eurosatellite venture in

Washington and were in trouble as soon as Howard became suspected of the leak. Somehow, you must have learned about the internal inquiry, and that was his death sentence. Because if the high priests grilled Howard about his contacts at NSA, God knows what else he might have finally spilled, and the whole plan involving Mikhail Siskin might have unraveled at the eleventh hour. So it seems my trip to Howard's place the day of his death was just coincidence, which makes me feel much better.

"Now, one thing I want to ask you, Lyle, and I'm sure the FBI are going to ask you too, is who's the Hispanic with missing fingers you hired to do all this? He's been a busy guy, hasn't he? In just about an hour we can call my contact in the New York field office, and maybe you can explain to him yourself—"

"I don't think so, Derek," said a voice over his left shoulder. Smailes wheeled to see Madge Ryan standing in the bedroom doorway, and at the same instant Pitkethly sprang at his waist, sending him sprawling backward. The gun spun out of his hand, bounced off the door, and landed at Madge's feet. She picked it up.

"Stand up, Derek," she said. "Look, I'm sorry about this, but I think we've been in the wrong all along. I think Lyle and his friends are right, that we're walking into a Russian trap . . ."

Smailes got to his feet. "Come on, Madge, don't be silly. Give me the gun." He took a pace toward her, but she raised it and trained it at his chest with both hands. "Don't make me use this, Derek," she said, in a voice he'd never heard before.

Pitkethly came toward him and pushed him down into an armchair. Smailes looked around him in disbelief. The sitting room had a completely depersonalized feeling, like a hotel room. Then it all hit him in a rush. Madge, the downtrodden spinster suddenly looking more perky and feminine. The source for handwriting samples, keypad codes and apartment keys, travel plans and everything else. She had buried the original memo in Van Deusen's in-tray, so Smailes would not know that Roberts the relief guard had been scheduled. She had been standing in the doorway when he had announced his plans to interview the guard in Newburgh. She had routed Kev Butterworth's call into Ralph's office, then overheard his plans to stop off in New York. She had withheld the information about the spare Mount Vernon key, so suspicion would fall on Booth, not her. She had been the feedback agent all along, not Ralph Van Deusen, and certainly not Clea Lynch. She had been privy to the Colin mission from its inception, and had betrayed all its details to Pitkethly, who had in turn fed them across to Siskin and Kott. Smailes looked across at her, standing in the doorway in her stockinged feet, her sad twill skirt and prim, box-pleated blouse. Poor, pathetic Madge Ryan.

"Look, Madge," he began gently. "You can't believe he's serious about you. He's just been using you to get the information he needed. The whole thing is a bust anyway —the coup attempt was crushed, the treaty signed and sealed. So now you're dead, Madge. You're as dead as any of the others who got in their way. Just give me the gun, and we'll explain the whole thing to the FBI and Roger Standiforth. He'll understand that—"

"Shut up, Derek," she cried, her voice almost breaking. "Don't try and trick me. Lyle and I are in love. We're going to be married. He's the first person who ever paid any real attention to me, who ever thought I was worth something. What do you think it's been like for me, working for that swine all these years? Coming to work and feeling physically sick day in and day out? And you, you and Graham Booth were no better. You always looked right through me, as if I wasn't there. Lyle's cause is a just one, and I have no regrets about helping him. I know he had nothing to do with Howard's or Kevin's deaths. They were both robberies, I'm sure of it," she said, her voice constricted by an edge of hysteria.

"Keep the gun on him, Madge," said Lyle, going into a small chest of drawers in the hallway and coming up with a wide roll of packing tape. "Stand up," he ordered.

Smailes got to his feet and thought desperately of

jumping Madge, but she seemed so close to breaking he thought she might fire if he tried it. There was a squawking sound as Pitkethly pulled out a length of tape, forced his arms behind him, and started binding his wrists.

Poor, pathetic Madge Ryan, Smailes said to himself bitterly. It was he, Smailes, who was the pathetic one, to allow his loathing of Pitkethly to cloud his judgment so badly that he had gone after him without backup. And Madge was right—he had never taken her seriously, barely even noticed her, which is why he had never recognized the incongruities in her behavior or identified her as the leak, which a simple process of elimination should have done. And now, here he was, trussed and helpless.

Pitkethly went into the pockets of Smailes' jacket and took out his car keys, attached to their official fob with the number plate marked.

"Where are you parked?" asked Pitkethly.

"Eat shit, Lyle," said Smailes.

"Well, it won't be too hard to find," he said, holding up the fob in front of Smailes' eyes. "Come on, Mr. Smailes," he said, taking the gun from Madge and grasping him by the elbow. "We're going for a little drive." The last thing Smailes heard as Pitkethly pushed him out the door was the sound of Madge Ryan, sobbing.

25

The hours between four and six A.M. were the only time the pace of Manhattan actually slowed, and as Pitkethly steered the car south in the gray wash of dawn they saw no pedestrians and only the occasional stray vehicle—a taxi returning home, a lone, inexplicable bus. Smailes licked his lips as he tried to contain his mounting panic. He was completely helpless, and not a soul in the world knew where he was. Pitkethly could plug him through the temple, stick the gun in his hand and drag him across to the driver's seat, and maybe even the British would think it a suicide. He strained against the binding of his wrists with all his force, but the effort was futile.

He found himself blinking back tears of rage, and cursing the stupid, arrogant folly of his attempt to bring in Pitkethly alone. In his blind hatred of Lyle as a potential rival for Clea, he had behaved like an amateur. It was all so primitive, his face burned with shame. He thought of trying to goad Pitkethly about his cynical manipulation of Madge, his enslavement to profit in the name of principle, but his mouth was so dry he didn't know how the words would come out. He looked away out of the side window, so Pitkethly would not see his humiliation.

The car hit a streak of green lights as it ploughed south down Ninth Avenue. Then, as it crossed Fourteenth

Street, Pitkethly turned right into the wasteland of the meat-packing district. Smailes stared out at the rutted, cobbled streets and the shuttered buildings skirted by cantilever crane joists and loading docks. There was not a soul in sight. Pitkethly turned left, then right again, then pulled in next to a truck painted with a sign that read BONNARO'S MEATS. Ahead at the end of the street Smailes could make out the causeway of the West Side Highway, and beyond, the gleaming steel cord of the Hudson River. Then his vision was obscured as a manhole cover beside the car gave out a gasp of billowing, municipal steam.

"Look out of your window, Smailes," said Pitkethly, and Smailes, no longer fighting back his tears, complied.

Derek Smailes knew he would not hear the report of the shot that ended his life, and he did not. His vision suddenly flooded red, and he heard what sounded like the shattering of glass, and then he tasted bile in his throat. He heard the wail of a horn, and turned to see Pitkethly's cheek resting against the steering wheel. The next thing Smailes knew, strong arms were pulling him to his feet.

"You okay, man?" asked a guttural voice. Smailes leaned against the powerful shoulder and sobbed. He caught the fragrance of an expensive cologne and stood away to confront the face of a muscular black man, who had tight curly hair and a thick black mustache. He held a large handgun in his right hand. Glancing behind him Smailes saw a red BMW pulled over at the curb, the driver's door thrown open. Its vanity plate read SHORTSTP.

At that moment, a powder blue Fleetwood drew up, and Rudy Kabalan leapt out. "Derek, what the fuck you doing?" he demanded. "Jesus, this was close. Hey, Ricky, you got a knife? Cut his hands free."

Shortstop went back to his car and retrieved a heavy wooden object. There was a menacing, percussive sound as he hit a catch and a six-inch switchblade appeared. He deftly sawed Smailes' hands free, then turned to Kabalan.

"Hey, this cool, man? You said drop the guy."

"Yeah, nice work, Ricky. Look, clear out. Go home. I'll give you a call later. Leave me that shooter."

Shortstop handed the pistol over. "Sure. Hey, you okay?" he asked Smailes again.

Smailes was shaking but felt a bizarre elation. "Yeah, I'm fine. Thanks," he said, rubbing his wrists.

Shortstop was back at the red BMW in three strides, then laid rubber as he gunned the car to the end of the street and turned north onto the highway.

Smailes turned to see Rudy using the pistol stock to break in the rest of the glass of the Ford's back window. Then he opened Pitkethly's door and yanked the inert figure back off the wheel. Smailes saw the fatal wound, two inches above the right ear. Rudy retrieved Smailes' pistol, which had fallen on the floor at Pitkethly's feet, and stuffed it into his pocket. Then he rubbed Shortstop's pistol carefully against his sweatshirt, wrapped the fingers of Pitkethly's right hand around the handle, and slammed the door. The whole exercise took less than thirty seconds.

"Looks like a suicide to me," he said with a shrug. "Come on, Derek. Let's go."

Kabalan steered Smailes into the passenger seat of the big Cadillac, drove to the highway, then headed south. "You okay?" he asked. "That was pretty damn close. Nearly got yourself killed. What the hell you doin' back in town so soon?"

Smailes shook his head and then was seized by a burst of uncontrollable, maniacal laughter. When he had gathered himself, he asked quietly, "Rudy, please tell me what's going on."

"Thought I told you in Oslo, just as you were climbing out of the Volvo. We were on to the guy. I'd have told you the whole thing if you'd have called, like I said."

Smailes shook his head. "Who's 'we,' Rudy?"

"Told you that too, months ago."

Smailes searched his memory. "That banker?"

"Right, Wilfred Thayer, chairman of Manhattan Liberty. I had a contract to keep tabs on the McLean Cartel for him."

"You knew Pitkethly was part of the cartel?" asked Smailes, incredulous.

"Naw, not for certain. Not till just now."

"Rudy, you'd better start at the beginning," said Smailes, as Kabalan guided the big Cadillac into the tunnel that ran beneath the southern tip of Manhattan and converted the West Side Highway into the FDR Drive.

"Yeah, right," Kabalan said. "The beginning? Okay, last fall, this button-down dude I never seen before approaches me for a job. It's a weird one—bugging a Western mission, planting a bomb in an official car. But that's not all that's weird. The bug is a dud, meant to be found, and same with the bomb—it's not intended to go off or injure no one. I turned him down."

"Go on."

"Well, then I play a hunch and I get an appointment to see Mr. Thayer, and offer my services to keep tabs on the McLean Cartel for him."

"Whatever for?"

"Use your head, Derek. All the commercial interests in this country, apart from the arms makers, want to see the coffin lid nailed down on the Cold War, and get those East-bloc markets opened up. Particularly the banks. Now, a bank is like a shark that's got to keep swimming to stay alive. A bank's got to keep lending, or it's dead. Those third-world loans they're all still holding? They're toilet paper. They're changing hands on the secondary market at fifteen, twenty cents on the dollar. You must have read about that development fund set up by the Bundesbank and the IMF? That's where the smart money's going today—East Europe. Ask yourself the same question. With the world economy stuck in a recession, who you gonna back to come through with the clutch payments? Nikolai Rostov or the president of Mexico? No contest, is it? But the banks have to wait for the green light from the White House, which in turn is hanging on the outcome of the arms talks. So I offer to keep watch on the cartel, make sure they don't gum up the works at the last minute."

"And Thayer accepts?"

"Listen, don't sound so surprised. Okay, so I dress

like a sleazebag and act like a rube, but there's a reason for it. I'm one of the best in the business, Derek, and I like to keep a real low profile. As long as most people don't take me seriously, that's fine with me. Those people need to know, they know. I'm playing a hunch that this job for Mr. Cleancut is some sting the cartel's working on, and the more I learn, the more I'm convinced. Remember, you told me about finding that bug in the New Year, so it seems like the Brits are the target. Then I heard about the limo bomb from a buddy at the FBI, which confirms it."

"Has he got a name?"

"Yeah, Lustig. Bob Lustig. We go back a long way. Why?"

"Never mind. Go on."

"Except, I can't ID the guy who called the original job. I figure he's got to be with the Company, the DIA or the Pentagon, or maybe one of the big manufacturers, but I can't get a fix on him. I even tried to find out who else he hired."

"After you turned him down?"

"Right. I had a meeting with Oscar Tufano, the day I gave you Malinovsky's hangout at the hotel on Lex. I figure Cleancut's gone down the list, and Oscar's probably taken it."

"Oscar Tufano?"

"Yeah, Oscar Two-Fingers we call him. He's a UCLA, and in the same business, generally. But a lot fewer principles, would do anything for money. I mean anything."

"UCLA?" Smailes asked.

"Unilaterally controlled Latino asset, the Company calls them. They got hundreds on the payroll."

"Go on."

"Say, you live in Brooklyn, right? You wanna go home, get cleaned up?" asked Kabalan as they sailed by the ramp for the Brooklyn Bridge.

"Yeah, okay," said Smailes.

"Manhattan Bridge okay?" asked Rudy.

"No, I'd double back if I were you," said Smailes.

"Right. Anyway, Oscar, he stonewalls me. But I get the sense he's lyin', he's taken the job. Then you confirm it, out at the house, when you tell me about the two-fingered Hispanic who did the original break-in."

"That's not all he did. He murdered Roberts and Butterworth, then set up the hit on Grundy back in England."

Kabalan screwed up his features, and shook his head. "Like I said, he's a psycho, he'd do anything." He paused to look out at the gray expanse of the East River before resuming.

"Anyway, I got Ricky on my payroll, doin' legwork for me, seeing if he can pin down a party of Button-down's description, but it's still no go. So then I play another hunch. Maybe it's much closer to home, I think, since we're talking UN missions. Maybe the party's a spook rotating through the UN. Then Ricky nails down a couple of prospects, and I confirm the guy, like, just a week, ten days ago. Just before all that shit hit the fan for you. I trace it back and sure enough, Mr. Pitkethly's a big player for several front groups. Mr. Thayer, he's thrilled to pieces, suggests we go straight to the FBI. I say, forget it, we don't have a package yet. Then you came out to Port Chester with your photos, and, hey—"

"The penny dropped."

"Yeah, whatever."

Kabalan steered the car up the Houston Street ramp, circled the island at the top and pointed the car back south. "So you see, I would have gone to Oslo anyway, as part of the contract for Thayer. But I thought, hey, if I can collect two fares for the same trip, I know it ain't the Brits' money . . ."

"I'm with you, Rudy. No problem."

"So then Siskin, he must have known they put the move on me right at the start, and maybe his last hope was that I was on his team after all, otherwise, how could he come out with that remark in the Volvo as we're driving away from the airport? Boy, I bet that gave you a jolt."

"It did. So Shortstop had the apartment staked out?"

"Yeah, we're taking rotating shifts with the long-range camera gear, trying to get shots of whoever he's hanging with, and maybe we'll get something concrete so we can reel him in."

The tires began to howl on the rutted asphalt of the Brooklyn Bridge roadway. "Hey, where's your place anyway?" asked Kabalan.

"First light after the bridge, make a left," said Smailes.

"So this morning, I get this frantic call from Ricky on his car phone, says a party answering your description has gone into the building. I throw some clothes on and jump into the car, but there's no way I can get down in time. Then, I got my own phone, see, luckily, so we stay in touch," said Kabalan, indicating the cradled car phone at his knee. "He tells me you're yanked out of there with your hands taped up, and I know we got a big problem. He tailed you down the West Side and when you both pulled over, I said, 'Go ahead, drop the guy,' if it looks like he's about to off you. Ricky always claimed he could handle a gun. Guess he proved it. Now where is it? Left here?"

Kabalan pulled over and looked across at Smailes awkwardly. "Well, I guess justice is done. I don't know we could have pinned anything on him, in the end. Say, who was the scrawny bimbo he was seeing, anyway?"

"The secretary in our office," said Smailes.

"Figures," said Kabalan.

"What are we going to do about the body?" asked Smailes. "That car can be traced directly to me, and it's not going to take a forensic genius to know it's no suicide."

"I'm goin' to leave that up to you, Derek, my friend. You're an inventive guy. Just return the favor and leave me and Ricky completely out of it, okay?"

"Okay, Rudy. I'll think of something," said Smailes, laughing despite himself. "Listen, tell me something."

"Sure."

"Why didn't you take the original job from Pitkethly? Didn't sound too dangerous."

"Business decision," said Kabalan with a sniff. "There's no future in the Cold War, anybody's gotta see that. I knew I could get a better price out of Thayer, too, if he saw my argument. Anyway, I just had this sense the job was goin' to turn real nasty, and I'm not into that shit." Rudy hesitated, drumming on the wheel with his fingers. "Which brings me to something else," he said.

"Yes?" said Smailes carefully.

"I'm getting out of this racket. Client base is shrinking, too much competition. Besides, I got a custody hearing next month, and I wanna convince the judge I'm respectable."

"Go on."

"I'm going into the fast-food business. I'm buying a health-food doughnut franchise in White Plains with the money from these last two jobs. I sign the lease today."

Smailes smiled, wondering aloud whether a health-food doughnut outlet wasn't a contradiction in terms.

"No way. Unbleached flour, maple syrup, vegetable oil, all that crap," said Kabalan knowledgeably. "It's gonna take off like a rocket. Called 'Healthnuts.' Well, Ricky's goin' to manage the place for me, and I thought, maybe you'd like to come in on the ground floor, as a partner. I'd give you twenty-five percent for, say, ten grand."

Smailes was genuinely touched. "Listen, Rudy, I'm flattered by the offer. I know we'd work well together, but I think my future's back in England. And I'm not ready to get out of the intelligence business yet. I'm barely getting started."

Kabalan stared away out of his window. It was now after six and traffic along the approach to the bridge was picking up. "Okay, I thought that's what you'd say," said Kabalan ruefully. He held out a meaty paw. "No hard feelings, about the Oslo thing?"

"How could I have hard feelings, Rudy?" asked

Smailes, grabbing his hand. "The two of you just saved my life. Hey, I'll call. We can go to a ballgame soon."

"You bet," said Kabalan, firing up the engine of the big Cadillac.

President Nikolai Rostov stood in the darkened living room of his hunting lodge, talking quietly with his GRU chief, Grigori Chumak. Lights suddenly streaked the bare branches outside, and both men turned to the elevated landing that led from the front door to the kitchen. Ivan Prokhanov, Rostov's bodyguard, appeared briefly at the kitchen entrance, then shook his head. Minutes later, the front door was flung open and Sonia Rostov entered, obviously in a state of high excitement.

"Nikolai! What on earth are you doing here?" she cried. "Why aren't you at Barvikha? Why don't you have more lights on? Hello, Grigori," she said as an afterthought, descending the wooden steps to the living room. She reached up to kiss her husband, who returned the embrace absently.

"Did you hear the Voice of America broadcast?" she asked. "President Wilkes said you have triumphed over the forces of 'evil and darkness.' Isn't that wonderful?"

"No, I didn't listen," said Rostov quietly. At that moment, more lights could be seen ploughing into the trees outside. This time, Prokhanov appeared on the landing and nodded. Quickly, Chumak said something into Sonia Rostov's ear and bundled her up the stairs into the kitchen. A minute later, the front door opened and General Alexei Dolghorukov entered, escorted by an aide carrying a briefcase. Rostov turned to face them as they slowly descended the stairs.

"So, Nikolai Sergeyevich, you have prevailed," said Dolghorukov, as he stood opposite Rostov. "I have kept my end of the bargain. Your political enemies are destroyed. Disloyal elements in the armed forces have been exposed and purged, and you are hailed as a hero around the world." He paused, and reached behind him to receive documents that his aide produced from the briefcase.

"Now it is your turn. Here are your false shipping documents. And here is our inventory of stored weaponry in the Urals system," he said. "And this is a list of my priorities once I assume the defense ministry."

"I don't think that will be necessary, General," Rostov replied in a voice like iron. "We can leave that equipment in mothballs. You know of the agreement we signed with the Americans at Lvov, I believe. This is sufficient guarantee of our security. And as for the defense ministry, you must be mistaken. When the world learns of your role in the failed rebellion, they will see you as I do, as both a traitor and a criminal."

Rostov turned away and strode over to the picture window to stare out into the night. The subsequent actions unfurled slowly, as if in slow motion. Momentarily stricken, Dolghorukov's expression contorted from one of incredulity into a cold, implacable hatred. Then he reached behind him into his aide's briefcase, and pulled out a service revolver. Aiming at the back of Rostov's head, he pulled the trigger. There was a loud click, then two shots rang out, and Dolghorukov buckled forward, mortally wounded. Ivan Prokhanov stood on the balcony, a smoking pistol held in both outstretched hands. Sonia Rostov forced her way back onto the landing, partially restrained by Chumak. At the sight of the dying general she shrieked and covered her face. Chumak clapped Prokhanov on the back, then descended the staircase quickly and shook Dolghorukov's aide's hand warmly, on whose face a thin smile was playing. Then he knelt to inspect the body of the general.

Sonia Rostov recovered herself and descended into the living room, looking from her husband, to Chumak, then back again. An awful realization had dawned on her.

"It was all a trick, wasn't it, Nikolai?" she said, in a voice shrill with fury. "Dolghorukov was working for you and Grigori all along, wasn't he? You engineered this coup to destroy your enemies, didn't you? Didn't you? Answer me!"

Rostov's face could be seen reflected in the dark glass. He had closed his eyes at the gunfire, but had not turned around. Now he opened his eyes at his wife's horrified accusations, his expression seeming pained and sorrowful at first, then stiffening slowly into a mask of determination and triumph.

26

Clea Lynch was seated on the settee in her parents' living room, pretending to read a magazine. She heard the thunk of a car door and her hand trembled slightly. Moments later, Derek Smailes strode into the room and walked quickly over to the drinks cabinet in the bookcase. Clea stood up and looked over at him. She was simply but elegantly dressed in a pleated skirt and a fawn cashmere sweater.

"Well, how did it go?" she asked.

"Is it all right if I help myself?" asked Smailes, not waiting for an answer as he manipulated the bottle of Dewar's. He poured a measure into a glass and took a swallow, finally turning to face her.

"Hi. All right, I suppose, considering. I've never seen him so angry."

"Roger Standiforth?"

"Right. I think he can forgive the caper in Oslo since I probably saved him from the greatest humiliation of his career. Lying to him about using Vasily Malinovsky as a resource, then the unauthorized trip back to New York— that really got to him. Until they heard from me, they didn't know that I hadn't defected to Moscow or something."

429

"Good grief, of course! Oh, darling, what did he say?"

"Well, he read the riot act at me for about twenty minutes and told me all the reasons he had for firing me. I made suitable expressions of humility and eventually he calmed down. Apparently, the FBI are going to accept the story that Lyle borrowed the car from Madge, then was murdered by persons unknown. They're pleased enough to have Malinovsky, it seems, and the inside dope on the McLean Cartel. But it sounds like Roger has had to do some fast talking."

"What about the others?" she asked compliantly.

"Madge has been taken up to Bovingdon, but it seems she's completely fallen apart and may have to be committed. Ralph has been cleared of any major infractions, apart from preventing me from calling Roger after I was nabbed in Brooklyn. Roger had apparently given strict instructions to let me speak with him, if I asked. I suppose Ralph wanted to make sure he'd head up the operation in Oslo. They're encouraging him to take early retirement, and in reality he's got no choice. Graham is being brought back to A Branch. But that's not the biggest news."

"What is?" asked Clea, her eyes averted.

"The PM has brought in a new man as DG—the former chief constable of South Glamorgan, imagine—and Price-Jones has resigned. Everyone's up in arms. Price-Jones is going to the Nuclear Energy Commission as head of security, but it's a demotion, it's not a knighthood position. It's obviously direct fallout from the Colin fiasco—Roger's probably lucky not to lose his job, too."

"Oh," said Clea.

"So how about you?" asked Smailes, noticing her manner. "Did you hear?"

"Yes," she said with forced brightness. "They called this afternoon. I passed the vetting and am officially approved as second secretary. Honestly, it's a big relief. Imagine what I thought when they started asking me all that stuff about Raul and his background—I couldn't imagine how they even knew of him! Then the questions about the clubs I joined at Oxford. It all seemed so odd, and I wasn't at all sure I'd convinced the chap by the end. But I suppose I really was a suspect, wasn't I?"

"Oh, I don't know about that, Clea," said Smailes, with feigned casualness. "But listen, that's not all Roger told me. The police have had to drop the inquiry into Howard's murder—there were too many cutouts on the contract, and they can't get any proof. So it doesn't seem like Lyle's hit man will ever face charges."

"That doesn't seem right," Clea said.

"That's exactly what I said, and you know what Roger replied? He just said, 'He'll be taken care of,' in this voice I'd never heard him use before. When I said I thought the British didn't go in for that kind of thing, he gave this little patronizing smile, and changed the subject."

Clea gave a shudder. "Honestly, that's creepy," she said mechanically.

Smailes finished his Scotch and set the glass down on the coffee table, giving her a puzzled look. Clea was still standing, brushing the nap of her parents' Bokhara rug with the toe of a new suede pump.

"So what is he going to do with you?" she asked quietly.

"I asked for head of station in New York, but he said no way, he wants me back in London, in K Branch, where he can keep an eye on me," said Smailes, with an involuntary smirk of triumph. Clea kept her eyes on the carpet.

"Oh. So you're not going back to New York? I just heard Felicity's moving in with Barry, you see, and I thought maybe you would want to move across from Brooklyn. It's a big enough place . . ."

"I'm sorry, Clea. He's adamant. There's no appeal."

She looked up at him suddenly, and spoke quickly. "Well, I could ask for a posting in London, you know. I know they'd consider it. In fact, they'd probably prefer it. They had only agreed to New York—"

"What do you envisage, Clea?" he asked. "A semi-detached in Caterham and a station wagon in the drive?"

She gave him an injured look. "Don't mock me, Derek," she said in a hurt voice.

Suddenly, Smailes understood Clea's preoccupied manner and knew exactly what he had to do, and the realization made him almost as terror-stricken as his dawn ride through Manhattan with Lyle Pitkethly. He picked up his glass, went back to the drinks cabinet and refilled it with a large shot. He took a swallow and advanced toward Clea, who was still brushing the carpet with her toe.

"Clea," he asked, his voice suddenly sounding strangely distant. "Will you marry me?"

She flew into his arms. "Of course I will, you darling idiot. I love you so much."

"You too. God, I love you. Far too much," said Smailes, returning her embrace, his voice catching.

"Whyever did it take you so long to ask?" she remonstrated.

"I honestly didn't think you'd have me," he responded.

"You're such a dope," she said. "I can't believe you couldn't tell. But I couldn't just come out and say. You had to realize it yourself."

They kissed and she held him close again. "Oh, Derek, I'm so thrilled you've been able to tell me what really happened. But do you really have to go off to Bovingdon tomorrow?" she asked.

"No," he said. "Viktor Kott has sought asylum at the consulate in Kingston, and Roger's going out to interview him. He leaves tonight."

"Goodness," said Clea. "So you thought all along that Mikhail Siskin was going to be the last defector, and now perhaps it's going to be his boss, after all."

"Mmm," said Smailes, drawing her close and running his hand into her hair. He didn't want to talk business anymore.

"Did you never really think I was a spy?" she whispered softly into his ear.

"No," he replied, feeling her shoulders sag in disappointment.

THE
CAMBRIDGE
THEOREM

by Tony Cape

Detective Sergeant Derek Smailes is drawn into a complex web of intrigue surrounding the not so obvious suicide of a Cambridge student, a mathematical genius who had devised a theorem to prove who *really* killed President Kennedy, and, at the time of his death, was investigating the infamous "Ring of Five," the Cambridge spy ring recruited by the KGB in the 1930's. Was there a trail to the unidentified fifth man?

Caught in the midst of an elite KGB hit squad, Smailes finds himself alone in the uncharted territory where MI5 and the KGB play out their brutal, desperate games.

"Cape successfully invades the realm of LeCarré and Deighton."—*Houston Post*"

"*The Cambridge Theorem* is a terrific way to start a writing career...it's a gold-plated winner."
—*The New York Daily News*